P9-CCU-180

PRIVILEGE

CHECK OUT ALL THE BOOKS IN THE
NEW YORK TIMES BESTSELLING PRIVATE
SERIES BY KATE BRIAN

PRIVATE

INVITATION ONLY

UNTOUCHABLE

CONFESSIONS

INNER CIRCLE

LEGACY

AMBITION

REVELATION

PRIVILEGE

BY

KATE BRIAN

SIMON PULSE

New York   London   Toronto   Sydney

This book is a work of fiction. Any references to historical events, real people, or real locales are used fictitiously. Other names, characters, places, and incidents are the product of the author's imagination, and any resemblance to actual events or locales or persons, living or dead, is entirely coincidental.

SIMON PULSE
An imprint of Simon & Schuster Children's Publishing Division
1230 Avenue of the Americas, New York, NY 10020

Copyright © 2008 by Alloy Entertainment
All rights reserved, including the right of reproduction
in whole or in part in any form.

SIMON PULSE and colophon are registered trademarks of
Simon & Schuster, Inc.

alloyentertainment
Produced by Alloy Entertainment
151 West 26th Street, New York, NY 10001

Designed by Andrea C. Uva
The text of this book was set in Adobe Garamond.

Manufactured in the United States of America
First Simon Pulse edition December 2008

2 4 6 8 10 9 7 5 3

Library of Congress Control Number 2008935041

ISBN-13: 978-1-4169-6759-0
ISBN-10: 1-4169-6759-1

This book is dedicated to Matt, Melinda, Mom V., and Mom S. Without your help, this one never would have gotten done.

Special thanks also to Lanie, Sara, and Josh. You know why.

PRIVILEGE

NEVER

"It's not fair."

It wasn't a whine or a complaint, just a statement. A statement of the obvious, as far as Ariana Osgood was concerned. As she stared out the window of the Brenda T. Trumbull Correctional Facility for Women, it was all she could think to say. Outside, the leaves on the trees swayed lazily in the warm summer breeze—a breeze she would be allowed to feel against her skin for exactly fifty-five minutes during midday recess. *Recess.* That was what the warden called it. Who ever heard of a teenage girl looking forward to recess?

"It's just not fair."

Across the wide oak desk, her "therapist" smirked. Shifting in his seat, Dr. Meloni leaned back, forcing his expensive leather chair to let out the loud creak that he *knew* made Ariana's skin crawl. Just outside the fence that encircled the grounds, about a hundred yards from where Ariana now sat, Meloni's precious Doberman, Rambo, barked nonstop, as always. The inmates of the Brenda T. listened to that damn dog bark all day long, every day. It was as if Meloni was trying to remind them that he was always there, always watching, even when they weren't in session with him. The man also couldn't be away from the dog for more than two hours at a time. He was always going out there and feeding him treats, cooing to the animal like it was a newborn baby and the apple of its father's eye. Revolting. Someone should have been analyzing *him*.

"What's not fair?" he asked.

Ariana flicked a glance at Dr. Victor Meloni, sitting there in front of his elaborately framed diplomas from Johns Hopkins and Stanford. Thick, leather-bound books sat on the shelves to his right, most of which she was sure he hadn't even opened, let alone read. Her lip curled at the sight of his fake tan. His overly gelled salt-and-pepper hair. His heavily starched blue shirt. His capped teeth.

Two hundred dollars a tooth, but can't spring for a pair of shoes with leather soles. Ariana could ascertain everything she needed to know about a person through his or her footwear. In the sixteen months she had been in residence at Brenda T. Trumbull just outside Washington, D.C., she had only seen Dr. Meloni wear two different pairs of shoes. The same exact style, one pair in black, one in brown. Clearly, the man thought that everyone he met would be so dazzled by the veneer of his face, they wouldn't take the time to notice his shoes.

But Ariana did. And they screamed white-trash-turned-scholarship-student-turned-poseur. He'd probably taken this job because it meant he'd have the chance to torture the daughters of all the deep-pocketed classmates who had never accepted him into their inner sanctum. And torture them he did. He smiled when they cried. Laughed in the face of their desperation.

Smirked . . . all . . . the . . . time.

"It's not fair, me being here for twenty years," Ariana said slowly, stating the obvious. Stating the point she'd made four thousand times before.

"Twenty years to life," he corrected, his blue eyes taunting.

"I don't think about that," Ariana said, averting her gaze again. Outside the window, the lake glinted in the summer sun. A lone sail-boat sliced across the window frame and disappeared.

"About what?" he asked. "The life part?"

He sat forward now. Interested.

"Yes," Ariana said. "It's unacceptable."

That was when Dr. Meloni laughed. Not just his usual amused chuckle, but a big, hearty, guttural laugh. Ariana tried not to cringe. She reached up and casually ran both hands through her soft, chin-length blond hair, securing it to the nape of her neck with an alligator barrette. She waited patiently for him to stop, curling her toes inside her state-issue white sneakers. It used to be that she would grab her own arm when she was tense, letting her fingernails cut into the flesh. Then one day last year Dr. Meloni had noticed this habit and pointed it out to her like he was oh so insightful. She hadn't done it in his presence since.

"Unacceptable," he repeated.

She looked him in the eye, her gaze unwavering. "Yes."

"You do realize you killed someone," Dr. Meloni said, in the tone adults use when scolding naughty children.

Ariana blinked, just barely betraying her internal flinch.

Thomas's blood. Thomas's blood. Thomas's blood. Just like that, she saw it on her hands. Under her fingernails. In her hair. She had made them chop it all off when she was waiting for trial and hadn't let it grow past her chin since. All that blood . . .

No. She mentally wiped it away. Gone. Back to the present. She focused in on Meloni's quote-of-the-day calendar. Today, for the twenty-ninth of June, was a Molière quote: "The greater the obstacle, the more the glory in overcoming it." Not a bad point.

"Yes. I do realize I killed someone," Ariana said, in a tone *she* reserved for idiots.

What no one here seemed to understand, or cared to hear, was that she hadn't meant to do it. Thomas Pearson had been the love of her life. He had been the only real thing she had ever possessed. It wasn't her fault that Reed Brennan had swooped in out of nowhere and stolen him away. It wasn't her fault that her best friend, Noelle Lange, had come up with the idea to kidnap him and tie him up in the woods to teach him a lesson after he'd humiliated Reed. And it definitely wasn't her fault that when she had gone back to show him how much she loved him, to show him mercy and untie him and set him free, he had chosen to mock her instead of thank her. Had chosen to tear her down and act like her devotion to him was worth no more than the mud under his feet. Had chosen to push her and push her and push her until she snapped.

If only he'd stopped when she'd asked him to.

"So you took the life of one of your schoolmates, one of your friends, and yet you don't think you deserve to be locked up for life," Dr. Meloni said.

"It was one mistake," Ariana replied.

One of three, but no one other than Ariana herself knew that.

"A mistake," he challenged, ducking his chin.

God, she was sick of this. Sick of him. Sick of his tiny little pea-brained, one-sided take on her and every other woman in this hellhole.

"You see everything in black and white, don't you?" Ariana snapped, her blood rising.

"And what you did was somehow gray?" he retorted.

"I'm not in denial. I know what I did and I'm sorry for it," Ariana said, her words clipped. "But this isn't how it's supposed to be. . . ."

She was supposed to go to Princeton. Supposed to take the train up to Yale to visit Noelle on weekends, or into the city to club hop with Kiran and Taylor. Supposed to join a secret society. Supposed to hobnob with literary geniuses. Supposed to graduate magna cum laude and snag the job as features editor at *Vanity Fair*. Supposed to live in a loft in Chelsea and meet some gorgeous artsy man who would sweep her off her feet and take her to exotic places like Thailand and India and Sri Lanka. Supposed to be proposed to on a mountaintop as the sun set in the distance. Supposed to have babies and take them home to Georgia to visit her family's estate and sit out on the porch and sip lemonade and watch them play tag under the same peach tree she used to climb when she was little.

This was her life. Her life the way it was supposed to be. It couldn't be over. The very thought made her heart constrict to the point where she actually thought she might stop breathing. Actually thought she might die over the futility of it all.

These were her dreams. Her *mother's* dreams. They couldn't be over. Not because of—

"One mistake," she said again.

Dr. Meloni stared at her. She was gripping the arms of her metal chair now, her heart pounding. As he stared, Ariana realized that she had just shown emotion for the first time in a year and a half of these daily sessions. She had let the pressure get to her. And Meloni was now smiling.

"One mistake that *ended* someone else's *life*," he said.

I know. I know this. I see him every night. Every night as I start to fall asleep. Every night I jolt awake in an ice-cold sweat. I haven't really slept in almost two years, thinking about how he made me kill him. How he didn't give me a choice. Isn't that torture enough?

"I just want this to be over," Ariana mumbled. She straightened her posture and stated it more firmly. "I just want this whole thing to be over."

Dr. Meloni leaned back in his chair again, the creak setting Ariana's arm hair on end, and let out an amused yet frustrated-sounding groan. He looked up at the wood beams that crisscrossed the ceiling and shook his head.

"It's always the same with you girls," he said.

"What's that supposed to mean?" Ariana snapped.

She didn't appreciate being likened to anyone else in this loony bin.

He glanced at her, then slowly stood up and slipped his hands into the pockets of his white coat. Watching her the whole time, he walked around his desk—the ancient wooden floor squeaking and cracking under his feet, and stood directly in front of her. For a long moment he stared down at her, his expression unreadable. Ariana stared back and felt an unexpected jolt of hope.

Oh, just try something, please. Touch me inappropriately. Try to hurt me. Whatever you're thinking, do it so that I can get your pathetic, low-rent ass fired.

Dr. Meloni leaned down and braced his hands on the arms of her chair. He brought his face within inches of hers. His breath smelled like soy sauce. Ariana wanted to recoil, but she forced herself to stay completely still.

"I have been working with psychopaths like you for the past twenty-five years," he said quietly. Up close, she could practically see her image reflected in those teeth. "You are not capable of change. If you were ever to be released from this facility, I am categorically certain that you would kill again. So no, Miss Osgood, you are never getting out of here. Not today, not tomorrow, not five years from now. Or ten. Or twenty. Not as long as I'm the one signing your chart. And believe me when I tell you I plan to stay in this job until they wheel my cold, dead corpse out that door."

He pointed at the solid metal door for effect. Ariana held his gaze. Held it and tried not to smile. Willed herself not to smile. He had no idea how wrong he was. How very, very wrong.

Finally, judging by the silence that his point had hit home, Dr. Meloni leaned back in satisfaction. His grin lit his entire face.

"Guard!" he shouted, his eyes still locked on Ariana's.

The door instantly opened, and Miriam, the bulbous Ward Two guard, appeared, filling the doorway. Miriam, with her dyed red hair and piglike nose, had an impressive collection of steel-toed boots. Shoes that meant business. Ariana had never even rolled her eyes at the woman.

"You can take this one back to her cell. I'm done with her," Meloni said disgustedly.

"Let's go," Miriam barked.

Ariana shoved herself out of her chair and walked across the room, biting down hard on her tongue to keep herself from tossing any sort of parting shot at Meloni. One wrong word, one angry glance, might give something away.

"See you tomorrow, Miss Osgood," Dr. Meloni sang in a teasing voice. "And the day after that . . . and the day after that . . . and the day after that. . . ."

He was still chuckling when the door slammed between them.

A GIFT

"It's such a lovely day. Isn't it such a lovely day?"

Kaitlynn Nottingham paused in the center of the prison yard. She tilted her pretty face toward the clear blue sky, closed her eyes, and took a long, cleansing breath. Her small, upturned nose, rosy cheeks, and long lashes were perfectly suited for a child's porcelain doll. A little someone to be cherished, coddled, cared for. An innocent someone who shouldn't have been locked up in the Brenda T.

How did we end up here? Ariana thought, her face creasing in consternation. This could not be her life: allowed to walk outside only under the watchful eyes of the gray-polyester-clad guards. Forced to wear these awful, shapeless denim trousers and itchy light blue button-downs—the short-sleeved summer version even more unflattering than the long-sleeved winter one. But most insulting of all were the clunky, square-toed sneakers she had to wear day in, day out. What sadist had designed those?

To add insult to serious fashion injury, Ariana and her fellow inmates weren't allowed to personalize anything. No accessories, no jewelry, not even a drop of perfume. Heaven forbid anyone exert any sort of individuality—it might make them start to long for other rights as well, like the right to wear an underwire bra, or to make a phone call at a normal hour of the day instead of during assigned slots late at night and in the early morning. Ariana reached up and fingered the gold fleur-de-lis necklace she wore tucked into the collar of her white undershirt. She'd been forced to bribe each and every guard on her ward in order to be allowed to continue wearing it. Even Dr. Meloni had let it slide once her father had slipped him a sizable check, which she was certain had paid for the Jaguar sedan he drove to work every morning with Rambo hanging out of the backseat. But the bribes had been worth it. Ariana was sure she would have gone slowly insane without the necklace. It was the only thing that kept her grounded. Reminded her that there was a reason to keep going. A family she needed to live for.

"At least they keep the grounds up," Kaitlynn continued, focusing on the positive, as always. "They put in summer blossoms this morning. Did you see?"

Ariana sighed as Kaitlynn pointed out the freshly planted flower beds. "Whatever you say, Little Miss Brightside," she teased, trying for a light tone and failing miserably. Yes, the grounds around the Brenda T. were lovely. Rolling green lawns, manicured gardens bursting with color and lined with natural stones, evergreen shrubs growing wild along the barbed-wire-topped chain-link fence that surrounded the entire yard. All very pretty.

But no matter how the groundskeepers tried to mask it, that fence was still there. Staring Ariana in the face. Appearing nightly in her already fraught dreams. Her worst and most unrelenting enemy. The enemy she'd have to conquer in just a few short days.

"I'm just saying, it could be worse," Kaitlynn replied. "We could be in one of those maximum security thingies with no view and no free time and all that gray. . . ." Kaitlynn shuddered.

"I like gray. I *feel* gray," Ariana told her, staring straight ahead as they walked.

Kaitlynn let her thick brown curls fall forward and gave Ariana a sympathetic look. Normally a look like that would have made Ariana bristle, but not coming from Kaitlynn. Kaitlynn had been there for Ariana from the moment Ariana had been shoved into their shared cell nearly a year and a half ago, the day after she'd been found guilty of Thomas's murder by reason of insanity. Kaitlynn had listened to her story. Had sympathized. Had given Ariana the room's one good pillow and let her keep it to this day. Kaitlynn was her only friend inside the Brenda T.—and maybe in the world.

Not that Ariana had expected to hear from Noelle Lange after everything that had happened. Or Kiran Hayes or Taylor Bell. But one card, one tiny little care package, would have been nice. They were probably too busy hanging out with Reed Brennan, being friends with Reed Brennan, taking Reed Brennan's side. . . .

"Ariana, stop!" Kaitlynn said, reaching for Ariana's arm with alarm. Ariana hadn't even noticed her fingernails digging angry grooves into the flesh of her forearm. She forced herself to breathe. Fine. She was fine. Thinking about her former friends—about *her*—always rattled Ariana. After everything that had happened, it was amazing how easily they seemed to have forgotten her.

"I'm sorry you had a bad session with Dr. Meloni," Kaitlynn said in a placating way. She tilted her head, a tell that Ariana recognized. It meant that Kaitlynn was going to tell a joke or say something witty. "But let's be honest. When have you ever had a *good* one?"

"Fair point." Ariana smiled, pleased that she had correctly predicted Kaitlynn's response. Ariana had been practicing reading people, noticing the habits and mannerisms that betrayed their intentions. She had made mistakes in the past—miscalculated—but she would *never* let that happen again. She was getting better, and this exchange with Kaitlynn proved it. But then again, Kaitlynn wasn't the most complex person in the world.

"And look around," Kaitlynn said, lifting a free hand. "It's beautiful out. Sunny . . . warm, not an ounce of humidity . . . a nice breeze coming in off the lake."

From her vantage point in the middle of the Brenda T.'s grassy area, Ariana stared off at Lake Page through the checkerboard pattern of the fence. Gazed at the boats crisscrossing the placid surface and the turrets of the castlelike Philmore Hotel on the far bank. Formerly the lavish estate of some early Virginia settler from Britain, the home had recently been purchased by the Philmore Family of Luxury Hotels and renovated into the most exclusive property in the greater Washington, D.C., area. Inside those stone walls vacationers awoke to cushy terry-cloth robes and decadent room service. They padded to the spa in cashmere slippers to indulge in warm stone massages, deep-pore-cleansing treatments, and mud baths. They took leisurely dips in the lake on the private beach and sipped champagne on the huge, rustic porch overlooking the water.

Right there. Right there people were living the life Ariana should have been living. The life she had lived until Reed and Noelle had found out what she had done that horrible night in the woods.

"Come on. Let's eat," Kaitlynn said, interrupting her wistful thoughts. She touched Ariana's shoulder, steering her toward a cluster of picnic-style tables. "You'll feel better once you get some food in you."

Ariana looked down at her bagged lunch—it was easier to carry outside than a tray—and took a deep, bolstering breath.

Only a few more days, she promised herself. *You can last a few more days. . . .*

As the two friends crossed to their usual table—a small, private one near the fence, with a partial view of the lake—Ariana became aware of a commotion a few yards off. Rambo, on his running line on the other side of the fence, was barking like he'd gone rabid and lunging for the chain link. On the inside, Crazy Cathy, one of the older inmates, was doubled over in tears, screaming the same three words over and over again:

"Hound from hell! Hound from hell! Hound from hell!"

Her short brown hair stuck out in all directions, as though she'd recently shoved her finger into an electrical outlet, which, Ariana thought, was not completely out of the question. Cathy began frantically clawing at her face as she screamed, her nails cutting a long, deep scratch in her cheek. Appalled, Ariana watched as two guards finally descended on Cathy and dragged her away from the fence. The dog, of course, kept right on lunging.

"That animal should be taken out to the lake and shot," Kaitlynn said, clucking her tongue. "He is just vicious."

Ariana dropped her lunch bag down on the table. "Now, Kaitlynn, you know that all of God's creatures serve some purpose," she admonished. Although if she hadn't needed Rambo, counted on him, Ariana would have shot the beast herself, just to punish Meloni. He loved that dog more than life itself.

"Not all," Kaitlynn said, easing her tall, lanky body down on the bench across from Ariana. She leaned her chin on her hand and sighed as she stared out at the lake. "I wonder what she's doing right this minute." A light breeze lifted her curls from her shoulders. "Probably lazing around at the country club pool, working on that skin cancer, and drinking herself into oblivion."

Ariana knew exactly who "she" was. Briana Leigh Covington. The object of Kaitlynn's obsession. The billionaire Texan oil heiress who had killed her own father to get her inheritance, then framed her best friend for the murder. The girl who hadn't even batted an eyelash when Kaitlynn had been sent away for life for a crime she had not committed.

"I got another letter from Grandma C. today," Kaitlynn said with a smile.

"Good," Ariana replied. "How is she?"

"It sounds like she's doing well," Kaitlynn replied brightly. "Heading up some new foundation, looking forward to the cooler weather in the fall. . . ."

Ariana smiled as Kaitlynn trailed off. She knew how much her friend looked forward to these letters. Grandma Covington was the only person who ever wrote to her. When Kaitlynn was thirteen years old, her parents had died in a plane crash and her aunt and uncle had refused to take her in because of a falling-out they'd had with her parents a few years prior. The Covingtons, who were old family friends, had welcomed Kaitlynn into their sprawling mansion, and Kaitlynn had instantly bonded not only with "Grandma C.," but with Briana Leigh as well. Everything had seemed perfect, until it all fell apart.

"Is she still living with Briana Leigh?" Ariana asked.

"Yes." Kaitlynn looked at the ground. "It must be so strange for her, living on the estate her son built. You know, now that he's . . ."

Kaitlynn swallowed. She couldn't even finish the sentence. Ariana's heart went out to her. Kaitlynn had been through so much even before being falsely accused of murder. First, her parents' death. Then her surrogate mother, Mrs. Covington, had died of cancer when Kaitlynn was fifteen, which had caused Kaitlynn's best friend, Briana Leigh, to become increasingly withdrawn, bitchy, and self-centered—all of which had come to a boiling point on the night Mr. Covington died. According to Kaitlynn, Briana Leigh's father had refused to write her a check for some ridiculous purchase, so she had snapped and shot him with his own gun in order to get her hands on her inheritance.

But since cold-blooded murderers were generally sent away for life, Briana Leigh had to find someone to frame for the murder. She had chosen Kaitlynn to take the fall, and Kaitlynn had been locked up in the Brenda T. ever since.

Even though she'd heard the story at least a thousand times, Ariana simply could not understand how any jury could look at Kaitlynn and find her guilty. The girl was pure innocence. Apparently not even Grandma C. thought Kaitlynn was responsible for the death of her only son. The old woman was the only person who had ever written to Kaitlynn since she'd been incarcerated—although Kaitlynn had never shared the contents of those letters with Ariana. Some things, Ariana knew, were simply too difficult to talk about.

And just to make the whole thing even more unbearable, Kaitlynn was now flat broke. Much of her own inheritance had been spent on her defense. Some had been used to bribe the judge into placing her at the Brenda T. What was left had been transferred to her cousin Robert once Kaitlynn became a ward of the state—Robert, who was the only son of the couple who had refused to take care of Kaitlynn when she was orphaned. So if Kaitlynn ever did get paroled, she would have to start from scratch.

The whole thing was just too unfair. Every time Ariana thought about it, her skin grew hot with anger.

"I wonder if she has any new friends," Kaitlynn continued, her words barely audible over Rambo's barking. "I wonder if she even realizes that she sent her only *true* friend away. . . ."

As Kaitlynn spoke, she slipped smoothly into her Texan drawl.

The accent always became more pronounced when Kaitlynn spoke about home, and especially about Briana Leigh. Ariana had noticed it on her very first day at the Brenda T. but had never pointed it out to Kaitlynn, lest her friend become self-conscious of the quirk. Ariana's Southern accent worked in much the same way. There were many people at Easton Academy who had never even realized she was from the South, but when she talked about her mother or her childhood—which was rare—the twangs and "y'alls" came right out without her even realizing it. Ariana also consciously threw them in when she needed something. Over the years she had found that when playing the damsel-in-distress card, it was more effective when that damsel was a Southern belle. As if women from the North were so much stronger and more capable. Right.

"Kaitlynn, you must stop obsessing about Briana Leigh," Ariana said as she removed her club sandwich from the paper bag. She smoothed the bag out on the table as a place mat, making sure all the corners were flattened, then set the sandwich down and carefully removed the wax paper, which she folded into a neat square. Kaitlynn automatically produced a large stack of napkins from the waistband of her state-issue jeans—cheap, light-wash, and made pocket-free in order to prevent the inmates from hiding contraband—and gave one to Ariana, who wiped each of her fingertips, one by one. "Obsession is unhealthy," she added.

Kaitlynn raised an eyebrow at Ariana's perfectly folded wax paper but stayed mum.

Rambo's barking had subsided into a constant snarl now that Crazy

Cathy wasn't rattling the fence and ranting at him. Ariana's shoulder muscles relaxed slightly, and she removed the bread from the top of her sandwich.

"I know I shouldn't think about Briana Leigh," Kaitlynn said, opening her own lunch bag. "But how am I supposed to stop? It's all wasted on her. All of it. The freedom, the cash, the *life*."

She dropped her head in her hands, the tips of her hair grazing the coarse grain of the picnic table surface. The only time Kaitlynn ever grew despondent was when she was talking about Briana Leigh Covington. Even over the past couple of grueling weeks as Kaitlynn had tried to find a lawyer who would appeal her case and failed (now that she had no money, attorneys weren't quite so interested in her), she had somehow stayed bright-eyed and peppy. But as she watched Kaitlynn now, Ariana's heart skipped a beat in sympathy. She took a break from her meal preparations and cleared her throat. Rambo started to bark feverishly again. He was getting closer to their table, but was separated as always by that horrible fence.

"Kaitlynn," Ariana said firmly. "Kaitlynn, look at me."

Her friend glanced up, already chagrined.

"Everything is going to be okay," Ariana told her. "One day, we are going to get out of here. And when we do, I promise you, you are going to get your revenge."

A warmth spread throughout Ariana's chest. A warmth of pride. Of strength. A warmth she clung to. It set her apart from the other inmates—the pathetic, the insane, the hopeless. It was going to set her free. Her *and* Kaitlynn. Because Kaitlynn clearly did not have the tools to free herself. She needed Ariana. And Ariana liked to be needed. To help those weaker than herself. To be the strong one.

Kaitlynn blushed and looked down again, tracing a knot in the wood with her fingertip. "I hate it when you say 'revenge.' It sounds so . . . medieval. I could never actually hurt anyone. Not even her."

Sometimes Kaitlynn amazed Ariana. How could anyone go through what she had gone through and not come out the other side just a little bit hardened? She reminded Ariana of the way she used to be, before Thomas. Before that Christmas at Easton. Before all the death and disappointment and heartbreak.

Tears stung Ariana's eyes at the thought of the girl she used to be. The girl she had been with Thomas. Stung at the memory of Thomas's playful smile, his searching blue eyes, his rough hands. But she quickly blinked them away.

"I know," Ariana said finally, placing the two halves of the wheat bread down on a napkin. Rambo was going berserk again now, his bark so close it felt like it was coming from inside Ariana's brain. "That's why I'm going to be there to help you."

Kaitlynn smirked, amused, as though there was no way either one of them would ever get out of the Brenda T., let alone both of them. Ariana bit her tongue.

You think I can't make it happen? she thought. *Just wait.*

"What would you do if you had Briana Leigh's money?" Kaitlynn asked, leaning her chin on her hand.

"Go to any school I wanted," Ariana said automatically.

"Really? With that kind of money you'd never have to see the inside of a classroom again," Kaitlynn said with a laugh.

Ariana shrugged. "I know. But I like school. I wish I could have finished."

She swallowed a lump in her throat as her thoughts turned to Easton Academy again. She'd been so close to graduation. Only one semester left. And she would have graduated with honors. Maybe even won firsts over Noelle again those last two quarters, what with Taylor gone from campus and unable to do Noelle's work for her. What a waste. What a supreme waste it all was.

But you're going to fix it, she reminded herself. *You're going to fix it as soon as you can.*

"What about you? What would you do with the money?" Ariana asked, taking a sip of her water.

"Travel," Kaitlynn replied. "My parents and I had this whole plan to see the world together, but we only got through Western Europe before they died. I'd see all the places we were going to see. Australia and the Far East and Africa and Russia and South America . . . just everywhere."

Ariana noted the wistful sadness in Kaitlynn's eyes and felt a pang in her heart. "You'll do it eventually."

"Yeah, right." Kaitlynn's hands came together in her lap and she looked down at them.

"You will," Ariana assured her.

She looked at her sandwich, at the exposed layer of roast beef on the top, and grimaced at the thick line of glistening fat running through it.

"Ugh. They really expect us to consume this?"

Pursing her lips in disgust, Ariana peeled the beef from the sandwich, taking with it a few curls of shredded lettuce, and tossed it into the bushes. She then carefully reassembled her meal, the sandwich now half its original size.

Kaitlynn shifted in her seat, and her tone took on a hint of concern. "Ariana, don't hate me for saying this . . ."

"What?" Ariana asked, eyebrows raised. She took a bite of her sandwich, enjoying the sudden silence. Her shoulders relaxed completely now as she looked around the courtyard. The guards all at their posts. Rambo licking his paws. The inmates either lunching or wandering around staring at the sky, the flowers, the grass. Oblivious, each and every one of them.

"It's just . . . maybe you should deal with that," Kaitlynn said, lifting a hand. "You know, your . . . eating habits."

Ariana blinked, chewing slowly. "My eating habits?"

"Well, it's just . . . you order a roast beef and turkey club every day, and then every day you throw the roast beef away."

"It's always too fatty," Ariana replied.

Kaitlynn bit her lip, as if carefully considering what to say next. "Ariana, you do know what the definition of insanity is," she said tentatively.

"Tell me." Ariana was enjoying this.

Kaitlynn looked around. She leaned into the table and lowered her voice, making sure only Ariana could hear. "It's doing the same thing over and over again, but expecting different results."

Her blue eyes were wide with unadulterated concern. So earnest it made Ariana want to giggle. But Ariana's self-control had always been her greatest asset. Except, of course, in extreme situations.

"I'm just worried about you. Maybe you should bring it up in group," Kaitlynn said.

Ariana nodded, touched by Kaitlynn's concern. "I'll think about it."

"Good."

Kaitlynn smiled. She picked up her own sandwich and took a big bite. Always polite, she waited until she had chewed and swallowed before speaking again. Ariana very much appreciated this behavior. Inside the Brenda T.'s walls, there was a lot of talking with one's mouth full. Or, for that matter, letting the food just fall right out the side of one's mouth while cackling or jabbering on.

"Know what this weather reminds me of? The summers at Camp Potowamac," Kaitlynn said, peeling the lid off her yogurt container. "Did I ever tell you about that girl Briana Leigh and I used to hang out with? Dana Dover? She was always talking about her friend Emma Walsh from home like she was some kind of Hollywood idol. . . ."

Kaitlynn launched into a story Ariana had already heard at least ten times before. The one where Dana got a letter from Emma that was essentially a breakup letter, saying they couldn't be friends anymore because Emma had a boyfriend now and she'd outgrown Dana. Dana had retaliated by writing a song to the tune of "You Are My Sunshine" called "You Are a Loser." She then got her entire bunk to sing the song into her video camera so that she could e-mail the video to Emma. It was all immature fun, and a distracting story to help whisk away the last remnants of irritation left over from Ariana's session with Meloni.

"'You are a loser . . . a big fat loser . . . ,'" Kaitlynn sang merrily under her breath.

"'*You're such a fatty . . . you block the sun . . . ,*'" Ariana sang along in her mind, having committed the tune to memory long ago.

It was an awful song. An awful and immature retaliation from a girl who should have just risen above and let her little friend Emma move on.

But then, everyone knows that teenage girls have a gift for cruelty, Ariana thought, feeling nostalgic for her former friends, her former life.

CREATURES OF HABIT

Ariana had learned a few things in her year and a half at the Brenda T. She had learned that people were creatures of habit. That if she paid enough attention to someone's tendencies—and she did have a thing for noticing details—she could predict what that person would do in any given situation. She found this discovery both spirit-crushing and very, very helpful.

It was spirit-crushing to learn that people lived by sad little routines day in and day out, because it made them far less interesting.

Helpful, because that predictability was going to set her free.

"Tracy? May I please use the bathroom?" Ariana asked, pausing outside the door to the common lavatory on Sunday.

Tracy Millet, the guard who lived to please, tried for a tough expression. As always, the effort just made her look more squirrelly and pinched than she already did. The other three inmates whom

Tracy had been escorting to the common room, Kaitlynn included, all stopped and waited.

"You okay, Osgood?" she asked.

Ariana tried not to stare at Tracy's dry brown curls, which sat atop her head like a plate of curly fries. She put her hand over her lower stomach and swallowed hard. "I'm not sure. I think they might have served bad yogurt at lunch."

"Ugh. Nasty," Donna Short said. The former child rapper, who'd been locked up for smashing in the teeth of some rival artist and was now in daily anger-management sessions, backed away from Ariana. For a girl who claimed to have been raised on the street, "Sweet D." seemed to have a low threshold for bodily functions.

Tracy's threshold, however, was even lower.

"Go ahead," the guard with a grimace. "I'll walk these three down and then I'll be right outside the door," she warned.

Ariana shoved the door open and entered the white-on-white-on-white bathroom. Everything from the tile walls to the marble floor to the porcelain toilets was bleached to a sheen. After making sure she was alone, Ariana yanked off her shoes and placed them on the counter next to the sink, feeling the chill of the floor through her white gym socks. She turned to the silver plate that served as an unbreakable (and unreliable) mirror, and stared into the mottled reflection of her blue eyes.

"One Mississippi . . . two Mississippi . . ."

Patience. Patience was the thing. Tracy was weak—pathetic, really. If Ariana stayed inside long enough, Tracy would cave. She would stand out there imagining what Ariana was doing and her leg would start to bounce. Then, after another minute, she would start to fiddle with her keys. Another minute and she'd be kneading the back of her neck with her palm. Finally, she would look both ways to make sure none of her superiors were around, and then stroll casually down to her post in the common room, where she would get sucked in by *Deal or No Deal* and all but forget about the diarrhea-ridden girl in the bathroom.

So Ariana kept counting. When she finally picked up her shoes ten minutes later and opened the door a crack to peek into the hallway, Tracy was gone. She was now standing on the inside of the metal-and-glass door to the common room, her back to the hallway. She could still turn at any moment and see Ariana, but Ariana had the sound buffer of the door and a good thirty yards of hallway between her and the guard.

Heart pounding in her ears, sneakers clutched to her chest, Ariana kept the door open but an inch and stared out. Her palms were clammy and she could hardly swallow. Everything hinged on this moment. If this didn't go exactly as planned, it would all be over before it had a chance to start.

Thirty more seconds, she told herself. And she started to count down. *Twenty-nine . . . twenty eight . . . twenty seven . . .*

Suddenly the door on the right of the bathroom was flung open. Ariana's heart flew into her throat. Nurse Knight was twenty-six seconds early. Dammit. So much for that reliable-creature-of-habit theory.

The rotund nurse stepped into the hallway and started for the common room, her thick white shoes squeak-squeaking on the linoleum floor. Ariana had only seconds or her plan would be trashed. She couldn't wait until tomorrow night. Tomorrow night would be too late. It was either act now or keep waiting—keep *rotting*—in the Brenda T.

Spurred by pure adrenaline, Ariana yanked the bathroom door open and raced in silent, socked feet to a door marked MEDICAL PERSONNEL ONLY.

It was about to click shut and auto-lock Ariana out. She flattened her hand against the door just as the metal of the latch touched the metal of the plate. The slight click sounded like an atom bomb explosion to Ariana, but she shoved into the room anyway. If Tracy or Nurse Knight were right behind her, so be it. She was not going to look back to find out.

Ariana breathed in. Waited. Nothing. No one was coming for her. The first phase of her plan was complete. She had made it inside the Drug Den.

The small, closetlike space felt like a meat locker, the air-conditioning jacked up so high her skin instantly began to tighten. All along one wall were metal cabinets with glass doors. Behind each door sat rows and rows of clear pill bottles, each filled to the brim with colorful little pills. Hundreds of thousands of little pills, all designed to keep the inmates under control, keep them sedated, keep them functioning like good little robots.

Ariana felt a flash of anger. Saw herself yanking the cabinets from the walls and tipping them over. Letting them crash and shatter and slam to the floor. *Screw them for trying to control us. Screw them for thinking they know what's best.*

But that wasn't why she was here. She gripped her forearm and breathed:

In . . . one . . . two . . . three . . .
Out . . . one . . . two . . . three . . .
In . . . one . . . two . . . three . . .
Out . . . one . . . two . . . three . . .

Until the fantasy faded away.

Her mind cleared. She focused. She was wasting precious time.

Ariana shoved open the sliding door on the first cabinet and quickly found a nice big bottle of the antianxiety drug Ativan. Thank God for alphabetization. She popped the top off and emptied at least fifty of the little white pentagonal pills into the bottom of her sneakers, then dumped the rest of the bottle into the garbage can. Holding her breath, she quickly rearranged the used paper towels and crumbled patient-care pages over the bottle to hide it, then shoved her feet into her now very uncomfortable shoes.

She carefully closed the cabinet door and breathed in. The hard part, she felt, was over. She had beaten the system. It was all she could do to keep from grinning. Shoulders back, chest held high, Ariana strolled into the hallway, letting the drug room door click shut and lock automatically behind her. Nurse Knight was nowhere in sight, and Tracy was so wrapped up in the TV, Ariana had to knock on the door of the common room before the woman even noticed her. When she did, she blanched, clearly realizing she'd fallen down on the job.

"Feeling better, Osgood?" she asked, opening the door.

"Much better, thanks," Ariana said with a pleasant smile. Her cheeks twitched, wanting to pull the smile wider, but she held back.

"Good. Because that's your last bathroom break for the night," Tracy said sternly.

Ariana walked into the common room, where the inmates were gathered on couches and chairs, reading or journaling or watching TV or staring off into space. She sat down between Kaitlynn and Crazy Cathy on one of the sofas.

"Everything okay?" Kaitlynn asked. "You looked pale back there."

"I'm fine," Ariana replied.

"I think she's gonna win the million," Crazy Cathy said, taking a break from chewing on the collar of her shirt. "I think she's gonna win. I think she looks lucky."

Ariana glanced at the TV screen and at the pretty housewife jumping up and down as she shouted out case numbers on a fluorescent stage. Normally, Ariana hated this stupid show and all the stupid people who never took the good deals when they were offered. Normally, she hated how Crazy Cathy always insisted every contestant was going to win. But tonight, somehow, none of it seemed as cloying. Tonight, as she sat with pills digging into the soft skin of her foot, all the dull predictability felt comforting. In fact, she was counting on it.

"You know what, Cathy?" Ariana said. "I think she's going to win too."

AN ATTEMPT

In the dead silence of night Ariana hit the floor with a thump, the side of her skull colliding with the cold concrete. Her shoulder exploded in pain. For a moment there was nothing but the sound of the final few pills skittering across the floor. And then:

"Ariana? Ari?"

Kaitlynn's voice filled the tiny cell. The light flicked on, a big after-hours no-no. "Oh my God. Ariana! What's wrong?"

The bedsprings squealed and Kaitlynn was on her knees. Her cold hand touched Ariana's cheek. Ariana didn't flinch. Her breath came in short, barely audible gasps, her chest motionless.

"Ariana! Can you hear me?"

There was a crunch. Kaitlynn had just knelt on one of the pills.

"What the hell—" There was a brief, satisfying pause. A rightly predicted pause. "Oh my God. Oh my God, no. No, no, no!"

Kaitlynn wrenched Ariana's torso up off the floor. Ariana's head lolled back over Kaitlynn's forearm. Her neck stretched painfully. Swallowing became impossible. Her body was heavy. So, so heavy. She felt her arms and legs go limp.

"Ariana, wake up!" Kaitlynn battered Ariana's face with a quick succession of stinging slaps. "Wake up, Ari. Please!"

Ariana's opened her mouth and let it hang that way. That did the trick. Told Kaitlynn she was not about to rouse. Ariana's friend dropped her unceremoniously. Her spine cracked against the hard floor.

That's going to leave a mark, Ariana thought.

"Guard!"

Kaitlynn slammed both hands flat against the door and beat the surface.

"Guard! Guard! I need help! It's Ariana! She's sick! Help! Help me please!"

Kaitlynn started to cry. Choke and cry and wail. All the desperation was affecting her voice. In a minute she was going to be so overcome she wouldn't be able to shout anymore.

Hold it together, Kaitlynn, Ariana silently pleaded.

"Please! Please help!" Kaitlynn croaked.

Then it started. First in Donna's room across the hall, then moving slowly from room to room on down. Everyone started to wake up. Started to grow restless from the commotion, wondering what was going on. Donna pounded on her door. Then Crazy Cathy got into the mix. Soon there was a whole chorus of shouting for the guards. Someone was singing. Another inmate slammed her own door with something much harder than her hands.

"Help! Help us! Please!"

Soon, the telltale sound of heavy, running footsteps. Jangling keys. Shouted directions. All protocol, all predicted.

"Stay on either side of the door," Tracy's voice told whichever guards were with her. "Hey! Shut up! Back to bed!" she shouted to the general population. "It's lights-out!"

The inmates only grew more raucous.

"Get back! Get back from the door!" Tracy shouted at Kaitlynn, sounding more in command than ever before. "Put your hands behind your head and face the wall on your knees!"

"Okay! Just hurry up! Please!" Kaitlynn's accent was as thick as peanut butter as she followed Tracy's orders.

The door was shoved open so hard it slammed back against the wall.

"Holy shit," Tracy said.

"Fuck. What did she take?" Miriam asked in the background. Apparently she was pulling a double shift today.

"Looks like Ativan," Tracy said, dropping down next to Ariana. "Get the doctor!"

Ariana's left eye was pried open. The eyeball rolled right into the back of her head.

"Shit. How much did she take?" Tracy shouted to Kaitlynn. She leaned over Ariana's body, placing her ear to Ariana's mouth. Short, weak breaths tickled her earlobe.

"I don't know! She fell out of bed and woke me up," Kaitlynn cried. "Is she going to be okay?"

Ariana's arm was dropped and it smacked against the floor. Luckily, her delicate wrist didn't crack. Tracy stood up and spoke into the walkie-talkie attached to her shoulder strap.

"We need a stretcher in cell number B twenty-two," she said. "She's breathing, but her pulse is weak."

Kaitlynn's bedsprings creaked as she was allowed out of her submissive position. She started to cry again, the sound of her sobs muffled by her pajama sleeve.

"Don't let her die. Please, God. Please don't take her away," Kaitlynn prayed.

Ariana wanted to tell her that everything was going to be okay, but now was obviously not the time. There was another commotion in the hallway. The room filled with emergency personnel. Someone stepped on Ariana's fingers.

"We have an attempt. Get her to the infirmary now!" Tracy ordered. "She may need her stomach pumped."

Ariana flinched. No one noticed, however, because they were too busy manhandling her onto a stretcher and elevating it until it popped up to waist level. These people needed to work on their bedside manners.

The stomach pump. She'd known it would have to happen, but hearing Tracy say it brought the reality home. The tube, the pain, the retching. Kiran had described it all to her once, and it sounded like pure hell.

But it was all part of her plan. The plan she'd been working on for too long for it to fail now. *If I want to start over, I'm just going to have to deal with it,* Ariana thought dimly as the overhead lights of the hallway began to fly by at perfect two-second intervals. Hoping that no one was watching her, she finally dared to take one deep, calming breath, fighting off the dizziness that threatened to overwhelm her oxygen-deprived brain. *I* will *deal with it. My new life depends on it.*

NEXT TIME

The fingers on Ariana's wrist felt like the icy cold harbingers of death. Ariana blinked slowly, groggily. A nurse was taking her pulse. The lights above her head were ugly, caged, fluorescent, and bright. Too bright. She flinched, squeezing her eyes shut again, and took a breath.

Her throat burned like a pit of fire. The convulsions threw her forward and her shoulder wrenched. Coughing uncontrollably, gasping for air, Ariana rolled her eyes around and found the heavy leather straps. Her wrists and ankles had been bound to the bed.

No, no, no, no, no. Get them off of me! Get them off!

Ariana wanted to scream at the startled nurse, but she couldn't even catch a breath. The memory of the stomach pumping rushed back to her. Being held down by two huge orderlies. The thick tube jammed into her throat, blocking out all air. She had tried to flail, tried to shove them off, but they had held her so firmly, like granite slabs lying on her arms and legs. She had thought she was going to die, and for the first time wondered what she'd been thinking. Whether this was all worth it. Then, once the awful, humiliating retching was done, she had closed her eyes and let the darkness come.

Tears spilled from Ariana's eyes and down into her ears. A woman placed her hand on Ariana's forehead and gently, but firmly, held her shoulders down. Colleen. It was Nurse Colleen. Ariana could barely make her out through the burning tears in her eyes, but this had been part of her plan—to land in the medical wing during Colleen's shift. She was the one semidecent person on the medical staff. The nurse brought a plastic cup full of cool water to Ariana's lips. Ariana gulped it down gratefully.

Everything was okay. She was right where she was supposed to be. Everything was going according to plan. Slowly her pulse started to relax.

"There you are . . . there you are . . . ," Colleen said, smoothing Ariana's brow with her fingers. The silver cross around Colleen's neck swung forward, hanging inches from Ariana's nose.

"Not a very nice way to wake up," Colleen said with a sympathetic cluck of the tongue. "That's what happens when your stomach's pumped. Your throat will be no good for a couple of days."

Ariana closed her eyes, calm spreading through her limbs. She could handle a little throat pain. The hard part was over now. In the past. It no longer mattered. This journey was all about the destination, not about the route she took to get there. All of this was happening for a reason. It was all part of her plan. She was in control—or as much as she could be, considering she was shackled like a zoo animal.

"What happened?" Ariana asked. Because that was what a person in her position should ask. Her voice was a croak, and the burning flared up again, but not as severely.

"What happened is you tried to kill yourself," Colleen said, strapping a blood pressure gauge around Ariana's upper arm. "You took some pills, honey. But don't worry, we got them all out of your system. You're going to be okay." Colleen had a sweet, soothing voice, much like Ariana's mother's and her grandmother's. The kind Ariana would have liked to hear read a bedtime story when she was young. Colleen had age lines around her mouth and eyes, and her dark hair was graying around the temples, but Ariana could tell she had once been pretty. How she had ended up in the godforsaken Brenda T., Ariana had no idea. But then, there were a lot of people within these walls who had no business being there.

"What day is it?" Ariana whispered, already knowing the answer.

Colleen held two fingers over Ariana's wrist, taking her pulse. "Monday. July second."

Perfect. Ariana looked around the tiny, white-walled room that would be her home for the next two days. There was a huge plate glass window next to her adjustable bed, affording a perfect view of the beach at the Philmore. The sun was just starting to come up and she could see the valets in their white pants and colorful polos arranging the lounge chairs and private tents for the guests. Ariana longed to be in one of those plush rooms across the lake, rather than inside this eight-by-eight box with its antiseptic stench and totally decoration-free walls.

Soon enough, she told herself. *Just two more days. You're almost there. Almost there . . .*

The blood pressure gauge tightened around Ariana's bicep, then deflated. Colleen made a note on her clipboard, then looked into Ariana's eyes. She seemed sad. Disappointed.

"Don't you know that your life is God's greatest gift?" she said.

Ariana bit her tongue to hold back a flare of anger. Of course she knew that. Of course she did. That was what all this was about. It was the assholes who ran this place who didn't seem to understand how precious her life was. She turned her face away from Colleen as if shamed by her words, when, in fact, she was trying to hide the ire in her eyes.

There was a quick rap on the door. Ariana glanced up as Colleen went to answer it. She caught a glimpse of Dr. Meloni's profile, framed by the high, square window in the door.

Just what Ariana had been dreading. Her hands curled into fists beneath the thick straps. She straightened her head on the thin pillow and stared up at the ceiling.

One last time. Just one last time . . .

As the door opened and Dr. Meloni stepped inside, Ariana breathed in and out deliberately.

In . . . one . . . two . . . three . . .

Out . . . one . . . two . . . three . . .

She could do this. She could deal with him. One last time.

"Hello there, Ariana," he said stepping into view at the side of her bed. He looked at the restraints on her wrists and smirked. "Comfy?"

"Why am I tied up?" She wished her voice didn't sound so uneven, so weak. She tried to make up for it with her eyes. Tried to stare right through him.

"You attempted to take your own life," he said, a teasing lilt to his voice. "This is standard procedure. We can't risk that you might try to harm yourself again. Or others."

He glanced over his shoulder. Nurse Colleen was still in the hallway, chatting with one of the orderlies. Dr. Meloni leaned in toward Ariana's ear. So close she could smell his disgustingly spicy aftershave, see the spot he'd missed on his neck while shaving. Ariana had to force herself not to squirm in her restraints.

"But here's the thing, Ariana. You didn't take enough pills to do any kind of damage. And do you know what I think?" He looked into her eyes. "I think you knew that. I think this whole thing was a farce. I think you're just a pathetic, spoiled little brat who couldn't get her way and wanted to get my attention."

Ariana pressed her lips together as a hot fury bubbled up inside of her. Of course she had known she wasn't taking enough pills to actually kill herself, but she hated that he had figured that out so easily. Not that she would ever admit it.

"I told you I just wanted it to be over," she said, looking him in the eye. "You didn't listen."

Meloni snorted a laugh. "Fine. You want it to be over so badly, then I have just one thing to say to you, Ariana," Dr. Meloni continued, standing up straight now. "Next time, try harder."

Ariana blinked. As much as she detested this man, as awful as she knew he was, this was a new level of sadism.

"Fine," she said through her teeth. "I will."

The door opened and Dr. Meloni lifted Ariana's chart from the end of her bed, pretending he had been going over it the whole time—faking it for Colleen. Ariana hated him more than ever in that moment. He was the doctor, the one in charge. He didn't have to mug for the nurse. This little charade did nothing but display his inner weakness. Ariana had always known it was there, but seeing it so plainly disgusted her.

"Just get some rest, Miss Osgood," Meloni said in a bright tone. "We'll have a nice, long session once you're off suicide watch. Talk all this through."

Or so you think, Ariana thought.

He dropped the chart and started for the door. Colleen held it open for him, but he paused.

"Put her on watch for seventy-two hours," he said.

Ariana's pulse all but stopped. She felt as if the restraints were tightening around her. Cutting into her skin. Pulling her down into some deep, dark abyss. She strained her neck to lift her head, chin to chest, so she could see them.

No. Not possible. Not acceptable. She had to be out by the morning of the fourth. Everything hinged on that date. *Everything.*

"Seventy-two hours?" Colleen frowned, holding her clipboard in both hands. "I can't do that."

"You can and you will," Meloni said ominously. "If she gets out before Wednesday, she'll be allowed in the yard for fireworks on the fourth. We can't reward this type of behavior."

Ariana's pulse was racing. She stared at Colleen. Felt almost dizzy. *Please. Please, no.*

Colleen placed her hands on her sizable hips. "I'm sorry, but I can't. The standard is forty-eight, and you know how the warden has been cracking down on procedures lately. I'm not going to lose my job on your whim."

Wow. Go, Colleen. Ariana had known there was a reason she wanted to be under Colleen's watch. Her eyes shifted to Meloni. Holding her head up was becoming difficult. She watched as his jaw worked. As he considered his options. Pull rank and make a scene, or back down. Luckily, his spineless side won out.

"Fine. Forty-eight it is," he said authoritatively. As if he had been the one making the decision. He turned and yanked the door open as wide as it would go, then stormed off down the hallway. Colleen rolled her eyes toward the ceiling and touched her cross before going about her business. Hiding a smile, Ariana dropped her head back onto the pillow and sighed.

Everything was okay. Everything was going to be okay.

"Colleen?" Ariana croaked. "Are these restraints really necessary?" she asked, slipping into her Southern accent. "Y'all know I'm not going anywhere, right?" She glanced meaningfully toward the door, knowing that at least one guard was standing watch in the hall.

Colleen considered and, probably on a power high from putting Meloni in his place, quickly loosened, then removed, the leg straps.

"Just promise me you won't try this again," Colleen said seriously as she unbuckled the wrist straps. "As long as you're drawing breath, you have the opportunity to repent. You have the chance for redemption."

"Thank you," Ariana said, touched. It was the first time in all her many days at the Brenda T. that she actually felt as if someone other than Kaitlynn cared about what happened to her. "I'll remember that."

"Good girl." Colleen patted Ariana's arm and doused the lights on her way out, enclosing Ariana in comforting darkness. "I'll be back in an hour to check on you."

The door clicked closed behind her and Ariana shoved her feet under the sheet and thin blanket that had been tucked tightly around the foot of the bed. She bent and yanked the covers out and pulled them up to her chin, then settled back and sighed. For the first time in a year and a half, she felt at peace. The other inmates always complained about suicide watch. How the staff checked on the patient every hour. How there was no rest. But Ariana was looking forward to it. Forty-eight hours in her own private room sounded like heaven. She loved Kaitlynn, but the girl could prattle on for hours, and right now Ariana could use some silence. Forty-eight straight hours of quiet contemplation. Forty-eight hours to rest up and prepare for what came next.

NEED TO KNOW

"Oh my God! Oh my God! Oh my God!"

Kaitlynn threw her bony arms around Ariana's neck and barreled her right back into the guard. Thrown off balance, Ariana laughed as Kaitlynn's curls tickled her face. She didn't even mind when the guard shoved them both into the center of the room, causing her shoulder to contract in pain—it was still sore from when she'd fallen on it the night of her "attempt." None of it mattered, because it was the morning of July 4. *Her* independence day. Finally. Her time inside the Brenda T. was about to come to a close.

"Are you all right?" Kaitlynn asked as the heavy door slammed shut behind the guard, locking them in together.

"I'm fine," Ariana said lightly, dropping onto her twin bed.

She was surprised at how good it felt to be back in her room. Even though suicide watch had been peaceful, the room she shared with Kaitlynn was much cozier than the infirmary. The walls were covered with posters of exotic destinations like Bali and Thailand and Sri Lanka on Kaitlynn's side, and tear-outs from fashion magazines on Ariana's, chronicling the spring and fall shows from the past year and a half. They had dozens of books they had taken out of the Brenda T.'s library lined up on a shelf under the picture window, and a reading corner they had constructed out of extra pillows and blankets they had accrued over the past few months. Most of all, Ariana had missed the brushed cotton blanket on her bed, her one little piece of luxury sent to her by her mother for her last birthday. The one in the medical wing had been much coarser.

Kaitlynn sat down beside Ariana on the bed, studying Ariana's face with her big green eyes.

"Oh my God. I was so worried!" Kaitlynn cried, her accent thicker than ever.

"Please, Kaitlynn—you're overreacting," Ariana said with a scoff. She kicked off her sneakers and wriggled her toes happily. She felt so rested after her time in the medical wing. She should have tried this faked suicide attempt long ago. It had been like a little vacay.

"Overreacting? You tried to kill yourself," Kaitlynn said, squeezing Ariana's fingers. "I was so freaked when you wouldn't wake up. I thought you were a goner for sure."

A goner for sure. She was so cute.

"Well, I'm fine," Ariana said again, wresting her fingers from Kaitlynn's too-tight grasp. She patted Kaitlynn's arm and leaned back, folding her pillow behind her neck to prop herself up.

Kaitlynn blew out a loud sigh and bounced around on the bed so she could face Ariana. She sat story style at the end and pulled Ariana's feet up onto her lap.

"Good. Because I do *not* know what I would do here without you," she said, rolling her eyes and holding her arms across her chest. "The last two days have been a nightmare. It was so lonely in here."

Ariana felt a pang in her chest but ignored it. Kaitlynn would get used to it. She would have to. And in the end, they would be together again.

"Did Meloni freak out?" Kaitlynn asked, her eyes wide.

Ariana snorted. "Hardly. We're *supposed* to have some massively long session tomorrow." Not that they would. "But would you believe he told me to try harder next time?"

Kaitlynn's jaw all but hit the concrete floor as she sat forward in shock. "He did not."

"He did! He's such a jackass," Ariana said, reaching up to touch her gold fleur-de-lis.

"Oh my God! We have to do something!" Kaitlynn blurted, standing up and letting Ariana's feet drop. "He can't say that to you! What kind of doctor is he? He's supposed to help you, not—"

"Kaitlynn, calm down," Ariana said, sitting up.

Kaitlynn started pacing the small room, her ranting growing louder with each word. "No! I will not calm down! He should be fired. We should have him fired. You're clearly depressed and he's supposed to help you. He can't tell you to *try harder next time*. That's sick. *Sick!*"

"Kaitlynn! Shh!" Ariana grabbed her friend's arms and glanced at the door just as the guard rapped her fist against it.

"Quiet in there!" she barked.

Ariana could feel that Kaitlynn was dying to say something, but Ariana stared her down and she stayed quiet. The guard moved on. Ariana allowed herself to breathe and released Kaitlynn's arms. She saw the white marks left by her fingers and felt badly for gripping her so tightly.

"Don't worry, okay?" she told Kaitlynn. "I'm going to deal with Dr. Meloni."

"So you *are* going to report him," Kaitlynn said, rubbing the spots on her arms.

"No. I just mean he's going to get what's coming to him," Ariana assured her with a shrug.

Kaitlynn's expression shifted. She eyed Ariana warily. "What does that mean—what's coming to him?"

Ariana decided it was time to change the subject. She didn't like the way Kaitlynn was looking at her. As if she was suddenly afraid of Ariana. Besides, her friend didn't need to know anything more. It was safer for her that way.

"Nothing. Can we please talk about something other than Dr. Meloni?"

She dropped down on her bed again and grabbed the worn copy of *Atonement* she'd been reading. Kaitlynn hesitated for a moment, then sat on the edge of her own mattress, facing Ariana across the three-foot span that separated their beds.

"How was the food?" she asked. "Is it really as good as they say?"

"Better," Ariana said with a smile. "I was allowed as much dessert as I wanted."

"Wow." Kaitlynn looked duly impressed.

"And you should have seen the view," Ariana continued. "I could see the whole lake from my window, including the beach at the hotel. I actually saw this couple making out in the middle of the night after they went for a swim."

Actually, they had gone skinny dipping and then had sex right out there on the beach for all of nature to see, but Ariana didn't want to shock Kaitlynn. The girl had never even been kissed before she'd been locked up in this hellhole.

Yet another precious experience stolen away from her by that bitch Briana Leigh Covington.

"A midnight swim," Kaitlynn said, looking wistful. "That must be heavenly. I would give anything to go for a swim in that lake. Just once."

She lay down on her bed, curling her knees up, and stared across the room. But this time, she wasn't looking at Ariana. She was gazing off into the distance. Into a future in which she might actually get to feel the cool water against her skin. Ariana knew this was one of her friend's favorite daydreams.

"We should make a pact," she said, sitting forward.

"A pact?" Kaitlynn snapped back into focus. The childlike idea of a pact was right up her alley.

"Yes. A pact," Ariana said, her eyes sparking, playing to her audience. "If we ever get out of here, we meet up at the lake, over on the east side where it's nice and shady, and go for a swim. You and me. Together."

Kaitlynn's eyes died a bit when she heard the plan, and Ariana felt a twinge of exasperation. Kaitlynn didn't believe it would ever happen. But it would.

"Yeah. Okay," Kaitlynn said sadly. "It's a pact."

They shook on it, and then they each leaned back on their own beds. Ariana was so giddy about what was to come she could hardly keep a straight face, but she knew that a girl in her position, someone who had just gotten off suicide watch and was now facing a grueling session with Meloni, would be anything but happy. She tried to put herself into an appropriate mood. What would she be doing right now? What would she actually say?

"I can't believe I have to spend all day tomorrow with Meloni," she groused. "He's probably going to give me some kind of electroshock therapy or something."

"Try not to think about it," Kaitlynn said, her voice bolstering. "Maybe it won't be as bad as you're imagining."

"I can't. I can't not think about it," Ariana said, playing up the desperation. "I hate him so much."

"Want me to tell you a story?" Kaitlynn suggested, propping herself up on her elbow.

Ariana smiled and laid her book aside. There was the Brightside Girl she knew and loved. "Definitely. One of your stories will definitely help."

"Which one? Ariana and Kaitlynn Take Manhattan? Ariana and Kaitlynn Do Paris? Ariana and Kaitlynn in the Maldives . . . ?" Kaitlynn was getting excited. There was nothing she loved better than the stories she made up about what the two of them would do if they were ever together on the outside.

"Paris," Ariana said, closing her eyes. "Definitely Paris."

"Okay. Paris it is," Kaitlynn said. Ariana heard her bed creak as she got comfortable. "We open the story on the banks of the Seine, where the local artists all clamor to paint our portraits. 'You are zee most beau-ti-ful girls we have ever seen,'" Kaitlynn said in a badly executed French accent. "'*S'il vous plaît!* Sit for us! It would be such an honor to paint you. . . . We will not even charge for the service!'"

Ariana laughed, covering her mouth with her hand.

"You turn away, blushing, and nearly trip over a man crouched next to his unopened easel. He looks up at you, and your eyes lock. He has the most gorgeous brown eyes you've ever seen in your life. It's love at first sight."

"Sounds perfect," Ariana said, opening her eyes. "But what about you?"

"Oh, he has a brother," Kaitlynn added quickly. "A much hotter brother."

Ariana laughed. "Of course he does."

"Of course," Kaitlynn added, laughing as well.

As Kaitlynn continued her story, Ariana's heart was a tangle of melancholy and excitement. She hated that she was going to have to leave Kaitlynn later today, but she was also happy because soon, they would both be free. Soon she was going to be able to make all these stories Kaitlynn had been telling her come true.

Her plan was going to work. It had to. Not just for her own sake, but for Kaitlynn's as well.

SO UNLADYLIKE

The night was warm and muggy, the air so thick with humidity it clung to Ariana's skin and made breathing a chore. Letting them out into the yard for Lake Page's Fourth of July fireworks was one of the warden's great gifts to his inmates. It was the only night of the year they were afforded such a privilege, and Ariana recalled that last year the prisoners had been beside themselves with giddiness. Tonight, however, the general population just seemed sluggish and annoyed, as if they would have preferred being left in their common rooms with their TVs and their air-conditioning. They groused and grumbled as they trudged across the lawn or dropped down on the grass to wait for the show. Ungrateful, every one of them.

Every one of them, save Ariana Osgood. Ariana couldn't have been more grateful. If she could have, she would have sent the warden a polite little note of thanks. What he didn't know was that he was aiding and abetting what Ariana hoped would be the first-ever escape from his precious facility. The fireworks and their noise were going to provide the perfect cover.

Now all she had to do was ditch Kaitlynn. Even though it pained her to do so.

"Did I ever tell you about that Independence Day when Grandma C. took all of us to the Texas hill country to spend the day on the river and watch the fireworks?" Kaitlynn said wistfully as they walked the yard. "Her father always used to take her there for the festivities, and she wanted to share it with us. Briana Leigh whined about it the whole time, of course. She wanted to go to the big barbecue picnic at the country club and hook up with Tad McMurray, but I loved it. I think that was the first time Grandma C. and I really bonded. . . ."

Ariana was only half paying attention to Kaitlynn's ramble. She was too busy scanning the yard for someone to distract her friend. Finally she saw E Cup—real name Maria Huff—strolling by, and grabbed her opportunity.

"Hey, Maria!" Ariana called out, interrupted Kaitlynn in the middle of a sentence. Maria looked over her shoulder, surprised. She and Ariana had spoken a total of three times.

"Yeah?" she said.

"C'mere." Ariana motioned with her hand.

Maria did so, shuffling her small feet. Maria was small all over. About four-foot nine, with toothpick legs, and arms that appeared as if they could be snapped like twigs. Everything was small except her breasts—her humongous fake breasts. She had been a call girl in Las Vegas in her former life: a high-paid call girl with a huge mansion in the desert and four cars and five Chihuahuas about whom she *loved* to talk. Maria had been living the life. Which made Ariana wonder what had possessed her to run over the proprietor of her strip club nine times with each of those four cars.

But then, one never knew what could make a person snap.

"What's up, Georgia Peach?" Maria asked, hands clasped behind her back.

"I was just thinking about my dog, Tara, back home and I remember hearing that you had dogs too," Ariana ventured, feigning interest. "What kind were they again? Shih tzus?"

Maria pulled an irritated face, her tiny features screwing up like a cartoon mouse's. "Ew. No. They're Chihuahuas. And my sister just sent me new pictures of 'em. Check it out." She pulled several bent photos out of her waistband and held them out for Ariana and Kaitlynn to see.

There they were. Five Chihuahuas all dressed up like ballerinas— tutus, crowns, and all. Ariana bristled. Animals dressed in human clothing was just so wrong. She felt humiliated on the dogs' behalf. Kaitlynn, however, loved it.

"Awww! Look at the little poochies!" she cooed, her voice going up an octave.

"Adorable!" Ariana forced herself to exclaim. She had seen Maria showing those pictures around to her table at breakfast that morning. As her tablemates cooed over them, Ariana had realized that God was on her side. She knew they would make for the perfect distraction tonight.

Kaitlynn reached for the photos, but Maria slapped her hands away. Kaitlynn drew her hands to her chest and pouted.

"Look, but don't touch," Maria warned.

For a breathless second Ariana thought Kaitlynn was going to walk away to sulk, but the dogs were too much for her to resist.

"What're their names again?" she asked Maria.

"This one's Betty . . . that one's Sam. The one with the lazy eye is Chita. You should have heard the way she was barking the last time I talked to my sister. I swear she knew I was on the phone."

"Oh, well, she knows her mommy! Of course she does!" Kaitlynn said, jutting out her lower lip in a precious way.

Slowly, Ariana backed away from the pair of dog lovers and ducked behind a crowd of women from Ward Three. Within ten seconds she had become just another one of the hundreds of dancing shadows on the lawn, and she allowed herself a quick moment to breathe. One obstacle down. Only a thousand more to go. But there was no telling how long Maria would keep Kaitlynn occupied. How long it would be before Kaitlynn came looking for her. Ariana wanted to glance back, take one last look at her friend, but she couldn't risk catching Kaitlynn's attention

Up above there was a loud crack, and suddenly the sky was illuminated by a thousand white sparks. Everyone in the yard reacted in some way. Oohing or ahhing or laughing.

"Pretty!" Crazy Cathy yelled, jumping up and down and clapping. "Pretty stars!"

Ariana's heart, already pounding, started to hammer in her chest.

Still, she managed to move slowly so as not to arouse the attention of any of the guards. Slowly, slowly, slowly, Ariana wound her way toward the table she and Kaitlynn shared every day at lunch. Her palms were slick with sweat. She wrinkled her nose and surreptitiously wiped them on her jeans. Sweat was so unladylike. But then, Ariana was about to get very, very unladylike.

On the other side of the fence, Rambo was going insane—petrified of the fireworks. It seemed that Meloni had decided to work late, as he so often did. Ariana pursed her lips. This was going to make things more difficult. Luckily, however, she had planned for this possibility.

Another explosion lit the sky. This one red, then orange, then yellow. Ariana watched the upturned faces of the inmates as they shifted from color to color. Her heart was pin-balling now, trying to slam its way out through her rib cage. Miriam stood not twenty yards away, chatting with another guard. Even as they gossiped, their eyes scanned the faces of the inmates. They were on their game tonight. Too on.

This is never going to work.

It has to work.

This is never going to work.

It has to work. There is no other way.

Ariana's hands trembled. She saw Miriam's gaze start to slide in her direction, and looked up at the sky just as a resounding *boom* brought a shower of purple and white sparks. In that moment she held her breath, certain that Miriam had read something on her face. That Miriam and her partner were on their way over to her right then and there. But when she slowly brought her eyes down again, the guards had gone back to their gabfest.

It was now or never.

Ariana took a sideways step toward the bushes. Crazy Cathy bounced and clapped. Rambo barked and growled. The sky exploded overhead, so loud that even Miriam jumped and looked up. Ariana seized her moment and dove into the bushes. Her knees hit the hard ground and she fell onto her stomach, slithering into a large hole that had been dug under the chain-link fence. Scrabbling like a rat, she dug her nails into the dirt and clawed her way forward.

Almost instantly, the sharp, rusted bottom edge of the chain link caught on the back of her crappy blue shirt. Ariana paused. The hole was not as deep as she had hoped. Could she shimmy back out and try to gouge out some of the dirt with her hands? As she hesitated, more explosions sounded overhead. Behind them, Ariana heard shouts. Her pulse screeched to a terrifying stop.

Were they coming after her? Had someone seen?

Lying there, chest to the dirt, Ariana started to panic. Her thoughts raced. Her vision prickled over with tiny black dots. They had seen. They had seen. They were all converging on her. Someone was about to grab her ankles and drag her back and—

No. She couldn't let it happen. She was not going back to that cell.

The very thought was enough to bring Ariana back to the task at hand. Her vision cleared. She took a deep breath, held it, and planted her face in the earth. Dug her fingers into the dirt on the other side of the fence, the side where she would be free, and pulled herself forward with all her might. Her legs flailed behind her, pushing her forward. Ariana sucked in her stomach and willed herself to become as skinny as she could possibly be, but still the sharp, rusted edge of the chain link tore through her shirt and pierced her skin. She dragged herself forward, crying out in pain—a cry masked by the fireworks—as the metal cut a long, jagged tear in her back. Tears streamed from her eyes, but she had to keep going. The next shove freed her from the fence, but she could feel a warm trickle of blood running down her side into the ground.

I'm bleeding. I'm bleeding. I'm bleeding. . . .

It doesn't matter. Shut up. You have to move. Just move!

The ditch was already sloping upward on the other side. Ariana arched her back, wincing at a new stab of pain, and pulled herself up. She looked back at the fence. Most of her torso was free. One last push and she'd be out. She could practically taste freedom. Taking a deep breath and grunting along with the next firework explosion, Ariana used every ounce of strength in her arms to pull herself up. The lace on her sneaker caught on the fence, and she yanked her foot with all her might. There was one last tear, and then she was free.

Chest rising and falling with her rapid breaths, Ariana dropped onto her back on the dirt, not even caring that she was exposing her cut to the ground. Overhead a red firework filled the night sky, followed quickly by a white, then a blue.

Ariana smiled. She was free. Finally, finally free.

That was when she felt Rambo's hot breath on her face.

Ariana flipped over and bolted up to a seated position, then immediately realized her mistake. Rambo took her sudden movement as a sign of aggression and lunged for her. Biting down on the inside of her cheek to keep from screaming, Ariana hurtled backwards and, by the grace of God, Rambo's running leash caught. She was mere inches outside his attack zone. But now he was barking like the angry, trained attack dog he was. His teeth were huge and sharp and dripping with saliva. Ariana could practically feel them piercing her skin, his strong jaw bearing down on her bones. Still, he was not nearly as scary as the fate that would befall her if someone came to check out his fit.

If they came, it would be all over. If they came, she was done. And Meloni's dog would have been the one to catch her. That was *not* going to happen.

Quickly, Ariana reached into her bra and peeled out the three slices of roast beef that had been fermenting there since lunch. Her nose wrinkled. So, so gross. But the moment she held them out to Rambo, he fell silent, sat down, and cocked his head with interest.

So, so worth it.

"There you go. Good boy . . . ," Ariana said, inching forward. She held the first bit out to him, but he didn't move. Meloni had trained his dog well, the bastard. "Go ahead, Rambo. It's for you."

He raised his snout and swallowed the slice with one gulp. Ariana slowly lifted herself off her knees and stood up. Rambo watched the roast beef. Blood dripped down Ariana's back into the waistband of her jeans. She used her free hand to hold what was left of her tattered shirt against the cut. The pain was excruciating, but she could deal with that later.

"That's right, puppy," Ariana said in a soothing voice. "I'm the one who's been tossing this stuff to you at lunchtime."

She held out another bit and the dog smacked it up happily, then licked her hand.

"You're welcome," she said affectionately, patting his head. "And thank *you* for digging for it and digging me out. I promise you I won't forget it. But for right now, I have to go."

Rambo tilted his head the other way, his ears turning in the breeze as more explosions crackled overhead. He looked at Ariana almost as if he understood what she was saying. That this was good-bye. For some strange reason Ariana's eyes filled with tears.

"Don't worry. I'll be seeing you again," she said.

Then she tossed the last piece of meat on the ground in front of him and ran like hell for the lake.

FEELING LUCKY

There were two cars in the driveway, but the cabin was dark. The owners were probably out on one of the many pontoon boats on the lake, hanging out after the fireworks. Ariana crouched on the private dock and quickly unwound the rope that held the tiny metal skiff in place. The little boat was probably some kid's first vessel, and she felt a slight pang at depriving him of it, but hopefully it would be returned. Besides, it was for a good cause. She liked to think the young boy would have approved of the intrigue that was going to surround his boat's fate. With a shove, she sent the skiff into the lake and watched for a moment to ensure that the wind would do its job and carry it toward the deeper water. Then she quickly turned and ran to a cabin two houses over. She paused for a moment, said a quick prayer, and turned the knob of the front door. Unlocked. Yes. Just as she had hoped. These vacation homes on the lake were all owned by happy-go-lucky, upper-middle-class families who trusted their neighbors.

Well, trust was for suckers.

Ariana slipped inside, crossed the sunken living room, and took the wide wooden stairs two at a time. She found the master bedroom at the end of the hallway and flicked on the light in the master bath.

Her reflection was a horror show. Hair knotted and matted with dirt. Brown streaks all over her face. Nails broken and lined with black muck. There was a cut over her right eyebrow and her shirt was torn to shreds. Not knowing how long she might have, Ariana peeled her clothes off. What little cash she had saved up over the past year and a half in prison—money she'd earned by selling off the food and magazines her mother had sent her—fell out of her underwear, where she'd hidden it. Ariana reverently placed the bills on the side of the sink. She could not lose that money. It was all she had.

She jumped in the shower and winced when the hot water hit her cut. She contorted herself in every direction trying to get the soap in and around the fresh wound. It stung so much she wanted to cry all over again, but she bit the urge back. Ariana had always prided herself on being tough after everything she had gone through with her family and Thomas, but she had never had to endure actual physical pain. This was new, but she could handle it. The last thing she needed was an infection. Hospitals were not an option.

Wrapping a towel around herself, Ariana raced back into the bedroom and shoved open the closet door. Her nose wrinkled. L.L. Bean, all the way. But still. There had to be something here she could work with. She grabbed an old, faded yellow Patagonia backpack off the floor, balled up her prison garb, and shoved it into the bottom.

She then dug to the back of the closet, hoping to find some clothes that were no longer favorites and therefore might not be missed. She selected a pair of cargo khakis and a white T-shirt, which she shoved in the bag as well, then added an Orioles baseball cap and a light blue sweater. She lost the towel and pulled her sweaty underpants and roast-beefy bra back on—she was not about to wear another woman's underwear—then yanked out a plain white V-neck sweater and a pair of jeans. The sweater fit fine, but the jeans were two sizes too big, so she cinched them with a leather belt she found hanging on a hook by the door, then shoved her feet into a pair of hiking boots a size too small.

"Huge ass, small feet. Fab." Ariana giggled to herself. Beggars couldn't be choosers. She couldn't have been happier to have been wearing the freak show's B-list outdoorsy outfit.

Back in the bathroom, Ariana stole a hairbrush, an unopened tube of lip balm, and a bar of soap, just in case. Satisfied that she had everything she actually needed to hold her over until she reached her destination, she shouldered the backpack and raced downstairs. Halfway across the living room, she heard voices on the front porch. Ariana froze, her heart hurtling into her throat.

A man laughed. Two kids were babbling on about the fireworks. She could see their shadows playing outside the front windows. Ariana whirled around and spotted the kitchen through an open doorway.

Back door. Please let there be a back door.

She stumbled on her way across the threshold, slammed her hip into a wooden chair at the kitchen table, and grasped for the door handle just as the front door opened. Ever so quietly, Ariana slipped out into the warm night air, letting the door click closed behind her. For the second time that night, she ran for her life.

Less than an hour later, Ariana stood in front of a bored, elderly teller who sat behind the window at the Arlington, Virginia, bus station. Her hair hidden under the Orioles baseball cap, Ariana was surprised at how calm she felt. But then, she had covered her bases. By now, Kaitlynn had to have found the note. By now, no one would be looking for her. At least not this far out of the facility.

"Help you?" the man said, barely lifting his eyes from his horse racing form.

"One ticket to Dallas, please," Ariana said, sliding the cash into the dip below the window. The dip that reminded her suddenly of the ditch Rambo had dug for her. The thought made her smile.

"What're you so happy about?" the man asked, not unkindly. He slid her ticket and change over to her.

"Nothing," she said, the smile widening. "You should bet the six horse."

For the first time his heavy eyelids raised a fraction of a centimeter.

"Yeah? Why's that?"

Ariana placed her ticket in the inside pocket of her backpack along with what was left of her money. Right next to the box of auburn hair dye she had purchased at the drugstore down the street.

"It's my lucky number," she replied.

She checked the schedule on the screen behind the man's head and saw that she would have just enough time to dye her hair before her bus began to board.

"Oh?" he asked, glancing down at the sheet again. "You feeling lucky today?"

"Very," Ariana said with a nod. "Trust me. It can't lose."

The man raised his bushy white eyebrows and circled the six horse on his racing form. Ariana turned and headed off for the private handicapped bathroom with a bit of swagger in her step. She had just done her good deed for the day.

SNAP DECISIONS

"Those colors *really* suit you," the perky blond Chanel cosmetics clerk said, grinning from ear to ear.

It was Friday morning and Ariana was staring at her reflection in the magnifying mirror that sat atop the gleaming glass counter at the Dallas Neiman Marcus. The gray shadows and black mascara that the girl had expertly applied really made her blue eyes pop. After looking at her eyes sans liner and mascara and only in mottled mirrors for more than a year, Ariana had forgotten how gorgeous they could be. The auburn hair was, of course, throwing her off, but the clerk had swept it back in a headband, and if Ariana tilted the mirror just so, she didn't have to look at it. Then she could see only herself.

And she looked beautiful.

Not bad for a girl who had just spent hours and hours on a Greyhound bus trying in vain to sleep as the loudmouthed man across the aisle gabbed on his cell phone. Unable to get a single moment of peace, Ariana had occupied herself with daydreams of what her life would be like now that she was on the outside. After securing her financial future, she would go back to Virginia and get Kaitlynn out of the Brenda T. Then the two of them would flee to Australia and lie low for a while before building a dream home near the water and living their lives as beach bums. It meant giving up the original dream— the Princeton, New York, *Vanity Fair* dream—the thought of which made her heart ache. But at least she and Kaitlynn would be together. At least they would be free.

Once she had the whole plan solidified in her mind, the jerk with the phone had finally passed out in his seat, but it had been too late for Ariana to sleep. The bus had pulled into the station ten minutes later, and Ariana had trudged into the Texas sunshine feeling exhausted and cranky. But with each passing moment under the soft lights of Neiman Marcus, surrounded by all the opulence and luxury, she was growing more and more comfortable and calm.

This was the moment she had been longing for all those months. The moment she began to feel herself again.

"Well? What do we think? Should I wrap it all up for you?"

According to her name tag, the clerk's name was Kelsi, which totally fit her annoyingly in-your-face demeanor. But Ariana had chosen her for a reason. The eager ones were always the most gullible.

Ariana looked down at all the tiny black lacquer compacts and tubes the girl had assembled before her. What she wouldn't have given to just whip out her old Neiman's credit card and buy the whole lot. But that wasn't an option. Instead, she was going to have to play the game. She leaned forward to avoid a group of gabbing girls her age, all laden down with packages. Still, one of them managed to whack Ariana in the back with the corner of one of her bags. She winced as her cut burned.

"I'm just not sure," Ariana said with a sigh. "I don't know if I'm ready to change my entire color palette."

"Oh, well, you don't have to change *everything*," the girl said quickly, brightly. "Sometimes a new gloss and a blusher do just the trick!"

"I don't know. I have to think about it. I've never been good at snap decisions."

Ariana pushed herself up off the cushy leather stool she had been sitting on for the past half hour. She knew that the girl didn't want to lose her sale. All that time she had spent making over Ariana would have been wasted if Ariana walked away with nothing. The desperation was evident in the girl's eyes as Ariana shouldered her backpack.

"Thanks for you time," Ariana said.

"Wait!" the girl hissed as Ariana turned to go. "I can give you a few free samples."

Ariana smiled to herself, but when she turned to face the girl, she was all interest.

"Really?"

Kelsi checked over her shoulder to make sure that none of her colleagues were listening in. They were all busy with other clients. Kelsi stepped out from behind the counter in her black smock. Ariana's eyes instantly flicked to her shoes. Black sling-back Michael Kors knock-offs. It figured.

"If you're not so good at snap decisions, maybe you'd like to try a few of these things out on your own," the girl whispered. "Then, once you're convinced, you can come back and purchase whatever you like. Just ask for me."

Ariana pretended to be relieved. "That would be perfect."

"You promise you'll be back?" Kelsi asked.

"I promise," Ariana said solemnly.

"Then I know I'll see you again!" the girl said brightly. "You have a very honest face!"

As Ariana hid a smile, Kelsi walked back behind the counter and opened a small paper Neiman Marcus bag, into which she deposited the samples she had used for Ariana's makeover—a trial-size mascara, a tiny compact of powder, a pot of cream blush, and a small lip gloss. She handed the package over to Ariana like a spy passing off some secret documentation.

"I predict you'll be back before the end of the day," she said confidently.

"Thank you *so* much," Ariana gushed.

Then she turned and sauntered off toward the escalator with a triumphant grin. This was going to be even easier than she'd hoped.

SHOPPING SPREE

The dressing room was large and plush, with mirrors on three walls and classical violin music playing at an unobtrusive level through speakers overhead. Ariana kicked off her too-small hiking boots and pressed her callused, blistered feet into the thick, soft carpet. She tipped her head back, closed her eyes, and let out a sigh. It had been almost two years since her feet had touched anything so soft.

Of course, even the carpeting wasn't quite as exciting as the prospect of new clothes. With a giddy zeal, Ariana attacked the selection of items she had snagged from the impeccably organized racks out on the floor. First, the underwear. She used the cuticle scissors she'd purchased at the drugstore to cut a tiny hole around the sensor on a Calvin Klein bra and a pair of La Perla panties and pulled them on. Her whole body shivered in delight. So nice to be wearing undergarments that didn't smell like roast beef. Then she pulled on a pair of Rock & Republic jeans and checked her reflection from behind.

There was her butt. She had forgotten what it looked like in the baggy denim she'd been wearing for the past year and a half. Topping off the jeans with a silky, light pink Marc Jacobs top, Ariana fastened the tiny pearl buttons, savoring the tickle of the luxurious, lightweight fabric against her skin. She lifted her blue eyes and looked at her reflection in the mirror. Her hair might have been a new, unfamiliar color, but her eyes welled with happy tears nonetheless. She sat back on the velvet bench along the far wall, indulging her overwhelming emotions for just a moment.

For the first time since she had busted out of the Brenda T., Ariana was starting to feel like herself again.

Fifteen minutes later, the sensors were gone from the jeans and top along with a wispy Thread dress, a few Three Dots tees, a pair of DKNY shorts, and a Chloé skirt. Ariana rolled the clothes up as tightly as she could, grateful that summer wear was so thin and manageable, and stuffed it all into her backpack along with a few more sets of underwear.

She quickly whipped out the Chanel lip gloss from the little Neiman's bag and reapplied. Then she slipped a leather Michael Kors clutch from under the pile of clothes on the bench, removed the sensor from that as well, and popped the lipstick inside. Admiring the purse in the mirror, Ariana sighed. She couldn't wait to finally ditch the bulky backpack and carry this sleek little bag instead. But for now, the backpack was serving its purpose.

Placing the tight hiking boots back onto her feet was like torture, but Ariana managed to get through it by daydreaming about her next stop—the shoe department. She opened the door to the dressing room and strode out with her chin held high, pausing to check out a colorful blouse some other shopper had left on the rack by the dressing room door.

If she just acted casual, no one would be the wiser.

On her way to the gleaming walkway between departments, Ariana's left foot twinged in pain, and she remembered that she wasn't done yet. If shoes made the woman, then she was still nothing but a grungy fugitive. She paused to check the store directory and was nearly knocked over by a pair of brassy ladies in huge flower prints carrying half a dozen bags each. The summer sales were on and the store was jam-packed with designer-hungry bargain-hunters. Normally not one for crowds, Ariana smiled as she realized her luck. The shoe department would be a madhouse.

Twenty minutes later, Ariana had gathered several pairs of sandals, sling-backs, boots, and flats and found one of the very few unoccupied seats in the center of the shoe department. All around her women jammed their feet into shoes from the sale racks, boxes and boxes piled up next to them. Ariana waited ten minutes, a totally unacceptable period of time, before one of the salesladies finally noticed her. She rushed over, all harried, with her curly hair floating out around her head like brown cotton candy, and heaved a sigh.

"So sorry, miss," she said, grabbing up the shoes Ariana had gathered. "Size?"

"Six," Ariana replied. "And please, don't worry about it. It's crazy here today."

"Tell me about it!" the woman said, taking a breath. "Thanks for understanding."

Ariana smirked as the woman scurried away. *As long as you understand when I deprive your department of a few hundred dollars' worth of shoes.*

As she waited, Ariana watched a tall woman across from her try on several pairs of expensive sandals without even bothering to put peds over her gnarled, callus-ridden toes. She wrinkled her nose in distaste and looked away.

"Here you go!"

The saleswoman returned and dumped ten shoe boxes at Ariana's feet. Instantly, three more shoe-wielding shoppers descended upon her, demanding sizes. She made a few notes and rushed off again without a second glance back at Ariana.

Perfect. Slowly, deliberately, Ariana opened each of the boxes. She didn't even need to try the shoes on. She had owned several pairs of shoes from these designers in her former life and knew that she was a perfect size six on their size charts. Quickly checking to make sure that none of the other shoppers were looking, Ariana slipped a pair of Coach flats into her bag. She followed them with a pair of leather Michael Kors sandals, black sling-backs, and some cute Kenneth Cole sneakers. Then she paused. The bag was full to bursting. If she tried to get anything else in there, it was either going to tear, or someone was going to notice the shape of a heel sticking into the vinyl and she'd get snagged.

Decisions, decisions.

Ariana eyed the rest of the shoes with longing. Finally, she decided on a pair of sensible black D&G sandals, which would go with almost anything. She pushed her feet into them and sighed. Not one of her painful blisters was aggravated by the straps. They were like heaven for her toes.

Quickly, Ariana placed her hiking boots inside the sneaker box, closed it up, and put it on the bottom of the stack. She then closed all the other boxes and looked around. Her saleswoman was helping a middle-aged woman with leathery skin strap on a pair of four-inch heels. Taking a deep breath, Ariana shouldered her now quite heavy backpack and strolled away from the shoe department.

On the way back through the women's clothing department, one of the saleswomen gave her an admiring smile—the sort of smile Ariana had been used to before her stay at the Brenda T. Ariana felt a flutter of pride. She was back. Really and truly back.

A SCARE

Ariana strolled the mall in her new sandals, heading for the exit at a deliberate pace. She knew that sooner or later that saleswoman was going to find all those empty boxes along with her crappy boots, and sound the alarm. Hopefully she wouldn't be able to pinpoint the nice girl with the auburn hair as the culprit, but one never knew. Her stomach growled as she passed by an upscale bar and grill. What she wouldn't give for some real food. . . .

"Ariana Osgood."

Ariana stopped in her tracks. Her heart fluttered so rapidly it made her cough. Who the hell did she know in Dallas? How had they recognized her? What was she going to do? Her fingers curled into fists as her vision prickled over. She was not going back. Never going back. Instantly, her mind started to concoct scenarios. There was an exit to her left—a small one, kind of dark and unused. A maintenance cart was parked off to the side. If she could lure whoever it was down there, she might have a shot at getting rid of them. There had to be something on that cart she could use. A plastic bag for suffocation, a stepladder as a club. . . . There were always ways. Ever so slowly, Ariana turned around, ready to do whatever it took to maintain her freedom.

But there was no one there. The voice was not coming from a person. It was coming from the TV behind the bar.

Her own smiling face stared back at her from the screen, a photo taken back at Easton during a schoolwide charity event. Ariana started to tremble as her empty stomach clenched. She hadn't eaten anything other than pretzels and water for the past two days—all she could afford on her meager stash—and suddenly she felt weak. Stepping forward, she leaned her hand on the back of one of the tall bar stools for support.

". . . body of Atlanta socialite Ariana Osgood has yet to be found, but we have now learned that the convicted murderer attempted suicide just days before her disappearance. When a new suicide note was found by her cellmate on the night of July fourth, a full-scale search of the facility was conducted. That was when prison officials found a hole beneath the fence surrounding the facility, which seems to have been dug out by a dog owned by one of the employees."

The camera focused in on the ditch. It looked so small in the light of day. Ariana's heart constricted as the memories of that night assaulted her, and she started to sweat.

I'm okay. . . . I'm okay. . . . It's over. I'm not going back. Never going back . . .

Her grip on the bar stool tightened and she forced herself to breathe.

In . . . one . . . two . . . three . . .

Out . . . one . . . two . . . three . . .

She glanced around, expecting to see a crowd forming around the television. Dozens of people rapt with interest. But the shoppers in the mall just kept right on about their business, window shopping, chatting on their cells, maneuvering their strollers onto the escalator. No one here cared. No one had noticed her.

"That same employee is now under investigation for his role in Miss Osgood's apparent suicide," the reporter continued.

The news feed flipped to footage of Dr. Meloni with his head bowed, ducking away from reporters as he headed for his Jag in the Brenda T.'s parking lot.

Never going back . . . Never going back . . .

"According to sources within the facility, Dr. Meloni was Miss Osgood's assigned psychiatrist, but after her last suicide attempt, he allegedly urged her to 'try harder next time.' "

Ariana's mouth twitched into a strained smile, despite the unflattering mug shot from nearly two years ago that now filled the screen. Even in her state of high alert she was able to appreciate this bit of news. Kaitlynn had done well. And Dr. Meloni was clearly being hounded by the press—a satisfying little development.

Suddenly Ariana felt a nudge at her shoulder. The lump of fear in her throat hardened, choking off her air supply. Someone had recognized her. Of course they had. She was standing right there, not ten feet from the television, staring at her own face. Her fight-or-flight reflex told her to drop everything and run. But then a little voice in her mind told her not to overreact. She had come too far to just run now. Controlling her rapid heartbeat, she turned around. A very cute, very scruffy twentysomething guy sat on the stool next to hers, nursing a beer.

"Crazy story, huh?" he asked, looking right into her eyes.

Her eyes. Her eyes. Ariana had to get her hands on some colored contacts. What if this guy recognized that the light blue eyes staring at him now were the same ones staring out from the TV screen?

"It really makes you think," he added.

Ariana took a breath. He didn't recognize her. Her mug shot was right in front of him, and yet this guy had no clue.

This was going to work. It was already working.

Suddenly Ariana realized how close she had come to the edge. When she had first heard her name, she had been ready to do anything to silence the person who had recognized her. Ready to kill. And the thought scared her. She had to squelch that side of herself. Had to make a new start now that she had a second chance. Taking lives was not an option. She knew that it was wrong.

Plus, where there was a dead body, there was usually a murder investigation. And she couldn't have that.

I will not lose control, Ariana promised herself right then and there. *I will* not *hurt anyone.*

"I know," Ariana said smoothly, making sure to keep her Southern accent buried. She glanced up at the picture of herself just before it was pulled from the screen. "Totally, totally insane."

A moment later he got up to go to the bathroom, leaving his credit card on the bar to pay for his drink. Southern men. So trusting. With the bartender's back turned, Ariana slipped the card into her pocket and casually strolled away. There had to be a quickie eyeglass place in this mall somewhere. Hearing her name and seeing her own face broadcast on national television had been enough to put a bit of a scare in Ariana. It was time for another change. She was not going to risk someone looking into her distinctive blue eyes and seeing Ariana Osgood.

NEW FRIENDS

Wearing her new skirt and a crisp white T-shirt, her auburn hair pinned back from her face to highlight her new green eyes, Ariana walked up to the gates of the Walker Country Club and sat down on the clipped grass next to the drive. Seeing a golf cart zooming toward the gates from the direction of one of the surrounding PGA-level courses, she cupped her ankle with both hands. Furrowed brow, concerned frown, shoe tossed carelessly on the grass: Clearly she was a girl in need of assistance.

The golf cart slid to a stop right in front of her, making the zipping noise Ariana recognized so well, and two older, distinguished-looking gentlemen in khaki pants and tasteful pastel shirts stepped out.

"Are you all right, miss?" the taller one asked. His lined face was red from the sun, save where his sunglasses sat on the bridge of his nose. He wore a white mesh golf hat, but it clearly had done nothing to shield him from the elements.

"I think I may have sprained it," Ariana replied, grimacing through her Southern drawl.

The second man, whose skin was smooth and had just a touch of a healthy tan, glanced up at the gates, still locked. "Were you coming or going?"

A warm breeze rustled the trees around the gates and Ariana's heart skipped an excited beat. She was going to get inside. This was going to work. Amazing how one day all she could think about was breaking *out* of a place, and a few days later all she could think about was breaking *into* another.

"Coming," Ariana said. "I was supposed to meet my friend by the pool half an hour ago." She gave them an endearing, embarrassed smile. "I'm afraid I'm a notorious latecomer."

The two men laughed and each offered her a hand. Ariana couldn't help but notice their exclusive Tag Heuer watches. Very nice. "Well, don't worry. We'll get you to her."

"Really? Oh, thank you ever so much," Ariana said, laying it on thick.

She let the taller man pull her to her feet and leaned into him as he helped her over to their cart. He grabbed her overstuffed backpack and placed it next to their golf bags on the rear rack. Ariana had come straight from the mall.

"All settled?" the tall man asked as Ariana carefully slipped her foot into the cart.

"Yes. Thank you. Really. Y'all are such gentlemen."

The two men glanced at one another, all puffed up and pleased with themselves. Ariana smirked as they took their seats and the cart jolted to life. Two minutes later they had entered their pass code into the keypad by the gate, and Ariana was in. She leaned back and enjoyed the view as they wound their way toward the main club-house. The grounds inside the exclusive club were impeccably kept, with beds of blooming flowers, towering pecan trees, and cacti dotting the cart path. Ariana thought of Kaitlynn and how much she appreciated good landscaping. She sighed, missing her friend. If Kaitlynn had known where she was headed right then, she would have been shocked off her prison bed.

A pair of security guards in white uniforms glanced at the cart as it drove by. Ariana's heart skipped a nervous beat, but she kept her expression placid, bored. One of the two young men nodded at her in acknowledgment—and appreciation—as she was whisked on by, and Ariana smiled the moment her back was to him.

She belonged. It was obvious to him that she belonged.

The cart pulled to a stop near the edge of an outdoor patio that overlooked one of the club's resort-style pools. Indigenous stones surrounded a huge, burbling waterfall and an in-pool bar. Ladies in wide-brim straw hats and designer loungewear sat around glass-topped tables, sipping ice water and picking at crisp salads. Ariana noted the large handbags, some carelessly yawning open at their owners' sides as they gossiped obliviously. These women were, of course, safe in their country club environment, surrounded by their own ilk. Ariana tucked a loose strand of auburn hair back into her bobby pin. That blind trust could be a girl's best friend. Ariana's white knights helped her to a thickly padded lounge chair under a wide umbrella near the edge of the water and ordered her an iced tea from the hovering waitress.

"Would you like us to look for your friend?" the doctor asked solicitously. "What's her name?"

"Oh, no. You've been kind enough. To be honest, she's probably not here yet," Ariana lied smoothly. "She's usually even later than I am."

The two men chuckled and said their good-byes, warning her to stay off her ankle for the day. Two minutes later Ariana was sipping iced tea and focusing on the task at hand. She hoped she had been deposited at the right pool. According to Kaitlynn's accounts, there were two on the grounds. Feeling a sharp pain in her arm, Ariana realized she was digging her fingers into her flesh, and she told herself not to stress. If it didn't happen today, there was always tomorrow. Tomorrow she could flag down another pair of gullible old men and start all over again.

Settling back into her seat, Ariana tipped her face toward the sun, looking every bit the bored teenage socialite, and tuned in to the group of girls a few chairs away. They were gabbing on about the latest Hollywood hookups and who was taking whom to the next cotillion. Wishing she had thought to swipe a pair of sunglasses at Neiman's, she tried to watch them without being obvious. None of them exactly matched Briana Leigh's description, but then Kaitlynn had been on the inside for more than two years. In that time appearances could change. Drastically.

"Your extra towels, Miss Covington."

Ariana's heart skipped a beat. She turned to the left to locate the voice and saw a valet handing three thick pool towels to a girl who had just emerged from the water. She was tall and curvy, her breasts barely contained by a sparkling pink string bikini. Her teased auburn hair was up in a high ponytail, and Ariana noted with interest that the color was very similar to the boxed shade she had chosen for herself. Huge Gucci aviators practically covered the girl's face, and as she approached the valet she shoved her too-tan feet into a pair of high-heeled gold lamé sandals. Ariana's nose wrinkled in distaste. If her plan was going to work, Ariana was going to need another makeover. A big, gaudy makeover.

The girl snatched the towels from the valet and flicked each of them open in turn, then threw two of them back in his face.

"These are too worn. Get me new ones," she snapped, settling into a chair two seats over from Ariana.

Ariana's eyes narrowed. This was definitely "the bitch." No doubt about it. Ariana had a habit of calling people out on their impoliteness. It was a quirk Noelle had often complained about. With this girl she had a feeling she was going to be biting her tongue. Often.

Still, her heart pounded with excitement. She was here. It was all happening. "Did that guy say, 'Miss Covington'?"Ariana asked as soon as the valet had scurried off. She sat up straight and placed her iced tea down on the table next to her. The girl looked over at Ariana, lifting her sunglasses and squinting. "Not *the* Briana Leigh Covington?" Ariana said. The Southern accent was gone again.

Briana Leigh's brow knit. "Do I know you?"

"No!" Ariana forced herself to laugh. "But you did know my friend Dana Dover. From Camp Potowamac?"

Ariana saw the recognition in Briana Leigh's eyes, but her expression was still one of annoyance.

"I'm Emma Walsh," Ariana said, placing her hand on her chest. "Dana and I have been in school together since kindergarten. She must have mentioned me."

Briana Leigh's blue eyes flicked over Ariana. "Sounds vaguely familiar. She *may* have mentioned you."

She put her sunglasses back on and leaned back in her chair again, clearly dismissing the intruder. Ariana's skin itched with annoyance.

"Well, she talked about *you* all the time," she gushed. "The fabulous Briana Leigh Covington from Dallas, Texas. I cannot believe I'm finally meeting you. She always said you were the most stylish girl at camp, but she didn't even do you justice!"

Slowly, Briana Leigh turned toward Ariana. She seemed to be mulling something over as she looked at her, then finally gave in.

"Well, Dana *was* always jealous of me. She probably held back on purpose," she said with a hint of a smile. She lifted her hand and snapped her fingers at a passing waiter. "Come have a drink," she said to Ariana. "You can tell me exactly what Dana said about me."

"Sounds perfect," Ariana said with a smile. She'd known she could crack her. Briana Leigh was just another Noelle—in bad clothing. Ariana stood up and, ankle miraculously recovered, walked over to join her new friend.

BEST SUMMER EVER

"Two more martinis. And tell the bartender to at least *try* to make mine dirty this time," Briana Leigh demanded, adjusting her bikini strap.

She slapped a fifty into the waiter's hand, ostensibly to keep him from pointing out that she and her guest were obviously underage. It was the third fifty-dollar bill this kid had pocketed since Briana Leigh's binge fest had begun an hour ago. Ariana stared longingly at his back pocket. She couldn't believe she had been reduced to lusting after a mere hundred and fifty dollars, but all she had left in her backpack was a twenty, two singles, and a handful of change.

Just be patient. All in due time . . . all in due time . . .

She refocused on Briana Leigh. If this went well, she would have all the money she could handle by the end of the week—the money this girl had earned by murdering her own father. The money she did not deserve.

Ariana applauded herself for having listened so carefully to all of Kaitlynn's stories. That diligence was going to set her up for life. And Kaitlynn as well, as soon as Ariana could safely make that happen. She shifted closer to the end of her lounge chair and wondered if she could possibly get away with tipping yet another martini into the pool without Briana Leigh noticing.

"God. How long does it take to pour vodka into a glass?" Briana Leigh added, snorting a laugh.

Ariana shot the waiter an apologetic smile as he collected Briana Leigh's empty glass yet again. Kaitlynn had not been joking when it came to Briana Leigh's champion drinking. The girl had downed more alcohol in the past sixty minutes than Ariana had ever consumed in a single outing—including the Legacy, where everyone indulged beyond what was normal. Briana Leigh's intake was excessive, especially for a random Friday afternoon. The plus side, though, was that drinking seemed to make her more chatty. Ariana was learning more about the girl with each empty glass.

"So why aren't you wearing your bathing suit?" Briana Leigh asked. She leaned over the arm of her chair and almost fell forward, catching herself at the last minute. "Bad wax?" she asked, lowering her voice to a confidential whisper.

"No. Nothing like that," Ariana replied. "I'm not much of a swimmer, actually." She couldn't exactly tell Briana Leigh that she didn't own one.

Briana Leigh nodded. "*I* had a bad wax this one time," she said, as if Ariana hadn't even spoken. She faced the pool again and let her arms hang lazily over the sides of her chair. "Told the girl to give me a landing strip and she did it at a total diagonal. I looked like a retarded streetwalker. So of course I had her fired."

Ariana bit down on her tongue. Hard. She could not criticize this small-minded girl. She simply could not. Not if she was going to get what she needed out of her.

"Don't you just *hate* when you have to have people fired?" Briana Leigh asked. "They get so whiny about it. Like my dog trainer. He swore to me he had house-trained my corgi, but the little bitch kept right on pooping in the house, so I had to have her put to sleep. And he acted as if *I* had done something wrong. Hello? It was his fault! If he'd done his job, I'd still have a dog."

Ariana felt like she was going to vomit. What was wrong with this girl? Putting a dog to sleep because of an inconvenience? How had Kaitlynn *ever* been friends with her?

Their drinks arrived and Ariana made a move for her bag. "Here. Let me pay for this round," she offered.

"Oh, please." Briana Leigh waved a hand before picking up her drink. "It all goes on my grandmother's membership account."

Ariana tried not to smirk at the mention of Briana Leigh's grand-mother. After the fond way in which Kaitlynn had spoken about her, Ariana could hardly wait to meet the old broad.

But she was getting ahead of herself.

"You're sure? I can pay for lunch. . . ."

An order that they had placed twenty minutes ago. Ariana was so hungry it took all her willpower to keep from checking over her shoul-der every two seconds to see if the waiter was coming yet.

"Shut up about it already," Briana Leigh said with a smile.

"Thanks, Briana. I promise I'll—"

"Do not call me Briana," Briana Leigh snapped, quickly shifting moods. "My *name* is Briana Leigh. That is the name my parents gave me, and I would appreciate it if you would use it."

Briana Leigh's blue eyes flashed dangerously and Ariana remembered that she was dealing with a murderer here. A quick-tempered, cold-blooded murderer. Her skin flashed hot with both fear and embarrassment as the girls to her right all stopped talking and turned to stare. She dug her fingernails into her arm and forced an apologetic smile.

"I'm sorry, Briana Leigh."

"Well, don't let it happen again, *Em*," Briana Leigh snapped with a laugh. As if shortening Ariana's "name" was somehow hilarious. When she finally stopped giggling at her own joke, she looked Ariana up and down. "You know, Dana always said her friend Emma was fat. You're not fat at all."

Ariana's heart skipped a beat, feeling snagged. So Briana Leigh *did* remember Dana talking about Emma. Had she just been pretending before, or had she just now remembered Emma Walsh?

She had to answer this accusation casually. If Briana Leigh got suspicious, it was all over.

"Yes, well, it's all about self-control," she said smoothly.

"Huh. I guess." Briana Leigh's eyes narrowed. "And you're from Chicago?"

Ariana's mouth was dry. Did Briana Leigh suspect something? "Yes."

"Which part?" Briana Leigh asked.

"The Gold Coast," Ariana answered instantly.

"You don't have a Chicago accent," Briana Leigh observed.

"I go to school back east, so I've gotten good at masking it," Ariana said, pretending to take a sip of her drink. Her fingers shook.

For a long moment Briana Leigh said nothing. Ariana's skin burned hotter and hotter, but she gazed out at the pool as if nothing was amiss. Was Briana Leigh suspicious, or just interested? Ariana couldn't be sure—which annoyed her. What had happened to her perceptiveness? Why couldn't she get a read on her? Finally, Briana Leigh leaned back in her chair and Ariana let herself breathe. She quickly, surreptitiously, removed the toothpick-speared-olives from her glass and tipped it over at the edge of the pool, dumping the alcohol into the water.

"So what're you doing in Dallas?" Briana Leigh asked, pushing her sunglasses over her eyes.

Stealing your money, Ariana answered silently. Heart in her throat, she quickly brought the glass to her lips, pretending she was finishing it off. She sucked an olive off the toothpick and her stomach growled, anticipating food—something it hadn't had nearly enough of lately. But if she could just pass Briana Leigh's little test, if she could just answer this question perfectly, that was all about to change.

"It's been a nightmare, actually," Ariana said, praying that Briana Leigh had a long enough attention span to listen to a story that wasn't about her. "My cousin invited me down for the summer to stay at her new ranch. She and her husband had it custom-built and said I'd have my own suite with private access to the pool. But I get there and the ranch isn't even finished. Instead of a suite, I'm sleeping in what's going to be the maid's quarters, and I have a blue tarp for a wall. Plus she keeps asking me to watch her kids, two terrors under the age of three. I mean, hello? I'm not a zookeeper."

Briana Leigh stared at Ariana from behind her sunglasses, her mouth hanging slightly open. For a long moment there was total silence and Ariana thought she had failed for sure. Briana Leigh could see right through her.

But then, suddenly, her mouth snapped closed.

"That is so wrong!" she said. "Your cousin should be taken out back and shot."

Ariana blinked. Was that an expression around here or what?

"I just don't know how I'm going to live like this another day," Ariana said wearily.

"Well, you're not," Briana Leigh told her.

"Excuse me?" Ariana raised her eyebrows.

"No one should have to live like that," Briana Leigh said firmly, looking Ariana in the eye. "You're going to come stay with me."

Yes, Ariana thought. She had done it.

"With you? I couldn't," Ariana said as she placed her empty glass on the table. "I mean . . . what about my cousin?"

"Screw your cousin!" Briana Leigh blurted, her expression incredulous. "All she wanted out of you was free day care. Skip the bitch and come stay with me. Seriously. I have this tremendous house all to myself and I am *so* bored."

"Really? You live alone?" Ariana asked, even though she knew this already.

"Well, there's my grandmother. But she lives in the guesthouse, so I'm practically alone," Briana Leigh said, swinging her legs over the side of her chair. "Come on! We will have *so* much fun!"

Ariana bit her lip, pretending to agonize over the decision—pretending that she hadn't been looking forward to this exact moment for months on end. It was all she could do to keep from grinning. Part one of her plan had gone perfectly, but it was just the beginning. She couldn't get ahead of herself.

"Well, if you insist," she said finally.

"I *absolutely* insist," Briana Leigh said with a nod. Then her whole face lit up with the first genuine smile Ariana had seen since they had met. "I'm so glad I bumped into you! This is going to be so much fun. I haven't had a friend stay over since . . ." Briana Leigh paused and put her hand over her mouth, swallowing with some effort. As if some bile had just risen up in her throat and needed to be put back in its place. "Well, it's been a long time," she finished quickly.

Ariana narrowed her eyes as Briana Leigh sat back again. She had been about to mention Kaitlynn. Ariana was sure of it. What had stopped her? For a moment the girl looked genuinely upset, but then she downed the rest of her drink and the indifferent expression returned.

"Your lunches, ladies."

The waiter placed two heaping plates of sandwiches down on the table and Ariana's mouth watered. She thanked the waiter and forced herself to count to ten Mississippis before she reached for her club sandwich. She took a slightly larger than polite–size bite and tried not to groan in ecstasy as she chewed.

Food. Real food. For as long as she lived, Ariana would never take it for granted again.

"I can't believe you eat roast beef," Briana Leigh said, biting into her own grilled chicken wrap. "I thought you were all about self-control."

"Well, I'll admit I haven't had it in a long time," Ariana mused.

"So why start now? Aren't you worried about regaining the weight?" Briana Leigh asked.

Ariana smiled. "Not at all," she said. "Roast beef has always been good to me."

SLUMMING

Saturday morning Ariana sat in the backseat of the black town car Briana Leigh had sent for her and stared at the thick trees outside the window. The driver had turned off the main road and onto Briana Leigh's driveway at least ten minutes ago. Ten minutes of winding drive through a forest of evergreens. The private road had to be at least a couple of miles long. Briana Leigh owned a lot of property.

"Are you a friend of the family, miss?" the middle-aged driver asked, glancing in the rearview mirror.

"A new friend," Ariana replied.

She wondered if he was the type of servant who would tip Briana Leigh off to the fact that he had picked Ariana up on the side of the road, rather than at the door of the huge under-construction ranch home she'd been standing in front of. She had found the house the day before, after she parted ways with Briana Leigh, knowing she would need to look authentic. At the end of the day at the country club, she had told Briana Leigh that she should at least go back to her cousin's to thank her and say good-bye to the kids—all so that she wouldn't look too eager. She didn't want to go straight home with the girl, lest she start suspecting that Ariana had planned to take advantage of her all along. Living above Briana Leigh's suspicion was key.

Ariana shuddered just thinking about the motel she'd stayed in—the motel she'd stiffed on the bill. She was sick and tired of slinking around, stealing, dodging checks. It was so distasteful. She was an Osgood, for goodness' sake. She shouldn't have to slum around like some kind of homeless person.

The car eased its way around one last curve and Briana Leigh's home came into view. Ariana nearly gasped in delight. Clearly, her slumming days were over. The modern ranch home sprawled out in front of her like a presidential compound, with huge plate-glass windows and slanted rooftops jutting toward the sky. There were three outer buildings and a stable surrounded by a huge paddock where a ranch hand was tending to half a dozen horses. Off to the right Ariana spotted two tennis courts and a huge swimming pool. To the left of the house, the property stretched out toward the horizon—fields full of wildflowers and stately trees.

In all Ariana's travels she had never seen such a beautiful private home. Not even Noelle's Upper East Side mansion compared. It looked more like a resort than a house. Briana Leigh clearly had money to burn. For the second time that day Ariana found herself salivating. Somewhere inside this ridiculously huge home was the information she needed to get her hands on Briana Leigh's millions.

Somewhere inside this house was the answer to all of her prayers. To her freedom.

Briana Leigh emerged from the front door as Ariana stepped out of the car, pulling her backpack with her. She shouldered the bag and took a deep breath as she looked around. Keeping up with Briana Leigh was going to be tough, especially with no money to her name. At least her new friend had sent the car, so Ariana hadn't been forced to spend the last of her cash on a cab. She had long since ditched her bar buddy's credit card, figuring he must have reported it stolen fairly quickly, but she had swiped another from some old lady's wallet on her way out of the country club that afternoon. Ariana would have to use this one wisely as well. One use and the woman would probably realize it was missing. A second use and the authorities would track her down.

More important, she had to find the information she needed fast or Briana Leigh was going to realize that Emma Walsh wasn't quite what she seemed.

"Hey, Emma! Get your butt inside!" Briana Leigh shouted. "That pasty skin of yours cannot handle our Texas sun, and I am *not* going to this party tonight with some red-faced freak."

The girl turned and sashayed back inside, leaving the huge door yawning open behind her. Ariana bit down on her tongue and followed.

This is all for a good cause, she reminded herself as she stepped into the airy entryway to Briana Leigh's exquisite home. *All for a very good cause.*

"Briana Leigh! Where have you been all day?"

Ariana paused in the center of the tiled foyer as an elderly woman in an automatic wheelchair zoomed in from the open archway to the south. Her heart fluttered as if she had just bumped into someone famous. It was Kaitlynn's beloved Grandma C. The woman looked tiny in her chair, but somehow not at all frail. She stared up at Briana Leigh through thick glasses, her pointy chin to the sky. Her white hair was pulled into the tightest bun Ariana had ever seen.

"At the club," Briana Leigh replied coolly, crossing her arms over her chest. "Why do you care?"

"We were supposed to talk about school this afternoon. I confirmed with you this morning, did I not?" Grandma C. demanded.

Ariana smirked. This woman was all business.

"So I forgot," Briana Leigh said, rolling her eyes. "We can talk about it tomorrow."

"We will talk about it right now, Briana Leigh," the old woman snapped.

"*Grandmother,*" Briana Leigh said through her teeth. "I *have* a *guest.*"

Briana Leigh turned toward Ariana, and Grandma C. followed her gaze. Her eyebrows shot up as she noticed for the first time that she and her granddaughter were not alone. She touched the pad on her wheelchair's arm and zoomed right up to Ariana.

"And who might you be?" she asked, her tone softened to one of mild interest.

"I'm Emma," Ariana said, extending her hand. "It's a pleasure to meet you, Mrs. Covington."

"Manners! Interesting. My granddaughter usually brings home nothing but heathens."

Ariana gave a polite chuckle—not too big, lest she offend Briana Leigh for laughing at such an obvious dig. Briana Leigh's grandmother never took her eyes off Ariana as she reached up and clasped her hand. Her grip was like iron. Impressive for such a tiny woman. "It's a pleasure to meet you as well," she said.

"Emma is going to be staying with me for a while," Briana Leigh said authoritatively, daring her grandmother to contradict her.

"If it's all right with you, of course," Ariana added, earning a sour look from Briana Leigh. But she couldn't help it. She had been trained from birth to be deferential to her elders.

Grandma C. clearly appreciated the effort. She gave Ariana an approving glance and nodded. "Good. Maybe you'll be a positive influence on my granddaughter while you're here. Make yourself at home."

"I will. Thank you," Ariana said. She now understood why Kaitlynn loved the woman so much. She was powerful and straightforward.

Grandma C. turned her chair to face Briana Leigh. "You and I will talk tomorrow morning," she told her. "Good afternoon, ladies." With that, she zipped out of the room, leaving Ariana with her hostess.

"Well. She liked you," Briana Leigh said in an acidic tone. As if the idea irritated her.

"Grandparents are pretty easy to work," Ariana replied, hoping Briana Leigh would believe that she was just putting on a front for the old woman. "It's nice to humor them, don't you think? They're so frail."

Briana Leigh smirked. "You've got style, I'll give you that," she said. "Come on. Let's go find you a room."

Ariana followed Briana Leigh out of the foyer and over to a wide staircase, appraising the gorgeous home as she went. She was glad she'd had a chance to meet Mrs. Covington. But she couldn't help wondering why Briana Leigh kept the woman around. Clearly the old lady irritated Briana Leigh. If the girl was such a cold-blooded killer, why not just feed the matriarch a mess of sleeping pills and earn her freedom?

There was a time when Ariana would have done that herself.

MOURNING

"That's all you brought?" Briana Leigh asked, glancing at Ariana's backpack as she opened the double doors to one of the guest suites.

"The airline lost my luggage," Ariana lied. "My cousin said she'd send it along as soon as it was delivered to the house."

"Well, you can borrow some of my old things in the meantime, I guess. You'll be a season or two behind, but beggars can't be choosers, right?"

Ariana's cheeks turned pink with irritation over having this pointed out to her face. Never in her life had she had to beg for anything. Not even inside the Brenda T. But this was just a brief moment in her life. A blip. If everything went according to plan, things would soon be back to normal. She forced herself to smile. "Thanks."

"Well, here it is." Briana Leigh lifted a hand toward the spacious, impeccably decorated guest room. Ariana already found herself savoring the view outside the huge glass doors that led to her own private balcony. Outside there was a gorgeous pond surrounded by wild-flowers, and behind it the sun was just dipping into view, headed for the horizon. "Meet me down by the pool when you're done unpack-ing. It's behind the game room at the back of the house. If you get lost, there's always some maid or other around to direct you. Did you at least get a suit when you went back to your cousin's?"

Ariana turned around as Briana Leigh headed out the door. "Actually, no. They were all in my luggage."

Briana Leigh rolled her eyes. "Fine. I'll have one of the girls bring you one of mine."

"Thank you."

"There should be some other stuff in the closet," Briana Leigh said, nodding toward a door near the head of the bed. "I always have the maids move the out-of-season stuff to other rooms so it doesn't get in my way."

Rather than, say, give it to charity, Ariana thought. "Okay. Thanks again, Briana Leigh."

"Don't mention it. Like I said, this is going to be fun!" The girl smiled for the first time since Ariana had arrived, then closed the doors behind her.

Finally alone, Ariana sighed with relief. She walked over to the king-size bed and fell back into its huge feather pillows. She smiled in delight as supersoft, eight-hundred-thread-count pillowcases enveloped her.

"I did it," she whispered to herself. "I'm actually here."

Opening her eyes, she noted the elaborate gold-and-crystal

chandelier overhead and grimaced. Ariana had never understood the compulsion people seemed to have to put dining room lighting in the bedroom.

She sat up and checked out the rest of her new home. On the east wall was a huge, ornate Victorian-style dresser, which her meager supply of clothes would never fill. Across the wide hardwood floor stood a large desk with a laptop and printer. Ariana got up to check out what she assumed would be the bathroom through the door opposite the bed. Instead she found a sitting room with two couches, a plasma-screen TV, and a well-stocked library of books and DVDs. She giggled in glee and turned back to the bedroom. There were two doors on either side of the four-poster bed. One led to a walk-in closet stuffed to the seams with clothing—from skinny jeans to colorful gauzy tops to overly sequined dresses. Most of it offended Ariana's simple sense of style, but considering the sheer abundance, there was probably something she could work with. She closed the door and opened the second door. A grin lit her entire face. The bathroom was modern and state-of-the-art, with a glass-encased stall shower and a separate Jacuzzi tub.

A tub. Ariana tingled at the very sight of it, picking up the Kiehl's products that were set up along the shelf. She hadn't had a tub in forever, and she could almost feel the warm bubbles tickling her skin. But that would have to wait for later.

Ariana headed back into the bedroom and crossed over to the desk, her heart starting to pound with trepidation. She took a deep breath and opened the laptop. It powered itself on instantly. Ariana stared at the blue-and-white backdrop on the screen, feeling sick with fear and anticipation.

"Just get it over with," she whispered to herself. "You have to know."

She pulled the chair out and sat down. Her fingers itched as she brought up the Google search screen, and she mistyped her own name three times.

"Dammit," Ariana said quietly. She held her own fingers and breathed.

In, one . . . two . . . three . . .

Out, one . . . two . . . three . . .

The breaths calmed her. The trembling stopped. Focused, she typed her name and hit search.

Instantly, dozens of articles from myriad magazines, newspapers, and gossip sites popped up. Ariana clicked on the first, a *New York Times* piece, and read slowly and carefully.

Following the evidence Ariana had planted for them—the footprints she had left in the soft earth leading to the dock from which she had launched the skiff—the FBI had dredged Lake Page for her body. They had, of course, found nothing. None of this was a surprise. But the following paragraph left Ariana's mouth dry.

"I don't care how long it takes. We are going to keep searching this lake until we find my daughter," Arthur Osgood said. "I don't care if I have to personally pay to have this lake dredged a hundred times. My daughter will have a proper Christian burial."

"Crap, Daddy," Ariana said, her accent sounding more pronounced than usual in the silence. She covered her mouth with her hand and leaned her elbow on the desk. Why couldn't her father just let it go? It wasn't as if he'd cared to see her when she was "alive." She knew that her father loved her in his own way—he had, after all, paid all that money to ensure she was placed at the Brenda T. rather than at some maximum security prison, and he had bought off all those people just so she could wear her fleur-de-lis—but he hadn't been up to visit her once since her incarceration. Why the doting father act now?

The rest of the article contained information about her childhood, her conviction, her sentence. A little bit about that awful mess with her sister last year at Easton and an editorial aside about how insanity obviously ran in the family, which made her want to call the newspaper and complain. Reporters were supposed to report, not make diagnoses.

Then Ariana came to a quote that stopped her blood cold.

"She was my baby," Lillian Osgood said via phone, through anguished sobs. "My one and only child. I don't care what you all think she did. She did not deserve to die this way."

A follow-up call was fielded by Mrs. Osgood's psychiatrist, who told this reporter that her patient would be making no further comment.

Ariana's heart expanded in her chest as tears welled in her eyes. One hand flew to the fleur-de-lis necklace as the other compulsively reached for the phone next to the computer. Her mother was in pain. She had to call and let her know that her baby was all right. But before she dialed through the area code, her logic kicked back in and she stopped herself.

No one could know she was alive. Not even her mother. *Especially* not her mother, who had a tendency to babble when drugged, which was most of the time. Ariana put the phone down again and covered her eyes as tears spilled down her cheeks. She was never going to speak to her mother again. Never going to see her or hug her or hear her sing her favorite lullaby. Ariana's heart filled with grief, overwhelmed by the loss. How was she going to do this? How was she ever going to get through all of this alone?

There was a quick rap on the door, and Ariana's head popped up. She quickly dried her tears with her hands and stood up, slapping the laptop closed.

"Come in."

A slight woman with white hair and a boxy gray uniform strode into the room, holding what appeared to be a scrap of purple nylon.

"Hello, miss," she said with a quick bow of the head. "Miss Briana Leigh asked me to bring this to you."

She held out the bathing suit. Ariana plucked it from her fingers and held it up, trying to discern where the many flosslike straps were supposed to go. Never in a million years would Ariana have ever been caught dead in such a revealing suit.

But then, she wasn't Ariana Osgood anymore.

"Thank you," Ariana said.

The woman smiled and scurried from the room. Ariana opened the laptop again and, with one final thought of her mother, quickly deleted the Google history. She could leave no evidence of Ariana Osgood behind. As of that moment Ariana Osgood was dead.

LACK OF TRUST

Briana Leigh had a manicurist on call. Other than Vienna Clark, an old friend from Easton Academy whose mother owned several upscale salons in New York and L.A., Ariana had never met anyone who had a manicurist on call. But the second Briana Leigh had seen the sorry state of Ariana's cuticles and toes, she had speed-dialed Libby Lane's Gold Star Salon. Now, as Briana Leigh lounged in the hot tub next to her indoor pool, Libby Lane herself sat at the end of Ariana's lounge chair, going to town on her calluses with a pumice stone.

Ariana would have been offended by Briana Leigh's audacity, if she hadn't been so very grateful.

"Your magazines, miss."

The maid who had delivered the bathing suit that was currently riding up Ariana's ass placed a stack of fashion mags on the slate floor between Ariana's chair and the hot tub. Ariana glanced at her hostess and, when the girl said nothing, uttered a quick, "Thank you."

The woman smiled at Ariana for the second time that day, and Ariana started to realize that those two words were a rarity around this house. All that money and Briana Leigh couldn't even spare a thank-you here and there to the people who took care of her evil, greedy, traitorous self?

No matter how hard Ariana tried, she just could not wrap her brain around the idea of killing for money. Especially one's own parent. Crimes of passion were another story. Those she could understand. She knew firsthand how a person could come to that. But what Briana Leigh had done was unthinkable. And what she'd done afterward— pinning the murder on her innocent best friend—was even worse.

She reached for the *Vogue* on the top of the stack and Briana Leigh gasped.

"Oh my God! What did you do to yourself?" she asked, gaping at Ariana's back.

Ariana winced, cursing herself for neglecting to cover herself up with a robe. She had been so distracted after reading her mother's quote that she had forgotten all about the ugly, jagged cut in the center of her back.

"Horseback riding mishap," she lied quickly, leaning back in her chair so that Briana Leigh would stop staring. "I was thrown and dragged. Only for a few seconds, but the damage was done."

Briana Leigh sucked air through her teeth. "That's nasty, Emma. You should have it looked at."

"I did. They said it's healing fine," Ariana lied. Time for a subject change. "So, Briana Leigh, where are your parents?" she asked casually.

She felt Libby Lane flinch, and the maid, who was now walking away, picked up the pace.

Briana Leigh stared straight ahead at the pristine blue water in the shimmering pool.

"My parents are dead," she said, her tone clipped.

"Oh my God! I'm so sorry!" Ariana said with a gasp. "What happened?"

Ariana caught a warning look from Libby as she began moisturizing Ariana's feet. Clearly Libby knew the scandalous story. At least the one the public had been fed—that after Briana Leigh's mother had passed away of cancer a few years back, Briana Leigh's father had started up a sordid affair with the very young Kaitlynn Nottingham. And that when Mr. Covington had tried to break it off, Kaitlynn had snapped and killed him. Little did these people know they were actually tending to the real murderer—a girl who'd offed her father just to get her inheritance sooner.

"I mean, you don't have to tell me if you don't want to . . . ," Ariana said, faking chagrin.

Briana Leigh sniffed and picked up the oversize *W* magazine. "No. It's fine. My mother got sick a few years ago and passed away, and then my dad died in an accident a year later," she said, as she flipped past a photo shoot of Katie Holmes. "Not the most interesting story."

Libby gaped up at Briana Leigh, and Briana Leigh shot her a silencing stare that sent her right back to work on Ariana's feet with renewed vigor. Ariana stared at Briana Leigh's profile. An accident? Right. That was one way to put it. Clearly Briana Leigh didn't trust her quite yet, considering she hadn't even shared the *lie* with her—that Kaitlynn had murdered Mr. Covington.

"I'm so sorry," Ariana said, her voice dripping with sympathy. "That must have been awful for you."

Briana Leigh lifted both shoulders. As if losing her parents was no big deal. Ariana had just suffered a similar fate up in her new bedroom a couple of hours ago, and she had a feeling her heart was never going to recover completely. Yet here this girl was, cold as stone.

"But anyway, I'm not alone. I have my grandmother," Briana Leigh said. "Of course, she *is* a total dictator, as you saw firsthand, so it's good that she lives in the guesthouse. If she was up here all the time I'd have no life. But I do have the staff. . . ."

At this she looked around vaguely at the man tending to the potted plants on the other side of the pool. The maid standing off to the side at a respectable distance, waiting for her next marching orders and looking bored. Briana Leigh got a far-off, almost sad look in her eye, and Ariana was surprised to feel her heart respond. What was that about? She shook her head slightly and immediately quashed the sentiment.

Suddenly Briana Leigh sat up straight and cursed under her breath. "Tabitha! My God! What are you trying to do? Boil me? Turn down the goddamn heat on this thing!"

Ariana glanced at the temperature knob for the hot tub. It was well within Briana Leigh's own reach. Yet the maid pushed away from the wall and practically sprinted over to adjust it.

"Sorry, miss."

"You can pay for my skin graft," Briana Leigh snapped.

Ariana couldn't believe the extreme shortness of Briana Leigh's fuse and reminded herself that it would be best to avoid pissing her off.

"So tell me about this party tonight," Ariana said, deftly changing the subject again.

"It's going to be intense," Briana Leigh said, instantly calm again. She leaned back into the contoured seat of the hot tub. "It's the launch party for this new band from Dallas, Renegade Conmen. Their first album is gonna be huge."

"Are we meeting up with your friends?" Ariana asked, remembering how Kaitlynn had wondered who Briana Leigh was hanging out with these days.

Briana Leigh averted her gaze, focusing intently on the *W* cover. "No. Well, everyone's away for the summer."

Code for "I have no friends," Ariana thought, feeling triumphant on Kaitlynn's behalf. Plus this would also make it much easier to get close to her. A girl with no friends needed one. Badly. No matter how nonchalant she acted about the subject.

"But you'll get to meet Téo!" Briana Leigh brightened.

"Téo?" Ariana said. "Who's that?"

Briana Leigh looked at Ariana as if she'd just landed from Oz. "Téo. DJ Téo? Have you been living in a convent for the last year?"

Something like that, Ariana thought, her thoughts flashing on her cell, the prison yard, the mess hall. Instantly her heart rate started to quicken.

No. Stop. It's over. She breathed in and out slowly, surreptitiously, so that Briana Leigh wouldn't notice anything amiss. Within seconds she was back in the present. Focused.

"He's only, like, the hottest DJ on the planet," Briana Leigh said, sucking at her teeth, which made Ariana cringe. "And he's also my boyfriend."

"*Really?*" Ariana feigned interest because she knew that was what Briana Leigh wanted. "What's he like?"

"Beautiful," Briana Leigh said, as if this were obvious. "Plus he totally adores me. He writes me love letters all the time. Real love letters on parchment paper, sealed with a wax seal he designed himself. Every time I get one I feel like Marianne Dashwood from *Sense and Sensibility*."

"Wow. I thought e-mail killed the love letter," Ariana mused, actually slightly impressed by this Téo. And also slightly impressed that Briana Leigh could reference Jane Austen.

"Not for us," Briana Leigh said. "He wants me to have something tangible as evidence of our love. He's so romantic."

"Very," Ariana agreed. Apparently DJ Téo had a poetic side. She wondered what he saw in Briana "Call-Me-Briana-Leigh-or-Die" Covington.

But of course she bit her tongue. Because her feet were tingling pleasantly, her stomach was full, and she had the prospect of an actual party ahead of her. Briana Leigh might have been a lying, conceited bitch. But she was already coming in handy.

THE RIGHT THING

"Love the paintings," Ariana gushed, standing in the middle of the amphitheater-size room that was Briana Leigh's bedroom suite. The walls were painted a deep lollipop pink, and all the accessories were black-and-white patterns. A polka-dot love seat, striped pillows, paisley drapes. The bed was done in pink, black, and white silks, and all the wainscoting and molding was painted black. But as offensive as the overdone theme was, none of it was as bad as the artwork. Covering the wall behind her massive bed were four huge original paintings of Briana Leigh herself, each done by a different artist—a different interpretation of the same sexy pose.

"Oh, yeah," Briana Leigh shouted out from inside her cavernous closet. "I'm thinking about having new ones done. I still had my mother's nose back then."

Ariana leaned toward the paintings and frowned. She actually preferred the old nose. It gave Briana Leigh character. Now her nose was

just a normal button. Kind of like Ariana's, actually. She had always
found her own nose a little boring.

"I'm gonna jump in the shower," Briana Leigh shouted.

Ariana's heart skipped a beat, anticipating a few moments alone.

"Okay!" she called back.

Ariana stood as still as stone, training her ear on the bathroom. As
soon as she heard the water running, she started rummaging through
the built-in cabinets along the wall. Expecting to find piles of sweaters
and T-shirts, Ariana was surprised to discover that the shelves inside
were lined with books. All sorts of books, from fiction to essays to
poetry to biographies. Ariana glanced over her shoulder toward the
bathroom door—Briana Leigh had just turned on the shower—and
studied the titles more closely. They were haphazardly arranged, but
they had all clearly been read. As she picked up one book after another,
she found that each one was worn or dog-eared or stained. Ariana saw
a copy of *Atonement*, the book she had been reading before her escape,
and snatched it up. She flipped to the chapter she had ended on and
saw that Briana Leigh had made little notes in the margin.

Ariana was intrigued. So Briana Leigh had a deep side. She put the
book down and kept looking, attacking the desk next. There were no
documents in the deep drawers—nothing but cute, colorful pens and
notebooks and all manner of disorganized desk accessories. No bank
statements in the top drawer, either. Then her eyes fell on the Palm
Treo sitting atop the desk, next to Briana Leigh's computer.

She didn't have time to power up the laptop and do a search, but
maybe Briana Leigh kept her account numbers in her PDA.

Ariana hesitated a moment, glancing toward the bathroom and the door to the bedroom, through which a servant could enter at any moment. But if she was caught with the phone in her hand she could always pretend she was simply making a call. She grabbed the PDA, her fingers shaking.

A rapid scan of the memo pad and task feature revealed nothing, so Ariana quickly searched the calendar for birthdates and memorized those of Briana Leigh, Téo, and both of Briana Leigh's parents. Once she finally did find Briana Leigh's account information, she would need the pin number, and one of these might serve.

Ariana put the phone down and paused to listen. With each passing moment her heart was creeping further and further up her throat, but there was no need to panic yet. The water was still running. She moved to Briana Leigh's dresser and opened one of the top drawers. Hundreds of pairs of mangled, unmatched socks met her. This girl was starting to remind her of Noelle, with her chaotic approach to storage. Digging around in the drawer, she felt her fingers touch something that definitely was not a sock.

Her eyes widened in glee as she pulled out a huge roll of cash, all hundreds. Jackpot. Swiftly, Ariana peeled off three bills and shoved them into her pocket, then carefully replaced the stash exactly where she'd found it—in the back right corner of the drawer. There was no way Briana Leigh would miss a measly three hundred. And now Ariana could breathe a little easier, even buy a round of drinks, without Briana Leigh catching on.

Ariana was just about to slide open the second drawer when she saw a brochure sticking out from under a tangled pile of scarves and necklaces atop the dresser. Her pulse quickened at the sight of the red-brick buildings, the word *Atherton* spelled out in an elaborate font.

This couldn't be what she thought it was.

Ariana slid the brochure out and held it up in both hands. It was a brochure for Atherton-Pryce Hall. Only the most prestigious boarding school in the entire nation. Home to dignitaries' sons and celebrity daughters. Princes and princesses and international oil heiresses and even the president's children. Atherton-Pryce Hall was the school everyone wanted to get into. It was the school that most of her friends from Easton Academy would have killed to attend.

Was Briana Leigh enrolled at this hallowed institution? How could a place with such impeccable standards accept a walking crime-against-fashion like her?

Suddenly the door to the bathroom swung wide and Briana Leigh strode into the room dripping wet, clutching a towel around her body. Ariana froze like a statue, her heart hurtling into her mouth. What would a psycho like Briana Leigh do to a person who was pawing through her things?

"Forgot my new conditioner," Briana Leigh said, snatching a bottle from her vanity table. She was about to stride right back to the bathroom when she paused and glanced at Ariana. "What're you doing?"

Ariana couldn't breathe. Her brain was suddenly blank, anticipating the wrath she had already witnessed in slight snippets that day.

Think, Ariana! Think, think, think!

"I just saw this sitting on your dresser," Ariana said finally. She held out the brochure. "Are you going to Atherton-Pryce?"

Briana Leigh groaned and her shoulders collapsed. Ariana breathed a sigh of relief. Briana Leigh had bought it.

"You mean the epicenter of boredom?" Briana Leigh said. "Unfortunately."

"Unfortunately?" Ariana repeated, casually flipping through the glossy pages. "Everyone wants to go there."

"Not me," Briana Leigh sniffed. "I want to be with Téo, and Téo is *here*. In Dallas. Besides, D.C. is, like, one huge slum. I'll probably be shot."

Ariana's teeth cut into her tongue. "The school isn't *in* the city." Ariana paged through the gorgeous photos of Atherton's campus—the rolling lawns, the bucolic countryside. "This place is incredible."

"Whatever. It doesn't matter. Grandma is, like, *obsessed* with me going there. She even threatened to cut me out of her will if I didn't enroll," Briana Leigh continued, adjusting her towel.

Ariana nodded, even though she didn't quite understand. If Briana Leigh cared about Téo so much, why not just blow the grandmother off? She was already independently wealthy thanks to her dad, whom she had murdered to achieve that very end.

"So you're going there in the fall," Ariana clarified.

"I have to. What Grandma says goes." Briana Leigh turned toward one of the many mirrors in her room and checked herself out, lifting her chin to inspect some unseen blemish. "Authority figures. Can't live with 'em . . ."

Can't shoot 'em, Ariana finished silently. Then her face turned beet red as she realized that Briana Leigh already *had* shot an authority figure. Perhaps that was why the girl had suddenly gone pale and hadn't finished the sentence herself.

"Anyway, you should get ready," Briana Leigh said. She grabbed the brochure from Ariana's hands and tossed it onto her bed. "You do have a bathroom in your suite, remember?"

"All right. I'll come back down when I'm ready," Ariana said.

"Good."

Ariana waited until Briana Leigh had closed the bathroom door behind her, then picked up the brochure again. After a moment's hesitation she went back into the cabinet and grabbed the copy of *Atonement* as well. Never in her life had Ariana left a book unfinished, and she wasn't about to start now. On the way down the hall to her room, she slowly paged through the glossy pages of the Atherton handbook, feeling as if her heart was being tugged from her chest at the sight of the austere buildings and studious-looking coeds. Atherton-Pryce Hall. God, that would be a dream come true. A diploma from this place meant a person could go anywhere, do anything. But of course Briana Leigh couldn't have cared less.

Curling the brochure into a cylinder in her palm, Ariana shoved open the doors to her suite. After being caged like a rat for the past sixteen months, there was one thing Ariana couldn't stand, and that was a person who didn't appreciate what she had. This girl had to be taken down, and fast—before Briana Leigh left for school in August, which was only a month away. Ariana did not like working under a ticking clock, didn't like the pressure it created, but she was more determined than ever to see this plan through.

It wasn't just the right thing for her or for Kaitlynn anymore. Clearly, bringing Briana Leigh Covington to her knees was simply the right thing to do.

EMBRACING THE NEW

As the car slid up to the curb in front of the historic Majestic Theater in downtown Dallas, Ariana glanced at her reflection in her Chanel compact. She was still surprised every time she saw the auburn hair framing her face, the green eyes staring back at her. A sour feeling of disappointment arose in her chest. Ariana had always been proud of her natural blond hair and her unusually light blue eyes. It was as if she had been stripped of her entire identity.

But that was, of course, the point. It was better to have no identity than to have no future. Sooner or later, she was going to have to embrace the new her. And as she looked out the window at the hundreds of would-be partiers lined up behind velvet ropes outside the Majestic's beautiful beveled doors, she felt a flutter of excitement. Maybe the embracing would start tonight.

"Let's do this," Briana Leigh said, sliding out onto the street.

Ariana carefully planted one high-heeled shoe on the pavement and rose from the car. It had been so long since she had walked in heels that she was afraid she might stumble, but the skill came right back to her. She saw a few guys on line check her out appreciatively and felt almost grateful. How could anyone like the way she looked in the tight, hot pink dress Briana Leigh had practically forced her to wear? At least Ariana had sneaked in a cropped white jacket that hid some of the ridiculous cleavage the dress's cinched bodice created. Wasn't anyone down with modesty anymore?

Briana Leigh strode right past the waiting hordes and sidled up to the larger-than-life bouncer, practically stepping on some poor girl in a white slip dress who had been about to walk through to the party.

"Hey, beyotch! Where do you think you're going?" A belligerent girl leaned over the ropes to shout at Briana Leigh. "We've been on line here for over an hour!"

"And with the look you're rocking, you'll be here for another," Briana Leigh said with a sneer. "*We're* on the list."

Ariana flinched as anyone within earshot reacted with offended groans and shouts.

"Briana Leigh Covington and guest. We're here with DJ Téo."

Again, Brian Leigh said this loud enough for all to hear. Showing off. Ariana lifted her chin and made sure not to meet anyone's gaze as Briana Leigh talked to the bouncer. Better to be aloof than crass. Aloof told the masses that she deserved to be where she was and that she wasn't about to apologize for it. The bouncer checked Téo's guest list and checked Briana Leigh's name.

"Enjoy, ladies," he said as he held the rope open for them.

Ariana shoved through the wall-to-wall revelers jamming the lobby area. The conversation was so loud she could barely hear herself think. She clutched her borrowed Coach purse to her chest to protect the precious cash she had stashed inside along with the new disposable cell phone she had bought during a quick trip to the mall on the way to the party. Briana Leigh had insisted that she needed new Christian Louboutin shoes to go with her new dress, so while Briana Leigh abused the salespeople at the very Neiman's Ariana had stolen from, Ariana excused herself to hit a cell phone kiosk in the mall. Any normal person had a cell phone, and for the past twenty-four hours Ariana had felt like a poseur without one.

"There he is!" Briana Leigh shouted the moment they made it through the doors and into the theater.

She was pointing at the stage area, but how she could see anything through the constant rain of bubbles and confetti and ribbons was a mystery. Ariana squinted into the strobe lights and tried to focus as loud dance music assaulted her ears and partiers slammed into her from all sides. There was definitely someone spinning up on stage, but Ariana could make out nothing other than his sideways baseball cap. Her pulse was starting to pound dangerously.

Where was the air-conditioning? And didn't this place have some kind of maximum occupancy guideline?

"Can we move?" Ariana shouted. "We're right in traffic here!"

Briana Leigh nodded and grabbed Ariana's hand. As they slid along the wall in the right aisle, Ariana was appalled at the things she saw. Girls in stiletto heels dancing on velvet chairs. Couples making out on the floor between seat rows, letting their drinks spill everywhere. Bubbles popping on chandeliers and wall sconces. How could the historical society have allowed this to happen? Wasn't this place protected?

Money. It was all about money. Enough cash could buy anything, anyone. The realization both disgusted and heartened Ariana. Once she got her hands on Briana Leigh's money, she was going to be banking on this fact. Somehow, she was going to have to buy herself a new identity, so some shady counterfeiter out there was going to make a serious load of cash off her.

"You okay? You look sick," Briana Leigh said, pausing about halfway through the orchestra seating. The music was much louder here, pumping directly into Ariana's skull through huge speakers set up at the corners of the stage.

"M'fine," she mumbled.

"Well, then relax. It's a party," Briana Leigh told her.

"Right."

Ariana turned around to scan the crowd and tried to find something, anything stationary, to focus on. Everywhere she looked, people were in motion. Girls danced in barely there skirts up on platforms dotting the stage. Waiters circulated with trays full of neon-colored drinks held precariously above the revelers' heads. People shouted and hugged and danced and sweated on each other. Ariana was starting to realize that she was not used to this. Even in her former life, she'd always had a little group of friends to attend parties with. A group that acted as a sort of lifeboat in the choppy waters. She didn't like the fact that she didn't know anyone here. That she didn't have a safe zone to retreat to—a place where she was in control.

Maybe this had been a bad idea.

"Come on! Let's get down front where he can see us!" Briana Leigh shouted, grabbing Ariana's other arm.

Ariana's shoulder exploded with pain as Briana Leigh yanked her into the crowd, moving toward the stage. It was her sore shoulder, the one she'd fallen on during her faked suicide attempt, and suddenly it all came back to her in stark flashes. The cold floor, Kaitlynn's screaming, the rough hands of the orderlies, being held down with the tube shoved into her throat. She couldn't breathe. She couldn't breathe. Couldn't—

No. Stop it. You're not there anymore. It's over. Over. Over.

As Briana Leigh wound around a group of randomly moshing skater-boy types, Ariana forced herself to breathe.

In, one . . . two . . . three . . .

Out, one . . . two . . . three . . .

It's a party. The first one you've been to in almost two years. Just relax. . . .

That was when Briana Leigh took a sudden turn and Ariana slammed right into a passing waiter. His tray went flying and empty beer bottles scattered everywhere, one shattering against the edge of the stage. Bits of glass ricocheted in all directions and the partiers within range shouted and scattered.

"Oh my—I'm so sorry!" Ariana cried.

Briana Leigh stopped, annoyed, still clutching Ariana's hand.

"No problem." The black-clad waiter gathered up his tray and stood. He ran a hand through his longish blond hair and looked around. "Everyone okay? No injuries?"

The partiers shrugged and went about their dancing. The waiter turned to Ariana and smiled. Her breath completely left her, but in a good way this time. His eyes were a gorgeous dark blue, and deep dimples anchored his lightly tanned cheeks. He wore a tight black T-shirt, and his arms were obviously defined. For the first time in forever, Ariana's heart skipped a few delighted beats. He took in her face and obviously liked what he saw. Ariana found that she simply could not help smiling back.

"All good?" he asked.

He even had a sexy voice. Ariana's smile widened. "All—"

"Oh my God! Let's go already!"

Briana Leigh yanked one last time on Ariana's arm, and before Ariana could take one more look at the gorgeous waiter, he was swallowed up by the crowd.

HUDSON

"I just don't get it. There are perfectly good schools here in Texas. Why does everyone feel the need to go to the Northeast? Like just because the schools have been there forever, they're innately better. That is totally backward thinking. Those schools are stuck in the past! They're archaic. And I, for one, like new. Progressive. Old school can kiss my ass."

The more alcohol Briana Leigh imbibed, the more crap spewed out of her mouth, and Ariana was starting to get tense. She smoothly pulled her cell phone out of her purse to check the time. It was a quarter to one. The band for which this party was being thrown had long since taken the stage, so where was Briana Leigh's beloved Téo? Ariana had been counting the minutes until he found them so he could bear some of the Briana Leigh burden.

"Where do *you* go to school, Emma?" Briana Leigh asked, taking a sip of her cocktail.

"Oh. I haven't decided where to go this fall," Ariana said. "But I know where I won't be going. I won't be going to Atherton-Pryce Hall."

She added this last bit just to distract Briana Leigh from prodding her further about her education. And it worked.

"I'll drink to that!" Briana Leigh said, lifting her glass to Ariana's. "Screw Atherton-Pryce Hall!"

"Screw Atherton-Pryce Hall!" Ariana echoed. Then she pretended to take a swig of her drink.

"What was that?" Briana Leigh said, narrowing her eyes. "Take a real drink."

"I did!" Ariana protested.

"Oh, please. You've barely had anything to drink since we got here," Briana Leigh said, waving a hand at Ariana. "Have you not noticed we're at a party?"

"This is my third martini!" Ariana lied, her eyes wide.

Briana Leigh rolled her eyes and trained her attention on the stage, crossing her slim, tan legs at the knee. The truth was that since Ariana and Briana Leigh had arrived at their VIP section—basically a roped-off set of ten seats in the balcony—Ariana had been nursing the same iridescent martini. The last thing she needed, given her precarious situation, was to have her logic impaired. Briana Leigh, of course, harbored no such qualms. Which was surprising. After all, Briana Leigh had some pretty dark secrets to protect.

Ariana glanced sideways at her benefactress. The girl could barely hold herself upright in the theater seat, and had to keep resting her cheek on her hand. Was she wasted enough to share a little info about her bank accounts? Subtlety, Ariana decided, was key.

"So, Briana Leigh, if all your friends are away, why didn't you go with them? I mean you obviously have the money to—"

"Téo!"

Briana Leigh jumped out of her seat so fast she almost tipped forward and plunged over the edge of the balcony. Heart in her throat, Ariana lunged from her chair and grabbed the girl's arm, pulling her upright. Briana Leigh laughed as she righted herself and Ariana rolled her eyes. She turned to find DJ Téo jogging down the steps toward the front row, girls on all sides checking him out and whispering to each other as he moved along. Ariana had to admit that, in an empiric sense, Téo was not unattractive. He was on the shorter side—maybe five-foot-eight—but had broad shoulders and large hands. With olive skin, dark hair shorn close to his head, and gleaming black eyes, he definitely had the exotic thing going for him. Plus, there was an easy confidence about him as he slapped hands with fans and signed autographs and smiled for photos, which Ariana admired.

Still, he was not her type. Ariana had always been into the more mysterious, tall, slender guys. She didn't do stocky and charismatic. Plus, his sneakers were way too tattered for her taste.

"Téo! Téo! Over here! Will you take a picture with me?"

A buxom blond girl who was falling out of her blouse grabbed Téo and shoved her camera at her friend. As the two of them posed, the girl made sure to press her ample breasts up against Téo's chest and pull his cheek to hers. Next to Ariana, Briana Leigh bristled.

"Hey! Get your own man, slut!" she shouted, leaning into the seat.

The girl didn't even hear Briana Leigh, what with the deafening music and the fact that she was a few yards off, but the people closer to their section laughed and pointed. Ariana cursed under her breath and pulled Briana Leigh back.

"Calm down. You're making a scene," Ariana whispered to her, almost feeling embarrassed on her behalf.

Briana Leigh huffed but didn't argue. She crossed her arms over her chest and waited with a pout until Téo was finally finished greeting his public.

"Hey, baby," he said, sliding his hand under the thick blanket of Briana Leigh's hair. He went in for a kiss, but Briana Leigh turned her face.

"What was that?" she demanded.

"What?" Téo said with a satisfied smile that told Ariana he knew exactly what Briana was talking about.

"That!" Briana Leigh flung an arm toward the fan who was sitting a few rows back, checking out the pics on the camera screen. "You were all over her!"

Téo slipped both hands around Briana Leigh's neck and tickled her cheekbones with his thumbs. He clucked his tongue and tilted his head as he looked into her eyes. "Aw, baby, come on. You know you're the only woman for me."

Briana Leigh's pout quickly turned into a smile, and then Téo pulled her to him and stuck his tongue right down her throat. Ariana looked away. Too disgusting for public viewing.

"Téo, this is Emma Walsh," Briana Leigh said, breaking away for a moment.

Ariana was ready with a polite smile, but Téo simply looked her over, said, "S'up?" and recommenced slobbering all over his girlfriend. Ariana sat down hard in her seat and swigged the last dregs of her now warm martini. She wasn't sure which was worse—listening to Briana Leigh babble or watching these two dry hump each other. Either way, this was going to be a very long night.

Just then someone dropped into the seat next to Ariana's, jostling her elbow from the armrest. She looked up, annoyed, and instantly recognized the arm. Her heart did a triple backflip. Hot waiter boy.

"Hey," he said with a grin as she hazarded a glance into his eyes.

"Hey." Ariana smiled as well, but couldn't stop herself from pointing out his faux pas. "This is the VIP section, you know."

His grin widened. "I'm aware. Yo! Téo!"

Téo broke off his kiss and Briana Leigh face-planted into his chest. He reached over Ariana to slap hands with the waiter. So DJ Téo knew the hired help. Interesting development.

"Shouldn't you be, like, serving us?" Briana Leigh said with a sneer. She was clutching onto Téo's graphic tee, ostensibly to keep herself upright.

"My shift just ended," he said. "I figured I'd watch the rest of the set with you guys, if that's okay." He said this last bit to Ariana, as if hers was the only permission he required. She blushed and looked away, focusing on the lead man on the stage, who was bouncing around with his guitar.

"I met Hudson up at UT a couple weeks ago at a gig," Téo explained.

Briana Leigh rolled her eyes. "Whatever." She pulled Téo to her again and mashed her face into his. Hudson smirked, looking at the couple as if they were just two crazy kids in love and he thought it was cute. Ariana suddenly couldn't stop staring at his face. It was so perfect. Not a mark or a blemish or a scar. Just perfect.

She could use a little perfect in her life.

"So. What's your name?" Hudson asked Ariana.

"Ar . . . Emma," Ariana said, her heart all but stopping. She had been startled by the question, snagged while staring. Hudson, however, didn't seem to notice her slip. For the first time all night Ariana was grateful for the noise. "Emma Walsh," she said. "From Chicago."

"Well, Emma Walsh from Chicago. I'm Ashley Hudson from Boston." He offered his hand, a plain silver band around his thumb. "Nice to meet you."

"Ashley, huh?"

"Mom loved *Gone with the Wind,*" he said with a shrug. "I go by Hudson for obvious reasons."

"I see."Ariana slipped her fingers into his and the warmth of his skin seemed to spread throughout her entire body. Her breath quickened. She looked into his eyes again and they sparkled.

"Want a drink?" he asked as one of the other waiters stopped by to check on the VIPs.

Ariana looked up at the hovering guy with his dyed red hair and multiple piercings. No, she did not want another drink. Look at how badly she had almost screwed up on just one. But Hudson was still holding her hand. The pleasant warmth was still humming in her veins. The band had just switched over to a lulling acoustic song. And she had just gotten out of prison, for God's sake. Shouldn't she be allowed to celebrate? Just a bit?

"Sure," she told Hudson finally. "I'd love one."

Half an hour later, Ariana was dancing. The music throbbed through her pores. She threw her bare arms over her head, her demure jacket long since lost to the masses, and closed her eyes. Her short hair whipped her face as she turned her head from side to side in time with the beat. All around her people screamed and shouted and laughed. Bodies collided, sweat mingled, drinks were spilled. And Ariana was loving every minute of it.

Why had it taken so long for her to let go? Letting go felt good. It felt amazing. She was free, after all. And not just free of the Brenda T., but free of herself. How had she not realized this blessing before? She was no longer Ariana Osgood. Nobody here even knew who she was, which meant that nobody here could really judge her. Ariana could do whatever she wanted. And what she wanted right then was to dance.

Suddenly someone slammed into her side, and Ariana was thrown right into Hudson's arms. He didn't even flinch as the full weight of her body hit him. Even stronger than he looked. Ariana giggled.

"Whoops. Sorry."

"Really not a problem," Hudson said with a smile. "At all."

He made no move to release her. He smelled both musky and Ivory-soap clean. Like a guy who had been working all night and had quickly washed up and changed into a fresh T-shirt before joining his friends. Not every guy would have made such an effort. Ariana stared into his gorgeous eyes and laughed. She was drunk. Drunker than she had been in a very, very long time.

They started to dance again, and Ariana moved boldly against Hudson, letting her body mesh with his, closer with every beat. Hudson smiled, but didn't seem to know what to do with his hands. He touched her waist briefly, then placed his hands on her shoulders, then gave up and just danced with them at his sides.

Ariana smiled. She had landed herself a gentleman.

"So, do you go to UT?" she shouted.

"No! I was just there for a music theory course," Hudson replied, bending toward her ear. "I'm gonna be a senior up at Harvard Prep."

Ariana nodded, impressed. A pre-Harvard boy.

"What about you?" he asked.

"I go to Easton," Ariana replied automatically.

"Easton Academy? Nice," Hudson said. "That's a good school."

All the blood in Ariana's body rushed to her face as she realized what she had just said. How could she have made such a stupid mistake? Was it just her knee-jerk need to prove to a Harvard guy that she was worthy?

Stupid, Ariana. Stupid, stupid, stupid.

She felt herself starting to recede into self-hatred, but then another dancer slammed into her from behind and she remembered where she was. What she was doing. This was just a random party on a random night. To Hudson she was just a random girl. He wouldn't even remember her fake name tomorrow, let alone where her fake self supposedly went to school.

Not every little thing had to have consequences, right?

"This may be totally out of line, but I have to say it. You, Emma Walsh, are insanely beautiful."

Ariana pushed away from him with a demure smile. So maybe she didn't need to be blond and blue-eyed to catch attention. "Thank you."

"Not out of line?" he said, raising his eyebrows.

Ariana shook her head. "Not at all."

Hudson tugged on her hand and lowered his lips to hers. She was about to pull away, but then her entire body sank into him. She wrapped her arms around his lean waist and pressed her lips against his. It was a perfect kiss. Warm and searching and soft and gentle. But even more so because of what it meant. It meant she was living. Really and truly living. Part of her had thought this would never happen for her again, that she had experienced her last first kiss all those months ago at Easton. But here she was, her heart palpitating, her skin on fire, her lips buzzing. Ariana smiled behind the kiss. She wished Dr. Meloni and his *nevers* could see her now.

"Stay away from me! No! Get *off* of me!"

Briana Leigh's voice cut through all the bliss and Hudson pulled away suddenly as a commotion erupted around them. Ariana looked up to find Briana Leigh bearing down on her, shrugging off Téo's pleas as she shoved people out of her path. The girl grabbed Ariana's upper arm in her viselike grip.

"We're going."

"Okay," Ariana said, shooting Hudson a startled look. "Let me just—"

"No. We're going *now*."

Briana Leigh pulled on Ariana's arm, but Hudson reached out and snagged Ariana's purse from her hand.

"Can't leave yet! I have Emma's purse."

"Give it back to her, waiter boy. I'm not kidding," Briana Leigh snapped.

Téo arrived at her side. The cocky posturing was gone and he was in full begging mode, palms upturned, posture slack. "Baby, just listen. I *have* to go. But maybe you could—"

"Ugh! That's it! I'm outta here!" Briana Leigh turned to Ariana. "You can find your own ride!"

She shoved through the crowd, disappearing almost instantly, and Ariana felt panic start to rise up through her chest. She couldn't let Briana Leigh out of her sight. If she didn't run after her and act the good friend, the girl might sour and freeze her out. She might not even let her back into her house if Ariana had to get her own cab. "Hudson, I'm sorry. I really have to go," she said.

When she turned to look at him, Hudson had her new cell phone out and was toying with the keyboard. His own cell was in his other hand and he was typing something into that as well.

"What're you doing?" Ariana demanded, on high alert. What if he noticed there were no contacts in her phone?

"There," he said, popping the phone back into her bag and handing it over. "Now you have my number and I have yours. This way if you don't call me, I can call you and demand an explanation."

Ariana was touched, but then she remembered this was a one-night thing. She couldn't have him hanging around. Ariana was in Dallas to make one connection and one connection only. After she got what she wanted out of Briana Leigh, she planned on disappearing. For good.

She had let her guard down, and this was the result.

"Talk to you soon," Hudson said, leaning in for a sweet, lingering kiss.

Ariana's heart was still beating in excitement as she sprinted after Briana Leigh.

VULNERABLE SIDE

"Ibiza! He's going to Ibiza! After giving me all that crap about going to stinking Atherton-Hill Prep because it's so far, he's going half a world away. And he doesn't even know when he's coming back!"

Ariana bit her tongue to keep from correcting Briana Leigh on the name of the exclusive boarding school. The girl was trashed and in full-on babble mode, so there was no point. Ariana did her best to remain upright as she supported most of the girl's weight on their way across Briana Leigh's bedroom. One of Briana Leigh's arms was slung around Ariana's neck and the other slapped limply at her side as she teetered in her gorgeous new Louboutins. Ariana had suggested she take them off in the car, which would have made this ridiculous trek *so* much easier, but the girl had insisted they would only be removed from her cold, dead feet.

Which Ariana was starting to consider.

"Here. Bed," Ariana said as they arrived at the foot of Briana Leigh's massive four-poster. She turned Briana Leigh around and dropped her on the end of the bed. Briana Leigh's chunky gold bracelet got caught in Ariana's hair as she started to fall back.

"Ow!" Ariana blurted, hurtling forward to keep from having a chunk of her hair ripped out.

"Sorry," Briana Leigh said with a pout as Ariana extricated her hair from the offending accessory. She finally stood up straight and smoothed the front of her dress.

"No problem," Ariana said. "It's fine."

"No. It's not. It's not fine," Briana Leigh said, gazing up at the ceiling with her bleary eyes. "Everyone leaves me. No one loves me enough to stick around. Am I that awful?"

She lifted her head half an inch off the bed to look at Ariana, who was now risking Briana Leigh's wrath by unbuckling the skinny straps on her shoes. Ariana paused, her heart constricting at the suddenly vulnerable expression on Briana Leigh's face. Ariana knew exactly how Briana Leigh felt. Exactly. The one person she had loved more than anyone in the world had left her too. Had not loved her back. And the pain had been unbearable.

Perhaps she had more in common with Briana Leigh than she had ever bothered to consider.

"Of course not," Ariana lied in a soothing tone. "You're great."

She placed Briana Leigh's shoes on the floor next to her dresser and fished a silky nightshirt out of the girl's pajama drawer. Back at the bed she pulled Briana Leigh up by the wrists and slipped the nightshirt over the slumping girl's head. Then, as Briana Leigh tipped even further forward, her head pressed into Ariana's waist, Ariana reached up under the nightshirt and unzipped her dress. As she went through the motions, Ariana felt a pang of nostalgia for Easton and the many nights she, Noelle, and Taylor had done this little dressing-undressing ritual for Kiran. She wondered if her old friend had ever gotten help for her alcoholic tendencies.

But you don't care, Ariana thought. *Because she doesn't care about you.*

Once the dress was unzipped, Ariana stepped back. Normally Noelle and Ariana would have lifted Kiran up so that Taylor could reach in and yank the dress to the floor, but this time Ariana had no help. She decided to just leave it. If Briana Leigh got uncomfortable enough, she would wriggle out of the thing herself.

"Okay. Time for bed!" Ariana said in a bright voice.

Briana Leigh crashed back onto the bed and rolled over. Face to the comforter, she half-crawled, half-slithered up the bed until her head was in the vicinity of the pillows. Ariana unfolded the cashmere throw at the foot of the bed and placed it over Briana Leigh.

"Thanks," Briana Leigh said, pulling the blanket up under her chin as she curled into a fetal position. "You're a good friend."

Ariana's mouth twitched into a smile.

"You're not going to leave me, are you?" Briana Leigh asked.

Ariana's chest welled with pride. She had already done it. Already made herself indispensable to Briana Leigh. But the pride was unexpectedly tinged with guilt. She realized with a start that she felt sorry for the girl. Clearly Briana Leigh had her lonely, vulnerable side. She was starting to depend on Emma Walsh, and all Emma Walsh was going to do was use her and bail.

"No. I'm not going to leave you," Ariana lied, a lump forming in her throat.

"Good." Briana Leigh closed her eyes. "I love you, Kaitlynn."

Ariana froze, hovering over Briana Leigh's bed. Her blood hardened in her veins, the guilt, pity, and sorrow instantly obliterated. For a moment she had forgotten why she was here—what Briana Leigh had done. Had been lulled by her loneliness. It must have been all the alcohol. Now, feeling suddenly sober as she stared down at Kaitlynn's mortal enemy, she could have torn her own hair out in penance for that lapse.

I love you? I love you? Ariana thought of her friend curled up on her bed in the Brenda T. while this murderous bitch cuddled into her imported Italian comforter in her multimillion-dollar compound. If Briana Leigh had really loved Kaitlynn, then what she had done to her was all the more evil. Trembling, Ariana's fingers slowly curled in. For the first time since she had broken free, she saw red.

DEAR KAITLYNN

Ariana took a step back from the bed and breathed.

In, one . . . two . . . three . . .

Out, one . . . two . . . three . . .

In, one . . . two . . . three . . .

Out, one . . . two . . . three . . .

It took several moments for her to come back to herself. For her pulse to stop rushing in her ears. She breathed in one more time, and the room snapped back into focus.

She could not harm Briana Leigh. That was not what this was about. As much as it pained her to think of it in these terms, she—and Kaitlynn—needed the girl.

But she would have given anything to be able to teach the girl a lesson. Maybe someday . . . Maybe someday she would have the chance. But not now. Not today.

Slowly, Ariana stepped away from the snoring heiress and made her way out of the room. As soon as the door was closed behind her, Ariana felt more in control. She had come so close to the edge. Too close. She had promised herself a new start. There was no way she was going to get that new start if she let herself cross over to the bad place.

The adrenaline rush had one benefit, however. It had cleared her mind of any residual effects from the alcohol. Ariana was fully awake and alert and saw everything around her with crisp clarity. Briana Leigh was completely passed out. This was her chance.

Ariana took off her shoes and jogged downstairs, the Southwestern-style tile floor frigid under her bare feet. The house was as still as a graveyard as she raced into the long hallway off the great room at the center of the Covington home. Briana Leigh hadn't given Ariana the full tour, so she had to stop to open each of the curved wooden doors along the way. Ariana found a pair of guest rooms, a gym, and what appeared to be some kind of indoor Zen garden. Here Ariana paused, taking in the lush greenery, the burbling waterfall and pond, the floor-to-ceiling windows, the Buddha sitting at the center of the room. It was all so soothing. She could picture Kaitlynn sitting here for hours. Maybe she would build a sanctuary like this in her new mansion. The one she planned to build for herself and Kaitlynn with Briana Leigh's money.

With a smile, she closed the door to the garden and continued the search. Finally, toward the end of the hall, she found a room that seemed promising. It was an office of some kind, outfitted with dark brown leather furniture and animal pelts and woven Native American tapestries, like an upscale western lodge. The desk in front of the picture window was huge and imposing, made out of roughly hewn oak. It was a man's desk. Briana Leigh's father's desk.

For a moment, Ariana paused in the center of the bearskin rug, feeling the ghost of Briana Leigh's father in the very walls around her. She wondered what he would think of her plan. Had he forgiven his daughter for murdering him in cold blood, or would he want to see the traitor get what was coming to her?

Ariana felt a thrill run up her spine, and somehow knew it was the latter. She opened the file cabinets and dug through the folders, giving herself several stinging paper cuts as she hungrily searched the pages and pages of documents, all having to do with Mr. Covington's many business deals. His money may have come from old oil, but he had his hands in a number of different flourishing businesses. After perusing all six drawers' worth of boring tax documents Ariana had not found what she was looking for.

She moved to Mr. Covington's desk. Nothing in the top drawer but several gold pens. The second drawer was full of blank white printer paper. Ariana was about to slam it shut when something out of place caught her eye. The corner of a piece of parchment paper, ivory, shoved into the center of the pile. Completely different from the rest of the pages in the stack.

Curious, Ariana dug the page free. There was writing at the top, only three words. Ariana squinted and held it up to the moonlight pouring through the window behind her. Her heart seized as the writing came into focus.

My dear Kaitlynn,

Ariana could hardly breathe. Someone had started a letter to Kaitlynn on this very page. Ariana studied the lettering. It was totally androgynous. Could have been a man or a woman. Maybe Briana Leigh had started to write to her friend in prison. An apology letter perhaps? Briana Leigh had already professed a preference for writing actual letters. It would have been poetic to write this particular missive in the office of the man she had murdered. The man at the center of the entire mess between her and Kaitlynn. Maybe she had made a start, lost her nerve, and stashed this here to come back to later.

Ariana slipped the unfinished letter back into the center of the paper stack where she had found it, just in case Briana Leigh decided to finish unburdening her heart. She didn't want the girl to find it was missing and get suspicious.

Taking a deep breath, she powered on the computer. Right on the desktop was a direct link to the Bank of Central Texas. Ariana smiled and double clicked the link. Of course, she needed a password to get in to the accounts. Quickly, Ariana tried the most obvious choices. Briana Leigh's name. Her mother's name. Her grandmother's name. None of them worked.

"Birthdays . . . birthdays . . . ," she whispered, the bluish glow of the screen lighting her face. "BrianaLeigh, four, fifteen."

She typed it in, and the bank's welcome screen greeted her.

"Yes! Yes, yes, yes," Ariana breathed, her heart pounding with excitement.

She placed her hand on the mouse and closed her eyes, letting the full force of her triumph wash over her. She could only imagine the huge dollar amounts that were going to greet her on the next screen. This was it. She was about to find out exactly how rich she was going to be.

Ariana opened her eyes and clicked on "Accounts." The page opened. There was only one account listed. A checking account. Worth $2,401.56.

"What?"

Ariana quickly clicked back and tried again. The same number greeted her. She scanned the page, looking for links to savings accounts or CDs or money market accounts. Anything. But there was nothing. Nothing but the tiny little checking account.

Her fingers gripped the mouse so tightly it slipped from her grasp. This wasn't right. It could not be right. Briana Leigh had millions. Hundreds of millions.

"Okay. Okay. Take a deep breath," Ariana told herself. "Maybe it's in a different bank. This must just be her petty cash account. You just have to keep looking."

She logged off the website and checked the desktop for other financial links. Nothing. Nothing in the recent browser history either.

"Dammit," Ariana said under her breath. She had been so close. So sure that her search was over. Where the hell was the rest of the money?

A footfall sounded in the hallway. Heart pounding, Ariana hit the power button and crouched on the floor behind the desk. Waited until the door was opened, then closed. Deciding it must have been one of the staff, Ariana waited another three minutes, counting the seconds off in her mind. By the time she was done, the many events of the day had come to rest on her shoulders and she suddenly felt exhausted.

Standing up straight, she stretched her arms over her head. It was three a.m. Time for a well-deserved rest. Tomorrow, the search would continue.

THE PROVERBIAL NAIL

The shaft of sunlight hit Ariana square in the face like a well-placed slap. Her temples were pierced with pain and she rolled away from the windows, squeezing her eyes even tighter.

"Time to get up, lazybones!" Briana Leigh trilled. She slapped Ariana on the ass and Ariana's eyes popped open.

*You can't kill her. You can*not *kill her.*

But she couldn't bring herself to force a smile, either.

"You're in a good mood," she said as Briana Leigh bounced into view. She was wearing lime green terry shorts with a white side stripe and a matching workout tank. Her auburn hair was back in a French braid, her sunglasses perched atop her head. How was this girl not hungover? She had drunk enough to level any respectable truck driver—and his wife. Ariana had sucked down all of three drinks and her head was pounding like a bass drum.

"Téo and I had a *long* talk and everything's going to be fine," Briana

Leigh said, bouncing from foot to foot. "Now get out of bed. I haven't had anyone to hit balls with in forever. You do play tennis, right?"

Ariana glanced over her shoulder at the blazing sun. She imagined it was at least a hundred and five degrees out there. All she wanted to do was stay inside with the air-conditioning and sleep for another five hours. But this wasn't about what she wanted. It was about what she needed. And she needed Briana Leigh to keep her around.

"Sure," Ariana said, shoving the comforter aside and swinging her legs over the side of the bed. Her head exploded with pain again. "Just let me throw some cold water on my face."

Ariana would have killed for a shower. In all her life she had never been seen in public without one. But she had a feeling Briana wouldn't stand for waiting. So this would be a first—a disgusting first—at Briana Leigh's hands. It made Ariana hate her that much more.

"I left a tennis outfit and racket on the dressing table."

Ariana looked over. Bright blue and red stripes. Totally garish, of course.

"Come on! This'll be good for you!" Briana Leigh cooed as Ariana slowly rose from the bed. This time she picked up her own tennis racket and used it to smack Ariana's ass. Ariana was not enjoying this new habit. "It's always good to get a healthy glow going before a big date."

Ariana paused on her way around the bed. She must have misheard.

"A big date?" she repeated.

"You, me, Hudson, Téo," Briana Leigh confirmed. "We're all going out tonight."

Ariana's heart both fluttered and dropped at the same time. An odd, contradictory sensation. She touched her face self-consciously, then crossed her arms over her chest, shoving her hands under her arms. There was no way she could see Hudson again, as much as she was suddenly longing to. Ariana knew herself well. If she saw him, she was going to let him in, and she could not let that happen. There was too much at stake.

"I don't remember being asked out on a date," Ariana said, trying for a light tone.

"You weren't," Briana Leigh replied, twirling the racket in her palm. "Hudson apparently couldn't stop talking about you, so Téo and I arranged the whole thing."

Ariana took a deep breath. She had to play this one carefully. She couldn't give a flat-out no. There had to be a good reason.

"Briana Leigh, the thing is . . . I'm not really interested in Hudson," Ariana said slowly, stepping forward. "He's not my type."

Briana Leigh's blue eyes flashed. "So?"

"So . . . I'd prefer not to go out on a date with someone I'm not interested in," Ariana said. "Why don't you and Téo just go?"

"Because he's Téo's friend and Téo wants us all to hang out," Briana Leigh said. Suddenly she seemed angry. Menacing. "And you're my friend, so you're going to do this for me."

It wasn't a question. Ariana's collarbone grew hot and she knew that her face was about to flush with irritation. She took a deep breath and beat it back.

"But I—"

"God, Emma! It's just one night!" Briana Leigh snapped, bringing the side of her racket down on the edge of the desk. The slam made Ariana flinch. This girl was *crazy*. "I *am* giving you a place to live."

A sizzle of fear raced down Ariana's spine. It was amazing how quickly and violently Briana Leigh's temper flared. Was that what had happened that day with her father? Had she been acting all carefree and happy one second, then blown his head off the next?

Ariana swallowed hard. She kept forgetting that she was living under the same roof with a psychotic murderer. From now on, she would have to be more careful. Briana Leigh had hit the proverbial nail right on its proverbial head. *Briana Leigh* was the one in control—not Ariana. Ariana hated to admit it, but it was true.

"Fine." Ariana managed a quick smile. "You're right. It could be fun."

"Good. Now get your ass in gear," Briana Leigh said with a grin, peppy once again. "Let's see how good the tennis instructors in Chi-town are!"

Ariana didn't know about Chi-town, but the instructors in Atlanta were pretty damn good. Still, should she let Briana Leigh win? Probably. As much as it pained her to consider it, taking a dive was the safer plan.

It would be a shame to die over something as silly as a tennis match.

ACTUAL FUN

"I've never done anything like this before," Ariana told Hudson as they strolled down the center of the crowded street in one of Dallas's historic districts. The full-skirted seersucker Ralph Lauren dress Briana Leigh had chosen for her fluttered in the breeze, tickling her knees. Considering the other options in Briana Leigh's wardrobe, this dress wasn't half bad. It made Ariana feel like she was the central character in some 1950s, small-town romantic play, with Hudson as her farm boy suitor. She scooped a small bite of ice cream out of her paper cup with her pink spoon and let the sweet confection melt deliciously on her tongue. The sun was finishing its long, slow trip toward the horizon, and a cool breeze tugged Ariana's hair back from her face. The sensory experiences were all so pleasant, she hardly minded the unwashed children with their painted faces and the screaming parents all around her.

"Anything like what?" Hudson asked.

"Like this." Ariana gestured with both arms to take in the whole scene. "This street fair thing."

Hudson paused, allowing a gap to open up between them and Briana Leigh and Téo, who were strolling up ahead, wearing the matching cowboy hats Téo had purchased for them from a guy at one of the many clothing stands. When Téo and Hudson had arrived at Briana Leigh's house midafternoon and announced that they were going to be attending the Taste of Dallas Festival, Ariana had balked. Her dates usually included five-star restaurants, classical concerts in the park, champagne, and respectful kisses at the door. A daytime street fair with arts and crafts vendors, restaurants hawking five-dollar tasting plates, and clowns on stilts generally didn't factor in. But now that she had spent a few hours there, Ariana realized that she was actually having fun. She wasn't sure if it was the weather or the food or the freedom or the fact that Hudson kept reaching for her hand—probably a combination of all four—but she was actually having fun.

"You've never been to a street fair? I'd think Chicago would have some good ones," Hudson said, incredulous. His ice cream cone dripped over his hand and Ariana automatically held out a napkin. Hudson thanked her and mopped up his hand, giving her an extra second to formulate a proper response.

"Oh, well, of course they do," Ariana said, figuring it was true. He launched the balled-up napkin toward a garbage can, missed, then rushed over to retrieve it and deposit it properly, all of which made Ariana smile. "It just wasn't something my family was into."

"Too upper crust for that, huh?" Hudson teased.

Ariana smirked. "How did you guess?"

"Just something about you," Hudson replied. "You go to Easton, and I just had a feeling it wasn't on scholarship."

Ariana's pulse quickened at the mention of Easton. So he did remember that tidbit she'd fed him. No good. Plus the scholarship thing now had her thinking about Reed Brennan, which instantly dampened her mood. She felt her face start to redden and looked at the ground.

In, one . . . two . . . three . . .

Out, one . . . two . . . three . . .

Okay. It's fine. You're fine.

"How's Harvard Prep?" Ariana asked, desperate to stop talking about herself. "Do you like it?"

"It's okay. It'll get the job done," he said, taking a bite from his cone.

"What job's that?" Ariana asked.

"Getting me into Boston Conservatory," Hudson said, running his free hand through his long blond hair. Most of it flopped right back into place. "They only accept three drummers each year, so it's not going to be easy."

"You play the drums?"

"And the guitar, the violin, the oboe, and a mean tambourine," Hudson joked. "But I want to focus on the drums in school. They're my passion."

"Wow. A five-instrument man," Ariana said with a smile, turning to face him.

"Impressed?" Hudson asked, his eyes sparkling.

Ariana smiled flirtatiously. "Maybe."

"Emma! They're line dancing over here! Let's go!"

Briana Leigh's hand closed around Ariana's wrist, and once again her arm felt dislocated. Ariana dropped her ice cream into the garbage can as Briana Leigh practically flung her up a set of stairs and onto a makeshift wooden dance floor. A dozen men and women in jeans and cowboy hats were all moving in perfect sync to some annoying twangy music being played by a six-piece band on a platform. Briana Leigh jumped right in, moving her feet in unison with the others, which couldn't have been easy considering she was sporting a tight, distressed denim Chanel mini and Jimmy Choos with four-inch heels.

"I don't know how," Ariana feebly protested, trying to inch her way off the stage.

"Come on! I'll teach you!" Briana Leigh shouted.

Téo laughed and clapped as he watched his girl get down. Ariana, however, was physically repulsed. She had never been one for synchronized dancing. All the girls at her small Southern private school had flocked to ballet and cheerleading and jazz classes when she was young, but her one go at tap had ended in disaster. Ariana had been so afraid of missing a step at the recital, she had frozen up and not moved a muscle throughout the entire number. Her mother had been forced to carry her home in tears. Her mom had never brought up dance lessons again.

Feeling the burning humiliation of that day as if it had just happened, Ariana turned and scurried right back down the steps. Hudson placed his hands on her stomach, stopping her. The intimacy of the gesture was not lost on Ariana.

"Go on. It looks like fun," Hudson said in her ear.

"I can't." Ariana shook her head. "I don't know it."

"I'll do it with you," Hudson said, taking her hand. "Come on. We can mess it up together."

This guy had no idea who he was talking to. Ariana had never *willingly* messed up anything in her life.

"Let's go, Emma!" Briana Leigh shouted, gesturing over her head.

Suddenly an unfamiliar sense of calm came over Ariana. Right. She wasn't Ariana Osgood anymore. She was Emma Walsh. For now, at least. And maybe Emma Walsh didn't mind getting a few steps wrong.

"You know what? Fine," Ariana said. "Let's do it."

She and Hudson stepped up onto the stage, to the whoops and happy hollers of the rest of the dancers, and fell in line with Briana Leigh. Staring at Briana Leigh's feet, Ariana did her best to match the steps, but soon found herself crushing Hudson's foot, turning the wrong way, and walking right into Briana Leigh's back.

"Sorry. I'm so sorry," Ariana said, embarrassed.

"It takes a few times through before you get it," Briana Leigh told her. "Here. Watch me. It's right, right, left, left, kick, turn, stomp, stomp."

Right, right, left, left, kick, turn, stomp, stomp.

Right, right, left, left, kick, turn, stomp, stomp.

Right, right, left, left, kick, turn, stomp, stomp.

"You try it," Briana Leigh said, stepping back.

Ariana looked at Hudson and they both went for it. Hudson

tripped over his own feet and almost fell off the stage. Ariana, however, executed the sequence perfectly.

"See!" Briana Leigh was all smiles. "You're a natural!"

Ariana found herself grinning from ear to ear. The day out had
apparently put Briana Leigh in a good mood and she was being
unusually nice at the exact perfect moment. The girl spent the next
ten minutes making sure Ariana had all the steps down, and soon the
two of them were dancing together, hamming it up like old pros and
throwing in hip juts and extra kicks for fun. Hudson gave up and
jumped off the stage to watch with Téo. Ariana felt his eyes on her
and made sure not to look at him, keep him wanting more. But her
skin grew warmer and warmer under his gaze, and she found herself
loving every minute of it.

When the song finally ended, Briana Leigh cheered and threw her
arms around Ariana.

"You sure you're not from the South?" she joked.

Ariana felt a sudden, unexpected twinge of guilt. She had felt so
free while she was dancing that she'd once again forgotten her mission
and started to enjoy her time with Briana Leigh. Ariana was starting
to understand why Kaitlynn had liked her—there was something dis-
armingly intoxicating about her. But Briana Leigh's rhetorical question brought her right back to reality.

"Nope. Not from the South. But that was fun," she admitted.

"See? You should always listen to me," Briana Leigh said lightly. Then
she turned and threw herself off the stage into Téo's waiting arms.

Ariana glanced at Hudson. He seemed willing to catch her, but she wasn't quite ready for stage diving and PDA yet. Instead she took the three stairs on her own and joined her friends.

"What next?" Briana Leigh asked.

"I don't think I could eat anything else," Hudson said, placing his hand on his flat stomach.

"No. No more food, please," Ariana added with a laugh.

All around them streetlights flicked on as the sun dipped below the horizon. The hanging paper lamps around the stage bobbed in the breeze. Ariana felt as if the laughter and conversation and music had softened along with the heat. A pleasant, content feeling overcame her just as Hudson's hand slipped into hers yet again. It was a feeling Ariana relished—so rare for her normally intense self.

Téo turned to Briana Leigh and Ariana noticed the serious expression on his face even before his girlfriend did. Something was up. She glanced at Hudson and he raised an eyebrow. He had seen it too.

"Well, since you asked, I do have an idea of what to do next . . . if you're up for it, Briana Leigh," Téo said.

Briana Leigh stopped looking around at all the people and frivolity. Her eyes widened as Téo got down on one knee, right there in the middle of the jostling crowd.

"Oh my God," Briana Leigh breathed.

"Oh my God," Ariana said as Téo whipped out a black double-hinged ring box.

"This just got way interesting," Hudson put in.

"Briana Leigh, I don't want you to have to worry while I'm away in Ibiza," Téo said, swallowing hard. He was clearly nervous but determined as well. His gaze was firm as he looked up at Briana Leigh's face and opened the box. "You're the only girl for me, now and forever. Briana Leigh Covington, will you marry me?"

Dozens of people stopped to stare. Ariana gaped at the ring. It was a perfect cushion-cut diamond with three baguettes on either side in an antique-style platinum setting. At least someone in this relationship had good taste.

"Are you kidding? Yes!" Briana Leigh cried.

Téo grinned as he stood up and Briana Leigh launched herself into his arms, wrapping her legs around his back. Ariana was surprised. She would have thought that Briana Leigh was the type to get that diamond on her finger ASAP, but she didn't even seem to realize the ring was there. She was too busy crying and kissing her new fiancé.

As the people around them applauded, Ariana looked at Hudson. He gave her a sort of nonplussed glance.

"Well, I don't have a ring," he said finally. "But I can offer you an iced coffee. . . ."

He tilted his head toward a Coffee Carma kiosk and grinned at her like he was offering a brand-new yacht. Ariana laughed.

"Come on. Let's leave these two alone for a little while," Hudson suggested.

"Definitely," Ariana said.

Hand in hand, they left the happy couple to their moment.

THE DREAM

Stars. Ariana had missed the stars. When she was a little girl in Georgia and her grandmother was still alive, she and her mother and her gran used to sit out in cushioned lawn chairs for hours, just waiting for that elusive shooting star. As Hudson settled in on the blanket next to her that night, Georgia and her family seemed so very far away. So far that they could have been on some remote planet circling one of the very stars she was now watching.

"Beautiful, huh?" Hudson said.

"Absolutely," Ariana replied with a sigh.

The moment the foursome had returned from Taste of Dallas, Briana Leigh had dragged Téo up to her room to thank him in God knew what way for asking her to marry him. Ariana had wanted to get as far away from the second floor as possible, so she had suggested the stargazing. After stealing a huge, cushy plaid blanket from an upstairs linen closet, she and Hudson had snuck out back and set up on the lawn near the shimmering outdoor pool, which, Ariana noted, was even bigger than the indoor one.

"It's so peaceful out here," Ariana mused.

Hudson shifted next to her and her skin sizzled as she braced for contact. But Hudson simply crooked his arm so that he could lay his head back in the palm of his hand.

"I love the sounds after dark in Texas," he said. "The night birds, the coyotes howling . . . You get nothing like that back in Boston."

Ariana smiled. A future music major like himself would notice nature's own lovely chorus.

"Tell me about music," she said, rolling over onto her side. She bent her arm under her head and propped herself up.

"What do you mean?" Hudson asked.

"Well, why music, exactly?" she asked. "How did you get into it? What do you love about it?"

Hudson pushed himself up as well, mirroring her pose. Even in the dim light coming off the pool area lamps, she could see the spark of excitement in his eyes.

"It's the only thing I've ever loved to do," he said. "I tried to get into sports as a kid because my dad wanted me to, but it never interested me. I would be running down the field in football, staring at the marching band, wishing I could try out the tuba or something. Got my helmet knocked off a few times that way."

He chuckled and Ariana grinned.

"It's like anytime I'm not doing something else, I have to be playing music or listening to music or writing music," he said.

"I used to write poetry," Ariana said wistfully.

"Used to?" Hudson prompted.

Ariana's heart clenched. Why had she brought that up? It wasn't something she wanted to talk about. She glanced at Hudson. His gaze was so intent, she realized that he wasn't going to just let it drop. But she couldn't tell him the truth. Hardly. She decided on a reasonable stretch of the truth.

"I used to keep these journals full of poems," she said, thinking of the standard-issue notebooks she'd been allowed to use at the Brenda T. "I'd write between classes, in the middle of the night, whenever something came to me. Then one day my father found them. A lot of the stuff was personal and some of it was kind of dark, you know?"

Hudson nodded.

"Anyway, knowing he had read that stuff just sort of made me freeze up. I haven't been able to write a word since," she said, picking at a pull in the blanket.

"God. That sucks," Hudson said.

"You have no idea," Ariana replied.

In fact, it had been Dr. Meloni who had told one of the guards to remove her current journal from her cell a few months ago. Then he had proceeded to read the poems to her in session, laughingly, trying to get her to analyze them herself. It had been one of the most degrading and humiliating experiences of her life. She hadn't written a word since.

"So what's the dream?" Ariana asked, trying to take the focus off herself.

"The dream?" he asked, his handsome brow knitting.

"Yes, the dream," Ariana said. "Do you want to play in an ensemble or are you going the rock star route? Or do you want to compose or play for a certain orchestra?"

Hudson blinked. It seemed as if he'd never really considered this question before. Then he grinned.

"Your dreams are very specific, aren't they?" he asked.

"Aren't everyone's?" Ariana replied, confused.

At that Hudson laughed, then leaned in to kiss her. Ariana was unsure what she had done to merit a kiss, but she didn't ask. Instead she let herself enjoy the moment. Every single touch sent a tingling sensation of giddiness through her core. How had she forgotten how incredible kissing could be? For so long the very idea of love had been so tied up with the idea of hatred and death. . . . She hadn't even considered the possibility of getting close to anyone.

But being close to Hudson felt so right. He didn't expect anything from her. Hadn't promised her anything. So there was no way for either one of them to be disappointed. No way this could turn for the worse. So Ariana simply focused on the now, on the kiss, and nothing else.

"So what's your dream then?" he asked when he pulled away. He touched her cheek with his fingertips, roughened from playing his various instruments.

Ariana sighed as she lay back down on the blanket and gazed up at the stars. She couldn't tell him the Australia plan, but she could tell him the original dream. The dream she'd had all her life. It would be nice to talk about it one last time. At that very moment a white streak cut across the sky, and she had to bite her lip to keep from pointing out the falling star like an excited little girl.

"First Princeton, where I'll major in English literature," Ariana recited, seeing it all play out in her mind as she had imagined it so many times. "Then a job at *Vanity Fair* in New York and a loft apartment in Chelsea on a quaint, tree-lined street. There, I will of course meet the perfect guy—"

"Wait a second, you haven't done that already?" Hudson protested, placing his hands to his chest in faux offense.

Ariana laughed. "Excuse me. I was talking," she scolded jokingly.

"Pardon me. Continue," Hudson replied, grinning from ear to ear.

The lightness in Ariana's chest was almost distracting in its perfection. She could get used to this feeling. This utter simplicity.

"Of course we'll get married, have two kids, and once I've established myself as a writer, I'll go freelance and we'll move the family back to the homestead in Georgia where—"

"Georgia?" Hudson interjected, his brow knitting. "I thought you were from Chicago."

Ariana's breath turned cold in her lungs. She hadn't just said that. She had not just said that. And, wait a second, had she started to slip into her twang? Dammit. She wasn't sure. What if he had seen her story on the news? Between her mention of Easton and now Georgia, he might definitely put two and two together and figure out who she really was. But a quick glance at Hudson told her he wasn't overly confused or alarmed. Just curious.

"I *am* from Chicago," she replied evenly, her gaze back on the night sky, her Northern accent perfectly intact once again. "But I have family in Georgia. My grandmother. I've always loved the plantation she lives on, so I'm hoping I'll get to move there one day."

"That's cool," Hudson said, lying on his back as well. "I've always wanted to go to Georgia and experience the whole Southern charm thing for myself. I hear Dallas doesn't quite do it justice."

"Definitely not," Ariana said, relaxing slightly. "Georgia hospitality is in another class."

"Well, maybe you'll take me to meet your grandmother sometime," Hudson said.

Her gran's gravesite flashed through her mind. Ariana would never get to visit that spot again.

"Maybe I will," she lied.

Hudson turned the conversation toward his class at UT and his plans for the rest of the summer, but Ariana barely heard a word for a good five minutes. She was too busy berating herself for her slip and concentrating on how to keep it from happening again. The last thing she could risk was Hudson finding out who she really was. She hated to think of what she might have to do to him if he did.

CARNIVAL NIGHTMARE

"Trust me. You need this," Briana Leigh told Ariana as she pulled her gold Cadillac convertible into a parking space at the Plaza of the Americas in downtown Dallas Tuesday afternoon. Her engagement ring flashed in the sunlight as she turned off the satellite radio, finally silencing the gratingly loud country-western station she'd been blaring throughout the drive. "Your luggage is obviously gone for good, and you can't keep wearing my old clothes."

No, I really can't, Ariana thought, looking down at the bright, tiered skirt she was currently sporting. What fascinated her was that all these awful clothes were by top designers. It was as if Briana Leigh hunted the boutiques each season for the worst pieces from each collection and filled her closets with them.

"You're right," Ariana said. "I definitely need some new things."

Her phone beeped and Ariana pulled it out of her small, borrowed purse. There was a picture message from Hudson in her in-box.

Speaking of new things . . . , Ariana thought wryly, as if Hudson was her new accessory. She opened the picture and smiled. Purple wildflowers filled the screen. The caption read, *Saw this and thought of you.*

Ariana's heart fluttered happily. Another point for Hudson. He was a true romantic. He'd gone back to Austin Sunday night, and Ariana actually missed him. As Briana Leigh hit the button to raise the ragtop roof, Ariana popped open the glove compartment. She took off her sunglasses and wedged them into the tiny space between the car manual and a box of Altoids, along with her cell. When Briana Leigh wasn't looking, she added her wallet to the mix, then slammed and locked the door.

"Paranoid much? This is, like, the safest street in Dallas," Briana Leigh said, gesturing out the window at the huge Le Meridien hotel across the street.

Ariana's cheeks turned pink. It was an old habit, removing the things she wouldn't need and locking them up in the car. Something her father had always done. And yes, he was paranoid, but for good reason. Everyone in their Atlanta suburb knew that the Osgood family, perched on their old family plantation on the outskirts of their sleepy Southern town, had more money than the rest of the households in the village combined. Her father had been mugged more than once and he had quickly learned his lesson. His theory was that if it wasn't on you, they couldn't steal it, and Ariana had adopted his lock-it-up ritual.

"Old habit," she said with a shrug.

"Whatever." Briana Leigh rolled her eyes. "Let's go."

Twenty minutes later Ariana found herself standing in a dressing room in a small, chic boutique, loaded down with the most hideous collection of garments she had ever seen—all florals and plaids and stripes in bright, offensive colors. It wasn't as if the store didn't carry some tasteful things. There were several, actually. But every time Ariana tried to sneak in a simple jacket or a straight skirt or a white top, Briana Leigh caught her and tossed the garment aside.

"Which one are you trying on?" Briana Leigh asked from outside the dressing room door.

"A Calvin Klein," Ariana replied, sliding her arms into the three-quarter sleeves of a gray shirtdress.

"What Calvin Klein? I didn't pick out any Calvin Klein."

Ariana gritted her teeth. "So have you and Téo set a date yet?" she asked, hoping to divert her. Briana Leigh had talked of nothing but her engagement for the past two days.

"Not yet," Briana Leigh replied. "I still can't even believe we're engaged. I'm going to have kids right away."

Ariana blinked. Briana Leigh was only sixteen. How could she be thinking about having children. "Really?"

"I always wanted a big family," Briana Leigh said, her tone wistful. "I never had any brothers or sisters . . . not really, anyway."

Ariana's heart skipped a beat. Was Briana Leigh thinking about Kaitlynn?

"And with my parents gone . . . I just want to start over," Briana Leigh finished.

Slowly, Ariana buttoned up the dress. It was the first time that Briana Leigh had sounded genuine. Hopeful. Not at all bitchy. It was as if she had just let her guard down, right there in broad daylight and without the help of alcohol. The girl actually had dreams.

There was a long moment of silence and then Briana Leigh suddenly rapped on the door. "I'm getting wrinkles out here! Let's see!"

And then the bitch was back. Ariana tied the ribbon belt on the dress and opened the door. Briana Leigh's face screwed up in disgust.

"What are you going for? Lame librarian?"

Ariana turned to look at herself. She liked the dress. It showed off her slim waist and toned calves and made her new hair color pop. Plus, it was totally her style. Understated. Refined. Definitely not lame librarian. But still, she couldn't contradict Briana Leigh. Ariana had searched the house twice since finding Briana Leigh's secondary checking account but had found nothing. She needed to keep staying at the mansion, meaning she needed to stay on Briana Leigh's good side, even if it meant being the second-worst-dressed person below the Mason-Dixon Line.

"You're right," she said, tugging at the ribbon belt. "I don't know what I was thinking."

Briana Leigh made a snorting noise of agreement. "Here. Take that off and put this on."

She shoved a pink-and-yellow Betsey Johnson frock at Ariana and slammed the dressing room door shut. Ariana sat down on the bench in her cubicle and looked into her eyes in the mirror.

"It's just temporary," she whispered. "When this is all over, you can come back here and buy anything you want. Better yet, you can go to Milan and buy anything you want."

Comforted by the thought of herself and Kaitlynn strolling past Milan's gleaming flagship stores loaded down with glossy designer bags, Ariana was buoyed enough to continue with her freak fashion show. As she slid the Betsey Johnson over her head, she mapped out her next search in her mind. She'd already ransacked the basement and Briana Leigh's parents' old bedroom, so tonight she was going to try the computer in Mr. Covington's office again. There had to be another bank, some other account she hadn't seen. Kaitlynn had said Briana Leigh had gotten everything when her dad died. There just had to be something Ariana was missing.

Ariana zipped up the dress and looked at her reflection. The frock was one-shouldered, tightly ruched, and way too short. Grimacing, she turned and opened the door of the dressing room. Briana Leigh's eyes widened in delight.

"What do you think?" Ariana asked, afraid of the answer.

"Now *that* is a dress!" Briana Leigh cried. "You should totally wear that out of here," Briana Leigh decided, standing next to Ariana to view the reflection in the mirror.

"Actually, I think I'll change back into the—"

"Shut up. You're wearing it." Briana Leigh ripped the tag off the dress to bring it up to the counter. "Get the rest of that stuff and let's go pay."

Biting down hard on her tongue, Ariana pushed her toes into her borrowed red sandals and gathered up the other garments Briana Leigh had chosen for her. As she placed them down on the counter, the older woman behind the cash register raised her glasses to her eyes.

"You've chosen some lovely things," she said to Ariana with a smile.

Right. If you want to walk around looking like a carnival nightmare, Ariana thought.

"I know," Briana Leigh replied haughtily.

Ariana smiled her thanks and reached for her purse. There was nothing inside but a lip balm and some other cosmetics.

"Oh my God. I'm such an idiot," she said, pretending to root through her bag.

"What?" Briana Leigh asked as the saleswoman paused in her ringing up.

"I must have locked my wallet in with the other things," Ariana said. "I thought this bag felt light."

Briana Leigh stared at Ariana, her eyes blank and hard. For a moment, Ariana felt the slightest twinge of fear.

"What kind of moron goes shopping without her wallet?" Briana Leigh asked, leaning her hand on the counter.

Ariana swallowed hard. This was not good. The girl was going to drag her back to the car to get her wallet. Ariana was going to have to use that credit card she'd swiped and just hope the old woman had yet to realize it was missing. Hope that she had enough credit to pay for hundreds of dollars' worth of hideous clothing.

"I'm sorry," Ariana said, glancing in embarrassment at the sales clerk. "I don't know what I was thinking. I guess I'll go change back."

She started to turn, but Briana Leigh's hand gripped her forearm. "Stop. You're not going anywhere."

Her back to Briana Leigh, Ariana closed her eyes and said a quick prayer. That the girl hadn't figured out that Ariana was freeloading. That she wasn't about to snap. That she wasn't going to kill Ariana too, the first chance she got. When Ariana turned around again, Briana Leigh was reaching into her own purse and pulling out her wallet.

"I've got this."

She slapped her American Express Black down on the counter and pushed it over with her fingertips.

Ariana flooded with relief. "Briana Leigh, you don't have to do that."

"Whatever," Briana Leigh said, brushing her off. "It's either this or I keep walking around with you in last year's collections. Talk about embarrassing."

Ariana controlled her humiliated blush and glanced back toward the dressing rooms, where a floor clerk was just removing the Calvin Klein from the hook where she'd left it.

Soon, she told herself, narrowing her eyes at Briana Leigh. *Soon you'll be free to do whatever you want.*

OVER

Ariana awoke early Thursday morning to the sound of a screaming wail and for a split second fully believed she was back in her cell at the Brenda T. She clutched the silky covers to her chest for a good long moment, waiting for her breath to return to normal. For her to realize that she was awake, alive, and still in Texas. Slowly, her mind focused on the noise. On the actual screaming, crying words.

"You have these people going through my things?" Briana Leigh wailed. "How could you?"

There was a response, but it was calm and even and at a much lower volume. Ariana jumped out of bed, grabbed a flowered silk robe from the closet, and slipped it on as she raced out of her room. In the hallway the commotion was much louder, and Ariana realized that Briana Leigh and her tormentor were standing in the great room downstairs. She paused at the end of the hallway where it opened up like a loft over the cavernous room below, and peeked around the corner.

The calm voice belonged to Grandma Covington. Ariana hadn't seen her in a couple of days—she'd been holed up in the guesthouse, nursing a cold. But she appeared to be better now. Sitting up in her wheelchair, Grandma C. was the picture of strength. She glared up at Briana Leigh with smoldering fury, as if she was facing off with the devil herself.

"Just tell me why!" Briana Leigh wailed, still wearing her flimsy nightgown, pushing her hands into her hair as she cried.

"It's for your own good," her grandmother said through her teeth. "And thank God I do it! Otherwise I never would have known that my only granddaughter planned on marrying before she even graduates high school!"

"But I love him!" Briana Leigh cried.

Ariana heard the anguish in Briana Leigh's voice and thought of that moment at the boutique the day before. How much Briana Leigh was looking forward to the future, to finally having a family. It made her heart ache for the girl.

Stop it. You're not supposed to feel sorry for her, she reminded herself.

"He's not appropriate," her grandmother replied, clucking her tongue. "And that is neither here nor there, because you will not be marrying anyone. You will go to Atherton-Pryce Hall and you will graduate on time. I have already phoned the headmaster, and he has agreed to give you the special attention you need. He will personally be sending me your report cards, as well as a weekly progress report."

"Great! You're going to have the headmaster spying on me too?" Briana Leigh cried.

"Yes. And come August, I'll be taking you to the plane myself so that we don't have another Paris incident," her grandmother said.

Paris incident? I wonder what happened there, Ariana thought.

"You can't do this to me," Briana Leigh said, trying to hold her quivering chin up. "You can't."

"You've brought this upon yourself," Grandma Covington said. "Ever since your mother died, your behavior has been deplorable. Your father may have tolerated it because he felt sorry for you, but it's about time you grew up and realized that you have responsibilities."

She flicked her wrist and something small and sparkling pinged against the tile floor, bounced a few times, and landed at Briana Leigh's feet. Ariana held her hand over her mouth when she realized it was Briana Leigh's engagement ring. So that was how her grandmother had found out. One of the help had snooped and uncovered the ring.

"May as well give that back to him," Grandma Covington said, using the controls on her wheelchair to reverse. The chair made a soft whirring sound as it worked. "I'm sure he can find some other willing girl to give it to."

Briana Leigh clutched her stomach and doubled over, sobbing. Ariana's heart automatically went out to her again. Her grandmother was so awful to her. This woman in no way meshed with the image of the sweet old lady Kaitlynn had painted for her. Had Grandma C. changed in the years since Kaitlynn had been imprisoned, or had the old lady favored Kaitlynn for some reason? As Ariana considered this, Grandma C. turned her chair and, without looking back, navigated her way across the great room and out the open back door. Briana Leigh picked up the ring in her trembling fingers and continued bawling, looking broken and pathetic. After she finally got hold of herself and dried her eyes, she lifted her head slowly and glared at the door through which her grandmother had gone. Then she slipped the ring back onto her left ring finger.

Good for you, Ariana thought. In that moment she couldn't help respecting the girl. She pushed herself away from the wall as Briana Leigh came barreling up the stairs. The girl stopped in her tracks when she saw Ariana.

"I heard the shouting . . . ," Ariana said with an apologetic shrug.

Briana Leigh sniffed and raised her chin. "Well, then you know I'm screwed."

"Why?" Ariana asked as Briana Leigh breezed right by her. She followed the girl into her room and stood in the center of the hardwood floor as Briana Leigh flung herself dramatically onto her unmade bed.

"Because! I have to go to Atherton! I can't marry Téo. She'll throw me out on the street! She'll disinherit me!" Briana Leigh said, sitting up straight and turning her palms out.

Ariana bit her tongue and cinched the belt on her robe. "So what?" she asked, sitting down on the edge of Briana Leigh's bed. "Let her disinherit you. You can take care of yourself."

Briana Leigh stared at her blankly. Ariana felt a flutter of uncertainty in her heart. For some reason the figure $2401.56 flashed through her mind.

"You do have your own money don't you?" Ariana asked, her voice sounding strained. "Your inheritance. From your parents."

Briana Leigh rolled her eyes and she fell onto her back again. "Uh, *no*."

Ariana felt as if the bright sun outside was mocking her. As if the four posts around the bed were tilting in around her, getting ready to clamp her down to the mattress and swallow her through the floor and into hell. So powerful, that one word.

No.

"What do you mean?" Ariana asked, fighting to keep her voice even. "Your parents didn't leave you anything?"

"Oh, no. They left me everything," Briana Leigh said in a bitter, sarcastic tone. "They just made sure that I wouldn't get any of it until I was twenty-five. It's held in a trust, and my grandmother controls it all."

"What?" Ariana breathed.

Suddenly she saw her whole world collapse around her. All her plans, her dreams, her future. Everything had hinged on coming here, gaining Briana Leigh's trust, and getting her inheritance. Ariana *needed* that money. But there was no inheritance. There wouldn't be one for another nine years.

Ariana's mind started to whirl, trying to find some logic. Something to latch onto. She had thought that Briana Leigh had murdered her father to get the cash. That was what Kaitlynn had always said. Had Kaitlynn been somehow misled? Or was it Briana Leigh who had been duped? Maybe she hadn't known about the trust clause until after her father was dead.

God, that must have sucked. Murder your own father and then find out it was all for nothing? Ariana knew the feeling, at least in a way. She had let Sergei die on that awful day nearly three years ago, had held him under the freezing water until he went limp, and had then learned that he was perfectly innocent. Ariana could only imagine Briana Leigh's face when the will had been read. It must have been classic. Suddenly she wasn't sure whether to laugh at Briana Leigh's misfortune or cry for her own.

"Yep. Until then all I get is a monthly allowance," Briana Leigh said, raising her hand to look at her sparkling diamond ring. She sighed and buried her face in a down pillow.

Ariana felt suddenly weak. She turned and lay back on Briana Leigh's bed, Briana Leigh's feet uncomfortably close to her cheek. Still, she didn't move. Couldn't have done so if she tried.

It was over. All over. There would be no starting fresh. No living the dream. What was she going to do now? Where was she going to go? She had no one. Nothing. Not a friend in the world.

Ariana's fingers closed around her forearm and squeezed.

In, one . . . two . . . three . . .

Out, one . . . two . . . three . . .

The breathing wasn't working. Ariana was starting to panic. Her vision spotted over and she felt sweat pricking under her arms, at the small of her back, along her temples. She had lost control of the situation. There was nothing she could do. Nothing at all.

REALITY

The sky outside Ariana's windows was just starting to turn pink, but she had yet to close her eyes. Sleepless nights had been a regular thing for her inside the Brenda T., but since she had been out, she had been so exhausted from the activity, the acting, the hope for the future, that she'd slept like a rock the whole week she'd been in Dallas.

Not this night, however. This night had been one of the worst she had ever experienced.

Letting out a deep sigh, Ariana rolled onto her back and stared at the revolting chandelier above her bed. What the hell was she doing here? Why was she torturing herself with Briana Leigh's company, bending backward to please her and her horrible fashion sense, if the girl didn't have any money? And what the hell was she going to do next? Where was she going to go?

All night long she had been asking herself these questions, and she had yet to devise an answer. Because there was nowhere. The moment she stepped off this compound, she'd be nothing but a fugitive with a crappy cell phone and less than three hundred dollars to her name. She supposed she could steal some of Briana Leigh's couture and a few pieces of jewelry and hock them, but that money would only last so long. She could go back to her parents, but if she did that, it would only be a matter of time before she was caught. It was simply too dangerous.

She needed Briana Leigh's millions. Needed the money so that she and Kaitlynn could truly disappear and start over. The thought of that money was all that had kept her going those last few months on the inside. It was completely inconceivable that she might leave here without it.

There was only one answer. All night long Ariana had kept return-ing to the obvious, but all night long she had shoved the thought into the back of her mind. She couldn't go there. She wouldn't. There had to be another way.

But now, in the dim light of dawn, she was starting to realize there was not. If she wanted her new life, she was going to have to make this sacrifice.

Taking a deep breath, Ariana let the cold hardness of the truth settle over her. Felt the weight of it in her veins. Let the reality seep into her mind. First she had to accept it. Only then would she be able to do what she had to do.

A moment later she shoved the covers aside, grabbed her robe, and was gone.

She walked calmly down the stairs and crossed the great room with a swiftness born of necessity. The back door slid open soundlessly and she was outside, crossing the stone patio in her bare feet. The air was already warm, and somewhere on the grounds a lawnmower roared. Ariana looked around to make sure none of the staff were in sight. She was alone.

The sliding backdoor of Grandma Covington's small bungalow was, thankfully, unlocked. Ariana opened it a few inches and turned sideways to slip inside, closing the door behind her with the tiniest of clicks. The cozy kitchen gleamed in the gathering morning sunshine, everything in its place. On her way through Ariana spotted a pill bottle and paused, snatching it up in curiosity.

Ambien. A full bottle. She pocketed half the pills. Past experience proved that something like these could come in handy one day.

Slowly, Ariana crept down the short hall, assuming the bedroom would be at the very end. On her way she passed by the open door to an office and paused. Sitting in the middle of the desk were two sets of legal-size papers. One was flagged with pink Post-its indicating places to sign. The temptation was too great. With a quick glance at the bedroom door, Ariana turned and stepped into the office.

Positioned on the west side of the house with the blinds drawn, the room was dimly lit. Ariana's eyes adjusted quickly as she picked up the papers and quickly scanned their contents. It was a will. Grandma Covington's will. Both a new version and an old. Ariana scanned the pages to find what had changed. Her eyes fell on Kaitlynn's name in the old version and her heart stood still. Grandma Covington had set aside two million dollars for Kaitlynn Nottingham.

Palms sweating, Ariana quickly scanned the new version.

"She's removing Kaitlynn from her will," Ariana whispered to herself. After the fond manner in which Kaitlynn had spoken about Grandma Covington, Ariana wasn't surprised that Kaitlynn had once been in her will. But Kaitlynn had been convicted of killing Grandma Covington's son more than two years ago. Why had the woman waited this long to take Kaitlynn out?

Suddenly Ariana felt a rush of realization. Maybe Grandma Covington hadn't believed that Kaitlynn was guilty. Maybe she had been hoping that her adopted granddaughter would be released. But since Kaitlynn had lost her chance at an appeal . . .

It all made sense. Suddenly, Ariana found a soft spot for the old woman growing inside her chest. This lady loved Kaitlynn just like Ariana did. How could Ariana murder the only other person in the world who cared about Kaitlynn?

She couldn't. It was as simple as that. Ariana breathed in and felt her mind start to clear. Once again she had let herself come far too close to the abyss. Once again she had been saved.

Ariana was just turning to go when she heard a whir and a creak. Her heart hit her throat and she made a move for the sliding glass door, but it was too late. Grandma Covington wheeled her way into the room and paused near the door.

This was it. The jig was up. Unless . . .

Ariana felt her hand close around the slim gold stand on the library lamp in front of her. She could still do it. If she had to.

"Briana Leigh?" Grandma Covington squinted in the darkness.

She wasn't wearing her glasses. "Is that you? What are you doing in my office?"

Ariana's grip loosened. She took a deep breath. Grandma Covington and her shoddy vision had just given her an easy out.

"Just looking for a pen, Grandma," Ariana said, perfectly mimicking Briana Leigh's slight Texan drawl. "I'll see you at breakfast."

Then, before the woman could question her further, Ariana slipped out the back door and onto the patio. She paused for a moment to collect herself, then shook her hair back and strolled toward the main house.

Kaitlynn would have been proud of her, she knew. Proud—and grateful. But that didn't change the fact that Ariana was screwed.

WASTED

Ariana watched from one of the extra bedroom windows as Téo picked up Briana Leigh in his Hummer later that morning. She wondered what Briana Leigh had said to him, if anything, about the confrontation with her grandmother. Was she the type of girl to keep it to herself and hope that it would go away, or would she get all dramatic and weepy and tell Téo everything?

She had a feeling it was the latter.

The second the roar of the engine had faded in the distance, Ariana grabbed her purse and headed downstairs. She snagged the keys to the Cadillac off the hook inside the mudroom and walked to the garage, where several choice autos were kept waxed and buffed and ready to go.

Ariana paused for a moment, wishing she knew more about cars. Which of these rides would be worth the most on the open market? The Bentley? The Ferrari? The vintage 'Vette? But even if she could somehow figure that out, she wasn't exactly versed in grand theft auto. She wouldn't have had a clue where to sell a car if she'd stolen one. And she had a feeling cars were easily traceable. Annoyed at her own naïveté, she got behind the wheel of the Caddy and zoomed out onto the driveway.

There was one thing she did know about, and that was fashion. Today she was going to utilize that expertise without Briana Leigh breathing down her neck. If ever there was a day for retail therapy, this was it.

On the way back to the Plaza of the Americas, Ariana cranked up the radio and tried to enjoy the feeling of the wind in her hair. She was going to have a little fun while she could, because in a couple of weeks, when Briana Leigh went off to Atherton-Pryce, Ariana was going to be homeless and broke. No more cars, no more mansion, no more three square meals a day. Unless she figured out a plan B, this could be the last time she would ever be this free.

At the plaza, Ariana parked the car and strode right to the first boutique she and Briana Leigh had hit a few days before. She had chosen the most understated outfit she could put together from the garments Briana Leigh had bought for her—an eggplant A-line skirt with a sleeveless ruffle-front blouse and bronze gladiator sandals. Altogether she'd felt almost presentable, but still not quite comfortable. As soon as she walked through the door of the boutique, she selected all the things Briana Leigh had refused to let her try on. She brought the whole armful back to one of the brightly lit dressing rooms and closed the door behind her.

"No one has told me what to wear since I was four years old," Ariana muttered to herself, stripping off the Briana Leigh wardrobe and tossing it on the floor.

Her cell phone beeped and she fished it from her purse. There was a picture message from Hudson waiting for her. With a smile, Ariana opened it and laughed. It was an extreme close-up of Hudson with an exaggerated sexy expression, one eyebrow raised and a saucy smirk on his lips. The caption read, *When can I see you?*

Ariana quickly texted back one word: *Soon.* Then she turned off her phone. She had important business to attend to.

As she slipped into a silky, light blue Nicole Miller dress, Ariana let out a sigh of relief. She turned to look at her reflection and smiled. There she was. There was the person she needed to be. There was really nothing better than retail therapy.

Except, of course, that she couldn't buy anything.

Ariana took the dress off and tried a black Michael Kors top paired with a sweet white eyelet skirt. Then she slipped into a rose-colored Elie Tahari dress. How could anyone look at these things and call them boring? Ariana felt sophisticated, beautiful, and refined. She should be the one making over Briana Leigh, not the other way around.

She would be so much more attractive in these things, Ariana thought, turning to check herself out from behind. She now understood how frustrated Kaitlynn was whenever she thought of Briana Leigh having all that money, even though Ariana now knew that Kaitlynn had been mistaken about the inheritance. Still, all Briana Leigh did was misspend the cash she did have on awful clothes, alcohol, and obviously pointless tennis lessons. If Ariana could even get her hands on Briana Leigh's allowance, the money would be put to much better use.

Half an hour later Ariana was through with her private fashion show. She sat down on the bench in the dressing room, back in the Briana Leigh–style clothes, and sighed, feeling morose as she looked at all the lovely things on their hangers. Life was so unfair. Even without that inheritance, Briana Leigh had everything. The Black AmEx card, the car, the cash. And here Ariana was, slumped in a dressing room, unable to buy herself even one little dress.

A tear slipped down Ariana's cheek. She had thought that this trip would make her feel better, but it was all so futile. There would be no Milan, no Australia, no future for her or for Kaitlynn. It was over. Her plan, her meticulously laid plan, had failed. She might as well have been back in that tiny room at the Brenda T., staring at the wall. Yes, she had gotten out, but without money she was just as trapped as ever.

A sob welled up in the back of her throat, and, try as she might to choke it back, Ariana couldn't stop it from coming. She pulled her feet up onto the bench and buried her face between her knees, muffling her tears.

She would never have a future. Dr. Meloni had been right. She was never going to be free. . . .

A few minutes later Ariana came up for air. She glimpsed her pathetic reflection in the mirror—mascara dripping down her face, eyes red and puffy—and suddenly she felt a flash of hot anger.

No. She was not a victim. She was in charge of her own life. There was a plan B out there somewhere. There was *always* a plan B. All she had to do was figure it out. And if she wanted a Calvin Klein shirtdress, dammit, she was going to have one.

Ariana's adrenaline took over. She dried her tears, grabbed the gray shirtdress, and strode out of the dressing room, slapping it down on the counter. Without even a hint of guilt, she pulled out her wallet and handed over two crisp one-hundred-dollar bills. As the saleslady wrapped the dress in pretty tissue paper and placed the gold sticker with the store's emblem on the bag, Ariana felt a rush of delight. She savored the moment. One little moment in which she had taken charge of her own life.

"Briana Leigh! Love the new haircut!"

A hand fell on Ariana's shoulder and she froze. Had someone just called her Briana Leigh?

When she turned around, the girl's face colored with embarrassment. She had bleached blond hair and a pair of red-rimmed sunglasses that did nothing for her ruddy skin tone. Plus she was wearing last season's Ugg boots.

"Oh my gosh. I'm so sorry! I thought you were someone else!"

Ariana shuddered. Without a word, she sidestepped the girl and strode out of the store.

I'd rather be dead than be Briana Leigh, Ariana thought as she used the key remote to unlock the Cadillac.

But a nagging voice in the back of her mind reminded her that, in a way, she *was* already dead.

THE TRUTH

Tears rolled down Ariana's face like big fat drops of failure. She couldn't stop crying. No matter how hard she tried, the sobs just came and came and came, racking her body as she lay atop the silken comforter on her temporary bed. Once she had started, there was no going back. Now she felt like she might cry forever.

One Calvin Klein dress had not helped the situation. Her lack of self-control had, in the end, only made her feel worse. She had to do something. Had to fix the situation. There was only one option left. That was, if she could actually bring herself to pull it off.

Ariana heard Briana Leigh's footsteps outside the room. She sat up and tried to wipe her face dry, but it was too late. Briana Leigh shoved open the door and came bounding in without so much as a knock. She was wearing the same outfit she'd left in that morning—a denim mini and a barely there tank. She froze the second she saw Ariana's face.

"Emma? What's wrong?" she asked, crossing the room.

It was the first time since Ariana had known her that she had actually showed concern for another human being.

"Nothing. I'm fine," Ariana said, sniffling.

Briana Leigh grabbed some tissues from the porcelain-covered box near the bed and handed them over.

"Please. You look like you've been crying for hours," Briana Leigh said. She stepped back and crossed her tanned arms over her stomach as she looked down at Ariana. "What's the matter?"

Ariana pressed the tissue to her nose. "It's just . . . I'm such an idiot." She hazarded a glance at Briana Leigh, who looked simply confused. Confused, but also concerned. Ariana took a deep breath and decided to take the plunge. "I've . . . Briana Leigh . . . I've been lying to you."

Suddenly a dark cloud passed over Briana Leigh's face. She took a step back from the bed, her shoulders curling forward. Like maybe she was a girl who had been lied to before.

"Lying about what?" she asked flatly.

"About . . . well, everything," Ariana said. She squeezed her eyes shut and decided to just blurt it out. "I'm not who I said I was."

The words hung in the room for a moment, enveloping them both in a heavy uncertainty. Ariana hazarded a glance at Briana Leigh's face. The girl was as still as a statue.

"What does that mean?" Briana Leigh said finally.

Ariana sighed. "I'm not the same person Dana knew. I'm . . . I'm . . . well, let's just say I'm broke. The other day at the store? It wasn't that I forgot my wallet. I don't have any money. Not anymore."

Her words were true. And it pained Ariana to say them out loud.

Briana Leigh blinked. Her body language relaxed slightly. "You're kidding."

Who would kid about such a thing? Ariana thought. But all she said was, "No, I'm not."

"What happened?" Briana Leigh asked.

Wide-eyed, Briana Leigh lowered herself onto the bed, picking up the tissue box and placing it between the two of them. Ariana got the sense that Briana Leigh was no longer concerned. That instead she was hungry for a good fall-from-grace story. Well, fine. Ariana would give her one.

Ariana pulled her leg up onto the bed and turned to fully face Briana Leigh. She toyed with the one clean tissue in her hand, folding it in half and creasing it, then folding it in half again. She couldn't tell her own story of woe for obvious reasons, but she had about a half-dozen to choose from that she had witnessed over the years. It was amazing how often wealthy families managed to fall into ruin.

"It was my dad. He kind of embezzled all this money from his company for, like, twenty years." Ariana tore her tissue in two and plucked another from the box.

"No!"

"I know," Ariana said, realizing that this was the first time she had Briana Leigh's complete attention. "My mom and I . . . we had no idea. We thought he was this perfect guy, you know? Always bringing home presents and whisking us away on these amazing vacations. Then one day a couple of years ago, he tells my mom he has a last-minute business trip and leaves first thing in the morning. Ten minutes later there are all these FBI guys practically ramming down the door. They searched our entire house, tore it apart, basically, and took all our computers and files and everything." A tear slid down Ariana's cheek. "It was horrifying."

Briana Leigh was visibly moved. "So your dad fled and left you guys to deal."

"Basically. Great guy, huh?" Ariana said with a sniffle.

"You must hate him," Briana Leigh said, twirling a piece of long auburn hair around her finger.

"I did. Maybe I still do. I don't know. It's complicated with parents, you know?"

Briana Leigh swallowed and glanced away. "Yeah. Definitely."

"Anyway, he didn't get very far. They tracked him down in California. He was about to hop a plane to Thailand, but they arrested him. Now he's in jail and the government seized everything. Our houses, our cars, our bank accounts . . ."

Briana Leigh stared at some far-off spot across the room. Ariana wasn't sure if she was losing the girl or if Briana Leigh was just taking it all in.

"After that my mother just became all withdrawn," Ariana continued. "She went on all these antidepressants and wouldn't even come out of her room."

Ariana thought of her own mother now. She was edging too close to the truth for comfort.

"And then last year she killed herself," she lied flatly.

"Oh my God." Briana Leigh snapped back to the moment. She looked at Ariana, clearly horrified.

"I have no one," Ariana said. A real tear dropped as the truth of those words hit home. It landed on the bedspread, turning the silky peach an ugly, wet brown. "Nothing. And I've been lying to you, even after you've been so nice to me. . . ."

Briana Leigh gave a slight nod, as if she was agreeing with this assessment of her own behavior.

"Anyway, I was just in town, and someone in a store thought I was you, and I just lost it," Ariana continued, wiping her eyes with the tissue. "I mean, all I could think about was how great it must be to *be* you. You have this house and all this security and a grandmother who loves you. Plus, you get to go to Atherton-Pryce in the fall while I go back to that shitty public school in Chicago. . . . Anyway, thinking about *that* made me realize how great you've been. I mean, who else in your position would take a random stranger in? And then I felt even more guilty and I just knew I had to tell you the truth. I'm so sorry."

Briana Leigh looked at Ariana, and her eyes were filled with tears. Ariana's heart skipped an intrigued beat.

"It's not so great being me," Briana Leigh admitted.

"What do you mean?" Ariana asked, finally drying her eyes.

"Remember how I told you my dad died in an accident?" Briana Leigh said, tugging at the hem of her tank top. "That wasn't exactly true either."

Ariana had to chomp down on the inside of her cheek. She was *finally* going to get the truth.

"It wasn't?"

"No. He was actually murdered," Briana Leigh said, looking down at her hands as she twisted the fabric. "By my best friend." A tear slipped down her cheek and Ariana chomped down harder.

So, not the truth, but the cover story. Still, it was better than that "accident" stuff. It was something.

"What?" Ariana breathed, trying to sound shocked.

Briana Leigh stood up and paced over to the dressing table, where, for the first time since Ariana had known her, the girl managed to stand in front of a mirror and not look into it. Instead she toyed with a light blue scarf Ariana had found in the back of the closet. She picked it up and wrapped it around her hand.

"Her name is Kaitlynn Nottingham and our families were friends. When I was eleven and she was thirteen, her parents died in a plane crash," Briana Leigh said, her voice full as she pulled the scarf tighter around her palm. "She came to live with us and it was like suddenly having an older sister. I was usually away at my boarding school, but when I was home, we had the best time."

Ariana watched Briana Leigh carefully. She knew all of this already, but she was curious as to how good a liar Briana Leigh was. Once she got to the fairy tale, would she have any tells?

"Kaitlynn lived here with my mom and dad and kept going to the day school she'd been in before her parents were killed. Then, after my mom died, Kaitlynn and my dad . . . they kind of had an affair," Briana Leigh said, her face turning pink with what appeared to be embarrassment. She glanced at Ariana in the mirror and Ariana feigned surprise.

"No way. Wasn't she kind of young?" Ariana said, forcing a horrified grimace onto her face.

Briana Leigh swallowed hard, disgusted. She tugged harder at the scarf. Her fingers were starting to turn red. "Sixteen. The only thing I can think is that my dad was so broken up over losing my mom, he just kind of lost his mind, you know?"

Ariana stared at Briana Leigh. There were no tells. No blinking or touching her face or looking away. And the whole scarf thing, it just seemed . . . genuine. Like she was trying to keep from crying out in anger. Trying to hold a hundred different awful emotions inside. A creeping sensation tugged at Ariana's heart.

"I'm sure that's what it was," Ariana said, realizing Briana Leigh was waiting for a response.

"When I was home for Christmas that year, I walked in on them. . . ." Briana Leigh paused and closed her eyes, unable to look at Ariana for this part. She yanked at the end of the scarf and gritted her teeth.

"Oh my God." There was a lump in Ariana's throat now. "What did you do?"

"I freaked. I told my father he had to end it or I would never be able to look at him again."

Here the tears really started to fall. Briana Leigh wept silently, her head bowed. Ariana waited in silence. The creeping feeling intensified. It was so powerful she had to acknowledge that Briana Leigh was telling the truth. There was nothing disingenuous about her. This moment . . . it was raw. Real.

"So he did. He ended it." She stopped yanking on the scarf and brought her trembling, purple fingertips to her forehead. "And she killed him."

Ariana felt as if she was about to throw up. What was she supposed to believe? Briana Leigh's confession seemed so genuine. Was it really possible that Kaitlynn had been lying to her all this time? That she was actually guilty? Had that note Ariana had found in Briana Leigh's father's office been started by *him*? Maybe he had planned to break up with her by letter, but had been interrupted by Kaitlynn and never had a chance to finish writing.

My dear Kaitlynn . . .

Ariana got up and crossed over to the desk, just to give her jittering nerves some sort of outlet. She pulled a piece of paper from the drawer and started to fold. Halves, then quarters, then eighths . . The systematic motion calmed her slightly. Allowed her to think.

Mr. Covington *had* started that letter. It made sense. So much more sense than the idea of Briana Leigh writing to Kaitlynn in prison.

"Oh my God," Ariana said breathlessly.

"It gets worse," Briana Leigh said, finally turning to face Ariana. She leaned back against the dressing table and took a deep breath. Ariana attempted to focus. She wanted so badly to be wrong now, instead of then. She wanted to find the lie behind Briana Leigh's eyes. Wanted to believe Kaitlynn, as she had so trustingly for the past year and a half. "During her trial . . . this awful, long, drawn-out trial, she tried to pin the whole thing on me. She said that I had done it so that I could get my inheritance and that I had framed her. But it was totally ridiculous. I loved my father and he always gave me everything

PRIVILEGE

193

I wanted. I didn't need my inheritance. Plus her fingerprints were on the gun, not mine."

Ariana blinked. Was that true? But then, something like that was easily explained. Maybe Kaitlynn had held the gun at some point, but that didn't mean she'd fired it. And Brianna Leigh could have been wearing gloves when she'd done the deed. . . .

"And I had an alibi. So they called me to the stand, and when I was telling the court where I'd been at the moment my dad was murdered, Kaitlynn had a fit, screaming about how I was a liar and a spoiled brat. The whole thing was just too awful. We were best friends and she took my dad from me. And then, as if that wasn't enough, she sent me this letter. . . ."

"A letter?" Ariana asked.

"From jail," Briana Leigh said. "Do you want to see it?"

Did she want to see it? Ariana was practically salivating to see it. She tried as hard as she could to keep her face placid. "Sure."

Briana Leigh left the room and Ariana found herself staring into the mirror. Staring into her unfamiliar green eyes as she tried to keep a handle on her emotions. This couldn't be. It just couldn't. Kaitlynn was not a murderer. Not sweet, innocent Kaitlynn. It was just not possible. There was no way Ariana could have been so very wrong about her.

Within moments Briana Leigh had returned. She handed Ariana a letter that was so worn it seemed as if it had been folded and opened and refolded hundreds of times. Instantly, Ariana recognized the standard-issue stationery of the Brenda T., with the prison's seal in the center of the top of the page. Her fingers trembled as she looked down at the hand-scrawled note.

Kaitlynn's handwriting. No mistaking it.

> *Briana Leigh,*
>
> *I thought you were my friend. I thought we were sisters. But clearly you care about no one but yourself. You broke my heart up on that stand. I was so sure you were going to stand up for me. Going to set me free so that at least we could be together. But you had to go and tell the truth? Do you even realize what you've done to me? My life is over. And it's all because of you.*
>
> *I'm glad I took your father away from you. I wish you could have seen the petrified, pleading look on his face when I shoved the barrel of the gun between his eyes. I know I'll never forget it. Because it was the moment I ruined your life, you ungrateful little bitch. It was the moment I made sure you'd be alone forever, just like I will be.*
>
> *Sweet dreams, BL.*
>
> *Love and kisses,*
>
> *Kaitlynn*

Ariana's hand dropped along with her heart. She couldn't believe that the Kaitlynn she knew had written such awful things, but there it was, staring her right in the face. She had been duped. Duped again by someone she loved. What was wrong with her? She had always prided herself on being able to read people, but clearly she was *always* wrong. Always wrong about the people closest to her. Her first boyfriend, Daniel Ryan, Thomas, Noelle, and now Kaitlynn. Everything she had believed for the past year and half had been a lie. She was so, *so* stupid. Her fingers closed around her forearm and clamped down.

For the second time in as many days Ariana saw her long-term dreams go up in smoke. There would be no perfect house with Kaitlynn in Australia. The Kaitlynn she thought she knew had never even existed. Ariana was so disoriented she had to sit down on the bed again to catch her breath.

Briana Leigh crouched to the ground and picked up the letter, which had fluttered to the floor.

"Scary, isn't it? I can't believe she was ever my friend."

Ariana swallowed against her dry throat and nodded. She knew the feeling.

"My father was all I had left. And now every single day that I'm in this house I'm reminded of him and of her and of what she did to us. . . ." Briana Leigh let out a long, shuddering sigh. "I can't take it anymore. I just want to get out of here and start over with Téo. Is that so wrong?" Briana Leigh said, her face desperate. "To want to start over? I mean, it *is* my life."

It sounded so familiar Ariana wanted to cry. Or laugh. Or throw something. She took a deep breath and tried to calm her frayed nerves. When her mind cleared again, she realized that, as awful as Kaitlynn's betrayal was, it made what she was going to do next so much easier. She no longer had to concern herself with fitting Kaitlynn Nottingham into plan B.

Buoyed by this realization, Ariana looked over at Briana Leigh. Everything hinged on what she said next. Everything.

Briana Leigh teared up again and Ariana shoved aside all her confusion and self-loathing, compartmentalizing it to deal with later. She pushed up from the bed, walked over, and hugged Briana Leigh. The girl hugged her back tightly—so tightly she almost squeezed the breath out of Ariana. It was as if Briana Leigh hadn't been hugged in years. Ariana closed her eyes and hoped she got the next words right.

"No. It's not wrong. But your life isn't over. You have Atherton-Pryce. It's only for two years and then you can do whatever you want," she said, pushing her hands into the back pockets of the jeans she had changed into after shopping. "I would *kill* to go to Atherton."

"Yeah. I suppose," Briana Leigh said automatically, drying her cheeks with her fingertips. "It's too bad you can't—"

Briana Leigh stopped and her eyes suddenly lit up. Ariana's heart stopped beating.

"Wait a minute."

Briana Leigh walked past Ariana over to the bed. For a long moment, her back to Ariana, she clung to the post at the foot of the bed, bringing her other hand to her mouth. Ariana could hardly breathe.

Please. Please, please, please . . .

Suddenly, Briana Leigh turned around. Her eyes were bright with excitement. "What if you go to Atherton in my place?"

Perfect, Briana Leigh, Ariana thought. *You got there even faster than I thought you would.*

She let out a slow breath. "What?"

Inside, Ariana was doing a happy dance. Even after everything she had just realized about Kaitlynn. Because her plan B was working. The plan B she had devised thanks to that loser bleach blond back at the boutique. The reason she had revealed her "lie" to Briana Leigh. But now, of course, she had worked it so that Briana Leigh would think it had been her idea all along.

"I'm serious!" Briana Leigh said. She looked around the room as if the details of the plan were falling into place all around her. "You go to Atherton-Pryce Hall and I'll go to Ibiza with Téo!"

"I think you've lost it," Ariana said, stepping toward Briana Leigh with a concerned look on her face. "How are we supposed to do that?"

"Easy!" Briana Leigh announced. "Nobody at the school has met me. I did my interview by phone. And even if they've seen a random picture here and there, so what? You said yourself some girl mistook you for me today. You definitely fit my description. The hair, your nose, our sense of style. We could be twins!"

Ariana pretended to be considering this for the first time. "But what about your grandmother?"

Briana Leigh rolled her eyes, growing impatient. "She'll still be getting progress reports and whatever—they'll just be about your performance, not mine! It'll be perfect!"

Ariana started to smile. "Do you really think we could pull it off?"

"Why not? And this way you don't have to go to some crap-ass public school and I don't have to leave Téo! It's a win-win!"

Slowly, Ariana lowered herself onto the bed. She looked up at Briana Leigh, chagrined. "I can't believe you would do this for me. After the way I've lied to you . . ."

Briana Leigh sat down next to Ariana and gave her an "oh, please" look. "Forget about it. You've been through almost as much as I have," she said. "How could I not understand?"

"To pull this off, we can't tell anyone. Not even Téo," Ariana warned.

"Duh!" Briana Leigh poked Ariana in the shoulder. "It'll be our little secret."

Ariana smiled. She was about to get everything she wanted. And maybe, just maybe, she had made a new friend in the process. Kaitlynn could rot in prison forever for all she cared. Briana Leigh was the victim here. Briana Leigh was the one who needed her help. And by assuming her identity, Ariana really would be helping her new friend. They would both be able to live the lives they'd always wanted.

"So, what do you think?" Briana Leigh asked, tossing her hair back. "Tomorrow we go to the DMV and get you your very first license as Briana Leigh Covington."

Ariana's smile lit her entire face. "Sounds like an amazing plan."

TOO FAST

Atherton-Pryce Hall. I'm going to Atherton-Pryce Hall.

Noelle would be so, *so* jealous.

Ariana imagined her old friend's face if she were to hear that Ariana was strolling the hallowed grounds of A.P.H. For once Noelle's legendary composure would crack. Her brown eyes would go wide. Her jaw would drop. She would, for once, be jealous of Ariana.

Why? Because the perfect, indomitable Noelle Lange had actually been rejected from Atherton-Pryce Hall. It was a little-known secret she had confessed to Ariana one drunken night during their hazing period at Billings House. She had been rejected, and, try as he might, not even her daddy, with all his money and connections, could get her in.

And now Ariana Osgood would be going there.

She was too giddy to sleep, thinking about the classic uniforms, the ancient library, the fresh-faced students, the cozy dorm rooms.

Ariana could picture them all as if she was already there. She imagined herself sitting on a beautiful lawn, reading *Walden* in the autumn sun, surrounded by friends. . . .

Friends. Kaitlynn's pretty face suddenly swam before her eyes, and Ariana's heart grew sour and black. Lying there in bed, she felt the deep humiliation of Kaitlynn's duplicity all over again.

"That bitch. That lying, psychotic bitch," she said through her teeth, flushing red hot from head to toe.

The anger grew so fierce she started to tremble. Clinging to a pillow, Ariana forced herself to breathe.

In, one . . . two . . . three . . .

Out, one . . . two . . . three . . .

Think about Atherton-Pryce. The future. The future is all that matters.

Gradually Ariana's pulse relaxed and she was back in her daydream. Floating on a sea of plaid wool skirts and falling leaves and thick textbooks. Lost as she was in her thoughts, it took a good few minutes for the music to seep into her consciousness. Once she heard it, she realized it had been playing for a good while. She sat up in her bed, her pulse skipping ahead. It was a violin. Almost eerie in its solitary beauty.

Ariana slipped out of bed and walked over to her bedroom door. When she cracked it open, the music didn't grow any louder. Not inside the house. Which had to mean . . .

A thrill ran down her spine as she turned toward the veranda. She tiptoed quickly over to the sliding glass doors and looked out. Her heart stopped beating. Hudson was standing beneath her window, wearing a white button-down shirt and jeans, serenading her with his violin.

It was, without question, the most romantic sight Ariana had ever seen. Could this day possibly get any better? She quickly checked her hair in the mirror and smoothed a few errant auburn strands. For a brief moment she considered covering up her white satin negligee with her robe, but then felt a thrill of naughtiness and decided against it. Hudson had gone to all this trouble, and besides, she was feeling carefree tonight. Why not let loose a bit?

Hardly daring to believe what she was about to do, she slid the door open and stepped, half-dressed, into the warm night air. Hudson's bow paused for only a moment over the strings, but Ariana could tell he was intrigued.

"What are you doing?" Ariana whispered. "Are you insane?"

"Just seemed like a good night for a concert," Hudson replied, still playing.

Ariana leaned into the railing around her veranda. The skinny strap on her right shoulder slid down over her arm. "And what do you expect in return for this concert?" she asked, feeling devilish.

Hudson stopped playing. "No expectations."

"Maybe you should come up," Ariana said, her heart pounding.

"Maybe?"

"No. You should definitely come up," Ariana replied.

Hudson quickly placed his violin in its case. "I'll be right back," he whispered.

Then he turned and ran off around the north side of the house. For a second Ariana was confused, but then Hudson returned, toting a ladder under his arm.

"I noticed this when I was sneaking around the house," he said, placing the top of the ladder against the side of the balcony.

"So why didn't you just bring it with you?" Ariana asked.

Hudson looked up at her. He was already halfway up the ladder. "Didn't want to be presumptuous," he said with a grin.

Ariana stepped back as he hoisted himself over the railing. She held her breath while his eyes trailed over her body, and wondered how see-through the nightgown might be in the moonlight. Her heart gave a thrill as she realized she didn't care. Let him see everything. She was letting go.

"You're gorgeous," he said.

Ariana grabbed his shirt, pulled him to her, and kissed him. He tripped forward as she backed into her room, pulling him with her. Before either of them could come up for air, her fingers were on the buttons of his shirt, shakily but purposefully working them open. As she pushed the shirt off his shoulders and ran her fingers down his chest, she let out a little gasp. His body was even more perfect than she had imagined.

Hudson pulled back, his eyes heavy.

"What? What is it?" Ariana asked, worried he was changing his mind.

"Nothing. I just wanted to look at you," he said.

Ariana smiled and sat back on her bed, inviting him to look all he wanted. Hudson slowly, deliciously approached and slid onto the covers next to her. He touched her face with his fingers before leaning down to kiss her again. Taking his time, he let his fingers travel down her neck and tickle her collarbone. Then he softly, cautiously, pushed the left strap of her nightgown down her shoulder. Ariana smiled beneath his kisses. She liked that he moved slowly. She wanted to savor every second of this.

Then he moved on top of her. Ariana froze.

Thomas's face flashed through her mind, so vivid he could have been right there with her. Thomas's weight over her. His crooked smile as he swooped in for a kiss. And then his blood.

His blood . . . his blood . . . his blood . . . *everywhere.*

Ariana sat up, shoved Hudson off her, and gasped for air.

"What? What did I do?" Hudson asked.

Ariana got up off the bed and straightened her nightgown. Just putting this distance between herself and Hudson cleared her mind. She looked at Hudson, at his concerned eyes, his gorgeous body, his perfect hands, and as much as she wanted to be with him, she knew there was just no way.

"I can't," she said, surprised by the sob in her throat.

She couldn't get that close to someone. Not after what had happened to Thomas. She couldn't get herself into a situation that might get out of control.

Hudson sat back on his heels. "Was it something I did?"

"No." Ariana forced a smile. She tried to regain her composure, tucking her hair behind her ears and looking at the ground for a moment. Deep breath. Better. "No. I just . . . I think I got caught up in the moment. I don't generally move this fast."

Not anymore. Not after Thomas.

"Oh. I'm sorry. I swear I didn't come here expecting, you know, sex," he said, getting up off the bed. He grabbed his shirt from where it had fallen, and Ariana was mortified to realize she had been the one to remove it. Talk about mixed signals.

"No, I'm sorry," Ariana said. "It was me."

"It's okay," Hudson said. He slid his arms into the sleeves and straightened the shirt on his shoulders. Then he walked over to her and leaned in for another sweet and searching kiss. "We can take it as slowly as you want."

Ariana smiled up at him, feeling inexplicably sad. "Thanks."

Hudson smiled. "Well. I guess I should go. Don't want the land-scaping staff finding my violin and calling the cops."

"That would be bad," Ariana said. *On many, many levels,* she added to herself.

"Good night, Emma Walsh," Hudson said, leaning in for one last kiss.

A single tear made its way out of the corner of Ariana's eye as he slipped through the door and down the ladder. She had just realized no one would ever again say her real name with that kind of tenderness again.

NEW BEGINNINGS

"You know, when you walked in here and told me you wanted extensions, I thought to myself, Girl, why fix what ain't broke?" Ariana's stylist, Deanna, crowed. "But you know what? You were right. Long hair suits your face!"

"Does it?" Ariana croaked.

Her mouth was so dry it felt like she'd been lunching on sand. Dressed in head-to-toe black, Deanna had dyed her own hair a fire engine red. Normally, Ariana wouldn't have let someone who had made such an obvious mistake with her own hair touch her precious locks, but Deanna was also wearing a gorgeous pair of leopard-print Giuseppe Zanotti heels, so she had decided to risk it. Now the woman grinned down at her all excited, and Ariana felt nothing but apprehension. Facing away from the mirror in the lush salon, she had been able to detach herself from what Deanna was doing. Kicked back in the soft white leather chair with her feet up and the smooth jazz playing through the speakers, she had let herself float off into a quiet, serene space where everything was as it should be. But now that Deanna was done, she realized she was afraid to see herself. Afraid to see the person she was about to become.

"Ready to see the new you?" Deanna asked, clicking her superlong acrylic fingernails together.

Ariana held her breath. The woman had no idea how squarely she had hit the nail on the head. A whole new Ariana. She stared at Deanna's face. Noted the laugh lines around her eyes. The small acne scar just under her right eye. The missing rhinestone on the lowest drop of her left earring. Finally, she felt calm. Calm enough, at least, to press forward.

"Sure."

"Here ya go!"

Deanna spun the chair around and Ariana opened her eyes. Long auburn hair fell in gorgeous waves over her shoulders. It didn't look fake at all. It actually looked pretty. When Briana Leigh had suggested the extensions, Ariana had hesitated. What if it brought back those memories that she tried so hard to keep locked up and buried away? What if every time she looked at herself, she saw Thomas's blood all over again?

But now she realized that was not going to happen. Because the girl looking back at her was nothing like the blond, blue-eyed Ariana Osgood of those days. The girl looking back at her was a green-eyed, auburn-haired Briana Leigh Covington.

Hi. I'm Briana Leigh Covington. So nice to meet you.

"Well? What do you think?" Deanna asked, whacking Ariana's shoulder.

Ariana swallowed back some bile and told herself that this was all for a reason. This was a good thing. This was going to allow her to have the life she wanted.

"I love it," she said. And somehow conveyed that she really did.

Just then a figure appeared in the mirror and Ariana's blood ran cold. Tall. Chin-length blond hair. Blue eyes. It was like looking at herself. The person she used to be. Suddenly she felt off-kilter. Like reality had turned itself upside down.

"Surprise!" Briana Leigh cried, rushing up behind Ariana's chair, her male stylist in tow.

Ariana fought for breath. Her sweaty palms clutched the arms of her chair. For a split second she thought that Briana Leigh had done it on purpose. Had made herself look like Ariana because Ariana was looking more and more like Briana Leigh. But then she realized that couldn't be the case. Briana Leigh had never seen Ariana as a blond. She had no idea how ironic her appearance was. Briana Leigh didn't realize how right she had been back at the ranch. The two of them definitely could have been twins.

"I thought you were just getting a cut," Ariana managed to say.

"I was going to, but then I thought, If we're getting new starts, why not go crazy?" Briana Leigh trilled. She strutted away from Ariana like a model and struck a pose, swinging her hair around so that it whacked her in the eyes when she turned. "Téo has always said he'd love to see me as a blond. Now he gets his wish!"

Ariana pressed her lips closed as jealousy overwhelmed her. God, she missed her blond hair.

"Why aren't you saying anything?" Briana Leigh asked, irritated. She brought her feet together and stood up straight. "I do look good as a blonde, right?"

Ariana blinked and tried to focus. "You look amazing." And she did.

Briana Leigh's smile lit the entire salon. Ever since their mutual confessions, her bitchy moments had been fewer and further between. But now it was clear to Ariana why Briana Leigh put on such a bitchy front. It was to protect herself. The girl had been betrayed in the absolute worst way possible by her best friend. "So do you."

Ariana's heart warmed. Maybe she could visit Briana Leigh and Téo in Ibiza over Christmas. It would be so nice to have someplace to go. A friend to visit. Someone to look forward to seeing . . . especially since she could never go home again. It was amazing how much her feelings for Briana Leigh had changed in the past day. But Ariana knew firsthand how crushing that sort of betrayal felt. Thanks to Noelle and now Kaitlynn.

"Ladies!"

Briana Leigh's stylist walked over and handed them each a flute filled with champagne. He had one for himself and one for Deanna as well. A strawberry slice floated in each glass.

"Let's celebrate," he said, tipping her glass forward. "To new beginnings."

Ariana's heart gave a little thrill as the four glasses clinked.

"To new beginnings."

THE DREADED DMV

Ariana sat in a warped plastic chair at the Department of Motor Vehicles that afternoon, trying not to cringe as Briana Leigh strolled around the waiting room checking out the new her in every reflective surface she could find. Ariana paged through a *Vogue* magazine and breathed in and out, keeping her nerves under control. This was going to work. Of course it was going to work. She had everything she needed. She just had to play it cool.

Or course it didn't help that the claustrophobic office had no air-conditioning and there was a stream of sweat coursing down the center of her back. Ariana hated to sweat. It was so animalistic.

"Briana Leigh Covington?" the large man behind the counter called out.

"Yeah?" Briana Leigh said.

Ariana's heart stopped as she sat forward. She turned away from the DMV worker and shot Briana Leigh a look that could have stopped a rabid pit bull in its tracks. Briana Leigh turned fuchsia.

"She's right here," Briana Leigh said loudly, walking over to Ariana and pulling her up by the arms. "Don't keep the nice man waiting, Briana Leigh."

Then she shoved Ariana forward. Ariana looked at the glowering DMV worker and rolled her eyes.

"Pardon my friend. Too much iced coffee," she said.

The man laced his fat, sausagelike fingers together and sighed through his nose. She could see the sweat stains spreading out on his shirt from his armpits and decided to breathe through her mouth. The oscillating fan on the shelf behind the man turned in Ariana's direction, but all she got from it was a piddling, stray breeze. His bulk was blocking the good stuff.

"You lost your license?" he said, raising an eyebrow.

Ariana took a deep breath. The key was not to babble.

"Yes," she said.

The man hit a few keys on his keyboard. Then he glanced at the screen and at Ariana. Then at the screen, then at Ariana. Her fingers automatically closed around her forearm. Sweat prickled along her brow and her underarms started to itch. He was checking Briana Leigh's old picture against the girl standing in front of him. This was it. He was going to call the police. Ariana glanced at the phone on his desk. Imagined she saw his fingers twitch in that direction.

"Says here you've got blue eyes," he said.

Ariana's throat was so dry she wasn't sure she could speak, but she was going to have to. She glanced over her shoulder. Briana Leigh's face was now buried in the *Vogue*. This was a huge risk, but it had to be done. She released her arm. Her fingers had left behind four long red marks on her skin.

"They're contacts," Ariana said quietly.

She leaned toward the putrid man and popped out the right contact, exposing her true eye color. He grimaced and hit a key on his computer.

"Never understood how people could stick their fingers in their eyes," he said.

Ariana bristled. If Briana Leigh had heard that she was definitely going to start asking questions. She quickly glanced over her shoulder. Briana Leigh was reading some article about Sarah Jessica Parker, her leg bouncing up and down with impatience. If she had overheard, she certainly wasn't showing it.

"All right, Miss Covington. Want a new picture?" the man asked.

Ariana replaced the contact and blinked a few times to make sure it was in place. "Definitely."

The man clucked his tongue. "You girls always do. Step in front of the camera."

He nodded to his left and Ariana slid over to stand in front of the blue backdrop. Now that she was past the inquisition, she couldn't believe how easy it had been. Somehow she controlled the huge, giddy smile that was trying to push its way onto her face and put on her prettiest closed-mouth smile instead. This was, after all, her first official photo as Briana Leigh Covington, one she would have to look at for years to come. She wanted it to be a good one.

Ten minutes later Ariana was holding an official Texas driver's license with her picture next to Briana Leigh's name. Briana Leigh pulled a pen out of her purse and signed the back of the license with a flourish. Ariana had always been good at forgeries—the note she had written to Reed from Thomas had kept the girl off her trail for a good couple of months—so she could have signed it herself, but she figured there was no reason for Briana Leigh to know about that particular talent.

"Nice to meet you, Briana Leigh," Briana Leigh giggled, handing the ID back to Ariana.

"And you, Briana Leigh," Ariana replied, grasping her friend's outstretched hand.

"This really is going to work," Briana Leigh said with a smile.

Ariana took a deep breath and felt totally at peace. "You know, I think it just might."

LOST

Ariana was looking forward to putting her new hair up and taking a nice, long, self-congratulatory lounge in the pool when Briana Leigh suddenly turned off the road onto a drive braced by two austere-looking gray pillars.

"What are you doing?" Ariana asked, looking up from her *Vogue*.

Suddenly the car emerged from between two thick hedges and all Ariana could see for miles were headstones. Headstones, mausoleums, freshly turned earth. The graves went on for miles. Instantly Ariana's palms began to sweat, and the air-conditioning seemed to be blowing heat. She could feel her breath grow short.

"I need to make a stop," Briana Leigh told her.

"Here? Why?" Ariana blurted.

She glanced at Briana Leigh's profile, her heart racing. Briana Leigh's gaze was trained straight ahead, her hands at ten and two on the wheel. What was this about? Had she somehow been wrong about

Briana Leigh? Had Briana Leigh forged that letter from Kaitlynn? Was she was bringing Ariana here to kill her? What better place to stash a body than a cemetery. Open graves everywhere, waiting to welcome their eternal guests.

"My parents are buried here," Briana Leigh told her.

Ariana swallowed. Of course. Briana Leigh had no reason to kill Emma Walsh. But her explanation calmed her only slightly. Maybe Ariana wasn't in danger, but still she felt as if the headstones were closing in on the car and blocking out the sun. She gripped her arm and tried to breathe.

"No," Ariana blurted. "I can't."

"Can't what?" Briana Leigh asked, glancing over at her from behind the wheel.

"I can't. I hate cemeteries," Ariana said, pressing one hand against the door and the other around Briana Leigh's headrest. Her feet were braced against the floor of the car so tightly she felt the strain in her knees. As if she could stop the car out of sheer force of will.

"Does anyone like them?" Briana Leigh asked, rolling her eyes. "Don't worry. You can wait in the car."

Ariana closed her eyes and forced herself to breathe.

In, one . . . two . . . three . . .

Out, one . . . two . . . three . . .

There was nothing outside the car but trees. Trees and grass and dead bodies . . .

In, one . . . two . . . three . . .

Out, one . . . two . . . three . . .

And flowers. Flowers in front of headstones. Flowers left by families who would never see their loved ones again. Flowers that the dead, rotting bodies below would never smell or see or appreciate because they were dead.

Dead, dead, dead.

They were judging her. All of them judging her from beyond the grave. Their cold, lifeless eyes glassy and vacant and wide. Judging her for what she had done. Thomas, Melissa, and Sergei had met untimely ends . . . all because of her.

Briana Leigh stopped the car and opened the door. The *bong, bong, bong* of the car door singed Ariana's already frayed nerves. "You know, Emma, I've never brought anyone else here before."

Ariana blinked, struggling for composure. She looked at Briana Leigh. "Not even Téo?"

Briana Leigh lifted a shoulder. "I don't want to get all morbid on him, you know? I want to keep him separate. But you . . . I don't know . . . I feel like you've been there, so you really understand."

Ariana swallowed hard. Briana Leigh was trying to tell her that she had become a good friend. Little did the girl know that she was actually here to use her because she had believed the stories of her former best friend. The one who had ruined her life.

"Believe me. I know what it is to lose everything."

"I'll be back in a second," Briana Leigh said, leaving the keys in the ignition. "I just want to say good-bye to my parents before I leave for Ibiza." She slammed the car door shut behind her, leaving Ariana alone.

In, one . . . two . . . three . . .

Out, one . . . two . . . three . . .

There's no one out there. No one watching you. Stop thinking about it. Stop. Stop. Stop. There is no past, only future. Think about where you're headed. A new life. A new school. A new start. The past doesn't matter. You have a future. You have a future now. . . .

After a few moments Ariana felt her fingers relax and her toes uncurl. The air-conditioning poured over her, cooling the sweat that now covered her skin. Suddenly she felt foolish and wished she hadn't let Briana Leigh see her weakness. She took one more breath and opened her eyes.

The brightness of the day assaulted her. Ariana looked around, trying to see past all the looming headstones, and found Briana Leigh. The girl was kneeling in front of a large, granite stone with two names etched into it, and she was talking. Ariana watched as she held out her hand, showing her engagement ring to the stone as if her parents could actually see it. Then she pulled her hand back and held it, gazing down at the diamond. And just like that, Briana Leigh started to cry. She was still talking, but tears ran down her face and dripped from her nose. Finally, she reached out her fingers and touched the cold stone, doubling over. She really was saying good-bye.

Ariana watched all of this, and her heart broke. It was clear that Briana Leigh had loved her parents. Really and truly loved them. Ariana suddenly knew this with an absolute certainty that was so simple it actually calmed her. Briana Leigh hadn't lied when she'd said she loved and missed her father. The pain, the anguish, the desperation she showed right now were perfectly real.

At that moment Ariana let go any lingering hope that Kaitlynn Nottingham was innocent, that perhaps Briana Leigh had somehow forged that awful letter. Kaitlynn was a liar. A murderer. And Ariana had to truly accept that.

Right there in that Dallas cemetery, while Briana Leigh said goodbye to the family Kaitlynn had taken from her, Ariana put her friendship with Kaitlynn where it belonged—in the ground.

Kaitlynn was the liar. And Ariana *hated* liars.

SLUTS

Ariana leaned back against Hudson's chest as he wrapped his arms around her from behind. This had never been part of the plan—meeting a guy, growing comfortable enough with him to publicly cuddle like this—but as unexpected twists went, it wasn't a bad one. They stood on the balcony level of the Curtain Club in Deep Ellum, looking down at the main floor, where hundreds of music lovers nodded their heads to the driving beat of the band onstage. Ariana committed the band's name to memory. They were a local Dallas group, and knowing a few things about them would help her look like the genuine Briana Leigh. It was all in the details.

"The new hair is very sexy," Hudson said in her ear, brushing some of her thick mane aside.

Ariana smiled sadly, wishing he could see her real hair. "Thanks."

She gazed down at Téo and Briana Leigh, who were slow dancing together toward the back of the crowd, even though the band was playing a frantic rock song. Kaitlynn was wearing a buttery tan leather jacket—a piece of clothing that Ariana actually would have worn herself—and with her new short blond hair, she actually looked sophisticated for once. It was Briana Leigh and Téo's last night together before Téo left for Ibiza, and clearly, they were making each moment count. In a few days Briana Leigh would be joining him there. Grandma C. would be escorting her granddaughter, along with Emma Walsh, to the airport, where they would board the Covingtons' private jet to Washington, D.C. Atherton-Pryce's school year didn't begin for another few weeks, so Briana Leigh had asked her grandmother if she could leave early to go stay with Emma's family, who were vacationing in Virginia, until term started. Grandma C. liked Emma Walsh so much that she hadn't even blinked before saying yes.

It was amazing how someone so shrewd could be so gullible. But, as Ariana had learned, it was all about what a person wanted to believe.

"What do you think of Briana Leigh's new look?" Ariana asked Hudson.

Hudson stood on his toes to see over the low wall to the floor below. "Eh. I've never been much for blondes."

A thump of dread shook Ariana's chest, until she realized she was no longer a blonde. She couldn't feel offended.

"Good," she said with a smile. She turned around in his grasp and wrapped one arm around his neck. With her free hand, she combed through the blond hair at his temple. "But I happen to like them."

Hudson grinned. "Good."

Ariana's eyes fluttered closed and their lips met. She had never

KATE BRIAN

enjoyed grungy clubs or loud, ear-splitting music, but this particular place was rapidly growing on her. Hudson took her hand and led her over to the creaky wooden bench along the wall, choosing a nice, dark corner. As he sat down, he pulled her right onto his lap and Ariana felt a thrill of excitement through her entire body. Before she could overthink anything, she was deep in a kiss that would have made her cluck her tongue and turn away if she had been on the outside looking in. But on the inside, all she could think about was Hudson. The minty taste of his mouth, the rough calluses on his fingers as they ran up her back under her shirt, the strength of his arms as he pulled her into him. So close she could feel the frenetic pounding of his heart.

Before long the band was playing their last, raucous note and shouting their good-byes to the cheering crowd. Before long, the patrons had filled the benches around them with drinks and loud chatter. Ariana felt a hand on her shoulder and turned, bleary-eyed, to find Briana Leigh laughing down at her.

"Time to go, sluts," she said.

Ariana's face burned. Her legs were wrapped around Hudson's waist and all their clothes were askew. The punk types next to her cackled and raised their plastic cups of beer in admiration. She glanced at Hudson and, feeling suddenly shy and embarrassed, slipped off his lap and straightened her skirt.

"Guess we should go then," he said, looking like he'd just woken up from a seriously long but satisfying nap.

All the way back to the ranch, Hudson held Ariana's hand in the backseat of Téo's Hummer. He ran his thumb back and forth over hers, sending pleasant tingles up her arm. But that was where they died. Because there was nothing pleasant about the feeling in her heart. She knew he was looking at her, but all she could do was stare out the window and grow more and more depressed.

"What are you thinking about?" he asked her quietly.

"Nothing," she lied. "What are you thinking about?"

She hazarded a glance at him and he gave her a sweet smile. "I was thinking about all the weekends I'm going to visit you down at Easton. Wondering where on campus you guys go when you want to be alone."

Ariana's stomach twisted for a million different reasons. Because this was exactly her fear—that Hudson was expecting more. Because she would never actually see Easton again. Because the last person she had sought out secluded campus spots with was dead. And because of what she was going to have to do.

Téo pulled up behind the Jeep Hudson had rented for the summer and killed the engine. Outside the car Ariana clutched Hudson's hand and held him back from following the others inside. He glanced back at her, a question in his eyes.

"We'll catch up," Ariana called after Briana Leigh.

Hudson turned on his heel on the drive, a quizzical look on his face. Ariana looked down at his shoes—perfectly buffed brown loafers—and her heart broke. Could he be any more perfect? Hudson must have sensed what was coming, because he removed his hand from hers. She automatically shoved her fingers under her arms, as if that would somehow replace the warmth of his skin.

"Hudson, you can't come visit me at Easton," she said, her eyes still trained on the ground.

He shifted his weight. "Why not?"

Ariana made herself look at him. He deserved that much. She forced herself to say the only thing she could think to say. The only thing that might actually keep him away. "Because I have a boyfriend."

Hudson took a step back and bent over slightly, as if he'd been punched in the stomach. His mouth curled into a stunned smile. Like he wanted to laugh at how stupid he felt. "You what?"

"I'm sorry, I . . . This was just a fling for me," Ariana said, feeling desperate. Feeling as if the lie were the truth. Suddenly, surprisingly, a picture of Daniel Ryan, her sophomore- and junior-year boyfriend, flashed through her mind, as if he were the one waiting for her back in Connecticut. Weird. But it made it easier to feel as if she was talking about someone real. "We're actually very serious and I just . . . I need to end this. Now. Tonight."

Hudson pushed one hand into his hair and looked away, off toward the darkened tennis courts. His expression was incredulous, and Ariana could practically hear his heart breaking. She hated that she had to do this to him and cursed fate for bringing him into her life now. Now, at the one point when she couldn't do this. When she couldn't be with anyone. When *she* wasn't even anyone.

But she couldn't think about that now. She had one purpose and that was her future. And Hudson could not be part of it. In a few days Emma Walsh as he knew her would cease to exist and she would become Briana Leigh Covington.

There was simply no good way to explain that to him.

"I don't believe this," Hudson said finally.

Smart guy, Ariana thought.

"I'm sorry," she said again.

He turned his back to her and she waited, listening to a coyote howling in the distance. The sound reminded her of their night under the stars and her heart clenched painfully. She waited for him to turn on her in anger. To tell her what a bitch she was. To call her a liar and a whore and whatever other choice words he could come up with. To glare at her with betrayed eyes.

But when he looked at her again, her breath caught. The only emotions in his eyes were sadness and longing. He took a step toward her and she didn't even flinch.

"This guy," he said, looking directly into her eyes, "this guy had better be worthy of you."

Ariana was so stunned she couldn't even formulate a thought. Hudson turned and got into his car and drove away, but she just stood there, in the exact same pose, her nails digging into her skin.

You have to start over. You have to start over, she reminded herself as a warm breeze tousled her long hair. But in that brief moment, the idea of starting over totally and completely sucked.

PURE EVIL

Ariana stood behind Briana Leigh on the tarmac at Love Field Airport as Briana Leigh said good-bye to her grandmother. Ariana wore a black strapless sundress with huge, colorful flowers all over the skirt, her extensions piled up under a floppy straw hat. Neither she nor Briana Leigh wanted Grandma Covington to notice her new hair. Not that the old bat could see three feet in front of her, but still. With so much at stake, extra precautions were necessary.

"Bye, Grandma," Briana Leigh said, bending down to hug the old woman. "You were so right to make me go to school. I don't know what I was thinking. Thank you *so* much for caring."

Behind her wide sunglasses, Ariana rolled her eyes. Briana Leigh was laying it on a tad thick. Grandma C. was old, but not at all stupid. The matriarch's mouth was twisted into a suspicious frown when Briana Leigh leaned back again.

"What are you up to?" she asked in her raspy voice.

Briana Leigh hesitated, than laughed, spreading her arms wide. "Nothing! Honestly. I just wanted to thank you."

The woman tilted her face back a bit to look Briana Leigh squarely in the eye. "Well, we'll see how much you're thanking me once I get those progress reports. I'd better see serious improvements in your grades, Briana Leigh."

Ariana tried not to smirk. The woman had no idea the number of A's and *excellent*s that were coming her way.

"Don't worry," Briana Leigh said, leaning down to give her grandmother a peck on the cheek. "I think you're going to be very proud of me this year."

"We'll see," Grandma C. said. "And don't go spending all the money I gave you on clothes and nights on the town. That money is for emergencies."

Briana Leigh's smile widened and Ariana hid a grin behind her hand. Her friend actually planned to use the fifteen thousand dollars her grandmother had given her to pay for a small oceanside wedding once she got to Ibiza. Ariana had hoped that Briana Leigh would give her some of the cash as well, but instead Briana Leigh had emptied the twenty-four hundred dollars from her checking account and given that to Ariana to use for incidentals. It was a start. And soon Grandma Covington would begin sending Briana Leigh's monthly allowance to her mailbox at Atherton-Pryce. All in all, Ariana would have more than enough money to live on.

Everything was working out as planned. Both Ariana and Briana Leigh were going to have the lives they wanted.

As the Covingtons said their last good-byes and Briana Leigh boarded the plane, Ariana stepped forward. She clutched the new Louis Vuitton travel case Briana Leigh had purchased for her in both hands.

"I just wanted to say thank you for letting me stay with you, and for letting me fly back east on your private jet. It's very generous of you, Mrs. Covington," she said. "I can't thank you enough."

Especially considering you're going to be paying my way for the next two years, she thought, biting back a Cheshire-cat grin. Of course, when it came to Princeton, she was going to have to figure out a brand-new plan, but she had two whole years to work on it, and she wasn't worried. Look what she had accomplished during sixteen months in prison.

"Miss Walsh, you seem like a very nice girl," the woman said, squinting.

"Thank you," Ariana said, pleased.

"Let me give you a piece of advice," Grandma Covington said, lifting a gnarled hand as if to point at Ariana. "Once my granddaughter is situated on campus, stay as far away from her as possible. That girl is a bad seed. Plain and simple."

Ariana's heart automatically thumped with foreboding.

"Let's go, Jonathan," Mrs. Covington said to the chauffeur standing at her side. "I want out of this sun."

The chauffeur grasped the handles on the back of her wheelchair and turned her until her back was to Ariana. She wished she could think of something to say in parting, but nothing came to mind.

Then the plane's engines whirred to life behind her and she realized that anything she said would have been lost in the noise anyway.

When she turned around, Briana Leigh stood at the top of the gangway stairs, waving at her to hurry up. Ariana wondered what, exactly, Grandma Covington had meant. Was it just because the two of them didn't get along, or did Grandma C. really sense something dark in her granddaughter? What, exactly, did the old matriarch think had actually happened the day her son was murdered? As much as she was dying to run after the woman and ask, Ariana knew that she couldn't. It was not her place. Mrs. Covington's thoughts on her son's death and her obviously complex feelings for Kaitlynn and Briana Leigh would have to remain a mystery.

Ariana rolled her shoulders back, placed her hand atop her hat to keep it from blowing off in the wind, and strode toward the family plane. As close as she had become with Briana Leigh over the past week, she was starting to feel that parting ways with her and her dysfunctional past was going to be a good thing.

PURGED

"How many of those have you had?" Ariana asked as Briana Leigh attempted to place an empty vodka and cranberry on the table between their two facing leather seats. She kept missing the edge of the table, so Ariana finally leaned forward, took the glass from the girl's hand, and put it down. Briana Leigh was sloshed and getting seriously messy. Ariana wrinkled her nose as Briana Leigh wiped her mouth with the back of her hand.

The new Briana Leigh Covington is going to have much better manners, Ariana vowed.

"I want to drink enough to be passed out on the plane to Ibiza," Briana Leigh explained, closing her eyes and tipping her head back.

Ariana tried not to sigh as she turned the page of that day's *Washington Post*. She had gone this long without criticizing Briana Leigh's habits. Why start now? Especially when Briana Leigh was giving her the biggest gift Ariana could have ever asked for: her life.

"What's with you and that newspaper?" Briana Leigh asked, sitting up again. She leaned her arm heavily on the armrest and snapped her fingers for the flight attendant, who immediately started mixing another drink. "You're so serious all of a sudden."

"Just want to know what's going on in the world," Ariana replied lightly, trying not to betray the pounding of her heart.

She turned the pages slowly, even though all she wanted to do was tear through the thing in search of any mention of her name. The moment she had seen the paper folded neatly on one of the airplane's tables along with the *New York Times* and *USA Today*, her pulse had started to race, but she had forced herself not to pick it up until now, when there was only an hour of flight time left in their flight. Otherwise, if the news was bad, she might have spent the whole flight obsessing and feeling ill.

The stewardess delivered another vodka and cranberry. Ariana turned to the last page of the local section and froze. There was the headline.

LATEST DREDGING OF LAKE PAGE INCONCLUSIVE
AUTHORITIES STEP UP HUNT FOR FUGITIVE TEEN

Ariana leaned forward, grabbed the glass from Briana Leigh's hand before it could reach her mouth, and took a swig. The alcohol burned its way down her throat and she winced.

"Hello, rude!" Briana Leigh snapped. She wagged her fingers at the stewardess impatiently. "If you wanted one, you could have just asked."

Ariana ignored her. She placed the drink down on the table and read the piece with dread in her heart. She learned that Dr. Meloni was still working at the Brenda T.—the investigation into the comments he had allegedly made about her suicide were unsubstantiated. Ariana hadn't mentioned him in her note, so there was no proof that his lack of professionalism had pushed Ariana to take her own life. He had been issued a warning by the warden, but that was all. *Lucky bastard.* He deserved to rot.

Meanwhile, Lake Page had now been dredged three times. Residents with homes on the lake were growing impatient, concerned about health issues. No one wanted their kids swimming in a lake that harbored a rotting corpse. The manager of the Philmore Hotel had reported several cancellations and suffering profits. Meanwhile, authorities were beginning to grow skeptical that such a corpse actually existed.

"We want visitors to the area to know that our lake is perfectly safe," said Christopher Hamm, PR director for the Philmore Family of Luxury Hotels. *"At this point, all experts agree that if no body has been found, there is no body to be found."*

Ariana's stomach was twisted like ten thousand pretzels. Her hand trembled as she reached for the drink again. Why wouldn't they just give up? Why were they so determined to find her body? And, honestly, so what if she had escaped rather than died? She wasn't going to hurt anyone. All she wanted was to start over. All she wanted was to be left alone. Why couldn't they just leave her alone?

"Did I mention the airport we're flying into is within miles of

Kaitlynn's prison?" Briana Leigh said, swigging from her new drink and looking out the window.

"Oh?" Terrified heat prickled Ariana's skin. Her hands were so sweaty the newsprint was coming off on her palms. What was she thinking, flying back to D.C., enrolling in Atherton? She should have been on a plane to Australia by now, not careening right into the belly of the beast. She reached back to pull her extensions off her shoulders and fan her neck with the newspaper.

And then she paused, all that new hair clutched in her fist. Suddenly an icy calm came over her. It didn't matter that she was going to be landing so close to the Brenda T. She had new hair, new clothes, new eyes. She had even managed a hint of a tan after spending every moment she could out by the pool. Every day Ariana looked more like Briana Leigh and less like herself. Plus, it wasn't as if she was going to go anywhere near the prison. No one was going to recognize her at Atherton-Pryce Hall. There was no reason for any of those people to suspect a thing.

Briana Leigh slipped her sunglasses on as she gazed out the window and Ariana smirked. The girl sitting across from her could have been the old her. Maybe the police would spot Briana Leigh at Dulles Airport and arrest her instead.

Amused by this mental image, Ariana felt her blood cool considerably. It was going to be fine. Everything was going to be fine. Even if the authorities did "step up the search," they would never look for her at Atherton-Pryce. There was simply no reason for them to go there.

"I wish my grandmother could see me getting on that plane to Ibiza," Briana Leigh said, snorting a laugh. "She would just die."

"Seriously," Ariana said, laying the newspaper aside. She took a deep breath, feeling more in control with each passing moment.

"Oh, no. You have no idea," Briana Leigh said. She was so drunk her words were slurring together. She swung her head around to look at Ariana and almost fell off her chair. Steadying herself with her hands on both armrests, she took a deep breath and focused. "I used to go to La Scuola Ferretta in Rome. Couldn't stand it. It was so freaking pretentious and the girls there hated me. They used to pick apart my Texan accent as if an Italian accent is *so* much better. Anyway, when I was thirteen, just after my mom died, my dad dropped me at the airport to go back to school and instead of getting on a plane to Rome, I hopped a flight to Paris."

Ah. The Paris incident, Ariana thought.

"Of course, after I didn't arrive at school, my father freaked out and called the airline. Eventually they figured out I was in France, so basically the entire Parisian police department was sent out looking for me. It was on the news there, and they searched all the five-star hotels. As if I was that stupid. I was using cash and staying in this tiny brothel-type place I found on the East Bank. It took them two days to find me. My grandmother said I almost killed my father."

Ariana let out a short laugh. Briana Leigh looked out the window again and took another swig of her drink. Her eyes were at half mast behind her sunglasses.

"Little did she know that a year later I actually would."

Ariana's stomach swooped so violently she was sure the plane had gone into a nosedive. She gripped her armrests and looked out the window. Nothing rushing past. Still cruising along. Her vision started to prickle over with the familiar black dots.

Breathe. Just breathe.

Briana Leigh could not have just said what Ariana had thought she had heard.

The girl leaned her forehead against the small ovular window. Tears coursed down her cheeks as she continued to cling to her glass.

"I killed my father. . . . I killed my father. . . ."

Ariana had to keep herself from lunging at Briana Leigh. To keep from grabbing her and shaking her and screaming in her face.

"My mother's dead. My father's gone. Kaitlynn's locked up down there in that horrible place," Briana Leigh continued babbling. "I'm all alone and it's all my fault."

So she really killed her father? The letter from Kaitlynn had seemed so authentic, but then, Ariana knew how easily these things could be faked. Briana Leigh had probably paid some guard or clerk to send her some letterhead and had written the letter herself, just to prove her own innocence should anyone ever question it.

Ariana's fingers closed around her forearm as she fought the urge to vomit. She felt so abysmally stupid. What was wrong with her? How could have she ever doubted Kaitlynn? Ever let Briana Leigh suck her into her psychosis? Ever let herself start to care about the psychotic bitch? This was what Grandma Covington had been talking about. The old bat was right—Briana Leigh was evil. No wonder Grandma C. had loved Kaitlynn more. She knew the truth.

Briana Leigh had murdered her father in cold blood and pinned it on innocent Kaitlynn. It was all true. She had simply fed Ariana the lie to keep up appearances, but now that she was on her way to Ibiza to start her new life, she was purging her heart. Ariana had thought the girl was saying good-bye to her parents in the graveyard; maybe she had been apologizing. And now the girl was drunk and thought she was talking to her new best friend, someone she could trust.

But she had no idea who she was talking to. No idea what "Emma Walsh" could do to her.

"I have no one," Briana Leigh repeated at a whisper.

It took all of Ariana's self-control to keep from smacking the girl across the face. Tackling her to the ground. Tearing her hair out. Ariana had almost forsaken Kaitlynn—innocent, sweet Kaitlynn— because of Briana Leigh's lies. She could have slaughtered the girl just for that. But she could do nothing. Not here. Not now. The authorities would be called—the authorities in D.C., who had been staring at her picture for a month now. Ariana would be headed back to prison before she could blink.

She had to keep playing the good friend. She looked around the plane's cabin, trying to distract herself. Noted the exact number of lights in the ceiling—twelve, six of which were on. Noted the flight attendant's shoes—patent leather, black. Noted a stain on the carpet on the far side of the plane. A spill of some kind, lightened by an attempt to clean it, but not quite gone.

Her breathing started to return to normal.

"Don't say that," she told Briana Leigh, making her voice sound sympathetic. "You have Téo. And you have me."

Gag. Gag. Gag.

Briana Leigh smiled slightly. Her eyes were starting to close. "Téo. Téo's waiting for me."

Ariana felt a sting on her arm and looked down. Her fingernails had drawn blood. She reached for her napkin and quickly covered up the tiny crescent-shaped wounds so that the flight attendant wouldn't see. Briana Leigh, meanwhile, began to snooze.

The plane dipped slightly. They were starting their descent. Ariana looked out the window, her teeth clenched, and silently berated herself. How could she have ever doubted her friend? The girl she had lived with for more than a year? The girl who had been there for her at the worst time of her life? Was she that fickle? A few weeks on the outside and a bond like that forgotten?

Never again, she vowed. *Never again.*

The plane dipped again, coming out of the clouds, and the earth became visible down below. Somewhere out there was the Brenda T. Somewhere down there was Kaitlynn, sitting alone, staring out at the lake and the Philmore Hotel, still daydreaming about that swim. That swim in the lake where the authorities were beginning to think they would never find Ariana's body.

Briana Leigh let out a slight snore and Ariana glanced over at her. There was a rivulet of drool running down the side of her chin. Revolting. Here Ariana was, prepared to give Briana Leigh a good name with her impeccable manners and her perfect grades and her focus on the future, and Briana Leigh was just going to lead the life of a lush in Ibiza, married to some crappy DJ, getting away with murder while Kaitlynn was locked up for the rest of her life.

The girl did not deserve to live. She simply did not deserve to live.

Ariana looked out the window again and her heart caught. They were flying over Lake Page now. She could see the brick walls of the Brenda T. on one side, the turrets of the Philmore Hotel on the other. A speedboat, apparently undeterred by the specter of Ariana's unfound corpse, cut a white V of foam across its pristine surface.

And just like that, an idea came to her. Ariana's veins sizzled with delight at the perfect deliciousness of the plan. If it worked out, everything would be fine. If it worked out, everyone would get the life they actually deserved.

The flight attendant paused next to Ariana's shoulder and whispered so as not to wake Briana Leigh. "We're starting our descent, Miss Walsh. Can I take your lunch plates?"

"One second," Ariana said. She grabbed one of the remaining wedges of her sandwich off the plate, then nodded. "All set. Thanks."

As soon as the flight attendant's back was turned, Ariana removed the roast beef from her sandwich and slipped it into the outside pocket of her purse.

THE NEW PLAN

By the time the plane landed, the sun was going down and Ariana had calmed herself into a cool, detached state of mind. She felt focused, placid, and filled with a sense of purpose she hadn't entirely felt since first arriving in Dallas. She had a plan to execute, and she was focused on that plan.

Briana Leigh, meanwhile, was so out of it she could hardly make it down the steps without the aid of the crew. The flight attendant had uncorked a bottle of champagne while the plane was taxiing down the runway, and Briana Leigh had downed three glasses. Now she gripped the corked, half-empty bottle in one hand as she tromped heavily toward the ground. Ariana slipped her huge sunglasses over her eyes and made sure her hat was secure. Now that she was so close to the Brenda T., she was taking no chances. Not until she was inside the gates of Atherton-Pryce Hall. Then she could finally relax.

The Covingtons' pilot met Briana Leigh and Ariana at the foot of the steps and grimaced when he saw that Briana Leigh could hardly hold herself upright.

"Maybe you should take these, Miss Walsh," he said, handing a set of car keys to Ariana. She immediately recognized the four-circle Audi emblem on the fob.

"And these are?" Ariana asked.

"The keys to my new car, *Emma*," Briana Leigh said with a laugh. She slung her arm around Ariana's shoulders and Ariana went rigid. "Well, *your* new car. It's kind of like a bribe to do well at school. Grandma covers her bases."

"She's drunk," Ariana said to the pilot, hoping it would explain what he had just heard—that the car was now hers.

"Well, good luck at school, Miss Briana," the pilot said.

Briana Leigh's eyes flashed. "It's Briana *Leigh*, you idiot! How many times do I have to tell you people?"

"Briana Leigh! Calm down," Ariana scolded, clinging to the girl. She shot the pilot an apologetic look. He simply looked amused, like he had made the faux pas on purpose. Clearly he thought that Briana Leigh's obsession with her name was ridiculous, just as Ariana did. "Where is the car?"

"Right over there."

He pointed toward the small terminal of the private airport, where a gleaming, steel-gray Audi convertible was parked.

"Nice! Shotgun!" Briana Leigh shouted. As if anyone else had been going to call it. She staggered toward the car, and the baggage men quickly hustled after her with all of her and Ariana's things.

"Good luck, miss," the pilot said to Ariana.

She smiled from behind her sunglasses. "Thanks."

Not that I need it, she added silently, narrowing her eyes at Briana Leigh. She had a plan. A foolproof plan. Luck would not be an issue.

Once in the car, Ariana locked her things in the glove compartment and turned on the GPS. Briana Leigh tossed the champagne bottle into the backseat, cranked up the stereo, and hit the button to release the car's roof.

"Whoo! Ibiza, here I come!" she shouted.

"Shhh!" Ariana scolded as she entered their destination into the car's computer. She glanced around at the Covingtons' crew, who were shuffling toward the terminal to relax while the jet was refueled. She hit the button again and reclosed the roof. There was no way her hat would stay on with the top down. "They're going to hear you."

"I don't care anymore," Briana Leigh said. "I can't wait to get the hell out of here!"

Ariana shook her head, clenched her teeth, and hit the gas. The sooner she got this over with, the better. She couldn't listen to Briana Leigh's shrill voice for one more second.

Speeding down the highway, Ariana opened the window and let the cool evening air rush over her. The familiar scents of the late-summer Virginia air filled her nostrils, and it was all she could do to keep from heaving at the memories that came whirling back. The chain-link fence, the itchy clothes, Crazy Cathy's screaming, Meloni's infuriating smirk . . . Ariana breathed in and let the memories come. Let her adrenaline intensify. She was going to need it very soon.

She took the exit for the country road near Lake Page. For the first time since getting in the car, Briana Leigh turned the music down and stopped singing.

"Where're we going? I didn't see a sign for the airport."

"That's because we're not going to the airport," Ariana replied, her fingers gripping the steering wheel tightly. "I have a surprise for you."

"What? Emma! I have a flight to catch!" Briana Leigh snapped.

Ariana took a deep breath. She stared straight ahead. "I know, but I wanted to thank you for everything you've done for me," she said, her voice utterly sincere. "I made a reservation for us at the Philmore on Lake Page. It's supposed to be the most exclusive resort in the area."

Briana Leigh clucked her tongue. "Like the people out here in Hickville USA know anything about a good spa." She shoved her hands under her arms. "What about Ibiza?"

"I got you a flight tomorrow," Ariana told her. "Come on. It'll be fun. It's a five-star resort. You'll love it. I swear."

Briana Leigh sighed and closed her eyes. "Fine. Just wake me when we get there."

"Oh, I will," Ariana said grimly.

Twenty minutes later, Ariana pulled the car onto a battered old one-way road on the east side of the lake, nowhere near the Philmore. She parked the car in the small clearing near the edge of the water, got out, and slammed the door. Briana Leigh flinched into consciousness. She looked around at the trees crowding the auto.

"What the hell is this?" Briana Leigh asked blearily when Ariana opened the door for her. She blinked several times but could barely focus her eyes. Ariana could see that the few Ambien pills she had crushed into Briana Leigh's champagne were finally taking effect.

"You're drunk. Let me help you," she told Briana Leigh flatly.

She reached into the car, wrapped her arms around Briana Leigh's waist, and yanked her out of the seat.

"Ow! Emma!" Briana Leigh attempted to swat Ariana's arm but missed. Briana Leigh paused and her eyes closed. She leaned against the top of the car for a moment, getting her bearings. "Why am I so dizzy?"

"Too much vodka," Ariana said, placing Briana Leigh's arm around her neck. "Let's go."

She helped Briana Leigh toward the old, creaky dock that jutted out into the water. On either side, a little clearing was cut in the reeds where kids had been coming for dozens of years to wade into the lake and swim out. Briana Leigh grew heavier as Ariana approached the dock. Her eyes were still open, but she was having a hard time keeping them that way.

"I don't get it. Where are we?" she said again as they finally reached the foot of the dock. "Where's the spa?"

"Right there."

Ariana stopped and pointed across the lake toward the west, where the Philmore Hotel rose like a castle out of the trees. Lights twinkled along the roof of the lakeside deck, and Ariana could hear bubbly piano music tinkling its way across the water. Briana Leigh leaned into Ariana's side and blinked at the hotel, confused.

"Know what's over there?" Ariana asked.

She turned and looked at the Brenda T. for the first time. Her entire body filled with burning fury at the sight of it.

"What?" Briana Leigh asked, totally clueless.

"That is the Brenda T. Trumbull Correctional Facility," Ariana said. "That is where your friend Kaitlynn Nottingham will be spending the rest of her life—thanks to you."

Briana Leigh's pupils were like pinpricks, even in the dark. She pulled away from Ariana and stumbled back a few steps before righting herself. Her hands pushed into her short blond hair as she wavered on her feet.

"What?" She let out a short, confused, angry laugh. "You have to be kidding me."

"No." Ariana said. "I'm not kidding you."

Briana Leigh blinked several times before she managed to focus on Ariana. "Why did you bring me here? You're sick!"

A searing hot flash of anger racked Ariana's core. Unable to contain herself a moment longer, she closed the gap between herself and Briana Leigh with two strides and grabbed the girl by her upper arms. For once it was Ariana who had the iron grip on *her.*

"You know what's sick, Briana Leigh? Killing your father and letting your best friend take the blame," Ariana said through her teeth. "What's sick is you living your life out here while Kaitlynn rots away behind barred windows!"

Briana Leigh shook her head. She tried to focus on Ariana's face. "What are you talking about? Kaitlynn deserves to rot. She's a certified psycho."

Ariana threw Briana Leigh to the ground. The thud was so satisfying that it made Ariana's pulse rush. What was the girl trying to pull? She had just confessed on the plane. She couldn't turn around and try to take it back now.

Briana Leigh slowly pushed herself up on her wrists and spat dirt from her mouth. "What the fuck is wrong with you?" she cried. She shook her head, still bleary, then held out a shaky hand. "Give me the keys! You're as crazy as she was!"

Ariana bent at the waist so she could get right in Briana Leigh's traitorous, lying face. "You are not going anywhere."

Then, as Briana Leigh's eyes widened, Ariana dug her fingers into the hair at the top of the girl's head and yanked as hard as she could. Briana Leigh screamed out as Ariana dragged her flailing body alongside the dock and into the water. Ariana wasn't worried about her being heard, however. She knew from experience that random shouts and screams were a common thing on Lake Page, thanks to the residents of the Brenda T.

"Let go of me!" Briana Leigh cried, her legs kicking out, splashing in the shallow water at the edge of the lake. Drugging her had been a good idea. The trip took enough exertion with Briana Leigh in her weakened state. If she had been at full strength, Ariana wasn't sure she would have been able to take her.

"What are you doing?" Briana Leigh shouted as Ariana pulled her into waist-deep water. Her arms and legs splashed around, grasping for something, anything to get hold of. "Emma! What the hell are you doing?"

Ariana turned the girl around and slammed her back against one of the dock's pylons, knocking the wind out of her. Briana Leigh's eyes went wide as she fought for breath.

"My name is not Emma," Ariana said, using that tone she reserved for idiots. "It's Briana Leigh Covington."

For the first time, sheer terror registered on Briana Leigh's face. As if she had just figured out that she was going to die. Ariana savored the satisfaction for the slightest of moments before plunging the girl's head into the water.

Briana Leigh, of course, struggled. Even all the alcohol and drugs couldn't kill her survival instinct, but they did dull her strength. Her legs and arms jerked while Ariana held her head under the water, using every ounce of her power to keep the girl down. Sweat popped up on her brow and under her arms. At one point Briana Leigh's nails dug into her skin. The whole thing was very unpleasant, really. And even though she had killed Sergei the same way, she wished she could have done it in a more humane way. Even as much as she hated Briana Leigh for what she had tried to do to Kaitlynn; as much as she hated her for her greed and her traitorous heart and her shallow ungratefulness for all she had; all that considered—drowning was still not a pleasant way to go.

But if Ariana wanted to kill two birds with one stone, this was the only way.

After the longest few moments of Ariana's life, Briana Leigh was still. Ariana turned her over in the water. Briana Leigh's cold, dead eyes stared up at her. Bile rose up in Ariana's throat. She shuddered and closed Briana Leigh's eyes with her thumb and forefinger, then turned and retched into the water.

You had to do this to survive, she thought, wiping her mouth with her trembling hand. *And you had to do this for Kaitlynn.*

Her moment of queasiness over, Ariana was ready for the next step in her plan.

THE UPPER HAND

In contrast to the insane rhythm of Ariana's heart, the night was incredibly tranquil. She pulled her car over to the side of the road and killed the lights, gazing out at the small, square cottage through the trees up ahead. The BEWARE OF THE DOG sign on the tall wooden fence was foreboding, but not as much as the maniacal barking coming from behind the gate.

Ariana smiled and got out of the car. It had rained recently, so she slipped out of her shoes to avoid leaving any discernible footprints in the wet earth. As she walked the few yards to the gate, she felt as if her body was on high alert. Her skin prickled with every breeze. She could distinguish every scent in the air—the fresh note of wet leaves, the tangy smell of barbecue coming from some backyard party. Crickets chirped, the wind rustled the trees, raindrops dripped from the gutters on the house, and the barking, the all-too-familiar barking, made the hairs on her arms stand on end.

But in a good way. An excited way. Ariana had taken a brief detour from her plan thanks to Briana Leigh's acting skills, but now she was back on track. It was all coming together.

Ariana quickly picked the lock on the gate, a skill she had learned not in prison, but from Gage Coolidge back at Easton. He who had picked many a well-stocked liquor cabinet. The lock easily popped open and the dog lunged. Ariana pulled the roll of roast beef from her purse. Wrapped inside were crushed Ambien. She held the meat out and smiled.

"Here, Rambo," she whispered.

The dog walked forward, took the meat, and nuzzled her hand.

Five minutes later Rambo was passed out in the backseat of the Audi. Ariana pulled out her untraceable disposable phone and dialed the cell number she had stolen and memorized more than a year ago. Dr. Meloni picked up on the first ring.

"Dr. Meloni here."

Ariana smiled. The self-importance was obvious in his voice. He probably thought there was some emergency at the Brenda T. Some crisis that only he could solve. But he had no idea what was about to hit him. It was all Ariana could do to keep from laughing. She had him right where she wanted him. Finally, she had the upper hand. Her only wish was that he could know that it was her. That he could feel the sting of it. But that could never be.

"I have your dog," she said, talking in low, controlled tones and mimicking a Boston accent for good measure. Meloni had heard her Southern drawl and her practiced Northeastern voice, but never a

Boston accent. "If you want him back, you're going to do something for me."

There was a short pause. In her mind's eye Ariana saw Dr. Meloni standing in the center of his outdated kitchen, listening for Rambo. She could just hear his heart skipping a scared beat. Her grin widened.

"Who is this?" he said.

"Do you really think I'm going to tell you that?"

Another pause. He was still listening. Hoping. "You don't have my dog."

But she could hear his footsteps as he crossed the room to check the yard.

Ariana giddily bit her lip. "Are you sure about that?"

She saw the outside light flick on and slid down in her seat, even though she was sure that Meloni wouldn't be able to see her car from his yard. The total darkness of these sparsely populated country roads was coming in handy.

"Rambo! Rambo, come here, boy!"

The anguished shouts carried through the quiet night. Ariana bit down harder.

A door slammed. Dr. Meloni fought his frantic breath. "What do you want?" he growled.

Ariana took a deep breath. Savored the moment. "I want you to have Kaitlynn Nottingham released from prison within the next three hours."

Meloni laughed derisively. "I can't do that. I don't have the authority."

"Oh, you'll figure out a way," Ariana said.

"You want me to break her out?" Dr. Meloni blurted. "You're nuts. I'll lose my job. I'll be arrested."

"That's up to you. If you are stupid enough to get caught, then yes, you might," Ariana said. "But you're not stupid, are you?"

Another long pause. Ariana listened to his breathing. The sounds of him no longer disgusted her. In fact, she found him suddenly amusing.

"I can't do it," he said. "I won't."

"I think you will," Ariana said.

She leaned around the backseat and snapped a picture of Rambo with her phone. The dog was snoozing with his tongue hanging out of his mouth, looking practically dead. It took two seconds to send the image to Dr. Meloni's cell phone.

"What the f—"

"He's not dead yet, but he's close," Ariana said slowly, deliberately. "Believe me when I tell you I have no qualms about ending his life. As dogs go, this one's kind of annoying. And think about this: If I subdued your Doberman this easily, just think what I can do to you."

"Okay," Dr. Meloni gasped. "Okay. I'll do whatever you want."

"Three hours," Ariana said. Then she disconnected the call before she cracked up laughing right in the man's ear. A laugh he would undoubtedly recognize.

Giggling to herself, Ariana watched as Dr. Meloni peeled out of his driveway in his Jaguar. She waited a few minutes, watching as they ticked away on the dashboard clock. Then she got out and roused a very sleepy Rambo. He teetered on his way back to the gate, but made it there in one piece. Ariana walked him over to his doghouse in the center of the yard and made sure he was curled up on his bed all comfy. Then she patted him on the head.

"Thanks again, buddy," she whispered. "You've been more help than you will ever know."

Then she raced out of the yard and locked the gate behind her.

THE ONLY WAY

The air had grown chilly by the time Ariana waded back to the dock with the skiff in tow. She had stolen it from one of the darkened houses on the lake and trudged through muck and reeds and slimy skittering fish until she reached her destination. She tied the boat off and slogged her way out of the water, shivering in the cool evening air. Her dress was dripping wet and ruined beyond repair, but she didn't mind. She hated it anyway. Way too former Briana Leigh for her tastes. Shaking the water off her hands and wringing out the skirt, she went over to the car and popped the trunk. From the several pieces of luggage she removed an ugly sweater Briana Leigh had chosen for her and the buttery, tan leather jacket Briana Leigh had worn to the Curtain Club—the only piece of clothing the girl owned that Ariana coveted.

She slipped her arms into the sleeves and savored the warmth. It belonged to her now. She was Briana Leigh Covington, after all. Everything in the car was hers.

After gazing longingly at the other dry clothes for a moment, Ariana decided it would be better not to change into jeans yet, since she had more dirty work to do. Might as well keep on the already ruined clothes. She took the jacket off again and tossed it into the backseat for later. Then she pulled on a Juicy Couture fleece zip-up and made her way into the woods to the clearing where she had left Briana Leigh's body. She covered the girl's face with the sweater, then dragged her over to the dock. Everything was ready. All she had to do now was wait. Ariana sat down next to Briana Leigh, her posture straight, and looked out over the water feeling perfectly at peace. The unpleasant murder aside, it was all working out as planned.

A touch more than two hours had passed since her phone call to Dr. Meloni when she heard someone approaching through the trees. Her heart hit her throat and she scrambled to her feet. Moments later, Kaitlynn emerged from between two pines, her curly hair back in a ponytail, her state-issued blue shirt untucked. Her eyes widened when she saw Ariana and she froze.

"Briana Leigh?"

Ariana laughed. She stepped closer to Kaitlynn, letting the moonlight cascade over her face. "Kaitlynn, it's me."

Relief colored Kaitlynn's skin. "Oh my God, Ariana! You're alive!"

The two of them ran forward and hugged. Ariana was so overwhelmed with happiness, she thought her heart might burst. Kaitlynn was free. They were together again. She had done it. She had come through on her promise.

"I knew you'd find me," Ariana said, pulling back but holding on to Kaitlynn's hands. "I knew you'd remember the pact and figure out where I'd be."

"All this time . . . I wanted to believe you were alive," Kaitlynn said, her eyes shining with tears. "But when I didn't hear from you—"

"I couldn't have written. They would have figured it out," Ariana explained.

No one other than Grandma C. had ever written to Kaitlynn, so a random letter would have been very suspicious.

"I know. I know," Kaitlynn said breathlessly. "Oh my God, I can't believe this is happening. When Dr. Meloni woke me up and smuggled me out, I thought I was dreaming." Kaitlynn paced back and forth as she talked, clearly so excited she couldn't stand still. "But then I was standing there outside the fence and he was telling me to go and I thought, Ariana. It has to be Ariana. So I decided to walk the eastern shore of the lake until I found you, and here you are!"

"Here I am," Ariana said with a grin.

"So what happened? How did you do it? Where have you been?" Kaitlynn asked. "How did you—"

Her last question died on her tongue. Ariana's heart turned. Kaitlynn had seen the body. Her face went slack and lost all its color as she glanced questioningly, warily, at Ariana. When Ariana remained silent, she took a couple of steps toward the body as if to confirm what she was seeing. Her hand flew up to cover her mouth and she froze.

"Ariana, is that—"

"Yes. It's Briana Leigh," Ariana said calmly.

She had to maintain an air of calm. It was the only way to keep

Kaitlynn's oncoming panic in check. She needed her friend to help her, and Kaitlynn would be no help if she broke down.

"You killed her?" Kaitlynn said, whirling on Ariana. Her expression was appalled. Terrified. "Ariana! Why?"

"I did it for you," Ariana said in a soothing tone, as if she was telling a nursery schooler why she needed to give in to nap time. "After everything she did to you . . . I couldn't let her get away with it. She had to be punished."

A tear spilled over onto Kaitlynn's cheek. A grateful tear? A disappointed tear? The crickets' song seemed to grow suddenly louder.

"Ariana—"

"Kaitlynn, she was pure evil . . . a waste of life," Ariana said, stepping forward to look right into her friend's eyes. Kaitlynn, however, averted her gaze. She couldn't stop staring at the corpse. "But her death won't be a waste."

Kaitlynn blinked. "What?"

Ariana took Kaitlynn's hands and tugged, forcing her friend to face her. Taking a deep breath, she tried to convey the seriousness of the situation with her eyes. Somewhere in the trees, a branch snapped. Ariana prayed it was just a deer or a raccoon, but her pulse quickened. "Kaitlynn, the police need to find my body."

At first, Kaitlynn didn't understand, but slowly her eyes widened. She tried to step back, but Ariana held her firm. A breeze rustled the trees and sent a chill down Ariana's beck.

"You can't be serious," Kaitlynn said.

"Serious as life in prison," Ariana said flatly.

Her palms were starting to sweat. Every second that passed was a second she couldn't afford. She was counting on Dr. Meloni's ego—on his survival instinct—to protect her. Counting on the probability that he wouldn't have a rush of conscience and confess what he had done. If he kept quiet, she and Kaitlynn had until seven a.m.—the first bed check—before anyone realized she was gone. But if he confessed, the cops could be after them at any moment. Ariana needed to get this over with and get out of there before that happened.

"We need to take her out to the center of the lake, weigh her down, and drop her in," Ariana told her friend, clutching her hands. Somewhere across the lake an outboard motor started up. Ariana's heart was in her throat. Then she heard a whoop and a laugh carry across the water. Just some college guys out for a drunken ride on the lake. That was all. "It's the only way they'll stop looking for me," she told her friend. "It's the only way I—we—can ever be free."

An incredulous noise escaped the back of Kaitlynn's throat. "You want me to . . . to touch her? I don't think I can do that."

"You can and you will," Ariana said. The engine noise grew dimmer. The boat was headed in the opposite direction. Ariana breathed a bit easier. "I did all of this for you. I got you out of prison. Now you have to do something for me. Unless you want me to go back to jail. Unless you want both of us to go back."

Kaitlynn appeared startled. "No. I don't want that."

"You have to help me," Ariana said desperately.

Something shifted in Kaitlynn's eyes. Sharpened. It was as if she had just realized she was free and, at the same time, realized how fleeting that freedom could be.

"You're right," Kaitlynn said finally. "Let's get this over with."

Ariana reached for her friend and hugged her. "Thank you," she said. "Now take off your clothes."

Kaitlynn understood without further explanation. She quickly removed her regulation Brenda T. blue shirt, white T-shirt, elastic-waist jeans, socks, and sneakers. Ariana grabbed a pair of jeans and a sweater from the bags in the car and gave them to Kaitlynn to wear. Together, they stripped Briana Leigh down and dressed her again in Kaitlynn's prison wear. As they worked, Kaitlynn never looked at Briana Leigh's face. Not once. Ariana's heart welled over the sacrifice her friend was making for her. She just hoped that Kaitlynn wouldn't have nightmares about this moment for the rest of her life. Ariana knew how horrifying that could be.

She waited until a moment when Kaitlynn's back was turned to remove the engagement ring from Briana Leigh's finger and slip it onto her own, the diamond turned in. Kaitlynn could not know that Briana Leigh had been engaged. Sweet as she was, it might make her feel real remorse.

"Okay. You get her feet," Ariana said once Briana Leigh was dressed.

As Kaitlynn hoisted Briana Leigh's legs, she glanced up. Her jaw dropped in shock.

"Her hair," she said.

"I know. She did that on her own," Ariana said with a smile. "Crazy, huh?"

Ariana wanted to bask in the lucky irony with her friend, but
Kaitlynn was too stunned to comment further. She walked awk-
wardly backward, struggling with Briana Leigh's dead weight, until
they were standing alongside the floating skiff. Together, they bent
at the waist and lowered the body into the boat. Then Kaitlynn
climbed in, sitting on the bench near Briana Leigh's feet. She was
still staring at the girl's face, as if she was understanding for the first
time that she was really dead.

"It's almost over," Ariana promised her, climbing into the boat.
"Just one more thing."

She sat behind Briana Leigh's lolling head. Her fingers trembled as
she reached around her own neck and unclasped the gold fleur-de-lis
necklace. The moonlight glinted on the pendant's smooth surface and
Ariana felt her heart tear down the center. It was the only thing she
had left. The only remnant of her old self.

"Ariana, no!" Kaitlynn gasped.

"I have to," Ariana said, speaking past a lump that had suddenly
arisen in her throat.

"But your mother gave you that," Kaitlynn said.

"I know." God, did she know. "But Meloni has seen it. He knows I
always wear it. If they find her with it, they'll be convinced she's me."

Closing her eyes, Ariana brought the pendant to her lips and kissed
it. She felt all the emotion of the past few weeks—realizing she was
never going to see her parents again, mourning them alone in front of
a computer, mourning herself every time she looked in the mirror—
and felt as if she could cry for days.

But she didn't have that luxury. She had work to do. Self-indulgence could come later. Taking a deep breath, Ariana pushed it all aside.

"I'm sorry, Mom," she said quietly. "I'm so sorry to put you through this."

Then she clasped the necklace around Briana Leigh's undeserving neck, untied the skiff, and pushed away from the dock into the cold, murky darkness of the lake.

USELESS

Ariana watched Briana Leigh's face as she sank below the surface of Lake Page. Her blond hair floated out around her head like a halo as she dipped beneath the greenish-brown water. Her skin looked waxy and pale.

"She could be you," Kaitlynn said, her voice morose.

Ariana shuddered, hoping the FBI would agree with Kaitlynn's assessment.

After that, everything went so smoothly it was like a dream. They rowed back to the house, tied up the skiff, and walked through the woods together. As they ducked under branches and stepped around muddy patches and puddles, Ariana felt more and more free. Soon the authorities would have their body. Soon the search would be successful, and Ariana Osgood would be officially declared dead. Before she knew it, it would all be over. She would finally be free to start her new life.

She only hoped it wouldn't be *too* soon. Ariana was supposed to have been dead for more than a week. In her estimation, Briana Leigh would have to go unfound for at least a week or two if she was going to look like she had been lolling at the bottom of the lake for that long. But there was nothing Ariana could do about that now. She was just going to have to wait and hope.

It was well past midnight when they arrived at the car. Ariana kept her ears trained for the sounds of sirens or dogs or shouting voices, but none came. There was nothing but crickets and the breeze and the occasional hoot of an owl. Undoubtedly Dr. Meloni was sitting in his house right now, petting his dear Rambo and wrestling with his conscience, trying to figure out what to do next. Tell the authorities that he'd helped Kaitlynn escape and have her found and dragged back, or wait until morning and hope that no one figured out his crime? The thought of his torture made Ariana smile.

At the car the two girls changed into dry clothes. Kaitlynn chose a pair of black cigarette pants and a white off-the shoulder sweater. Ariana took out her coveted Calvin Klein dress and sighed happily as she belted it around her waist. Kaitlynn removed the rubber band from her hair and shook out her curls. Together they leaned back against the trunk of the car. If anyone were to happen along, they would be just two friends out for a moonlight chat by the lake.

"The hair suits you," Kaitlynn said with a smile.

"You think?" Ariana asked. She lifted the heavy extensions over her shoulders in a gesture that made her think of Noelle Lange. "I'm still getting used to it."

Ariana looked at her friend with a pang. She had yet to tell Kaitlynn that she was going to Atherton-Pryce now—that they were going to have to go their separate ways—but she decided she should wait until they were far away from the Brenda T. Until they were safely tucked away in a place where they could talk and come up with a plan for Kaitlynn. Because now that Ariana had spent so much time daydreaming about Atherton-Pryce, about the fact that she could still have everything she had always wanted, she wasn't willing to give it up. She could only hope that Kaitlynn would understand.

"We should probably get going. The farther we get away from this place, the better."

"Agreed." Kaitlynn crossed her legs at the ankle and sighed as the breeze tossed her hair back from her face. "So. Where's the money?"

Ariana arched an eyebrow. "Figured out what my plan was already?"

"Isn't it obvious?" Kaitlynn asked with a shrug. "Why else would you have gone straight to Briana Leigh? The money, the body. It's perfect."

Ariana smiled. "Thanks. But I hadn't planned on using her for the body until it became absolutely necessary. And unfortunately, there is no money."

Kaitlynn stood up straight and crossed her arms over her chest. "What do you mean there's no money?"

Her voice was sharp. Angry. Never in Ariana's life had she heard Kaitlynn sound angry. Not even when Christmas had passed without so much as a card from the aunt and uncle and cousin she still had on the outside—the ones who had refused to take her in when her parents died. The ones who now had control of all of Kaitlynn's family money.

"It turns out there was a clause in her dad's will," Ariana said, walking around to the backseat with a towel. She wanted to clean out Rambo's dog hair. The new Briana Leigh Covington did not drive around in a hairy car. "She wasn't getting any of the inheritance until she was twenty-five."

"That's bullshit!" Kaitlynn shouted.

Ariana paused, leaning halfway into the car. *That* was definitely annoyance. She stood up again and looked over the car at her friend.

"Don't worry. I've got fifteen thousand in cash that Grandma Covington gave to Briana Leigh for emergencies. That should be enough to—"

Kaitlynn let out an irritated squawk. She walked around the side of the car and faced Ariana. Her brow was creased in consternation. Ariana stared at her friend. She felt as if she had missed something. As if she was playing catch-up.

She hated that feeling.

"You're telling me that you spent all that time with that bitch and you didn't even get your hands on the money?" Kaitlynn spat, her teeth clenched. "You have to be kidding me!"

"Kaitlynn, calm down," Ariana said, wrapping the towel around her fist. "I told you—"

"I don't believe this!" Kaitlynn seethed. "God, I should have known better. If you want something done right . . . But I couldn't do it myself, could I? You were my best shot!"

Ariana's heart slowly turned to stone inside her chest. She suddenly felt cold. Very, very cold. "What are you talking about? Handle what?"

"This!" Kaitlynn flung her hands out as if to encompass the whole world. "I *couldn't* go myself because Briana Leigh knows me. I had to send someone else," she ranted, pacing the dirt clearing. Her growing voice startled a few night birds from the trees. Ariana's heart seized up in her chest at the noise. She attempted to focus, but she simply could not. She couldn't believe what she was hearing. "So I fed you all the crap you'd need to know to get in with Briana Leigh and gave you my whole sob story and you ate it up. All of it. It *was* the perfect plan, Ari. Because *I* thought it up!"

The world started to spin in front of Ariana's eyes. She brought her hand to her head and tried to stop it, but it was no use. The person in front of her was supposed to be her friend. Supposed to be innocent, naive Kaitlynn Nottingham. But at that moment the person in front of her was unrecognizable. Fury lined her pretty face and she spat when she talked. The transformation was utterly horrid.

It hadn't been Ariana's plan. It had been Kaitlynn's plan all along. Kaitlynn had planted it inside Ariana's mind, just like Ariana had planted the identity-switching plan in Briana Leigh's head, making her think she'd come up with it herself.

Ariana's stomach turned and bile rose up in her throat. *Wrong again, Ariana. You were wrong again. . . .*

"But now, as it turns out, you used me to get the body you wanted and now you're leaving me high and dry," Kaitlynn ranted.

It wasn't possible. It just was not possible.

"Kaitlynn, why?" Ariana said, her mouth dry. Her heart was pounding so hard she could barely speak past its frenzy.

Kaitlynn stepped toward Ariana. "Why? Because I killed Derek Covington. He broke my heart, so I killed him. I took out his prized antique Winston revolver and I shot him right between the eyebrows. It was me. And if you weren't such an idiot, you would have figured that out by now."

Ariana's vision clouded over so fast she had to lean into the side of the car to stay on her feet. Her blood sounded like a freight train in her ears. Suddenly all she could see was Briana Leigh's face as she sank beneath the surface of the lake. It brought back with utter clarity the sight of Sergei Tretyakov's face. She had held him under as he clung to her hands—begged for help before sinking to his death. All for nothing.

She had killed the wrong person. Again. She had killed Briana Leigh for no good reason. Just like Sergei. All for nothing.

Not again. Not again not again not again.

"But she told me," Ariana whispered hoarsely, barely clinging to consciousness. Her fingers trembled. Her knees were rubber. She could hardly breathe. "She told me on the plane that she killed him. That it was her fault."

Kaitlynn clucked her tongue. "It was. If she hadn't told him to break up with me, he'd still be alive. But she had no idea what it's really like to kill someone, did she, Ariana?"

Ariana squeezed her eyes closed. Briana Leigh hadn't been confessing. She hadn't been unburdening her heart. She had been drunkenly babbling. Feeling sad and guilty over the loss of her father.

And Ariana had killed her for it.

How could I have been so wrong? How could I have been so gullible? She felt so stupid. So humiliated. All those stories Kaitlynn had told her—she had believed every last one of them. Kaitlynn had played her for months, and she had simply let her. So much for her ability to read people. It was nonexistent. Kaitlynn was right. She *was* an idiot.

But she wasn't powerless.

Ariana opened her eyes. Kaitlynn was turning away in disgust. A hot rage surged through Ariana—so hot it seared her skin. All she could see was Kaitlynn. Everything else—the car, the trees, the lake, the night sky—all of it faded to black. Kaitlynn had used her. She had lied to her for sixteen months, day in and day out. She had forced Ariana to kill an innocent girl. Something she'd sworn she would never do again. And now she was calling her useless?

With a guttural growl that echoed off the lake, Ariana lunged forward and shoved Kaitlynn with both hands. Kaitlynn shouted in surprise and fell to her knees. Ariana pounced on her and grabbed her by the hair, just as she had done with Briana Leigh.

"You miserable lying bitch!" Ariana seethed, feeling the frizzy texture of Kaitlynn's curls between her fingers. Savoring the pain on the girl's face as she wrenched her forward. She turned toward the lake. It was Kaitlynn who deserved to die. Kaitlynn who deserved to suffer a horrible, undignified end. And Ariana was going to make it happen.

"Get off me!"

Kaitlynn whirled around and backhanded Ariana across the face. Stunned, Ariana slammed into the side of the car and fell backward onto her butt, taking a handful of Kaitlynn's hair with her. For a moment she had forgotten that she was dealing with someone who wasn't drugged. Someone who wasn't tied up. Someone who could defend herself.

Someone who could kill.

"Ow!" Kaitlynn held her hand to her head and gaped at the hair in Ariana's fist. "You bitch."

Before Ariana could even move, Kaitlynn had jumped on her and slammed her head back into the hard-packed dirt. Ariana kneed the girl in the stomach and used the moment of shock to roll her attacker off her, but Kaitlynn grabbed Ariana's foot before she could scramble away. Ariana hit the ground again, face-first. Kaitlynn pressed her knee into the small of Ariana's back and gripped her hair, shoving her face into the dirt.

Ariana couldn't breathe. She struggled, wagging her head back and forth, trying to grab behind her and get hold of Kaitlynn, but nothing worked. She was using up what little oxygen she had, starting to black out.

No. I'm not going to die this way. I just got my life back. No . . . no . . . no . . .

Just when she was about to helplessly give in to the oncoming darkness, Kaitlynn released her. Ariana lifted her chin and gasped for breath. She got a lungful of dirt and her throat burned. Coughing like mad, she turned over and looked up at Kaitlynn, who was now rummaging through the car. Hot tears coursed down her face as she fought for breath. She was still struggling to get her knees under her when Kaitlynn loomed over her once more.

"This is where we part ways, *friend*," Kaitlynn said through her teeth. She raised the half-empty champagne bottle Briana Leigh had lifted from the plane. "Thanks for nothing."

Ariana let out one pathetic screech before the bottle cracked against the back of her skull and everything went black.

A PROMISE

The sky was purple.

That was all Ariana was able to register before her head exploded with pain. She groaned and gripped the back of her skull, rolling over onto her side. Every bone in her body seemed to ache and there was an awful taste in her mouth.

Dirt. She was lying in dirt.

Suddenly everything came rushing back and Ariana shoved herself to her knees. The buzz of a motorboat's engine assaulted her ears, and she winced as a new bolt of pain shot through her skull. Lake Page was coming alive. The search for Ariana's body was revving up again.

I have to get out of here, Ariana thought. *Now.*

She scrambled to her feet and turned around. The car. The car was still there. And there appeared to be some kind of note shoved between the window and door. Pressing her lips together, Ariana grabbed the piece of paper, torn from one of the notebooks she had bought for her new school year.

Be seeing you soon! Kaitlynn had written. She had even drawn a smiley face next to it. Ariana balled the page up and threw it on the ground. Kaitlynn had probably realized the car would be too easy to trace. Smart girl. Evil girl.

Ariana's fingers curled at the very thought of what Kaitlynn had done to her. She was going to kill that bitch. She looked down at her Calvin Klein dress, stained with dirt and blood, and her jaw clenched. She was going to murder that bitch the first chance she got.

Grabbing the keys from the ground, Ariana raced to the back of the car and popped the trunk. Empty. Kaitlynn had taken everything. The clothes, the laptop, the jewelry, the cash—even the toiletries and towels and makeup. The yawning void of the trunk stared up at Ariana, mocking her. Heart in her throat, she slammed it closed and got behind the wheel.

Please. Please, just this one thing . . .

She unlocked the glove compartment and reached into the back. Her fingers found her purse and the velvet bag she had stashed there the night before. Instantly, her pulse relaxed. Kaitlynn hadn't thought to check it. The Osgood paranoia had paid off this time.

Just to reassure herself, Ariana overturned the velvet bag. Dozens of priceless jewelry pieces tumbled into her palm, all lifted from Grandma Covington's bedroom the night before she and Briana Leigh had left. Ariana grinned. Hocking these would pay for a new wardrobe and computer. Her heart tingled with pride as she congratulated herself for thinking ahead. She opened the wallet and looked over her Briana Leigh Covington IDs, then looked for the twenty-four hundred dollars from Briana Leigh's checking account, which she had stashed in there, as well as the credit cards Briana Leigh had given her. All present and accounted for.

Kaitlynn hadn't seen any of this. Which meant she still didn't know exactly what Ariana's plan was. Ariana hadn't had a chance to tell her. Thank goodness. And unless Kaitlynn had realized that Ariana's new hair was supposed to serve some purpose, she was clueless. The thought that she knew more than Kaitlynn on at least one score soothed Ariana even further.

She turned the rearview mirror toward her to look herself in the eye and caught a glimpse of tan leather in the backseat. Her heart skipped a happy beat. Kaitlynn hadn't seen the jacket either. That was definitely going to come in handy for covering up her bloodstains until she could buy some new clothes.

Popping her green contacts out of her eyes, Ariana looked at herself in the mirror again.

"Briana Leigh Covington," she whispered to herself. "Hi. I'm Briana Leigh Covington."

She still couldn't get comfortable with the sound of it, but, in the words of Briana Leigh herself, beggars couldn't be choosers.

Ariana's heart squeezed suddenly. Briana Leigh had hidden feelings of loss and guilt and loneliness behind her bitchy veil. She had been so trusting. So generous. Yes, Ariana had been doing her a favor, but she had been so quick to give up control of her whole identity, just so that "Emma Walsh" could go to a good school. Could have a life.

And now she was dead. Needlessly dead. All because of Kaitlynn Nottingham.

"I'm so sorry for what happened, Briana Leigh," Ariana said, gazing out at the lake. "But don't worry. I'll take care of her. Sooner or later, she'll pay for this. I promise."

Then she started up the car, threw it in reverse, and turned around, speeding away from the lake and all the demons it held.

SOME CRAZY

Ariana stepped inside the lobby of the Philmore Hotel and Spa and breathed in deeply. Breathed in the scents of opulence. The fresh lilies bursting from crystal vases. The pungent wax on the gleaming marble floor. The clean leather and velvet furniture. The Chanel No. 5 of the distinguished-looking middle-aged woman at the concierge desk. She took in that breath and tried to calm her terrified excitement.

This was where she belonged. This was the life she deserved.

But would these people recognize her? If anyone had seen her photo ten million times, it was the staff of the Philmore. Just standing inside the gold-trimmed door was risky. But Ariana simply could not stay anywhere else. She had to be near the lake. Had to keep her eye on the proceedings. It was the only way.

She lifted her head and strode toward the registration desk, her brand-new Louis Vuitton trunk—filled with neatly folded designer items, thanks to Grandma C.'s jewels—zipping along behind her.

The thirtysomething man behind the counter looked up at the auburn-haired girl in D&G sunglasses approaching him. Ariana saw his eyes flick over her outfit, sizing her up with one glance. He took in the Miss Sixty jeans, the Donna Karan blouse, the leather jacket, the diamond studs (the one item of Grandma Covington's she had kept). He smiled, not a trace of recognition in his eyes. There was nothing but approval.

"Good afternoon, miss. Welcome to the Philmore," the man said. "How may I help you?"

Ariana placed her Calvin Klein clutch on the desk and smiled apologetically. "I know it's last minute, but I was hoping you might have a room available," she said with a slight Texan accent.

"Absolutely, Miss . . . ?"

"Covington," Ariana said with a smile. "Briana Leigh Covington."

"Yes, Miss Covington. And what type of room would you like?" he asked, typing away on his keyboard. "We have several levels. Luxury, luxury suite, deluxe luxury suite with lake view—"

"Lake view? Really?" Ariana's heart skipped in excitement. "I assumed those would all be booked at the height of summer."

The man glanced around, then lowered his voice. "Haven't you heard?" he whispered.

"Are you talking about that girl who went and drowned herself?" Ariana leaned in, the picture of curiosity.

"Yes," he said, leaning toward her. He clucked his tongue in distaste. "I'm not supposed to tell the guests, but personally, I think our clientele should be given all the facts and allowed to make an informed decision."

Ariana nodded seriously, even though inside she was laughing. Little did this guy know he was talking to the very ghost of Lake Page.

He stood up straight again, with an amused smile on his lips. "So. Still want a lake view?"

Ariana slapped a credit card down on the desk. "Book it."

The clerk's eyebrows raised in surprise, but he was also clearly impressed.

Ariana grinned. "Now where can I make a spa appointment?"

THE BODY

Every morning for two weeks, Ariana sat on her private veranda overlooking the lake as she ate a gorgeous breakfast of fresh fruit and eggs. Every morning she sat, filling a notebook with practiced handwriting, and watched as FBI agents and their crews searched the lake, their dredging boats moving slowly across the placid surface. A few private cruisers launched half a dozen divers every morning as well, and Ariana could only assume these were paid for by her father. She tried not to think of him sitting in his office at the house in Atlanta, receiving the daily three-word reports: No body found.

Around noon, when the crews took their lunch break, Ariana would indulge in a spa treatment or a massage. But she would be back on the veranda by midafternoon, watching. Always watching.

She had been a resident of the Philmore for exactly fifteen days when her cell beeped. It had been silent for so long, the sudden noise startled her. Only one person had the number. Fingers trembling, she picked up the phone and read the text from Hudson.

> 3 wks. Figured u'd b busting down my door by now from missing me so much, but nada. Went to BL's but ur not there. Where r u? I need to see u. I'll come to u. Just tell me where you are. —H

Ariana's heart skipped around like a bouncing ball inside her chest. Her fingers itched to text back, but she forced herself to turn off the phone. She could not make contact with Hudson. He was the only person who could threaten her new life. He and Téo, who had not only met Emma Walsh but knew that Briana Leigh was enrolled at Atherton-Pryce. But she had a plan to deal with Téo. A plan she would put into play as soon as she knew she was safe.

She had just placed the phone back in her bag when it happened.

"We found something! A body!" someone yelled through a bull-horn.

Instantly speedboats rushed to the center of the lake from all directions, descending on one of the dredgers. Ariana leaned forward with interest, her heart trying to pound its way free of her body. She tried not to look too intrigued as a diver popped through the surface of the lake. He removed his mouthpiece and his voice carried over the water.

Ariana couldn't help standing up, placing her notebook aside, and going to the railing. She told herself that any normal person staying at the hotel would do the same. Her fingers trembled as she gripped the iron rail.

The people on the boats were all shouting, conferring, pointing, issuing orders. Ariana forced herself to breathe at a regular pace as she waited. Time stood still. An eternity seemed to pass. And then, finally, the body emerged.

Shaking, Ariana turned and grabbed the binoculars she had purchased at a local hunting and fishing outpost. Holding her breath, she zeroed in on the corpse. The prison garb was tattered and muddy, the sneakers gone. The skin was veiny and the face bloated beyond recognition. The blond hair was matted in muddy tangles all around the gruesome face.

The crew tied the rope from a pulley mechanism around Briana Leigh's body and turned it on. With a groan, the mechanism lifted the corpse from the water. Ariana dry heaved when she saw the way the arms and legs hung limply forward, the head jerking around like a rag doll's. She covered her mouth and looked away, imagining that it was, in fact, her out there. That she had met such a tragic, messy, undignified end. Her parents were going to be devastated. Her mother might never recover.

What did I do? Ariana thought, pressing her eyes closed. *What did I do?*

A motor roared to life below and Ariana swallowed hard. She had to watch this. Had to make sure it all went as planned. When she opened her eyes again, the boat was whisking its way toward the far shore. Several unmarked police cars sat in wait, obviously having been alerted that something had been found. Ariana focused the binoculars on the cars. Her heart caught when Dr. Meloni emerged from the back of one of the SUVs. He walked to the edge of the lake and waited.

So this was the person they had brought to identify her body. Kaitlynn's escape had been all over the news for the past two weeks, and there had been talk about shutting down the Brenda T. now that two inmates had busted free in as many months, but Dr. Meloni had never been mentioned as a person of interest. Not once. How he'd managed to sneak under the radar was a mystery to Ariana.

She trained the binoculars on the great doctor, her hands aching from the force of her grip. The boat docked. Dr. Meloni was escorted to the vessel and helped aboard. She watched as he knelt over her body, covering his mouth and nose against the stench. He looked her over and shook his head. Shrugged his shoulders. Ariana felt sick. He was going to ruin this whole thing. He was going to say he couldn't be sure.

But then, something caught his eye.

Slowly, Dr. Meloni reached inside the collar of the light blue shirt and pulled out the fleur-de-lis. He stared at it for a long moment, in total shock. Then he dropped it, stood up, and backed away. He said a few words to the officer who was obviously in charge, and both men nodded.

Meloni was probably spouting some crap about how well he knew her. How she never took that necklace off. How she had an almost unhealthy attachment to it and all it represented. How she never would have given it to anyone else because she was pathologically OCD and couldn't let go of the past.

"Surprise, surprise, doctor," Ariana whispered triumphantly. "Maybe next time *you* should try harder to understand exactly what your patients are capable of."

Finally, the body was lifted up and placed into a black body bag. All Ariana could do now was hope that Meloni's identification would be enough—that they wouldn't perform any further tests on the body. But she knew her parents well enough to know that they wouldn't want her corpse defiled any further than it already had been. Hopefully they would use their considerable power to make sure that her body went untouched from here on. After all, the authorities had just found the body of a blond teenager dressed in prison garb, wearing Ariana's signature necklace. Who else could it be?

Ariana forced herself to look one last time at Briana Leigh's bloated face. She let the remorse wash over her. Let herself feel the loss of innocent Briana Leigh Covington. Even felt a pang for Téo, waiting all alone in Ibiza for the past weeks, having no idea what had happened to his fiancée.

Then she took a deep breath, closed her eyes, and shoved it all aside. There was nothing she could do about that now. All she could do was honor Briana Leigh by living the life the girl was meant to have.

As the body bag was zipped up, Ariana got up from her chair and began to pack her things.

It was done.

THE END

Easton, Connecticut, looked exactly the same. Not that Ariana had been away very long, but she had been through so much, she somehow expected everything to have changed. But there were the quaint little boutiques, the tiny exclusive restaurants like Latour and Frattelli's, the cute old-school police station with its orb-topped lampposts out front. Even the people on the street seemed the same to her. Lunching ladies with their tiny dogs lounging in their purses, wealthy boys on skateboards dressed all grungy like they couldn't afford Hugo Boss, teenage girls squealing into their cell phones as they swung their shopping bags.

It was all so quaint and sunny and happy. It didn't feel like the right place for a funeral.

Ariana hid a smile as she turned her Audi down Elm Street and St. Peter's Episcopal Church came into view. Several black limousines were parked outside along with dozens of cars. The doors were open and Ariana could hear the organ playing its somber tones. She would have given anything to be a fly on the wall inside, but the church was too small. Too cozy. And most of the people inside had known her since birth. The risk was simply too high.

With a longing sigh, Ariana turned at the next corner and headed for Coleman Park—a large square at the center of town containing a duck pond, dozens of benches for lounging, and a few colorful play areas for children. She shook her head as she tooled around, searching for a parking space on the pristine, tree-lined streets. Leave it to her mother to plan her funeral in Easton. After days of scouring the obituaries, Ariana had found the details of her final party in the *Atlanta Journal-Constitution*. She was to be cremated and her ashes spread in Easton's Coleman Park—Ariana and her Billings sisters had helped renovate the park as part of a community service project. A small accompanying article had quoted her mother as saying that Ariana had spent the happiest years of her life at Easton Academy, but that since the institution had refused to let the family scatter her ashes on the premises, this was the next best thing.

It was *so* Lillian. Her mother *would* believe that Ariana's happiest years had been at Easton, because that was where her mother had always wanted her to be. But if Ariana had had her way, she would have been buried on the family plantation—the place where she had spent the few happy times together with her mother and father and grandparents and cousins. Maybe one day Briana Leigh Covington would buy the old place from the Osgoods and actually make that dream come true.

Ariana parked the car on the street, directly across from one of the entrances to the park. She was about to lock up her purse but stopped herself. That was an Ariana Osgood thing to do. She wasn't Ariana Osgood anymore. Briana Leigh Covington wasn't nearly as cautious. Perhaps she should try to shed some of the old paranoia. She placed the black clutch under her arm, straightened her wide black hat and sunglasses, and got out of the car with her valuables still inside her purse. A pair of police officers were loitering near the edge of the pond; Ariana assumed they were stationed there for crowd control. She found a spot near an ancient elm tree several yards behind them and waited.

Before long, the procession of cars made its way to the park. Several Easton police officers arrived to close down the road and make it easier for the mourners to get through. Ariana knew her father must have paid a pretty penny for that kind of service. She wasn't exactly Easton's favorite former resident.

Standing at a safe distance from the pond, Ariana was able to see each of her guests as they arrived. Her uncles and aunts and cousins—the young ones looking uncomfortable in their formal suits and dresses. Her father's colleagues, checking their BlackBerrys as they emerged from their chauffeur-driven cars, clearly counting the minutes until they could get back to their lives. Then a silver Mercedes convertible pulled up and Ariana's heart collapsed when she saw the stone-faced brunette behind the wheel. It was Noelle. Noelle had come to her funeral.

Ariana's chest flooded with a thousand different emotions. Anger, sadness, abandonment, glee, nostalgia. Noelle lifted her thick brown hair over her shoulders as she got out of the car, wearing a tasteful black suit and black heels. Then she turned around to wait as a red vintage roadster pulled up behind her. When Kiran Hayes and Taylor Bell emerged, Ariana had to hold her hand over her mouth to keep the emotion at bay. Taylor had gained some weight, but wore it well in a black dress and belted jacket. Kiran looked as gorgeous as ever, her hair cropped short, a pillbox hat and veil atop her head. Kiran and Taylor held hands for support as they approached the rest of the mourners, but Noelle, of course, didn't need any such help. She followed behind her friends, her head held high. The only betrayal of any emotion was when she quickly lifted a handkerchief to her nose, but she just as quickly folded it away.

Ariana watched her friends and all emotions blurred into nostalgia. These were the girls with whom she had spent some of the most incredible times of her life, and she ached to talk to them. She wanted to tell them what she had been through, that she was so mad at them for never visiting her in prison, but that she was so grateful they were here now. The knowledge that she couldn't do any of this was almost too much to bear.

Instead, Ariana forced herself to focus on the later arrivals. She was surprised when Daniel and Paige Ryan showed up. Wondered what that was about. Then was disappointed when none of the other guys arrived. No Gage, no Walt Whittaker, no Josh Hollis or Dash McCafferty or Trey Prescott.

They were probably still mad at her. Probably still hated that she had stolen Thomas Always-up-for-a-Good-Time Pearson away from them. Ariana swallowed that bitter pill and shoved it aside.

And then, the moment she had been dreading. Her parents' arrival.

Ariana took a deep breath. Silently let the tears come. Her father carried her urn, his eyes steadfastly trained straight ahead as he supported her mother with his other arm. Support that she needed, bent and sobbing as she was. Her blond hair had gone white, wispy, and thin and was piled atop her head. The black barrette that held it there was barely clinging to what little it had to cling to. As they reached the center of the park where everyone was gathered, her mother let out a loud sob that sent whispers through the crowd.

It broke Ariana's heart.

I have to see this, she told herself, fighting the urge to turn back to her car and drive away from it all. *I have to see this if I'm really going to start over.*

Ariana's father handed her mother's arm over to her uncle James, then stood before the gathering with the urn. From the distance, Ariana couldn't hear what he was saying. She took a few tentative steps toward the back of the crowd, longing to hear her father's voice, to know what his parting words to her might be. It was dangerous, she knew, but how could she resist? It was a natural curiosity. Not everyone got to attend their own funeral.

She was about thirty yards from the back of the crowd, telling herself she should stop now, when her cell phone let out a loud, obnoxious beep.

There were a few annoyed whispers as people looked around to see who would be so rude as to not silence her phone at a funeral. Ariana cursed herself for not having locked up her purse, or at least turned off her phone. She fumbled for the phone and silenced it with the touch of a button. She quickly turned around, but not before she saw Dr. Meloni at the back of the crowd, turning her way.

"Shit," Ariana said under her breath. What was he doing here? She had read that, once her body had been found, he had been fired from the Brenda T. for his apparent role in her suicide—right after the warden had been canned for running a prison from which two teenagers had been able to escape within two months. How could Meloni have the audacity to show up at her funeral after that? More important, had he seen her?

Ariana quickly strode away. With every step she could feel Dr. Meloni bearing down on her. His breath on her neck. His hand just millimeters from her shoulder. It was over. He had seen her. She was done. Three steps from the edge of the park, Ariana couldn't take it anymore. She took a deep breath and turned around.

But there was no one there.

She scanned the mourners for Dr. Meloni but couldn't pick him out from all the other black-suited men. She had been spared.

Lesson learned.

Safely behind the wheel of her car, she turned her phone on again. Her hand shook as she looked down at the screen, knowing exactly what she would find. A text from Hudson. He had texted her dozens of times since his first message on the day her body had been found.

She hadn't responded to a single message, but that hadn't stopped him. This one, however, made her blood run cold.

Fine. U don't want to reply, I'll just come see u. On my way to Easton now. See u soon. —H

Ariana grabbed her arm and squeezed. This was not good. Hudson was coming to Easton. He would go to the school and find out that not only was Emma Walsh not currently enrolled, but she never had been. What would he do next? Would he give up and go home, or would he try to track her down? Find the actual Emma Walsh from Chicago who had gone to school with Dana Dover from Camp Potowamac and learn that she was actually some middle-class chub who had never even heard of Easton?

And if he did all that, what would Ariana be forced to do in return?

Ariana swallowed a hard lump in her throat and tossed the phone onto the passenger seat. She couldn't think about that now. The best thing she could do for herself and for Hudson was put as much distance between herself and Easton, Connecticut, as possible. There would be no more visits to her past. Visits to her past were obviously too dangerous. From now on, Ariana's focus was on the future. With one last parting glance at her former friends, her former family, her former world, Ariana pulled her car into traffic and never looked back.

THE BEGINNING

It all starts here.

Ariana paused outside the imposing iron gates. Paused and took a deep, satisfying breath. She closed her eyes and let it all soak in. The clean, fresh air. The cool breeze carrying the slightly musky scent of the oncoming autumn. The popping of luxury car doors and the shouts of students greeting one another after a long summer apart.

It all starts here.

Ariana turned and slid the package out from under her arm. She looked over the handwriting on the slip, satisfied that it was indistinguishable from Briana Leigh's. All that practicing on the veranda at the Philmore had done the trick. Téo would never know that the breakup letter was not from his betrothed. Would never suspect the format in which it arrived, since the two of them had been writing real letters to one another since the beginning of their romance. She hoped the ring she had nestled inside would arrive safely and that he would find some worthy girl to give it to someday. Placing the package carefully into the FedEx box on the sidewalk next to the gates, she took a deep breath. Briana Leigh's ties were officially cut. It was up to Ariana now to decide who Briana Leigh Covington would become. This last task finally completed, she shook her hair back from her face, grasped the handle of her rolling Louis Vuitton trunk, and strode through the gates onto the campus of Atherton-Pryce Hall.

Breathless with anticipation, Ariana nevertheless managed to keep her gait to a stroll, to take it all in. The low, redbrick buildings with the arched, multipaned windows gleaming in the sun. The cherry trees lining the walkways, which would no doubt burst forth with big, beautiful blossoms in the spring. The cocky boys, already clad in their blue blazers and gray slacks as they slapped hands with one another on the lawn. The huge fountain at the center of campus, bubbling happily as underclassmen gathered around to check their schedules against one another's or gossip about who hooked up with whom over the summer.

Ariana was surprised at how giddy she felt and realized for the first time how close she had come to losing everything. How very near she had come to the brink. Never again. Never again could she take all this for granted. She promised herself right then and there that she would turn over a new leaf. She had earned her second chance. Had worked and sacrificed and suffered for it.

Her fingernails dug into the skin of her bare forearm and she winced. Hadn't even realized she had been doing it. Slowly, deliberately, Ariana breathed in the crisp, cool air and felt her pulse start to relax. Her fingers uncurled. She was finally where she belonged. It was time to focus.

As she made her way around the fountain, she saw them. They stood with their shoulders back, noses up, looking the plainer girls up and down derisively as they scurried around like excited hamsters. Even though everyone wore the same pleated uniform skirts and fitted blazers, they looked more sophisticated than the others. There were a dozen in all, clustered into little groups. But of the twelve, the trio at the center was different. Special. They stood in a shaft of sunlight that seemed to shine just for them, and every so often the girls in the other klatches would look over at them with interest and envy. These were the girls Ariana was looking for.

The tall one at the center—raven hair, exotic olive skin, regal nose—was clearly in charge. The others spoke, whispered, or laughed toward her, but she never moved for anyone. She stood perfectly straight and poised, like a ballerina. Her dark hair was back in an unkempt ponytail and the tie of her uniform hung loose around her neck. She wore expensive yet broken-in Prada boots that had no place in her preppy uniform but somehow still worked. Long, delicate gold earrings grazed her collarbone. The whole look said she didn't care, but was perfect nonetheless. The girl to her left—pale skin, short blond hair cut above the ears, big bright eyes—was the most gorgeous girl Ariana had ever laid eyes on, even if she could stand to lose a few pounds. Everything about her was big. Big enamel hoop earrings. Oversize leather D&G bag. Tons of bracelets clinking around on both arms. A watch with a face so huge Ariana could almost read it from yards away. Her shoes were open-toed wedges. Definitely European. Definitely a designer Ariana didn't know, which was intriguing. The third girl was Asian. Tiny. Impeccably put together. Black hair back in a velvet headband hanging straight down her back like a knife. Not a wrinkle or crease on her shirt. Everything brand-new. She wore sensible yet stylish Roger Vivier flats, black with a big buckle over the front. Very nice.

Ariana took one look at them and knew she was home.

But suddenly, somehow, a skitter of nerves assaulted her heart. These people didn't know her. They didn't have to instantly accept her. What if she messed it all up? What if something went wrong? This was her life. Her *new* life. After everything she had been through, she couldn't screw it up now. Everything was riding on this moment.

Just be yourself, honey, she heard her mother say in her ear, just as she had on that first day at Easton so many years ago. *Just be yourself, and I know they'll love you.*

She had, after all, been an outsider then, too. The only girl from Georgia in her freshman class at the tony New England prep school. And look how easily she had been accepted there. Look how well that had all turned out.

Relatively.

Now, standing in her street clothes among all these uniformed strangers, Ariana felt her heart squeeze with longing for the sound of her mother's voice, but she quickly shook it off. Her mother would have been proud if she knew where Ariana was right now, how she was taking charge of her life. That was going to have to be enough. Taking a deep, calming breath, Ariana lifted her long auburn hair over her shoulder, put on a big smile, and strode confidently forward.

Easton was in the past. Noelle and Billings and Thomas were in the past. Her mother, even, was in the past.

It was time to start the first day of the rest of her life.

She stepped up to the dark-haired girl in the Prada boots and smiled. "Hi. I'm Briana Leigh Covington," she said. "But you can call me Ana."

Visit the official home of

WWW.PRIVATENOVELS.COM

Where Kate Brian fans chat, win prizes, *and*
find out what happens next!

From bestselling author
KATE BRIAN

❤ ❤ ❤ ❤ ❤

Juicy reads for the sweet and the sassy!

Sweet 16
As seen in *CosmoGIRL!*

Lucky T
"Fans of Meg Cabot's *The Princess Diaries* will enjoy it." —*SLJ*

Megan Meade's Guide to the McGowan Boys
Featured in *Teen* magazine!

The Virginity Club
"*Sex and the City: High School Edition.*" —*KLIATT*

The Princess & the Pauper
"Truly exceptional chick-lit." —*Kirkus Reviews*

❤ Published by Simon & Schuster ❤

meet
th@shleys

there's a new name in school

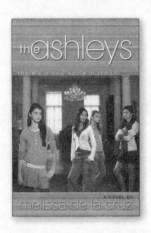

from the bestselling author
melissa de la cruz

e.l.f
eyeslipsface.com

Shh... special offer
for Privilege fans

Get the look of Privilege
at eyeslipsface.com

Fans like you receive* $5
toward your next purchase with
COUPON CODE:
PRIVILEGE

*Restrictions may apply

See Ariana's makeover
& enter to win your own at
eyeslipsface.com/privilege

Grand Prize:
- You and a friend win a trip to NYC
- While there, you get a
  professional makeover
- Head home with a full
  supply of e.l.f. beauty products

e.l.f.
eyeslipsface.com

To enter, and for official rules, go to eyeslipsface.com/privilege

No purchase necessary. Starts 12/30/08 at 12:01 p.m. EST. Ends on 2/10/09 at 11:59 a.m. Open to legal residents of the fifty United States and the District of Columbia who are 13-25 years of age. Void in Alaska, Hawaii, Puerto Rico, Guam, the U.S. Virgin Islands, and where prohibited by law. Subject to official rules. For official rules go to www.eyeslipsface.com/privilege

P9-DNK-968

PRAYING WITH SAINT LUKE

CARLO CARDINAL MARTINI

PRAYING WITH SAINT LUKE

VERITAS

Published 1987 by
Veritas Publications
7-8 Lower Abbey Street
Dublin 1

Italian language edition published 1983 by
Edizioni Paoline
Via Paolo Ucello 9
20148 Milan
Italy

Copyright © 1987 Veritas Publications

ISBN 0 86217 283 7

The Scripture quotations contained herein are from the *Revised Standard Version Bible*, copyright 1946, 1952, 1971 by the Division of Christian Education of the National Council of the Churches of Christ in the USA, and are used by permission.

Translation: Luke Griffin
Cover design: Eddie McManus
Cover photograph: Robert Allen Photography
Typesetting: Printset & Design Ltd, Dublin
Printed in the Republic of Ireland by
Mount Salus Press Ltd, Dublin

Contents

PREFACE — 9

INTRODUCTION — 11

1. THE CLIMATE OF PRAYER — 13
   Prayer of being — 15
   Conditions for prayer — 19
   Entrance to prayer — 22
   The rhythm of prayer — 23

2. PRAYING WITH SAINT LUKE — 29
   Mary's prayer — 31
   The prayer of Simeon — 38
   Jesus' prayer of rejoicing — 44
   Jesus' prayer in Gethsemane — 53
   Jesus' prayer on the Cross — 58
   The Christian's prayer — 64
   Prayer of the community — 71

3. MILESTONES ON THE WAY — 77

PREFACE

In September 1980 The Archbishop of Milan addressed to the clergy and laity of his diocese his first pastoral letter entitled *The Contemplative Dimension of Life*.[1] Its reception indicated that it represented a response to a need and, as a result, various initiatives sprang up all over the diocese.

A group of young Catholic activists[2] asked the Archbishop to teach them to pray by praying with them. This was the beginning of the school of prayer in the Cathedral which took place on the first Thursday of every month until June 1981. These young people wished to share their experience of praying with the Archbishop and hence the present book.

It is not a book on prayer — rather an account of an experience of prayer. This explains the directness of style of these pages. We retained the colloquial style in the hope of remaining as faithful as possible to what took place in the Cathedral.

The meditations which we have reproduced were preceded by hymns and readings from the Scriptures. Following on the Word of God there were periods of silence and, for those who wished, the Sacrament of Penance was available. We ended with some common prayer. None of this part of the experience has, of course, found its way into our pages.

1. *La dimensione contemplativa della vita.*
2. Members of Catholic Action.

INTRODUCTION

It is our intention to undertake a 'prayerful journey' together. We will use Luke's Gospel for it tells us more about prayer than the others. It speaks of Jesus' prayer, in a desert place at daybreak *(Lk 4:42)* or of his prayer on the mountain during the night *(6:12)* and the Gospel also speaks of prayer during his Baptism *(3:21)*. Luke's Gospel also speaks of our prayer; it records the parable of the importunate friend *(11:5-8)* and of the widow and the dishonest judge — all telling us that we should continue to pray without ceasing.

Apart from this Luke gives us examples of prayer. It is on these examples that we will reflect. There are three examples of Jesus' prayer — the hymn of Jubilation, the prayer of Jesus in the Garden and his prayer on the Cross. There are also three prayers by human beings: the Virgin's Magnificat, the prayer of Simeon and the Christian's prayer, the Our Father. Towards the end we will meditate on a prayer of the community as reported by Luke in the Acts of the Apostles.

Before beginning to pray we should be aware of the difficulties which we may encounter, and of those things that may impede the harmony between our spirit and the Spirit of God.

One difficulty that weighs greatly on me these days is the thought of the sufferings of so many of our brothers and sisters. Even more am I upset by the thought of those who have to face sad events of life, whose faith is thus shaken, and who wonder then why God does not intervene.

These, and indeed the many other difficulties we might

experience, can be overcome by bringing them to our prayer which otherwise would not be real, but would be artificial, cut off from life as it is. Silently and in the presence of God let us express what we feel — the very difficulty we have in placing ourselves in his presence and in knowing the God who has revealed himself in Jesus crucified.

Let us therefore begin:

O Lord, God of Mystery, we know you so little. Indeed there are times when we feel we know you even less. We feel we are struggling with you as Jacob struggled with the Angel; perhaps we are struggling with the image we have of you. We cannot comprehend you, we cannot succeed in understanding you.

O Lord, reveal your face; show us the face of your crucified son. Grant that in this face we may learn to understand something of the immense sufferings that are afflicting so many parts of humanity. Grant that we may know you as you really are, in your Son, crucified for us, in his death, in his agony and in his resurrection.

AMEN.

1

THE CLIMATE OF PRAYER

Prayer of being

I am always uneasy and hesistant when it comes to speaking about prayer. I feel that prayer is one of those subjcts about which one cannot speak: exhortation, invitation and advice are possible; prayer is such a personal and intimate reality, so much part of what we are, that merely speaking about it together becomes difficult unless the Lord creates for us an atmosphere for prayer.

Let me then begin with a prayer:

> Lord, you are aware that I do not know how to pray. How then can I speak to others about prayer? How can I teach them anything about prayer. You alone, O Lord, know how to pray. You prayed on the mountain in the night. You prayed on the plains of Palestine. You prayed in the garden of your agony. You prayed on the cross. You alone, Lord, are the teacher of prayer. And you have given each of us the Holy Spirit as our personal teacher. Trusting in you alone, Lord and Teacher, Adorer of the Father in spirit and in truth, with confidence in the Spirit who lives in us, we hope to encourage one another to exchange your gifts to us.
>
> Prayer makes it possible for us to speak with you, Lord Jesus, Our Saviour, to speak with your Father and the Spirit, to speak in simplicity and truth. Mother Mary, teacher of prayer, help, guide, and enlighten us on the road that you have walked before us in knowing God the Father and his will.

What can I say to you this evening on our theme of prayer? I had thought of a number of starting points and in particular of two short fundamental theological premises which I wish to recall. I will then endeavour to respond to a concrete question: how do we help ourselves and others to rekindle the spark of prayer in our hearts? The spark is the work of God but we must nourish it carefully.

a) My first premise is taken from Psalm 8. Prayer is an extremely simple reality. It springs from the mouth and the heart of the child. It is the immediate reaction of our heart when we are confronted with the truth of existence.

> How great is your name, O Lord our God,
> through all the earth!

> Your majesty is praised above the heavens;
> on the lips of children and of babes
> you have found praise to foil your enemy,
> to silence the foe and the rebel.

> When I see the heavens, the work of your hands,
> the moon and the stars which you arranged,
> what is man that you should keep him in mind,
> mortal man that you care for him?

> Yet you have made him little less than a god;
> with glory and honour you crowned him,
> gave him power over the works of your hand,
> put all things under his feet.

> All of them, sheep and cattle,
> yes, even the savage beasts,
> birds of the air, and fish
> that make their way through the waters.

> How great is your name, O Lord our God,
> through all the earth!

This happens in many ways, perhaps in different ways, for each individual. It may well be a walk in the mountains, a moment of quiet rest in the forest, a piece of music that distracts us from the harshness of reality, that takes us out of ourselves.

16

These are instances of the truth of existence, privileged moments in which we are liberated from the hustle of niggling interferences and from the continuous slavery of routine. We breathe more deeply. We feel something moving within us and then, in these moments of natural grace, in these happy moments of self-fulfilment it is easy, not to say almost instinctive to raise our voices in prayer: 'O thanks be to God', 'O Lord how great you are'.

Each one of us has, I believe, some experience of these privileged moments. Perhaps through a series of happy circumstances we have found ourselves praising God from the depths of our being: this is natural prayer, the prayer of existence.

All our prayer, all our education for prayer springs from this principle: Anyone who authentically lives through his various experiences feels the immediate and instinctive need to express himself in a prayer of praise, of thanksgiving of offering.

b) Above and beyond this truth, which is the prayer of existence, there is that other level: the prayer of *Christian* existence. It is not merely my response to the reality of being which surrounds me. Nor again is it a response to the feeling of authenticity which I sense within myself. It is rather the Spirit who prays in me.

The basic text to which we refer is the second part of chapter 8 of the Letter to the Romans (8:14-27): the Spirit prays in us. These two truths must be borne in mind. 'From the mouths of babes and sucklings you have brought praise.' Prayer is then a very simple reality, which arises, given the proper circumstances, when a person, even a youth, child or adolescent, is faced with the reality of being, the truth of existence, especially in conditions of peace and calm and serenity. But another truth follows: as Christians it is not we who pray, it is the Spirit who prays in us.

Education for prayer, therefore, lies either in our effort to maximise those conditions which favour the experience of authenticity or in looking within ourselves for the voice of the Spirit who prays, so that we can give him room and articulate his prayer.

Without this premise there is no Christian prayer, it is the Spirit within us who prays. This is the most central and typical characteristic of Christian prayer. I remember Fr Mollat, one of our greatest exegetes of St John, posing the question as to what was the characteristic of Christian prayer that differentiates it from the prayer of all other religions and indeed from all the natural prayers of which man is capable. His answer was the one found in the fourth chapter of St John's Gospel — 'prayer in spirit and in truth'. In the language of St John 'truth' signifies God the Father who reveals himself in Jesus Christ. This is the very nub of what differentiates Christian prayer from the prayer of all other religions, be they ever so sublime. We can learn a great deal from the prayer of other religions, we can discover so much that is valuable in our effort to come closer to God. However, what remains specific to Christian prayer is that it is a direct gift from God, who sends us his Spirit who enables us to pray in truth, the truth which is God's revelation of himself in Jesus.

This is actualised in the liturgy when we conclude every prayer with the formula 'through Christ Our Lord in the unity of the Holy Spirit'.

This is the prayer to which we have to be educated. We would have failed in this task if we were to limit our efforts to stimulating sentiments of praise, admiration, thanksgiving and petition, and did not bring these sentiments into the rhythm of the Spirit who prays in us.

The question 'How can I help you to pray?' now becomes more specific: 'How can I help to discover in us the movements of the Spirit who guides us?' 'How can I help to discern the movements of the Spirit of Christ who is within us, the Spirit who is the great source of all our prayer?'

I now come to a few more specific questions that each person can measure against their own experience and then refine and adapt them. The suggestions which I offer have to do with three attitudes:

1. The conditions of prayer as preliminary conditions.

2. Entrance to prayer as the moment of entry into prayer.
3. The rhythm of prayer as the rhythm of permanence in prayer.

Conditions for prayer

It is important that we start from the following fact: each one of us has a personal, unrepeatable condition for prayer. It is unrepeatable not merely because it is 'mine' as a person different from others but also because it is 'mine' at this moment and therefore unrepeatable in time. This is true even though each of us may have particular prayer forms which are notably personal.

The question is: How do I recognise my particular condition, that state which for me is most conducive to prayer? How do I bring about this condition, cause this state to emerge?

Firstly, some negative remarks. Let us ask ourselves what this state or condition is *not*. It is not a state that is induced by other people's prayers, by various prayer models, by books on prayer. All of these are excellent — the books, prayers learned from others and repeated, the lives of saints that allow us to share their experience. The problem is that these may raise our enthusiasm, but only momentarily. We read the wonderful pages of Teresa of Avila, of John of the Cross, and we feel the need to become part of the rhythm of their prayer, to share their experience. For one, two, or even three days a week, we seem to live off these lights. A prayer from St Augustine, an extract from his Confessions, a few splendid pages of Madeleine Delbrêl are capable of creating in us a certain affective and emotional empathy. This is excellent and is all part of the process of education, but does not lead us to the discovery of our own personal state or condition for prayer. It could even be illusory; we might be led to believe that we had already acquired who knows what capacity to pray.

But then the effects of this reading of these words and of other people's prayers vanish and we are left with our original poverty and our own aridity. Thus they are models, indicators of shared experience; they are not sufficient or of much use in enabling us to discover our own personal actual condition for prayer. In a positive way, then, how are we to find our condition for prayer, our starting point?

I give three brief suggestions.

My condition for prayer requires:

    a) A position of the body;
    b) An invocation from the heart;
    c) A page of scripture which I can take as a model.

a) My condition for prayer requires a position of the body

What I am about to say may appear a little idealistic and is in any case difficult to put into practice, but it may at least serve as a point of reference. We ought to try this experiment: Let ourselves 'go' for a while and thus, totally relaxed, ask ourselves: if now, at this moment, I were really to express what I feel and desire most profoundly, what bodily attitude would I assure in order to give expression to my prayer?

We should then see if some attitude suggests itself. It may be the *orans* position, the arms raised aloft or the hands joined in invocation; it might be the position of prayer so beloved of the orientals, forehead on the ground or, indeed, that of Jesus in the Garden on his knees with his face on the earth; the hands may be outstretched in the welcoming gesture of one who stands afar and waits like the father for the return of the prodigal son, the attitude of one who expects or asks for something.

These are simple things, and they might seem foolish if we did them publicly; however, this is how we express ourselves; our gestures are part of our expression. And, as Jesus says, when in silence we close the door of our room, and we pray to the Father in secret *(Mt 6:6)* then we should from time to time express ourselves more freely: we can fall on our knees with our foreheads on the ground, we can raise our arms spontaneously or open them like one who is waiting to receive, or we might adopt an attitude of submission. In any case it is important that precisely through the experience of our own body we should lay bare our deepest desires.

20

b) My condition for prayer is a cry from the heart

We should try asking ourselves this question: If I had to cry out at this moment, and give expression before God of my deepest need, of what is closest to my heart, how would I express myself? Let whatever comes, come freely; It might be the invocation 'Lord, have mercy on me' or indeed 'Lord, I can't go on anymore'; 'Lord, I praise you'; 'Lord, I give you thanks'; 'Lord, come to my aid'; 'Lord, I am finished'.

Jesus, too, at a crucial moment in his life cried out: 'My soul is sorrowful into death' and again: 'Father, I give you thanks for you always hear me'.

Among these invocations from the heart we should look for the one that corresponds best with what we feel, one that can act as the starting point for our prayer, one that best suits our actual situation. Of course this invocation can be enriched by other people's prayers; it can be helped to grow in depth through the inspiration of others who have prayed before me and perhaps better than I. My particular invocation may appear poor and very simple; it is a blade of grass, perhaps a tiny one when compared with the majestic trees of prayer of the saints. But what I am placing before God is my blade of grass, my very simple prayer.

Jesus reminds us of the words of the publican in the Temple: 'Lord, have mercy on me a sinner'. There is a man, who had authentically discovered his condition for prayer, and returned to his house justified. One short phrase was enough to lay bare his soul. It was then a cry from the heart.

c) My condition for prayer is a page from scripture in which I find an echo

Let us ask ourselves this question: if I really want to express what I feel, what to ask from God, what I would like to ask him for; if I were really to describe my situation in his presence — with what person or figure in the Gospel would I identify? In what Gospel scene would I place myself? Would I be like Peter who, after his initial courageous act of jumping into the water, cried out: 'Lord, I cannot do it'? Might I mingle with the Apostles faced by the crowd who asked them for bread: 'O Lord, where shall we go, what shall we do'? Or again perhaps I might find a reflection, an echo in some other scene from the Gospel or in the words of a Psalm that gives voice to my state of mind.

It is very important to find and indeed to educate others to find these starting points. We can work on these points and starting from them we can develop dispositions for prayer and an authentic attitude of dialogue with God. This dialogue is not based on an artificially induced state but on the intimate truth of the person.

Entrance to prayer

It is in this area, perhaps, that mistakes are made most readily. We are often led to believe that it is important to begin in some way or other. A quick sign of the cross. That's how it's done. . . . This gets things underway, brings about a little order. It is a great mistake to think that we can thus initiate dialogue with God; it means plunging imprudently into the adventure of prayer without due preparation.

This is, perhaps, one of the main causes of experiencing difficulty in prayer: we have not gone through the proper entrance. Just as in our churches there is an entrance atrium, so also in prayer, particularly in prolonged prayer, we need a special preparatory phase, a moment of absolute silence.

We ought to help even today's youngsters to observe a moment of absolute silence as a starting point for prayer. I would add that something more is necessary: I would call this entrance phase the return to zero: the imagination, our very being, are brought to zero, in the same way as an odometer is set at zero at the beginning of a journey.

What do we mean by this? In my view it is extremely important that we begin to pray not only by observing a moment of silence, of rest, of pause, but also by clearly recognising that we are not able to pray. 'O Lord, it is you who pray in me; I do not know where to begin; it is your Spirit that will guide me'.

All presuppositions, everything we feel that we have learned and possess, all these must go on entering into dialogue with

God. We must enter into prayer poor, stripped of our possessions. When we come before God we must always be absolutely poor. If we do not observe this our prayer suffers, it becomes heavy and burdensome, laden down with elements that interefere with it.

We must come before God genuinely poor, naked, without any pretensions. 'O Lord, I am not able to pray, and if you allow me to remain in your presence avid and waiting, very well, but let me be grateful for the waiting, for you are beyond my comprehension. You are the Immense, the Infinite, the Eternal; how then can I speak with you?' This is what emerges in many Psalms, those authentic models of prayer which, of course, we have afterwards to make our own.

Let us therefore begin our prayer with a 'zeroing' of ourselves. We can manifest this internal state in many ways; a moment of silence, of adoration on our knees; a moment of reverence and exterior respect — kneeling adoration — all indicating that we are entering a situation in which we have nothing to bring and everything to receive.

I enter into a dialogue in which the word enriches me in my poverty. I enter as a sick person who needs a doctor, as a sinner who needs to be justified, a poor man who needs enrichment; 'The rich he sent empty away, the thrones of the mighty he overturned' (this refers also to those mighty ones who believe that they know how to pray, that they have achieved that capacity).

We should make the plea of the blind man our own: 'O Lord, that I may see'. May I be able to understand, may I be enabled to pronounce the words that the Spirit suggests to me.

The rhythm of prayer

Prayer, like life, has its own rhythm. Prayer is sustained by this rhythm and can be prolonged without provoking tiredness. We have numerous and extraordinary examples of young people who continue to pray for hours. Years ago we would not have thought such a thing possible. But the evidence is there for all to see. It is a marvel worked by God.

These people have found the correct rhythm. Just as in

walking, once you find the right pace, you can go on for miles without getting tired, so in prayer it is vitally important to find the correct physical, psychic and interior rhythm. What is this rhythm? Our basic rhythm, our own interior musical beat as it were, is that of breathing. This is the fundamental rhythm of life, the basic beat of existence.

For this very reason the monastic tradition of the Greek church and, to a greater extent, the Yoga and Buddhist traditions in the East have laid great emphasis on breathing techniques. They have pushed technique to the point of being able consciously to control their breathing rhythms. Though this may appear complicated it does have positive aspects.

I would underline this point. The 'Jesus Prayer' is the oriental form of prayer which is closest to the Christian tradition and therefore the easiest for us to assimilate. This prayer (see *The Way of a Pilgrim* and similar texts) consists of an invocation repeated slowly on the same rhythm as breathing. The invocation itself is extremely rich in meaning. 'Jesus Christ, Son of God, have mercy on me'.

According to the teaching of the oriental monastic tradition this invocation should pass from the head to the heart, enter into the rhythm of breathing and enter into and pervade the entire person. We Westerners tend at times to have a mechanical approach to this experience; We adopt more the external forms, which can lead to exaggeration or deviation. This could lead to exaggeratedly curious results. It therefore goes without saying that people have to adapt this kind of prayer to their own needs.

In any case a 'breathing pattern' for prayer does exist. It is a rhythm which, once acquired, stays with us, allows us to persevere joyfully and with interior satisfaction, in our dialogue with God; it fills the heart and brings us to face the truth of our inner selves.

Another very simple technique is that of the rosary. The rosary is a slightly more complicated western version of the oriental technique of repetition.

It began in Italy in the Middle Ages and has now become very widespread. It is not, however, an easy prayer. From my own experience as a child and adolescent I seem to recall a feeling of boredom and distraction, having the impression that prayer was imposed from the outside. The rosary was not explained and therefore it was difficult. It is, in fact, a prayer that requires a certain calm, a certain relaxation; it requires a certain rhythm that allows us to enter into a real state of prayer instead of a mere recitation of the words.

For those who may find difficulty in praying the rosary, or who may have abandoned it and are afraid to take it up again, I would offer what may appear to be very simple advice. Nevertheless, I feel it may help in the rediscovery of this prayer.

The rosary can, if we have a little time at our disposal, offer the same advantages as the Jesus Prayer referred to above. By limiting the prayer to the recital of a few words repeated and pondered in our hearts, we are indeed very close to the model of prayer which the orientals call the 'Jesus Prayer'.

When I want to enter this atmosphere of prayer I select an invocation from the rosary and repeat it slowly a number of times. An example might be in the first decade. I would simply repeat 'Holy Mary, pray for us'. These very simple words, repeated slowly ten times, while much shorter than the complete recitation, gradually penetrate our being and thus dispose us to longer and fuller prayer. There are many ways in which we can draw ourselves into prolonged prayer. We should not concentrate on quantity but on a true rhythm which nourishes our spirit and penetrates our being.

We could make many other remarks on the rhythm of prayer. Basically, it is this rhythm which governs the structure of the Psalms. The poetic technique used in the Psalms is known as parallelism. It can be antithetic parallelism — something is affirmed in the first part of a verse and its opposite is stated in the second part; or again it can be synthetic parallelism — the first part affirms something and the second restates another aspect of the same reality. This 'going and coming' corresponds to the rhythm of breathing, to the rhythm of alternating choirs, to the rhythm of call and response. By entering into this reality we get a better understanding of many things presented to us in the

Scriptures. It is only very gradually that we come to have deep insights into humanity and the authentic reality of the human person which emerges from different forms of prayer.

A final word of clarification. It might appear that learning to pray is equivalent to a patient mastering of a certain number of techniques. It might appear to depend on the acquisition of self-control, of a certain calm, of a way of breathing, of some greater powers of penetration. This indeed is the aim of Yoga techniques — the acquisition of greater self-control by individuals.

If we were to believe this to be the aim of prayer then we would indeed be very seriously mistaken about Christian prayer. The aim of Christian prayer is not self-control or self-possession, even though prayer does bring about a more authentic self-awareness, a more balanced, rounded, reflective person and promotes attentiveness and far-sightedness. These qualities are the fruit of an education in prayer. Without doubt the person who prays gets things in perspective and tends to make more mature judgments. But all this is not the aim of prayer and if we were to make it the aim we would have completely distorted the meaning of education in prayer.

What, therefore, is the peak and the meaning of Christian prayer? It is given to us by Jesus in the midst of his agony: 'Father, not my will but thine be done', or again when hanging on the Cross: 'Father, into thy hands I commend my Spirit'. This is the peak of prayer.

Any education in prayer that does not achieve this peak or at least tend towards it, any education that does not lead people to place themselves with faith and love in God's hands, at some stage, leads to illusion and straightaway is a cause of religious deviation. It is not enough to counsel people to pray a lot. A person could in fact spend a lot of time at prayer and yet be religiously deviant with a distorted sense of values. Prayer, like all human realities, is exposed to the risk of distortion and deviation. In fact there are no human realities which we cannot spoil through our egoism. Prayer too has a human ambiguity.

We cannot afford to forget the aim of Christian prayer: it is that each one of us, like Jesus in the garden of Gethsemane, might be able to put our lives in God's hands: 'Here is my life, it is in your hands'.

It is only then that prayer reveals what we really are — beings who have their origin in God and whose destiny is to find our real selves by placing ourselves, through the gift of faith, in the hands of our Father.

Prayer becomes the expression of perfect faith, the total handing over of my life to God. Abraham is an example of perfect prayer. On hearing the voice of God he left his home country. Even if we have no idea what particular prayer he may have said, we do know that he courageously handed himself over at the voice of God and followed the call that was given to him.

Because this is the summit of prayer my pastoral letter insists on the relationships between prayer and the Eucharist. It is in the Eucharist that Christ hands himself to the Father for us and it is in the Eucharist that we are invited to become part of this great movement of self-giving by entering into and sharing in the gift of Christ himself.

Each one of our prayers then becomes preparation for, and a lived actualisation of, the Eucharist. Authentic prayer puts each one of us at the service of others. The giving over of our lives to God is not accomplished in the abstract, as it were, by alienating us from the world. On the contrary it means giving our lives to God so that he may make us fitting instruments for the service of our brothers and sisters. This is the culmination of Christian prayer: education for service, for being totally at the disposal of others, for putting ourselves unconditionally at the service of our brothers and sisters.

Unconditionally, because God who is absolute and unconditioned, has called us to be givers without condition and, in revealing himself to us, has transformed our lives. Here we have the basic of not only the relationship between prayer and the Eucharist but also the relationship between prayer and life.

The touchstone of authenticity of prayer is not a turning in on ourselves or the quest for personal gratification but is rather, our openly and clearly putting our lives at the disposal of all those who need us, of those who are suffering, the very poor and the most needy. We, as it were, achieve self-possession with a view to putting ourselves at the service of others.

This is the kind of prayer in which we wish to engage and in which I, with your help, also wish to engage: my desire is to be evermore at the service of others.

2

PRAYING WITH SAINT LUKE

1. MARY'S PRAYER *(Luke 1:39-56)*

In those days Mary arose and went with haste into the hill country, to a city of Judah, and she entered the house of Zachariah and greeted Elizabeth. And when Elizabeth heard the greeting of Mary, the babe leaped in her womb; and Elizabeth was filled with the Holy Spirit and she exclaimed with a loud cry, 'Blessed are you among women, and blessed is the fruit of your womb! And why is this granted to me that the mother of my Lord should come to me? For behold, when the voice of your greeting came to my ears, the babe in my womb leaped for joy. And blessed is she who believed that there would be a fulfilment of what was spoken to her from the Lord'.

And Mary said
'My soul magnifies the Lord,
and my spirit rejoices in God my Saviour
For he has regarded the low estate of his handmaiden.
For behold, henceforth all generations will call me blessed;
for he who is mighty has done great things for me.
and holy is his name.
And his mercy is on those who fear him
from generation to generation.
He has shown strength with his arm,
he has scattered the proud in the
imagination of their hearts,
he has put down the mighty from their thrones,
and exalted those of low degree;
he has filled the hungry with good things,
and the rich he has sent empty away.

He has helped his servant Israel,
in remembrance of his mercy,
as he spoke to our fathers,
to Abraham and to his posterity for ever'.

And Mary remained with her about three months, and returned to
her home.

The episode of the Visitation, followed by the Magnificat, will
be where we stop first in order to learn how Mary prayed. I would
like to reflect on it with the same spirit as that shown by a
contemporary poet:

With what voice you sang, O Mary,
The ancient Psalms
Appeared to shine
With light anew
The hills are melted
And all the poor
Do praise you still.

And I would like to pray: 'O Lord, who through the gift of your
Spirit have inspired Mary with this prayer of praise and
thanksgiving, grant to us and to all the poor of this world who
still listen to and resonate with this prayer, that we may be able
to repeat it with that affection and fullness of joy and praise with
which Mary your mother first sang it'.

Annunciations of life
In the first instance let us try to understand the meaning of the
whole episode which acts as a context for the Magnificat. The
episode is placed between two annunciations and two accounts
of births: the annunciation to Zechariah and the annunciation
to Mary which occupy the main part of chapter 1 of Luke; the
accounts of the birth of John and of Jesus from the latter part
of chapter 1, and chapter 2.

Almost as an interlude between these annunciations and
accounts of births we find the episode of the visitation and the

Magnificat which allows us to enter into the mystery of Mary's human psychology; the episode leads us to an understanding of what happened in Mary, the emotions she felt after her sudden and unforeseen involvement in God's plan through the recent extraordinary event in her life.

Joy and bewilderment

How did Mary live through these events, what happened to her? After the annunciation by the Angel Mary is one to whom a great secret was confided: it changed her life; it involved her profoundly; it would lead her to an experience utterly different from anything she could have imagined. She carried this secret in her heart and could not share it with anyone.

It is certainly a joyful secret capable of filling her with happiness, but at the same time it is tinged with sorrow and bewilderment.

Matthew's Gospel gives us a hint of how this annunciation weighed on her: how would she explain to Joseph, her husband, what had happened? How would she make it credible? How would she make understood the mystery of God which had been manifested in her? Mary found herself in one of those peculiar situations; she had within her a great secret, at one and the same time a source of joy and anxiety; she would like to talk about it, make herself understood, but she does not know how or to whom. In this solitude, thoughtful and pained, she takes the road to Judaea to help Elizabeth.

We are all familiar with this type of situation. We find ourselves burdened with knowledge of something without, however, the consolation of having someone to talk to about it. We have no confidence that anybody else might be able to understand our own intimate joy or sorrow.

Friendship with Elizabeth

Mary makes her way to the mountain country of Judaea and on entering Zechariah's house greets Elizabeth. 'And when Elizabeth heard the greeting of Mary, the babe leaped in her womb. Elizabeth was filled with the Holy Spirit and she exclaimed with a loud cry, "Blessed are you among women, and blessed is the fruit of your womb!" ' Suddenly, without any need for words, Mary feels that her situation is understood: she senses that her secret has been grasped, that another person, with the help of the Holy Spirit, has understood what has happened to her: the mystery of God has been finally understood by others, understood with love, tenderness and trust. She feels welcomed and profoundly understood and gives free rein to all those emotions which up to that moment were pent up inside her. Now that another person has divined her secret, Mary experiences a sense of inner freedom and so speaks out what she has hitherto kept within her. The warmth of a genuine friendship and the understanding of a sympathetic heart enable her to give expression to her feelings. And so her hymn bursts forth, the fruit of her long meditation during her journey (to Judaea).

It is hard to overestimate the value of a friendship in which we are understood, helped to unwind, one which allows us to open up and speak out what has been bottled up within us, good and perhaps bad. All that matters is that we speak and share.

Full of joy Mary expresses herself in singing and rejoices.

A hymn of joy
The first thing we notice in a careful reading of Mary's hymn is that it begins with the subject 'I' — my soul, my spirit. At the beginning she is at the centre — it is her experience, her joy, her emotional outburst. But immediately the subject changes: My spirit rejoices in *God,* because he (and from here on the subject is God). . .

    . . . for he has regarded the low estate . . .
    he has done great things . . .
    his mercy is on those . . .
    he has shown strength . . .
    he has scattered the proud . . .
    he has put down the mighty . . .
    he has exalted those of low degree
    he has filled the hungry with good things . . .

the rich he has sent empty away . . .
He has helped his servant Israel.

The structure of the hymn begins with a personal experience. Mary speaks out what she feels inside her — I magnify God, I rejoice — only to switch immediately to a description of what God does. There is perfect fusion between the personal, the subjective, the immediate experience of the person who prays, and the contemplation of God's plan in which the person is inserted. Later on in the hymn Mary speaks of herself again: he has done great things for me. . . he has shown strength. . . he has scattered the proud. . . but now she sees herself within the plan of God, caught up in the great mystery into which she has entered.

Contemplating God in the world
Let us ask ourselves if we would be able to repeat Mary's statements. Might we not be tempted, on looking at what is happening around us, to succumb to scepticism and desperation and state rather the exact opposite. Might we not say that the proud prevail, the mighty domineer over us from their thrones, the meek are trodden underfoot, the hungry grow more numerous, their hunger more desperate, and the rich grow ever richer. What we call the realism of the facts becomes overturned in Mary's contemplation of the plan of God.

Is Mary describing what is merely an ideal or are we failing to grasp all the dmensions of reality? In a certain sense both are true. In fact some of the Psalms, unlike the Magnificat, tell us that truth has disappeared, that everyone lies and exploits his or her neighbour. These Psalms express realistic conclusions on the misery and suffering of the world but they are the opposite of Mary's description.

The fact is that Mary looks at history from the standpoint of hope. Her perspective is that of the Kingdom and in a humanity swamped in a sea of suffering and injustice she contemplates the coming of God who even now is transforming our miserable human existence.

We ask ourselves then, how can Mary carry out this prophetic action? On what does she base her courageous contemplation of history in which emerge signs of the Kingdom, and signs of hope which give meaning to a suffering humanity about to be transformed, indeed upended, by the arrival of the same Kingdom?

Personal experience

Mary can take this stance because she has tasted salvation. She has experienced Yahweh as Saviour of her life. In one dizzy instant Yahweh has transformed her, raised her to a new level of existence, capable of new heights of hope and love and of a new relationship with God and man.

'God my Saviour': From this standpoint, this experience of salvation, Mary can look in a new way on her surroundings and on history. Mary looks over the entire history of Israel, she sees the marvels that God has performed for the salvation of his people and in this vista she reads what Vatican II calls 'the signs of the time', signs of hope, signs of the Gospel, everything anticipating the Kingdom of God, emerge from the experience of her own life.

We cannot know the God of the Gospel unless we have experienced salvation. The Virgin Mary has this experience; she knew the God of the Gospel; she can proclaim God and look at the world's history from the standpoint of humanity.

Our Magnificat

Here then is the prayer which this page of the Gospel suggests: 'Since you, O Lord, are the God of my Salvation, how can I sing the hymn of my personal Magnificat? What personal experience of salvation reveals you to me as the great God, the God of the Gospel, who changes my life, charges me with hope, makes me capable of seeing reality in the light of the Kingdom, and puts me firmly on the side of justice, of the humble, of the poor?

Singing the hymn of Mary, shall I join those who are still listening for it?

The ancient Psalms
Appeared to shine
With light anew
The hills are melted
And all the poor
Do praise you still.

Placing ourselves before Mary's prayer let us ask ourselves what could our Magnificat be? What words will we use? To what events will we allude? What marvels has the Lord prformed for us that give us grounds for praising him?

Each one of us should take courage and open our heart to discover the high points of God's intervention in our lives. Let us think of the love and the good things bestowed on us by others, those encounters that have filled us with joy and faith, from our Baptism right up to this very evening during which we have met the God of our salvation together. This is the God who saves us, the God who sends the rich away empty and has filled the hungry with good things. First of all we are the poor and hungry ones, but there are so many others who await him.

Let us ask ourselves: from what pain or secret joys has our meeting with God and with others freed us? What splendid realities will become apparent in our lives if we take the side of hope and of the Kingdom? What would God ask of us if we take the side of the poor?

2. THE PRAYER OF SIMEON *(Luke 2:25-35)*

Now there was a man in Jerusalem, whose name was Simeon, and this man was righteous and devout, looking for the consolation of Israel, and the Holy Spirit was upon him. And it had been revealed to him by the Holy Spirit that he should not see death before he had seen the Lord's Christ. And inspired by the Spirit he came into the temple; and when the parents brought in the child Jesus, to do for him according to the custom of the law, he took him up in his arms and blessed God and said:

> *'Lord, now lettest thou thy servant depart in peace*
> *according to thy word;*
> *for mine eyes have seen thy salvation*
> *which thou has prepared in the presence of all peoples,*
> *a light for revelation to the Gentiles,*
> *and for glory to thy people Israel.'*

And his father and his mother marvelled at what was said about him; and Simeon blessed them and said to Mary his mother:

> *'Behold this child is set for the fall*
> *and rising for many in Israel,*
> *and for a sign that is spoken against*
> *(and a sword will pierce through your own soul also),*
> *that thoughts out of many hearts may be revealed'.*

'Lord, now lettest thy servant depart in peace according to thy word; for mine eyes have seen thy salvation which thou hast prepared in the presence of all peoples, a light for revelation to the Gentiles, and for glory to thy people, Israel.'

This prayer begins with the word with which our reading began *now,* at this moment: what we are living and experiencing *now* is the starting point for all all our prayers. This short opening word of Simeon's prayer — *now* — in the Bible means the instant of one's life in which God manifests himself. Now, at this moment God wishes to manifest himself in our lives in spite of all, indeed through the very opaqueness that furrows our experience.

Simeon starts from his present experience, from what he is now living.

An old man and a baby

In the first place let us underline the sheer humanity of this meeting. The old man holds the child in his arms — the torch of life somehow spanning two generations. Holding this child in his arms, the old man knows that it is his own future which he holds. He is happy that in his own arms he embraces the continuity of his own life. He has hoped, he has believed and now his hope, in the shape of a baby, is here, full of vitality and future promise.

There is something profoundly human in this scene. The old man rejoices that others will continue his work; he is happy that in his own decline there is indeed a reawakening, a rebirth, a future that is opening up.

If we were to take only this much from the reading it would be in itself an important lesson for life. It is not easy for the old man that is in each one of us to welcome the new, to take the baby in our arms. There is always the fear that the baby will not survive, that he will not share the same ideals, that he will betray our ideals and in so doing put us aside and take our place.

The old man Simeon, holding the baby, is a marvellous sight, for he represents each one of us brought face to face with the 'newness' of God. This 'newness' of God is like a baby and we, with our old ways of doing things, our fears, our jealousies, our preoccupations, are brought face to face with the 'newness' of God. Will we hold the baby in our arms, welcome him, make room for him in our lives? Will this 'newness' really enter into our lives or will we try to put the old and the new together hoping that the newness of God will cause us minimum disturbance.

This then, is our first prayer: 'O Lord, grant that I may welcome you as the New One into my life, that I may not be afraid of you, that I may not try to fit you into my scheme of things, that I may not imprison you in my own mental attitudes, that I may be transformed by the newness of your presence. Grant Lord that, like Simeon, I may welcome you in your newness, in all that is true, new and good around me. May I welcome you in all the babies of this world, in every life, in every germ and newness with which you surround me, in society, in my heart.'

A message of personal salvation

If we repeat and let the words of Simeon echo within us we will become aware of what they are. These are the key words of the experience of salvation: peace, the Word of God, salvation, light, glory, Israel and the peoples of the world. In three lines we have a compendium of biblical theology.

These key words are found in numerous passages of the Bible. For example, in chapter 10 of the Acts of the Apostles when Peter speaks in the house of Cornelius: 'Truly I perceive that God shows no partiality, but in every nation any one who fears him and does what is right is acceptable to him. You know the word which he sent to Israel, preaching the good news of peace by Jesus Christ — he is Lord of All'. (*Ac 10:34-36*)

The word of God, peace, the good news of salvation, the universality of salvation and, in the background, Israel. We could reflect prayerfully on each of these elements. I will dwell for a moment on the last one: the opposition which in reality is complementarity between Israel and all peoples.

Divine salvation, which is brought to us through this Word and which brings peace, comes through his people whose glory is God's word, and then it becomes a light for all the nations. According to God's mysterious plan, his word which brings peace and salvation passes through the few but is destined for many. It passes through the mystery of election or choice through which a few are called on behalf of 'others', a few are consecrated so that they become a light for 'others'.

40

This is the mystery which we are sharing together this evening. We have come here, called to deepen our experience of prayer, not for ourselves, but as a group on behalf of all peoples. The experience of God which is granted to us ought to serve to illuminate all those with whom we come in contact. We are at the service of all those whom we shall meet tomorrow and during the coming days, placing at their disposal our experience and in particular our experience of overcoming difficulties through the mediation of the Word of God.

'Glory of your people Israel and a light to illuminate all the Gentiles!' This comes from the word of God and from that salvation which is in Jesus and which is communicated to us as the common heritage of all.

Eyes that know how to read

The structure of Simeon's prayer is very simple. There is an imperative, 'lettest thou thy servant depart in peace'; then a series of reasons, 'for mine eyes have seen the salvation, prepared in the presence of all the people, and for the Gentiles, and the glory of Israel'.

This presupposes strong interior tensions, a life lived in suffering. It indicates a man of faith, who has eked out his existence in justice and in fear of the Lord, living according to the Law, but never seeing the object of his hope.

Now he can pray as he does because for many years he has desired the glory of his people. He had seen his people humiliated, afflicted and oppressed and yet he hoped. He awaited the light that would illuminate all the nations as promised by Isaiah and meanwhile the nations trod Israel underfoot. He had seen the cruelty, the atrocities of the nations and he was torn between sorrow and hope.

Now he sees! This is the unique experience that gives rise to his prayer.

Now he sees a child and he speaks of salvation. In the eyes of others his experience means nothing. But to him, enlightened by faith and the Holy Spirit, it means that he 'sees salvation'.

Simeon was granted that grace which in scripture is called

'the opening of the eyes' or the 'opening of the heart'. He was able to read in the simple event of the Child Jesus being brought to the Temple by Mary and Joseph, the presence of God's salvation being made manifest. His awaiting ends in peace. The light of the Gentiles has not yet been made manifest to the nations, the glory of Israel is not yet present, but in that mysterious sign Simeon sees salvation.

This prayer of praise and thanksgiving erupts: 'Lord, it is enough! I have seen all that I have desired and my heart is overflowing: all my desires have been fulfilled!' His long wait gives way to the contemplation of salvation.

Newness of life

Having seen how Simeon prayed and seen how his prayer came from his heart, let us ask ourselves how we might model our prayers on his example. Do we in our innermost heart await salvation, do we desire to see the glory of his people and the light of the Gentiles? O Lord, is my desire for you, for your glory, for the light of the nations, for justice, for truth, for peace, really so great that, like Simeon's desire, it tears me apart?

If we leave room for silence, I believe that from our hearts will spring a veritable shout filled with desire: 'Come Lord! Lord, enlighten, be the glory of your people! Lord, let us see your face, allow us to witness your justice and your truth in our midst'.

The grace of the opening of our eyes springs from this desire. 'Open my eyes, O Lord, so that I may know how to see the signs of your salvation in our midst. Grant that in my life, in my experience of the Church, and of my brothers and sisters, in my prayer, in the experience of the Eucharist and of the Holy Spirit who fills our hearts — in all these may I know how to see the sign of your salvation: this baby to be held in my arms, this newness welcomed into my life'.

'O Lord, grant that I may not close my eyes, saying this baby does not exist, this is no salvation, this is no newness. Open my eyes so that I may see and understand how your salvation is in our midst and that all I need to do is welcome it with open arms'.

What then does this mean for us, to open our eyes? What does it mean for me to overcome habits, banal and superficial judgments on persons and things and instead to discover the newness of God; to discover his truth and his joy, the power of the Love of God, to go beyond appearances and suffering, to go beyond all that can cloud the eyes and the vision?

Thus a prayer of contemplation and of thanksgiving will be born in our hearts and our very lives will be light and salvation for those who await it.

3. JESUS' PRAYER OF REJOICING *(Luke 10:1-24)*

After this the Lord appointed seventy others, and sent them on ahead of him, two by two, into every town and place where he himself was about to come. And he said to them, 'The harvest is plentiful, but the labourers are few; pray therefore the Lord of the harvest to send out labourers into his harvest. Go your way; behold, I send you out as lambs in the midst of wolves. Carry no purse, no bag, no sandals; and salute no one on the road. Whatever house you enter, first say "Peace be to this house"! And if a son of peace is there, your peace shall rest upon him; but if not, it shall return to you. And remain in the same house, eating and drinking what they provide, for the labourer deserves his wages; do not go from house to house. Whenever you enter a town and they receive you, eat what is set before you; heal the sick in it and say to them, "The Kingdom of God has come near to you". But whenever you enter a town and they do not receive you, go into its streets and say, "Even the dust of your town that clings to our feet, we wipe off against you; nevertheless know this, that the kingdom of God has come near". I tell you, it shall be more tolerable on that day for Sodom than for that town.

'Woe to you, Chorazin! woe to you Bethsaida! for if the mighty works done in you had been done in Tyre and Sidon, they would have repented long ago, sitting in sackcloth and ashes. But it shall be more tolerable in he judgment for Tyre and Sidon than for you. And you, Capernaum, will you be exalted to heaven? You shall be brought down to Hades.

He who hears you, hears me, and he who rejects you rejects me, and he who rejects me rejects him who sent me.'

The seventy returned with joy, saying, 'Lord even the demons are subject to us in your name'! And he said to them, 'I saw Satan fall like lightning from heaven. Behold I have given you authority to tread upon serpents and scorpions, and over all the power of the enemy; and nothing shall hurt you. Nevertheless do not rejoice in this, that the spirits are subject to you; but rejoice that your names are written in heaven'.

In that same hour he rejoiced in the Holy Spirit and said, 'I thank thee, Father, Lord of heaven and earth, that thou hast hidden these things from the wise and understanding and revealed them to babes: yea, Father for such was thy gracious will. All things have been delivered to me by my Father; and no one knows who the Son is except the Father, or who the Father is except the Son and any one to whom the Son chooses to reveal him'.

Then turning to the disciples he said privately, 'Blessed are the eyes which see what you see! For I tell you that many prophets and kings desired to see what you see, and did not see it, and to hear what you hear, and did not hear it'.

'In that same hour Jesus rejoiced in the Holy Spirit' (*Lk 10:21*). By prefixing 'that same hour' the evangelist connects Jesus rejoicing with the immediate context of the pericope. Matthew (*11:25*) dos not give any particular context. Luke begins the chapter with a missionary action; he then follows with an account of a charitable action, (the parable of the Samaritan) and ends with contemplative prayer. In this context then — mission, charity and the neighbour, Mary's contemplative prayer — Luke highlights the prayer of Jesus.

Rejoicing and joy
According to the text, this prayer is one of rejoicing: Jesus rejoiced. We have already found the same expression in other prayers which we have examined. In the Magnificat Mary says: 'My Spirit rejoices in God my Saviour' (*Lk 1:47*), repeating the canticle of Hannah. 'My heart rejoices in the Lord' (*1 Sam 2:1*). The same word occurs in another liturgical canticle which is well known, a hymn of thanksgiving for a city that has been spared and freed: 'I will greatly rejoice in the Lord. My soul shall exult in my God.' (*Isaiah 61:10*)

Before Jesus' time there are people and situations that give rise to this sentiment of rejoicing: the canticle of Hannah, the canticle of thanksgiving for Jerusalem, and Mary in the Magnificat.

Rejoicing takes place when one is faced with an unforeseen joyful event and, being transported out of oneself, is at the same time aware of a deep and intimate sense of joy. It is an interior emotion caused by an unexpected, surprising, pleasant event outside ourselves. A distant one returns unexpectedly and the reunion causes rejoicing and joy. We are awaiting bad news, are overcome with pessimism and suddenly we are told that all is well; we rejoice.

Let us try to understand the difference between the rejoicing of Hannah, Mary, Jerusalem and Jesus.

Mary rejoices because 'God has regarded the low estate of his handmaid': we are dealing with a reality that touches her directly and changes her life. *Hannah* rejoices because she who was sterile has given birth: in her case too her life has been changed unexpectedly and joyfully. The city of *Jerusalem* rejoices because 'God has clothed me with the garments of salvation': its situation has changed. Whoever prays and rejoices in this manner has experienced the power of God acting on his poverty, has felt the change from the depression and pessimism of a dead end to a new situation of openness, of a free heart and of bright horizons.

Creative joy

Our text has two words that do not appear in the parallel texts which we quoted. 'Jesus rejoiced in the *Holy Spirit*'. With this addition Luke underlines the trinitarian dimension and allows us to see the fullness of God's power which is revealed for our salvation. The Father is present, Lord of Heaven and earth, the Son, to whom all things are given and the Holy Spirit in whom Jesus rejoices.

We can say something more in order further to understand what the Evangelist means by 'Jesus rejoiced in the Holy Spirit'. It means that Jesus rejoices in his innermost being, in what is most profound in his unique relationship of love with the Father.

46

His joy springs from his inner self, from that fullness of the Holy Spirit which he alone enjoys. It does not depend on some event, some fact, some outer reality.

This rejoicing in the Holy Spirit is experienced by Jesus but we too can share that experience. It is an experience that is born within ourselves and is grounded in the presence of the Holy Spirit in us. A joy springs up in us that is not motivated by some random event even though when reading subsequent events in God's light the joy can be related to them. It is first of all the joy of really being ourselves because the Spirit within us manifests the Father's love and because the charity of God is poured out in our hearts.

Joy which is in the Holy Spirit is not tainted, is not false, is not reactive to something external. It is creative: it is born from what I am through the gift of God. It is communicable: born from within me I can communicate it in an original way to others and thus become for them, in turn, a source of joy. A new quality is brought to my life and to the lives of these around me, a new quality that is not brought about by circumstances, not disturbed by changes in humour, not subject to the ravages of tiredness and boredom for it comes froma spring created within me by the Spirit.

The Holy Spirit who is within us is the origin of that joy about which Jesus speaks, which nobody can take from us, the source of that peace which the world cannot give. This is the meaning of the mysterious saying of Jesus — 'It is more beautiful to give than to receive'. (*Ac 20:35* — Paul's discourse at Miletus). It is more beautiful to give joy than to receive it for in that giving we live out that profound creativity which is the result of the life of the Spirit in us.

Jesus rejoicing
'I thank thee Father, Lord of heaven and earth, that thou hast hidden these things from the wise and understanding and revealed them to babes.' The occasion is the success of the mission of the seventy disciples. Jesus' joy springs from his intimate participation in the life of the Father in the Holy Spirit and he

expresses it on the occasion of events that manifest the hand of God at work.

The disciples, in spite of their initial fear, not unlike the Hebrews before their entry to the Promised Land, find that their efforts have been successful. Their joy is a reactive one dependent on circumstances, in this case the success of their mission.

They returned full of joy, saying, 'Lord, even the demons are subject to us in your name' — nothing could resist us, we have seen that the power of your word overcomes the evils of the world: we are happy because of the success that has crowned our endeavours.

Jesus' reaction to this news is totally unexpected: a prayer of praise to God: 'I thank you Father because you have hidden these things from the wise and understanding and revealed them to babes'.

Jesus does not comment on the general positive outcome of what has happened: he presents it through polemic — wise men and children, hiding revelation and uncovering revelation.

The gift of the Kingdom
We shall reflect very carefully on these few words, because they are a compendium of the Gospel and of the mystery of the God of the Gospel who manifests himself in Jesus.

We find two sets of opposites: hide and reveal, the wise and children. Hide from the wise, reveal to children.

Jesus has already proclaimed: 'To you it is given to know the mystery' — or, better, the mysteries — 'of the Kingdom of God' (*Luke 8:10*). Thus the generic expression 'these things' should be understood as 'the mysteries of the Kingdom of God', not only the Kingdom, but also its mysteries; not only the Kingdom as the manifestation of God's love but also the Kingdom which is manifested in a way that to us is paradoxical and mysterious.

The paradoxical and mysterious manifestation is indicated by the contraries: revealed-hidden, wise men-children. The Kingdom is revealed, it is a gift and not the fruit of research. The Kingdom can also be subject to research, it can give rise to analysis, but it is never the fruit of research or the prize gained by analysis. It is a gift which God manifests and for which we must humbly ask: 'Lord, manifest your Kingdom; upon me, upon us may your mercy be manifested'.

Precisely because the Kingdom is revealed it can also be hidden from those whose eyes and hearts are closed. If we do not receive it as a gift or if we refuse it, the Kingdom remains hidden as does the whole salvific meaning of existence and of life, so that life itself becomes bitter. The request of the blind man at the entrance to Jerusalem is an adequate expression of what we mean. 'O Lord, grant that I may see', 'Lord, enlighten me, grant that your mystery may not be hidden from me.

The opposition between the Kingdom hidden or revealed underlines the free nature of the gift through which it is made known to us.

There is a further point. The opposition between wise men and children tells us that the mystery of the Kingdom is revealed to those who feel they need others and do not believe in their own self-sufficiency. The person who feels the need for other people is willing to receive a gift; those who believe in their own self-sufficiency hide behind what they think they know and do not receive the mystery. Once again we are reminded of the set of oppositions in Mary's prayer: 'you have sent the rich away empty; you have put down the mighty; you have filled the hungry with good things'.

Jesus' joy is not immediately based on the success of the mission of the seventy disciples. It is born of his contemplation of that success in so far as it manifests the hand of God wonderfully at work.

Welcome the gift
We can further ask why he insists on a polemic way of expressing the manifestation of God who hides from the wise and reveals to children? I think we will find the answer in prayer. The Lord will give us to understand that in these words we are being told something about the God of the Gospel. We should always endeavour to understand the God of the Gospel because we carry around the concept of the God of the philosophers or of reason.

49

We should leave room for the God of Jesus Christ who reveals himself in history and manifests himself in our lives.

The mystery of the God of Jesus Christ is one of communication, of sharing himself with us; it is a mystery of love which presupposes a capacity which knows how to receive. The Son of God is, in the first instance, the one who knows how to receive! 'All things have been given to me by my Father'. Jesus himself has received everything from the Father: the mystery of the human person lies in being open, little and conscious therefore of the need to know how to receive the gift of God.

Jesus' rejoicing in the Holy Spirit has its roots in an interior joy which becomes creative and so justifies the saying of Jesus that 'it is more beautiful to give than to receive'. In the Christian mystery all is based on knowing how to receive; both aspects are united in the experience of faith. It is a beautiful thing to give because in the first place we have received from God in abundance the gift of his Son and of the Holy Spirit; it is a beautiful thing to forgive for in the first instance we have been pardoned by the Father through the death and resurrection of Jesus; it is a beautiful thing to open ourselves to others for in the first instance God has opened himself to us and has communicated himself to us in Jesus Christ.

The event of salvation is the basis for all our attitudes about morality, humanity, communication and friendship. All this is expressed concisely by Jesus in his most simple prayer: 'I thank thee Father, Lord of heaven and earth, that thou hast hidden these things from the wise and understanding and revealed them to babes.'

Prayer of praise
Jesus prays with rejoicing and praise. He allows the creative joy that springs up in him to be seen. We too are invited to make room for the creative joy that springs up in us: it is to come forth despite the blockages of our ill humour, weariness, boredom or intolerance; it is the truth of our real selves — praise and rejoicing — that is to gush forth for the benefit of others. Jesus prays with

rejoicing and praise. Then, looking around, he rejoices and praises for others. Here we have a new element compared with the prayer of Mary or Hannah who praised for themselves.

Do we know how to give praise for others, rejoice for others; do we pray through contemplating the works of God as accomplished in others? There are some for whom it is easy to praise God since they represent high points in the work of God. It is easy in the case of saints of the past or indeed in the case of a Mother Teresa of Calcutta and her work or on hearing the testimony of some missionary.

We are, however, invited to be inventive in broadening our praise: we should rejoice in God for priests and religious sisters who have given us examples of faith, charity and service. We should praise God for our parents, for those who may be placed over us, for the friendships that are given to us and for all those poor and simple people who know and love God more than we do. We should praise God for those who serve him in silence and humility; for those who serve him publicly and solemnly; let us give praise for the Pope and for what the Lord achieves through him, for his apostolic endeavour throughout the world.

We should learn to praise the Lord for the many whom we have perhaps never considered in a good light but have only criticised. Let us open our hearts in praise for them and above all for those who work in the Church, like us, even better than ourselves but in a different fashion so that sometimes we do not agree on the ways and means of serving the Church.

If we learn to pray in this fashion with our lips and with our hearts, we need to be set free by God from all bitterness, disillusionment and resentment, from every desire to judge others; God must open our eyes so that in our midst we may see the work of salvation.

Prayer and forgiveness
A final reflection may help us to continue in silence our meditation on another part of the passage from Luke. The following cities are mentioned — Tyre, Sidon, Chorazin, Bethsaida, Capernaum — each of which is a symbol of a

civilisation, a lifestyle and a mentality. It is strange that the towns most stigmatised by Jesus are the little ones: Chorazin, Bethsaida and Capernaum, and not the bigger and more famous cities. Jesus uses a very fundamental criterion in judging — the degree of self-sufficiency and lack of openness to truth. Tyre and Sidon were certainly famous, problem-ridden and also dishonest, but compared with the smaller towns they were aware of their poverty and felt the need for help. The measure which Jesus proposes is not a rigorously moral judgment; it is an evangelical judgment which is valid for civilisations, cultures, peoples, groups and individuals. We are not asked for the number of the sins we have committed. Above all we are asked if we need help, if we are open to the gift of God, if we are willing to open our hearts to the words of love and pardon offered by the Kingdom.

Let us pray together so that each one of us may have this openness of mind, may bring it along with us so that it becomes a way of life, a mentality, a capacity to open our ears and our hearts to the message, to the Word of Jesus. Then indeed we will be able to rejoice because the word of the Gospel will have been heard by many.

4. JESUS' PRAYER IN GETHSEMANE *(Luke 22:39-46)*

And he came out, and went, as was his custom, to the Mount of Olives; and the disciples followed him. And when he came to the place he said to them, 'Pray that you may not enter into tempation' And he withdrew from them about a stone's throw, and knelt down and prayed, 'Father, if thou art willing, remove this cup from me; nevertheless not my will, but thine be done'. And there appeared to him an angel from heaven, strengthening him. And being in an agony he prayed more earnestly; and his sweat became like great drops of blood falling down upon the ground. And when he rose from prayer, he came to the disciples and found them sleeping for sorrow, and he said to them, 'Why do you sleep? Rise and pray that you may not enter into temptation'.

The verb 'to pray' occurs a number of times in this passage from Luke. 'Pray that you may not enter into tempation', 'Jesus, falling to his knees, prayed', 'and being in an agony, he prayed more earnestly', 'he rose from his prayer'. Then Jesus concludes by admonishing his disciples: "Rise and pray that you may not enter into temptation".

Jesus' two almost identical admonitions are a frame for the passage; in the centre we have his own personal prayer. This prayer is presented as beginning with: 'Jesus knelt down and prayed'; its high point is: 'being in an agony, he prayed more earnestly'; at the end, 'he rose from prayer'.

The second theme running through the passage is that of temptation which is repeated twice: 'Pray that you may not enter into temptation'.

Let us ask ourselves what this temptation consists of, and what is the relationship between prayer and temptation.

Temptation and prayer

The immediate meaning, at least of temptation, is not a stimulus to evil. It is much more subtle, more dramatic and more dangerous: it is the temptation to flee from one's responsibilities, the fear of making a decision, the fear of facing up to a reality that requires a personal decision; it is fear of facing the problems of life, of the community, of our society.

It is the temptation to flee from the real, to close one's eyes, hide oneself, to pretend to hear and see nothing lest we get involved; it is the temptation to laziness, the fear of getting started, the temptation which prevents us from doing what God, the Church and the world calls us to do.

Thus the exhortation to pray that we might not enter into temptation means: Pray that you do not enter into an environment of comfortable compromise, of cowardice, of disinterest which becomes the choice of not choosing, of the decision not to decide, of flight from responsibility.

This situation is portrayed by the actions of the Apostles; they sleep for sadness; they sleep in order not to see.

There are other biblical episodes that underline this flight from reality. The priest and the Levite who pass by the wounded man on the road from Jerusalem to Jericho. They close their eyes and go on their way, flying from the demands of responsibility.

Even the great Prophet Elijah, brave to the point of foolhardiness, was overcome by this temptation to withdraw. In the first book of Kings, in fact, it is said, that 'Then he was afraid, and he arose and went for his life' (*1 K. 19:3ff*). Yet it was this same Elijah who alone, on Mount Carmel, faced up to the 450 Prophets of Ba'al; he appeared to fear no one and yet in an instant he is overcome by this tempation and flees from reality.

It is the self-same temptation which affects Jonas who runs away because he does not want to face up to his duties as a prophet. It is the temptation which overtakes each one of us when we close our eyes and our ears so as not to see or hear the needs

54

of those around us. Withdrawal and disengagement when in fact reality calls us to courageous involvement!

Jesus' exhortation to pray that we might not enter into temptation makes it clear that prayer is not flight; it is not a refusal of responsibility, a taking refuge in our own privacy. Prayer is facing up to temptation, to fear and to responsibility. Prayer is doing as the Samaritan did — stopping and bending over the wounded man. Prayer is that boldness that faces up to important decisions.

This is the relationship between prayer and temptation which we find in this text.

Body and prayer

'Jesus knelt down and prayed'. Kneeling was not a usual position for Jesus. In the temple one normally stood for prayer. Kneeling for prayer is indicative of particular earnestness and the phrase is found elsewhere in the Bible. Describing the death of Stephen, the author of the Acts of the Apostles says 'And he knelt down and cried with a loud voice, ''Lord do not hold this sin against them'' ' (*Ac 7:60*). At the decisive and dramatic moment of his death, Stephen knelt and prayed.

The fact that Jesus knelt tells us another important thing: there is a relationship to be lived and rediscovered between the body and prayer, between gesture and prayer. Some of these more ordinary gestures are already familiar to us from the liturgy. We stand, we kneel, we sit, we raise our arms for the recitation of the Lord's Prayer. But it remains important that each one of us in our own private prayers discover the relationship between prayer and gesture, between prayer and the body. Jesus lived out this relationship: 'He knelt down and prayed and said ''Father, if thou art willing remove this cup from me, nevertheless not my will but thine be done''.'

Father, if thou art willing. . .

His prayer encompasses two fundamental realities. In the first place there is the exclamation 'Father' which expresses the Son's total trust in the Father whom he loves. Secondly there is the expression of deep, violent desires: 'Remove this cup from me, if it is thy will', 'not my will be done but thine'. Jesus allows two objectively conflicting desires to be voiced; they are two conflicting realities, but he is not afraid to express them since he knows them to be unified in his prayer which requests: 'Not my will but thine be done'.

To pray in a moment of trial is to allow the emergence of anguish and dread, the fear of what faces us and runs counter to the desire which we have to be at the disposal of others, to make a decision and to face up to reality. The division in us is unified in prayer and we are fitted for the struggle and for courageous decisions. The frenzied conflict in us prevents action, paralyses us with fear, causes decisions to be put off and excuses to be found. All of this when tempered in the furnace of prayer is unified and we are enabled to pick up the pieces, make decisions and say meaningfully 'Thy will be done'; 'let what is involved in your calling be fulfilled in me.'

The text further tells us that Jesus' unifying prayer of abandonment arose from a state of anguish and agony. The words of Pascal come to mind: 'Jesus is in agony until the end of time, in his church, in humanity'. We can therefore unite ourselves with the anguish, agony and distress of all the people of the world, near or far, who suffer and are sorely tried. Jesus, through his own trials, conquers all our trials for us until the end of the world; his anguish conquers ours. Our fear of deciding, of becoming involved, of being willing to lose our lives for the sake of others, is conquered by his prayer in agony.

Jesus manifested his agony so that he could be profoundly close to us. He did not mind his weakness and fragility showing so that we might learn not to fear ours. Nor should we be afraid of our weakness showing for in our fragility the work of God is made manifest.

Prayer and life
Contemplating Jesus praying on his knees, abandoning himself for the Father, showing his innermost desires, passing through anguish and overcoming it, let us ask ourselves how we pray

when faced with the decisive choices of life. We might ask ourselves three questions while rereading the text.

— Is my prayer a flight or is it courageous contemplation of what God is asking of me?
— When I pray do I unify my desires and internal conflicts in asking for the will of God which strengthens me in moments of trial?
— Do I feel the strength of Christ who prays in me, his victory over fear and anguish, or do I feel that this is my own strength, that the victory is mine?

In answering these questions let us ask the Lord to teach us to pray: Grant that in our prayer we overcome all fear that prevents us from opting for you and for our brothers no matter what it costs, no matter how frightening. Grant that our prayer may represent a victory for faith. In it may your power which has overcome the fear of death be triumphant.

5. JESUS' PRAYER ON THE CROSS *(Luke 23:33-49)*

And when they came to the place which is called The Skull, there they crucified him, and the criminals, one on the right and one on the left.

And Jesus said, 'Father forgive them; for they know not what they do'. And they cast lots to divide his garments. And the people stood by, watching; but the rulers scoffed at him, saying, 'He saved others; let him save himself, if he is the Christ of God, his Chosen One'! The soldiers also mocked him, coming up and offering him vinegar, and saying, 'If you are the King of the Jews, save yourself!' There was also an inscription over him, 'This is the King of the Jews'.

One of the criminals who were hanged railed at him, saying, 'Are you not the Christ? Save yourself and us!' But the other rebuked him, saying, 'Do you not fear God, since you are under the same sentence of condemnation? And we indeed justly; for we are receiving the due reward of our deeds; but this man has done nothing wrong'. And he said, 'Jesus, remember me when you come into your kingly power'. And he said to him, 'Truly, I say to you, today you will be with me in Paradise'.

It was now about the sixth hour, and there was darkness over the whole land, until the ninth hour, while the sun's light failed; and the curtain of the temple was torn in two. Then Jesus, crying out in a loud voice, said, 'Father, into thy hands I commit my spirit!' And having said this he breathed his last. Now when the centurion saw what had taken place, he praised God, and said, 'Certainly this man was innocent!' And all the multitudes who assembled to see the sight, when they saw what had taken place, returned home beating their breasts. And all his acquaintances and the women who had followed him from Galilee stood at a distance and saw these things.

According to Luke's Gospel the last words uttered by Jesus in his life are a prayer. Jesus dies while praying: 'Father, into thy hands I commend my spirit'. This is a prayer that he knows from memory. This most dramatic of moments is neither the time nor the place to compose a prayer. From his heart erupts what is most familiar, but it is too a cry from within him.

These words are taken from a Psalm: 'In thee, O Lord do I seek refuge; let me never be put to shame. In thy righteousness deliver me'. And then, 'Into thy hands I commit my Spirit; thou hast redeemed me, O Lord, Faithful God'. (*Ps 31:1,5*).

Biblical prayer

The verses of the Psalm which come from the heart and memory of Jesus were composed centuries before his time. He might have considered them distant, written by men of a different world, a different culture and mentality. Yet this ancient Psalm becomes Jesus' prayer: it is identical with his own experience. It is as if in that moment it became the perfect expression of his situation. Facing death, the most meaningful words which Jesus feels the need of uttering are words of the Bible.

During our 'journey' we too have tried to find ourselves in these ancient prayers spoken by others so many centuries ago: we read our own experiences in them; we can feel ourselves understood and interpreted through them. We have tried to learn what are the right words which would express what was, or is, really deepest within us. We must always remember that these biblical prayers were written also for us. When we use these centuries-old prayers, we find a way of expressing ourselves more authentically: we can sense that God gave them to us as a means of communicating with him and with others; with these prayers we can say what we could not explain either to ourselves or to others. When at the supreme moment of his life Jesus prays he teaches us to entrust ourselves to the Word of God using his own prayer.

The loneliness of witness

The Psalm which Jesus proclaims is one of total confidence. Jesus gives himself to God, he performs an act of total abandonment to the Father.

What he is now living is not merely a dramatic situation: it is the final act of death. It is a death of utter, total and bitter solitude. The Gospel account is at pains to underline the fact that none of those around him understood and the account which leads up to this final word of Jesus strongly emphasises that he has been abandoned by all. These who might have been expected to understand him, or at least to have remained close to him, have not done so. The ordinary people remain to stare, the leaders scoff, the soldiers mock him, and even one of the thieves, hanging on a cross beside him, insults him. It is striking to see how these persons — leaders, soldiers, criminals — represent not only categories of people who think differently: they are natural enemies; not one of them is for Jesus.

All would seem to say to him that his is an absurd death, serving no purpose; it is rather a mistaken gesture and so no one seems to support him. The loneliness that he feels is not merely that of being misunderstood but is the loneliness of being mocked and scoffed at in the very thing that is most important to him: salvation. The refrain of those around is always the same: 'save yourself', 'let him save himself'. This key word thrice repeated is really the key to the entire mission and preaching of Jesus; it is, in fact, the word which Luke has taken as the central reference point of his entire Gospel. In the fourth chapter Luke presents Jesus at the beginning of his public ministry in Nazareth as quoting from scripture — the word of salvation — 'Every man shall see the salvation of God'. With this announcement of salvation Jesus' mission is inaugurated.

The evangelist closes his second book, the Acts of the Apostles, by stamping it, as it were, with a seal, everything he had narrated. Again we have the word of salvation: 'God's salvation is now being offered to the pagans'. (*Ac 28:28*)

Now at the final moment when Jesus is dying, it is precisely this message of salvation which is being called into question. The people cry out: 'If you are really able to save, begin by saving yourself. How can you give salvation if you cannot save yourself'.

The argument seems irrefutable. If Jesus cannot save himself he cannot be credible. Jesus is alone and is being attacked precisely about the core of his mission — to bring salvation. He is being asked to use, for himself, in his own favour, the power that he says he has. If he uses this power and comes down from the cross then they will believe that he is the Messiah.

But Jesus does not use this power. Had he done so, he would have been testifying to a pagan god: a god who holds power only to distribute it so that each one might have more power; a god who uses power for his own benefit, and gives it to people so that they might use it for themselves. If he came down from the cross, they would believe indeed, but in a god of convenience, in a false image of God.

Abandonment to the love of the Father

Jesus chooses not to come down from the cross. It is true that he will thus die, alone and abandoned. He will have, however, borne witness to God who gives life, to God who is at the service of humanity. He will have borne witness to God who is Love. Good that is done in the world comes from the fact that someone goes beyond what is measured, beyond calculations, beyond what reason lays down.

The prevalent attitude towards death is one belonging to a world which fears for the future, fears to be life-giving: there is then an inexorable descent into a progressive tasting of death, into a sadness at all manifestations of existence. Many things going on around us are thus explained — we live in a culture that has lost its taste for risk, for gambling on a future in God, for self-commitment into the hands of the Father.

Jesus commits himself: 'Father into thy hands I commit my Spirit'. His prayer expresses that final abandonment in which we might find again our authentic selves but we cannot. From time to time we imagine ourselves capable of that abandonment. Faced with some situation that requires a leap of faith, we soon discover how far beyond us is the prayer of Jesus: it is an ideal we cannot reach.

'Let us pray.' 'O Lord, I am incapable of offering you Jesus' words of abandonment; say them in me. You, Lord Jesus, who with the fullness of your Spirit dwell in me, pronounce in me your prayer, implant it within my heart. Grant that I know how to see my entire life in the light of that prayer; let me look again at all my activities, at everything to which I am called, my future, my very choice of vocation and of commitment'.

This is the background against which we can understand the final words of Jesus. He comes up against an ultimate and definitive challenge: it is his mission and he is determined to remain faithful until the very end. In this isolation, which from the outside seems to spell total failure, Jesus reacts by exclaiming: 'Into thy hands, Father, I commit my life'. Thus he bears witness to the God of the Gospel, the God of faith, the God who is to be blindly trusted, the God into whose hands we too are invited to commit our lives, our past, our present and our future.

Faith and prayer

The basic question that arises from this scene and from this word of Jesus is: In what God do I believe? In a God in whom I can hope for a certain success, for an alliance which I could use to my advantage? Or do I believe in the God who gives life provided I totally commit myself, my life's undertaking and my future totally to him? Do I believe in the God who will give me back life a hundredfold, for even if the evidence points to death, there is the certainty of life with the Risen One? Jesus has said in the Gospel: Whoever loses his life will find it. On the other hand whoever wishes to find his own life, wants to remain closed in himself, does not trust, that person will lose his life.

There is a second question: Is my prayer just one that arises from a need? Or is my prayer one of trust?

When the Lord guides us towards the high point of prayer, the prayer of trust by which we commit our lives into his hands, then we have reached the basic, fundamental, primordial attitude of existence. The meaning of human existence is to commit ourselves, to know how to trust. In the presence of your cross, O Lord, and faced with the power of your resurrection, I am aware of my poverty and my wants. I ask you to impress on my heart your supreme abandonment for in it you have truly revealed God. You, O Lord, did not wish to deceive us, you did not wish to come down from the cross but through your prayer the Kingdom of the Father sprang to life around you. The centurion glorified God, the crowds returned beating their breasts convinced of discovering some extraordinary event, new and unforeseen. Before revealing yourself in the glory of your resurrection you first revealed yourself, by committing your life into your Father's hands.

Help us to understand that a gospel existence, which reveals a self-abandonment to the Father already is a manifestation of the true power of God, not a power for our use or for self-aggrandisement, but the power of God which is for service.

From this prayer we pass to service and the gift of offering up ourselves, for these prayers are an expression of basic attitudes and a fundamental experience of Christian conversion.

6.   THE CHRISTIAN'S PRAYER *(Luke 11:1-4)*

He was praying in a certain place, and when he ceased, one of his disciples said to him, 'Lord teach us to pray, as John taught his disciples'. And he said to them 'when you pray, say: "Father, hallowed be thy name. Thy Kingdom come. Give us each day our daily bread; and forgive us our sins for we ourselves forgive everyone who is indebted to us; and lead us not into temptation" '.

The prayer which Luke presents, and the actual occasion on which Jesus taught it, are both very well known to all of us.

And yet every time we take up this text we find ourselves somewhat disarmed and surprised as if coming face to face with something we still do not know.

Let us therefore ask the Lord: You who taught the disciples to pray after having prayed yourself, teach us now this evening to pray, to pray with you, to pray in you; teach each one of us to live prayerfully the words which you put on our lips.

The discovery of the Father
Our first experience is of a somewhat confused rote learning. We received it in childhood, taught to us in an atmosphere of love. Even if we did not understand the words we repeated them from memory, happy to have whatever meaning they had for those who handed them on to us: our parents, our teachers, the priest. Whoever taught us to pray handed on more than words; they also passed on to us a lived experience. Welcoming it as a sign of communion with those who prayed before us we are thus inserted into that immense river of prayer which, from its

source in Jesus, flows through the Apostles and the intervening centuries to reach our day.

Following our childhood years there was perhaps a moment of discovery. For me it was the discovery of the word 'Father': God, who is called Father, God the Father, as a new horizon of my life, God who is really our Father.

The adolescent welcomes this particular aspect of the prayer which creates an affective relationship with the infinite, the deep reassuring paternity of God. With the discovery of the paternity of God one gradually grows to understand the Our Father as the prayer of the Kingdom, as 'God's designs laid upon us'. Intuitively we learn the meaning of 'Thy Kingdom Come', the future horizons that it opens up for us. We give ourselves wholeheartedly for this Kingdom, making God's designs our own. This is the discovery of the young person; the Our Father is the prayer of the disciple, who wants above all the Kingdom of justice, of truth and of perfect brotherhood.

There is a further phase, or at least there has been for many of us — the adult phase. The prayer of the Kingdom becomes the prayer of the poor, of the person who plods along within the Kingdom, weary and needing bread and daily sustenance, and the strength to face difficulties. The adult looks for the Kingdom of the Father starting from his own acknowledged frailty.

We have drawn a rough outline of what might be the history of the Our Father for us and of our entry into this prayer. Perhaps a number of the aspects which we described have not yet become part of life's experience for many of us; they remain only words. For this reason let us make the following preliminary reflection.

Teach us to pray

The preamble to the Our Father gives the situation which gives rise to a request. Jesus prays and the disciples ask him to teach them to pray.

Jesus prays in order to enable us to pray. Today we can pray because he has prayed and we learn to pray by inserting ourselves into his prayer.

Jesus was praying: his prayer must have had some quality of great intensity, visible even to those seeing him. From the text we note that the disciples did not dare interrupt; 'when he had finished' the disciples, who up to this were amazed, astonished, awed and fascinated by the manner in which he prayed, now approached him. The Greek text would almost indicate that we should translate 'during a break'. During this intense prayer Jesus allows himself a break, during which the disciples have a request. Their request is an important element in the preamble to the prayer; in order to learn to pray we must *want* to pray and we must *ask*.

As St Paul says, 'We do not know how to pray' and therefore we have to say 'teach us to pray'. In his Gospel Luke tells us that the disciples make this request rather late in the day. We are already at the eleventh chapter and well into Luke's description of the life of Jesus. Jesus has already been portrayed as praying — at his baptism (*Lk 3*), and when crowds came to him to be cured, Jesus went into the desert to pray. (*Lk 5:16*) Luke supposes that the disciples would have been struck by this almost violent withdrawal by Jesus from the pressing crowds in order to pray. Even in the sixth chapter, prior to choosing his disciples, Jesus spends the night in prayer on the mountain.

Why then does Luke put the request only at this point? It is surely because the evangelist is here outlining the process of the interior formation of the disciples, hence a fitting context for an instruction on prayer. Perhaps Luke also wants to underline the fact that the request derives from the disciples' continued experience of seeing Jesus at prayer.

In an analogous fashion in the Church, questions concerning prayer arise when we see others praying; when praying with others we are aware of an inexplicable quality surrounding us: it fascinates us; we want it for ourselves. Desire is a preamble to prayer; this desire often springs from example and leads on to a request.

Words that provide a synthesis

There is something paradoxical about the text. On the one hand it contains a number of very basic words: name, Kingdom, hallowed, come, bread, sins, temptation, and some of these are key words in the New Testament. On the other hand, though apparently simple, these words are not easily explained.

For centuries, experts have discussed the meaning of the word *hepioúsion* which qualifies the word 'bread'. It occurs in no other place in the New Testament and is very rare in Greek literature. Up to now no one can say precisely what it means; various options are given — 'daily', 'for today', 'for tomorrow', 'substantial'. The most obvious meaning is perhaps 'daily', but we are not certain philologically that this is the only possible translation.

Again, 'Hallowed be thy name' is a strange expression; 'lead us not into temptation' is an extremely pregnant phrase whose very brevity requires lengthy explanations.

The Our Father then is a prayer made up of very basic words, each alluding to the entire reality of the Kingdom of God. They are a compendium of the Gospel: (So rich are they in meaning that they 'explode', for they contain a synthesis of the teaching of Jesus.) A literal, word-by-word explanation would lead us to a reading of almost the entire Gospel.

The climate for prayer

This is the first phase of prayer. To say 'Father' does not mean that we are making an effort of the imagination, or that we have a certain idea of God, but rather more simply that we enter into Jesus' way of prayer.

All the prayers of Jesus that have been handed on to us in the Gospel begin with the word 'Father'. 'I thank thee Father, Lord of heaven and earth. . .' (*Mt 11:25*); 'Abba, Father all things are possible to thee; remove this cup from me' (*Mk 14:36*); Jesus' two prayers on the cross as reported by Luke: 'Father forgive them'; 'Father, into thy hands I commend my spirit' (*Lk 23:34,36*).

In the eleventh chapter of John we read, 'Father, I thank thee that thou hast heard me' (*v. 41*); in chapter twelve, 'Father, save me from this hour', 'Father, glorify thy name' (*vv 27-28*); still in John from what is called the priestly prayer, 'Father. . .I have manifested thy name. . .keep them in thy name, which thou hast given to me (cf. *Jn 17*).

If every prayer of Jesus that has been handed down to us begins with the invocation 'Father' this can only mean that we have here the first step, the climate for prayer and the horizons within which it takes place. Inviting us to pray in this way and pouring the gift of prayer into our hearts, Jesus makes his horizon ours. Ideally all the invocations of the Lord's prayer ought to be prefixed with the invocation '*Father*': '*Father*, hallowed be thy name', *Father*, thy kingdom come', '*Father*, give us this day our daily bread', '*Father*, forgive us our trespasses. . .'.

With this fundamental invocation, 'Father', we find the right tone, the proper attitude of availability, of trust, of self-commitment, of certainty about being heard, of victory over fears, and of a straightforward relationship with God.

Desire for the Kingdom

'Hallowed be thy name, thy Kingdom come' — these wishes mark, as it were, a second phase. I shall dwell particularly on the second phrase — a prayer for the full realisation of the divine plan. In requesting the arrival of the Kingdom we express a wish, a desire, a restlessness for the manifestation of all that we mean by the word Kingdom. This has a thousand names, and we include them all without detailing them in our prayer: justice, brotherhood, triumph of life, victory over death, a situation where tears will have passed away, an ability to love one another totally, the fullness of the Body of Christ realised in the Church, real unity of humanity. . . with this expression, 'Thy Kingdom come', we anticipate, we desire and we await God's designs in history.

Thy Kingdom. Not a kingdom that would be the fruit of my imagination but the one that you prepare for us, you give us, you ask us to bring about daily. It is your design and so it has characteristics that could only be yours: fullness, totality, truth, purity, clarity, brightness.

We sense all of these realities as we try to bring them about. The Kingdom, indeed, is made concrete in our human projects, in our vision of the Church and of society, in our human relations lived in the fullness of the Gospel and in the image that we have of the new world to be built. But it is yours, we receive it from you as you reveal it to us, always greater than our desires, always more sublime than our requests.

In this tension — the Kingdom which we bring about from day to day and the Kingdom which God gives us and which is always greater than our own project — prayer activates us. It is prayer which makes us ready to face up to the possible conflict between our vision of the Kingdom and the Kingdom which God in his infinite and mysterious wisdom gives us. This was the conflict faced by Jesus in the Garden of Olives; 'Father, not my will but thine be done; thy Kingdom come, not mine'.

This phrase of the Lord's prayer places us directly in the spirit of our baptism; with it in fact we begin to live out the reality of our baptism.

Three requests

Requests mark the third phase of our prayer. What do we need so that the Kingdom may come, so that God's designs may be realised? What do we need if this is to be effective and possible? If we had to write the Our Father no doubt we would have produced a long list of conditions both internal and external. Jesus, in Luke's account, mentions only three.

So that the Kingdom may come *we need perseverance today, sustained by daily bread.*

We need mercy and mutual pardon, which will be shown in our capacity to welcome each other and in the numerous times that God pardons our constant falls and inability to realise the Kingdom.

We need God's support so that *we may not succumb to temptation* when the moment of trial comes and the Kingdom seems dimmed around us.

69

In the first part of the Lord's prayer we are described as anticipating and desiring the coming of the Kingdom. In the second part we are described as poor pilgrims of the Kingdom.

The truth within us
Now we can compare the three phases of prayer with what we feel within us.

In our heart, is the first *word* addressed to God, the name 'Father', and do we repeat it with trust, self-abandonment and tenderness?

In our heart, is the fundamental *desire* the fullness of God's designs to which we are called to dedicate our lives through our baptism and through our presence in the whole reality of the world in every form of service to others, to the Church and to society?

In our heart, have we a humble sense of ourselves so that we can *ask* for whatever is essential and suited to our weakness?

Let us unite ourselves with all our brothers who together with us experience this weakness and poverty on their journey to the Kingdom. I am thinking in particular of victims of violence and kidnap, of all those whose lives are heavily burdened to the point of being almost intolerable, of so many brothers and sisters who are seriously ill. They need the daily bread of hope and the breath of strength that will allow them to welcome each day as it comes.

Then there are those who do not share our vision of the Kingdom; because they do not believe that God's designs are operative in their lives, they have no future, no direction, no particular reason for committing themselves to a better tomorrow.

We should pray with all people, particularly with those whom we meet every day, and with whom we would like to share our desires, our invocation of the Father and our experience of the divine paternity which Jesus has given us to live out.

7. PRAYER OF THE COMMUNITY *(Acts 4:23-31)*

When they were released they went to their friends and reported what the chief priests and the elders had said to them. And when they heard it, they lifted their voices together to God and said, 'Sovereign Lord, who didst make the heaven and the earth and the sea and everything in them, who by the mouth of our father David, thy servant, didst say by the Holy Spirit,

> *"Why did the Gentiles rage,*
> *and the peoples imagine vain things?*
> *The kings of the earth set themselves in array,*
> *and the rulers were gathered together,*
> *against the Lord and against his Anointed"* —

For truly in this city there were gathered together against thy holy servant Jesus, whom thou didst anoint, both Herod and Pontius Pilate, with the Gentiles and the people of Israel, to do whatever thy hand and thy plan had predestined to take place. And now, Lord, look upon their threats, and grant to thy servants to speak thy word with all boldness, while thou stretchest out thy hand to heal, and signs and wonders are performed through the name of the holy servant Jesus. And when they had prayed, the place in which they were gathered together was shaken; and they were filled with the Holy Spirit and spoke the word of God with boldness'.

This is a prayer of the Christian community which found itself facing temptation; for the first time it was threatened by an enemy power that aimed at stifling the liberty of God's Word.

71

The Word in chains

The Acts recount how, in fact, Peter and John were brought before the tribunal; they were interrogated and threatened and ordered to speak no longer in the name of the Lord. Peter and John return to the community and it is at this point that the prayer is offered. It is a prayer that is born in a moment of opposition and persecution. The situation has not yet reached the point where the Apostles are suffering bodily harm; they have not been assaulted or tortured. Nevertheless it is already a time of tension. It is typical of that atmosphere in which the freedom of the word of God is being hampered. The occasion of the prayer is not actual harm inflicted on the belivers as such but rather the fact that the word of God is being chained, impeded by force and suffocated by threat.

The community's response

What does the community do when faced by this threat? It had a number of options open to it: meetings, consultations, analysis, action plans, strategies, distinctions between moderates and intransigents. . . . They may well have done some or all of these things, but the Acts of the Apostles do not tell us. The purpose of Acts is to describe the essential elements of an ideal community: when faced with a crisis, this community prays.

Here we have grounds for reflection. Prayer is presented as the central expression of the community, its principal way of facing up to difficulties.

If, therefore, a community when faced with a hard situation takes the responsibility of praying together, it does what affirms it; it finds its real identity; it adopts the right attitude that is over and above all other ways of acting or reacting.

Personal response

This reflection leads us to a question: When do I feel most at ease in the community, in what situations do I really feel most myself?

My personal answer as a bishop is that I feel perfectly at ease in a community which prays, which listens to the Word of God

Prayer of petition

The second part is indeed a prayer of petition. The community has finally understood that what has happened to it is not a disaster but rather that it has been inserted into the suffering and persecuted Christ.

It asks just one thing: to be able to proclaim the Word openly. It feels a responsibility before the world for the Word and asks to be enabled to proclaim it. We are surprised that they do not ask for success, nor do they ask for an end to the persecution, an end which would see the malfactors triumphantly defeated. The community asks to be able to continue courageously to proclaim the Word in its entirety with the humility and perseverance required for announcing the Gospel.

Then it requests cures, miracles and marvels. The first is the fundamental petition of a community that is conscious of its duty to evangelise, to bring the Word to others.

The second is a petition for a proper context for this proclaimation — the communication of the message in a way that will show forth the transforming power of the Spirit of God in human existence. Not, then, mere abstract principles.

Cures, miracles, marvels: a world changing; hearts changing; lifestyles transformed; people who hated each other now extending pardon; those people who dreamt of a future of personal success now feeling the need to consecrate themselves to something for which it is worth giving their lives. These are the transformations that are a concrete sign of the effectiveness of the Word.

What the community asks for is to be able to preach the Word and at the same time to be able to change minds and hearts so that there would be consistency between the Word proclaimed and the surrounding reality. The power to change things which is asked in prayer is one which overcomes our instinctive fear of change, of commitment to new ways that change into a zest for life the inclination towards and the power of death.

In prayer, let us ask for that courage that comes from the Word of God. What does this courage mean for us? In what sitautions does our courage fail? What personal and other situations need to be changed if there is to be consistency between the word that is spoken and the Word that is heard?

3

MILESTONES ON THE WAY

At the end of our prayer meetings we might ask ourselves what meaning they have had for us.

— For me, they have been above all one of my most beautiful events of the year. In them I really experienced the Church as Church.

— It has been important that we used the Word of God as our starting point for prayer which thus became our response to God who spoke to us. If during the year we have seriously committed ourselves to using the Word of God as a basis for our prayer, then we have made great strides forward.

— A third important point is that we have *prayed together*: I have understood something that goes beyond the sum of our individual efforts. In our praying together I have lived and felt the mystery of God in our midst; the mystery of God being welcomed, not the results of our own efforts. We have mutually shared each other's faith.

— The meetings have also been a bodily expression of prayer. We have experienced listening, proclamation, singing, silence; the different rhythms in which prayer is expressed. We have understood better that, since we are bodily beings, prayer includes movement so that our bodies too are involved in worship.

— Finally, I was struck by the relationship we sought between prayer and penance. This too is significant, for prayer purifies and leads to purification. Without this continuous effort at purification prayer could be in vain just as all the activities of Christian life could be futile if contaminated by ambition and a desire for personal success. Only by penance and purification do we come before God in our poverty of sinfulness so that he may love us in his mercy.

Let us therefore give praise to the Lord for all the gifts he has showered on us and let us ask the Spirit to come upon us and accomplish in us that deep purification which is necessary if in our poverty we are to welcome the infinite mercy of God.